Python First:
The Joy of Success

Printed Companion to the
Python Digital Pack from StudyPack.com

Atanas Radenski
Chapman University

To Fred from Atanas.
1st Python Tutorial @ Chapman.
June 12, 2007

Llumina Press

© 2007 Atanas Radenski

All rights reserved. No part of this publication may be reproduced or transmitted in any form or by any means electronic or mechanical, including photocopy, recording, or any information storage and retrieval system, without permission in writing from both the copyright owner and the publisher.

Requests for permission to make copies of any part of this work should be mailed to Permissions Department, Llumina Press, PO Box 772246, Coral Springs, FL 33077-2246

ISBN: 978-1-59526-713-9

Printed in the United States of America by Llumina Press

Library of Congress Control Number: 2006911184

Foreword

"Python First" is an introduction to computing through an interactive and easy to learn programming language, Python. It is designed to make computer science in general, and programming in particular, more accessible and exciting to learners. "Python First" is ideal for beginners or for learners with little prior experience in computing.

"Python First" is published in two forms: digital and paper.

A comprehensive digital "Python First" study pack is published and maintained online at the Study Pack site, http://studypack.com. The digital pack features detailed e-texts, a wealth of detailed self-guided labs that learners can complete on their own, sample programs, extensive quizzes, and slides.

This book offers a paper version of all e-texts and labs from the "Python First" digital pack. The book is intended to be used as a paper companion to the digital pack. In the book, all e-texts and labs are published in the same format as they appear in the digital pack.

To make full use of this paper companion, the reader should access sample programs, quizzes, and slides at the Study Pack site, in addition to searchable e-texts and labs. To do so, one needs to enroll - for a modest fee - in a "Python First" digital pack at the Study Pack site. Study Pack provides an on-going access to the most up-to-date online edition of the complete "Python First" pack - for no additional fee. No paper book alone can offer such a benefit.

In early summer of 2006, the first full edition of the "Python First" pack was published at the Study Pack site. Since then, instructors from various schools began adopting "Python First" for their courses. Custom packs for such courses are hosted on the Study Pack site, while the courses themselves are taught at the schools' campuses.

Note that "Python First" is available to individual learners as well. Although most students use "Python First" on Windows platforms, quite a few do the same on Macintosh OS and Linux platforms.

Are you a learner who wishes or needs to take a "Python First" course? If you are and if you enjoy traditional books, then this "Python First" printed companion is for you. Note that it is only a companion and you will still need to enroll in a digital "Python First" pack.

Foreword

To learn more of "Python First", please visit the Study Pack site at http://studypack.com, or send an email to info@studypack.com.

Atanas Radenski

Contents

Foreword   iii
Preliminaries   1

    Lab A [Preliminaries]   8

Introduction   13

    Lab A [Introduction, Optional]   32

    Lab B [Introduction]   34

    Lab C [Introduction]   39

    Lab D [Introduction]   45

    Lab E [Introduction]   50

    Lab F [Introduction]   52

    Lab G [Introduction]   54

    Lab H [Introduction, Optional]   58

    Lab I [Introduction, Optional]   59

Program Control: Selection   61

    Lab A [Program Control: Selection]   86

    Lab B [Program Control: Selection]   90

    Lab C [Program Control: Selection]   93

    Lab D [Program Control: Selection]   96

    Lab E [Program Control: Selection]   99

    Lab F [Program Control: Selection, Optional]   101

    Lab G [Program Control: Selection, Optional]   102
    Lab H [Program Control: Selection, Optional]   104

Lab I [Program Control: Selection, Optional]　　　105

Program Control: Repetition　　　**107**

　　　Lab A [Program Control: Repetition]　　　144

　　　Lab B [Program Control: Repetition]　　　148

　　　Lab C [Program Control: Repetition]　　　153

　　　Lab D [Program Control: Repetition]　　　158

　　　Lab E [Program Control: Repetition]　　　162

　　　Lab F [Program Control: Repetition, Optional]　　　165

　　　Lab G [Program Control: Repetition, Optional]　　　166

　　　Lab H - Challenge [Program Control: Repetition, Optional]　　　167

　　　Lab I - Challenge [Program Control: Repetition, Optional]　　　168

Functions　　　**169**

　　　Lab A [Functions]　　　201

　　　Lab B [Functions]　　　206

　　　Lab C [Functions]　　　209

　　　Lab D [Functions]　　　213

　　　Lab E [Functions]　　　216

　　　Lab F [Functions, Optional]　　　219

　　　Lab G [Functions, Optional]　　　222

　　　Lab H [Functions, Optional]　　　224

　　　Lab I [Functions, Optional]　　　225

Lab K [Functions, Optional]	226

Lists and Dictionaries — **229**

Lab A [Lists and Dictionaries]	268
Lab B [Lists and Dictionaries]	274
Lab C [Lists and Dictionaries]	278
Lab D [Lists and Dictionaries]	280
Lab E [Lists and Dictionaries, Optional]	282
Lab F [Lists and Dictionaries, Optional]	284
Lab G [Lists and Dictionaries, Optional]	286
Lab H [Lists and Dictionaries, Optional]	288
Lab I - Challenge [Lists and Dictionaries, Optional]	290

Strings, Files, and the Web — **291**

Lab A [Strings, Files, and the Web]	336
Lab B [Strings, Files, and the Web]	342
Lab C [Strings, Files, and the Web]	347
Lab D [Strings, Files, and the Web]	351
Lab E [Strings, Files, and the Web, Optional]	354

Graphics and Interfaces — **357**

Lab A [Graphics and Interfaces]	402
Lab B [Graphics and Interfaces]	408
Lab C [Graphics and Interfaces]	412

Lab D [Graphics and Interfaces]	418
Lab E [Graphics and Interfaces, Optional]	420
Lab F [Graphics and Interfaces, Optional]	422
Lab G [Graphics and Interfaces, Optional]	423
Lab H [Graphics and Interfaces, Optional]	424

Classes   425

Lab A [Classes]	452
Lab B [Classes]	457
Lab C [Classes]	461

Review   465

Lab A [Review]	493

Preliminaries

Is this Course of Study for You? Course Goals and Outcomes; The Origin of the Python Programming Language; Why Start with Python? The Online Study Pack; Things to Do with the Study Pack; Acknowledgements

Is this Course of Study for You?

This course of study is a short, dependable way of learning, understanding, and mastering the science of computing. The only prerequisite for the course is basic computer skills such as file editing, file management, and web browsing. You will learn how to write interesting programs in a productive, easy-to-use programming language, Python, a language that is a rising star in information technology.

This course of study is the right choice for you if:
- You are considering a career in information technology.
- You have chosen a field of study that requires an introduction to computing.
- You are a software user who wants to get deeper insight into system and application software.
- You want to learn computer programming for fun, profit or both.
- You know how to program in traditional compiled language(s) - C++ or Java - but want to learn effective programming in a dynamic interpreted language, such as Python.

Course Goals and Outcomes

This course of study has the following main goals:
- to teach a broad introduction to algorithms, programs, programming languages and environments.
- to introduce the imperative, functional, and objects-oriented programming paradigms.
- to discus a variety of numeric and symbolic computing recipes.
- to introduce Internet-based computing.
- to discuss the architecture of graphical user interfaces.
- to introduce computer graphics.
- to give you a chance to enjoy and be satisfied with computer programming.

- to smoothly prepare you for the study of mainstream commercial languages, such as Java and C#.

In this course of study, computer programming is a superb vehicle for a technical introduction to computing, rather than a subject of study. In other words, this course does not solely target 'learning to program', but also focuses on 'programming to learn'. It is important and beneficial to master the art of computer programming for various reasons:
- Learning how to program is a sound, dependable introduction to the foundations of information technology in general, computer and information sciences in particular.
- By becoming a computer-programming insider, you will secure good intuitive understanding of any software you may have to deal with, now and in the years to come. This can open exiting professional opportunities for you.
- Creating programs can be very entertaining and satisfying, especially in a powerful and easy to use language like Python.

Programming a computer may often look like magic. Parts of your thoughts and ideas go into a program that runs, exists, and behaves independently, an amazing incarnation of a valuable and interesting part of you. You may feel that by programming you clone a part of your mind and soul that will continue to exist in the future.

The Origin of the Python Programming Language

In the realm of programming languages, the Python language is what the python snake is in the realm of snakes: powerful, flexible, beautiful, and mostly harmless to humans. The language, however, was not named after the snake. The name 'Python' is short, unique, and mysterious, inspired by the 'Monty Python's Flying Circus', a BBC comedy series that was at one time widely popular.

Guido van Rossum, the father and godfather of Python, conceived of the language in 1990 while at the National Research Institute for Mathematics and Computer Science in Amsterdam, the Netherlands. Currently Python is developed and maintained under the ownership of the non-profit Python Software Foundation.

In the beginning, Python was developed and promoted as the language of choice for true beginners, but Python turned out to be well-suited for real world computing as well. Tens of thousands of programmers are now using Python for a wide variety of business and science projects. Python is even growing in popularity at high-profile organizations such as Yahoo, Google, Disney, Nokia, and the US Government.

Why Start with Python?

What is Problematic with Purely Commercial Languages?

Would it be practical for a new driver to start learning how to drive in an eighteen-wheeler? The majority of students start out in a light vehicle, usually a passenger car.

Introductory computing education and driving education are comparable because both involve significant practical components. One cannot learn how to program without using a programming language to develop real programs; likewise, one cannot learn how to drive without gaining actual driving experience with a real vehicle. The choice of a programming language for introductory programming is as important as the choice of a vehicle for a beginning driver.

The majority of computing students take introductory computing courses based on purely commercial languages, such as Java or C++. While students with good preliminary background usually succeed in such courses, many others become disappointed or fail. The main problem is that purely commercial languages are designed for large-scale software development, rather than education. Commercial applications are complex, as are the programming languages designed to support them. For beginner programmers, the complexity of commercial languages creates a very steep learning curve.

What is Problematic with Purely Educational Languages?

Languages designed exclusively for education at one time dominated introductory computing education. Prominent examples of such educational languages are Pascal, Basic, and Logo. These languages were simpler and smaller than commercial languages, making them more manageable for anyone interested in learning how to program. With these languages, students can succeed and enjoy programming. In the age of the educational languages, learning to program was fun.

While these educational languages were good for beginning computing education, they were not suitable for commercial software development. Indeed, educational languages were not meant at all for large-scale software development but were exclusively intended to be used for educational programming. While students normally create relatively small programs, commercial programmers work on large and complex programs; educational languages were not equipped to support such programs. Because purely educational languages were unattractive to commercial employers, those languages were gradually dropped from most institutions' curricula. As a result, mainstream commercial languages currently dominate introductory computing curricula.

The Python Advantages

Python is neither a purely educational language nor a purely commercial language. Guido van Rossum originally designed Python for education, but its swift rise in popularity among practical programmers became the driving force in its evolution. Guido van Rossum heralds Python as both a good teaching language and a language for major application development. Python is not just a teaching language, but is also suitable for developing large real applications.

Python supports *various computing styles*: imperative, functional, and object-oriented. Those who learn how to work with Python will be well prepared for further study in other languages.

Python's syntax is straightforward and elegant without being overly simplistic.

Python offers a small kernel of efficient high-level features that easily combine into interesting, useful programs.

Python's learning curve is gentle.

Python is interactive and fun.

Programmers at all levels, from beginners to experts, choose Python for its incomparable *productivity*: programs written in Python tend to be shorter than equivalent programs in common languages, such as C++ and Java. Program size matters: it is easier to manage a 2,000-line program in Python than the equivalent 10,000 line C++ or Java program. This smaller program size – along with and a few other factors - makes the development of Python programs faster than in Java or C++.

With Python, you can get things done quickly.

Python First then Mainstream Java

While Python is gaining recognition among educators and software developers, it has not yet reached the level of the truly mainstream languages, C++ and Java. The adoption of a non-mainstream language for introductory computing courses may face some psychological resistance: some school administrators are concerned with teaching students a language that is not dominant in business and academia. Some students share these reservations, mostly because existing computer science and computer engineering curricula require the knowledge of mainstream languages. Students are expected to be trained in mainstream languages for the existing upper-level curriculum that require the knowledge of such languages. Some instructors view the need to train students in mainstream languages as an obstacle to the adoption of the Python language.

This problem can be solved with a sequence of two courses of study: a gentle Python-based first course and a comprehensive second course that is based on a mainstream language, such as Java or C++. These two courses can serve most computer science and computer engineering curricula by teaching beginning concepts with Python then teaching higher level computing proficiency with Java - or another suitable mainstream language.

The Online Study Pack

A comprehensive online study pack supports this course of study. The study pack includes the following learning content modules:
- E-Texts
- Slides
- Detailed Self-Guided Labs
- Quizzes
- Discussion Forums

The author of all learning content modules included in the study pack is Atanas Radenski.

You will be able to use the study pack online at your convenience, any time and anywhere. You are also entitled to printing or saving single copies of all learning modules for your personal use.

In addition to the online study pack, you will use a standard Python implementation that is freely available on the Internet at http://www.python.org.

Things to Do with the Study Pack

The following is a list of recommended activities, which will make your work with the Study Pack successful and rewarding. For each topic, you should read the **Slides** and the **E-Text,** work on the **Lab Assignment**, submit your labs according to the **Lab Submission Instructions**, submit an online **Report**, and take the **Quiz**.

Step 1: Skim the Quiz

Looking at the Quiz without taking it is a good first step. Click on the *Quiz* link, then click on the *Attempt quiz now* button. You do not have to submit your answers at this time – just skim the Quiz.

Step 2: Read the Slides and the E-Text

Thoroughly acquaint yourself with the Slides and the E-Text for the topic.

Step 3: Work on the Lab Assignment

Study the Lab Assignment then perform all activities. You do not have to submit individual labs before you finish your work on the entire Lab Assignment.

Step 4: Submit all completed lab work online

Follow the Lab Submission Instructions to submit online all completed lab work for the current topic. You need to submit your work from *all labs* for a topic *at once*. You get credit for your labs after you submit them. To claim your lab credit, you must submit an online Report for the topic as outlined in Step 5.

Step 5: Submit online Report

In the online Report, you answer questions to report your lab work. The instructor then assigns credit to you accordingly. This self-claimed lab credit is provisionary, and the instructor may reduce it if submitted labs do not comply with requirements for lab assignments. All credits for submitted labs are subject to correction by the instructor.

The report allows you to receive (1) *full credit* for work that you completed in full according to the requirement, or (2) *partial credit* for work that you did not finish as required. If you have done some work on a lab but have not completed the lab by the time it is due, report it accurately as partially completed to receive partial credit for it.

Step 6: Take the Quiz

Your final step for each chapter should be to take the Quiz. Multiple attempts are permissible; only the last score matters. When taking the quiz, you may search the E-text for terms that appear in the quiz.

Lab assignments and quizzes allow multiple online submissions. You can submit your work as many times, as you wish until the deadline, but only the last submission counts. Lab assignments and quizzes are learning tools as well as evaluation tools. The author designed quizzes and lab assignments to help you learn and prepare for exams.

Acknowledgement

The Moodle course management system supports this course of study. Thanks are due to Martin Dougiamas who leads the development and maintenance of Moodle at http://www.moodle.org.

Lab A [Preliminaries]

Objective; Overview of the Online Study Pack; Creating an Account for the Online Study Pack; Browsing the Online Study Pack; Participation in the Open Forum; Taking the Quiz; Logging Out; Compressed (Zipped) Folders

Objective
This lab will acquaint you with the online study pack.

Overview of the Online Study Pack
A complete online study pack supports this course of study. The online study pack includes various learning modules, such as E-Texts, Lab Assignments, Quizzes, and Discussion Forums.

With the online study pack you will read various materials online and submit quizzes and lab assignments online.

Moodle course management system supports this course of study. Atanas Radenski has authored the learning contents modules for the study pack.

Creating an Account for the Online Study Pack
To use the online study pack, you need an account with a username and password. You can create this account when you first access the online study pack. Skip this part if you already have an account. If you have not opened an account yet, perform the following steps.
- Use a browser to open the online study pack.
- Click the *login* link in the upper right corner of the screen.
- Follow the instructions on the right half of the screen to create your account.
  - Be sure to submit a correct email address in your profile.
  - If you change your email address, remember to enter the new email in your profile in the online study pack.

Browsing the Online Study Pack
- Click various links to browse the online study pack and to acquaint yourself with its structure and contents.
- Open and read the Things-To-Do resource.

- Open and skim the Quiz.
  - You do not have to submit answers at this time.
- Open and read the E-text for the current topic.
- Browse other available resources, such as the References.

Participation in the Open Forum

After following the above steps, you are expected to participate in the Open Forum. You must:
- Identify *one particular way in which computers can be beneficial to you professionally or personally*. Elaborate on the topic you choose by giving examples and presenting some rationale.
- Provide some information about yourself to your peers.

Post a message in the Open Forum.
- You may choose to reply to another person's message, if your opinion is related to that person's message. Alternatively, you may start a new discussion topic.
- To reply to a message, read the message. Use the *Reply* link at the bottom of the message to post your response.
- To start a new discussion topic, use the *Add a new discussion topic* link; do your best to come up with an informative discussion *subject*.

You are encouraged to participate in the Open Forum, where you can join existing discussions or start new ones. You can use the Open Forum to ask for help on difficult labs, make suggestions for improvements of the online study pack or bring up any other relevant topics.

Submitting a Report

At this time, you should submit an online Report. In your submission, you answer questions to report your work; the system assigns to you credit accordingly. Such self-claimed lab credit is provisionary and is subject to correction by the instructor. Multiple report submissions are allowed until the deadline; only the final one matters.
- Click the *Report* link in the Preliminaries topic.
- Check the Report deadline in the newly opened page.
- Click the *Attempt quiz now* button.
- Fill in answers in the Quiz form.
- Click *Submit all and finish*, then click the *OK* button.
  - Wait for the study pack to respond with a review of your submission.

Taking the Quiz

Next, take the Quiz. Multiple attempts are allowed until the deadline; only the last score matters.
- Click the *Quiz* link in the Preliminaries topic.
- Check the Quiz deadline in newly opened page.
- Click the *Attempt quiz now* button.
- Supply answers to the Quiz form.
- Click the *Submit all and finish* button, then click *OK*.
  - Wait for the study pack to respond with a review of your submission.

Logging Out

Before you go, logout from the online study pack. *Logout* links are available on many study pack pages. You can always find a *Logout* link on the home page. After you logout, you should also logout from the operating system (such as Windows).

Compressed (Zipped) Folders

During this course you will use *compressed (zipped) folders* for various purposes.
- More specifically, useful sample programs are posted on the online study pack as compressed (zipped) folders.
  - As part of your Lab Assignments, you will have to download and uncompress such folders.
- In addition, completed labs are submitted as compressed (zipped) folders.
  - In order to complete Lab Assignments, you will have to create and upload such folders.

The following brief introduction to compressed (zipped) folders intends to give you initial technical background on the subject.

Benefits of Data Compression

Data compression methods allow reduced file size, in order to reduce storage space and network transmission time. *Zip compression* is a particularly popular compression.

Features of a Compressed (zipped) Folder

A *compressed (zipped) folder* is a folder compressed by zip compression.

A compressed (zipped) folder exhibits some properties of single monolithic files and some properties of regular uncompressed folders. More specifically:
- A compressed (zipped) folder can be submitted in Web forms at once as a single monolithic file.
- A compressed (zipped) folder can be browsed like a regular folder.
- Applications can open files from compressed (zipped) folders, but normally they cannot save them directly into these folders.

Built-In Compression Support

Contemporary platforms provide built-in support for compressed folders. In recent editions of Windows, for example, you can create and browse such folders using the platform's built-in *File Browser.*

Compression Utilities

On older platforms, you need to install and use special compression utilities, such as (1) *Win-Zip* for earlier versions of Windows, or (2) *Zip* and *Un-Zip* for Unix.

Terminology may vary in different platforms. For example, folders may be called directories, and *compressed (zipped) folders* may be called *compressed (zipped) files* or *archives.*

Introduction

Sample Programming Problem: Temperature Conversion; Algorithms, Programs, and Programming Languages; Sample Program: Temperature Converter; Programming Concepts; Language Structures; Program Execution Scenario; Writing Readable Programs; Tokens Matter; Errors in Programs; Working with Numbers; Sample Function: Travel Time Calculator; Synonyms

Sample Programming Problem: Temperature Conversion

Consider the following programming problem: we want to develop a *Temperature Converter* program that can be used:

- To transform any temperature measured in *Fahrenheit* to the equivalent temperature in *Celsius*, and
- To transform any temperature measured in *Celsius* to the equivalent temperature in *Fahrenheit*.

The following *conversion equations* relate *Fahrenheit* and *Celsius* temperatures:

*Celsius = (5.0 / 9.0) * (Fahrenheit - 32)*
*Fahrenheit = (9.0 / 5.0) * Celsius + 32*

Exercise

Assume that you do not know the above equations and search the Web to find them, or their equivalents.

Exercise

You use the above conversion equations to perform the conversions necessary to fill in the following conversion table. Do not write a program for this exercise.

Fahrenheit	Celsius
32	
100	
-40	

	0
	100
	-40

Algorithms, Programs, and Programming Languages

Instead of using a mathematical notation to define temperature conversions, we can employ natural language. Here we use English:

- To convert any temperature measured in *Fahrenheit* to the equivalent temperature in *Celsius*, perform the following steps:
  - Subtract *32* from the *Fahrenheit* temperature.
  - Divide *5.0* by *9.0*.
  - Multiply the results from the previous two steps to determine the equivalent temperature in *Celsius*.

The above description is an example of an *algorithm*, a description of actions that can be performed by a human to obtain a desired result. Note that the original conversion equations serve the same purpose. They too are examples of algorithms.

Algorithms can be expressed in various notations in various languages. Cookbook recipes are popular examples of algorithms expressed in English, Bulgarian, or any other language. These algorithms utilize simple mathematical notation to define ingredient quantities and method of cooking. Many cooking recipes appear complex, even illegible, to the untrained eye, yet they provide clear instructions to an experienced cook. Similarly computer algorithms seem utterly foreign to the untrained eye, but they provide clear instructions to a computer easily read by a trained programmer.

When algorithms are to be executed by computers, they must be transformed into programs. *Programs* represent algorithms in artificial *programming languages*.

Unlike to spoken, natural languages, programming languages are strict, unambiguous. Programs must also be strict and unambiguous to be executed by computers *automatically* and without human interference (that might be otherwise needed to resolve ambiguity). Because computers execute programs automatically, program execution is fast, dependable, and predictable.

Writing programs is generally more difficult that writing algorithms. It is easy, for example, to write an omelet recipe, but it is difficult to program a computer to prepare omelets. Algorithms are intended to be executed by humans who can understand and interpret vague, incomplete, even erroneous recipes, and still get the desired results. This is why algorithms need not be formal or overly specific. However, computers cannot execute programs that are vague or incomplete. This is why programs, in contrast to algorithms, need to be very formal and specific as to all details of execution.

The first digital computer, ENIAC, became operational in 1945. Since then, hundreds of programming languages have been developed, but only a few of them have established themselves in practice. Languages like Java, C, C++, and Visual Basic have all become widely used, with their advantages and shortcomings well known. The development of programming languages is a quest for improvement and perfection. Languages like Perl, PhP, and Python have gained acceptance with the promise to make programming more productive.

Python is the language of choice for this course. The benefits of Python are offered in the *Preliminaries*.

> Exercise
> Search for the definitions for the following terms on the Web:
> - Algorithm
> - Program
> - Programming Languages
> - Python programming language
>
> Hint: Search the Web for a good online computer dictionary, then search the dictionary itself, or search the Web directly then browse for the best search results.

Sample Program: Temperature Converter

The following *Temperature Converter* program is written in Python. The program can be used to convert any temperature measured in *Fahrenheit* to the equivalent temperature in *Celsius*, and vice versa.

```
def F2C():
    Fahrenheit = input('Enter degrees in Fahrenheit: ');
    Celsius = (5.0 / 9.0) * (Fahrenheit - 32);
    print Celsius;
```

```
def C2F():
    Celsius  = input('Enter degrees in Celsius: ');
    Fahrenheit  = (9.0 / 5.0) * Celsius + 32;
    print Fahrenheit;
```

The *Temperature Converter* program can be *executed* by a computer, to make various temperature conversions. A sample program execution is depicted in an example below, while a general program execution scenario is discussed in detail later.

Example

A possible execution of the *Temperature Converter* program may look like this on the screen of your computer:

```
>>> F2C();
Enter degrees in Fahrenheit: 32
32 Fahrenheit = 0.0 Celsius
>>> C2F();
Enter degrees in Celsius: 0
0 Celsius = 32.0 Fahrenheit
```

The following Python-to-English translation provides insight into the meaning of the *Temperature Converter* program.

Python-To-English Translation

Python Program	Common English Meaning
def F2C():	The name of this algorithm is *F2C*. (*F2C* is an abbreviation for 'Fahrenheit to Celsius conversion'.) The algorithm consists of the following steps:
Fahrenheit = input('Enter degrees in Fahrenheit: ');	F2C Step 1. ◦ Ask the user to *'Enter degrees in Fahrenheit'*; ◦ Wait for the user to *input* a value; ◦ Assign that value to a variable named *Fahrenheit*.

Celsius = (5.0 / 9.0) * (Fahrenheit - 32);	F2C Step 2. ○ Evaluate the expression *(5.0 / 9.0) * (Fahrenheit – 32.)*; ○ Assign the value of the expression to a variable named *Celsius*.
print Celsius;	F2C Step 3. Print on the screen the value of variable *Celsius*.
def C2F():	The name of this algorithm is *C2F*. (*C2F* is an abbreviation for 'Celsius to Fahrenheit conversion'.) The algorithm consists of the following steps:
Celsius = input('Enter degrees in Celsius: ');	C2F Step 1. ○ Ask the user to *'Enter degrees in Celsius'*; ○ Wait for the user to *input* a value; ○ Assign that value to a variable named *Celsius*.
Fahrenheit = (9.0 / 5.0) * Celsius + 32;	F2C Step 2. ○ Evaluate the expression *(9.0 / 5.0) * Celsius + 32*; ○ Assign the value of the expression to a variable named *Fahrenheit*.
print Fahrenheit;	F2C Step 3. Print on the screen the value of variable *Fahrenheit*.

In plain English translation, the *Temperature Converter* program is a collection of two algorithms: *F2C* and *C2F*. Each of the algorithms is defined by as a sequence of executable steps.

Programming Concepts

Python, like other programming languages, introduces its own terminology. For example, algorithms are called *functions* while executable algorithmic steps are called *statements*. The following table offers the common English meaning of principal programming concepts. Many more concepts will be gradually introduced throughout the course.

Concept	Example	Common English Meaning
Program	*Temperature Converter* (see above)	Collection of one or more algorithms
Function	F2C, C2F, input	Algorithm
User-defined function	F2C, C2F	A custom algorithm that is defined by the user of the programming language, i.e. the programmer
Built-in function	input	Algorithm that comes implemented within the programming language and is readily available to the programmer

Function definition	def C2F():
	    Celsius = input('Enter degrees in Celsius: ');
	    Fahrenheit = (9.0 / 5.0) * Celsius + 32;
	    print Celsius;
		Complete algorithm specification supplied by the programmer

Statement	Celsius = input('Enter degrees in Celsius: ');	Executable algorithmic step

Language Structures

Programs are built of various linguistic structures of the Python language that serve different purposes. For example, the purpose of a *print-statement* is to output information to the user, while the purpose of a *function header* is to give the name of a new function. The following table describes the purpose of the language structures encountered in the *Temperature Converter* sample program. Many more language structures will be gradually introduced as the course progresses.

Structure	Example	Purpose
Assignment statement	Fahrenheit = (9.0 / 5.0) * Celsius + 32;	Evaluates an expression and assigns the result of the evaluation to a variable.
Variable	Celsius, Fahrenheit	Refers to a value that can change during program execution.

Print-statement	print Celsius;	Outputs a value to the screen.
Function header	def C2F():	Starts a function definition by giving the function a name. The name of the function can be used for function invocations.
Function body	Celsius = input('Enter degrees in Celsius: '); Fahrenheit = (9.0 / 5.0) * Celsius + 32; print Celsius;	Provides a block of statements to be executed when the function is invoked. Note: These statements must be indented and aligned.

Program Execution Scenario

You can execute any Python program, such as the *Temperature Converter* program, by means of the *Python system*. The *Python system* is a comprehensive Python software package for Windows, Macintosh, and Linux. It is available free from http://www.python.org.

The *Python system* includes various components, including a *Python interpreter*, an *Integrated Development Environment (IDLE)*, and documentation. Unlike some popular languages, Python does not use a compiler.

In this course, the *Python system* will be used to develop and execute your Python programs. The Lab Assignment for this topic explains how to download and install the *Python system* on your computer and introduces the Integrated Development Environment (IDLE).

Exercise
Search for definitions of the following terms on the Web:
- Interpreter
- Compiler

To execute the *Temperature Converter* program and other similar programs, follow this scenario:

Step 1
Create a *program file* containing the complete program. The *Temperature Converter* program file consists of the definitions of two functions, *F2C* and *C2F*.

Step 2

Run the program file. When you run the *Temperature Converter* program file, you define the two functions from the program, *F2C* and *C2F*, to the *Python interpreter*. This does not execute the function bodies.

Step 3

Invoke any of the defined functions as many times as you wish. When you invoke functions *F2C* and *C2F*, the *Python interpreter* executes the corresponding function bodies.

The above scenario uses the *Python interpreter* in two modes: *file input mode* and *interactive mode*. In file input mode, the *Python interpreter* runs programs previously saved. In interactive mode, the *Python interpreter* executes statements that are typed directly at the interpreter's *interactive prompt*, >>>.

Note

You can create program files by means of the *Python editor*. This editor is a part of the Integrated Development Environment (IDLE), a component of the *Python system*. You may use an alternative editor if you prefer. Note that extension '**.py**' is required for Python program files.

Example

In interactive mode, the *Python interpreter* displays its interactive prompt, >>>. At the prompt, you can enter an invocation of function *F2C*. The invocation is formed of the function name followed by parentheses: >>> *F2C()*. For this invocation, the *Python interpreter* executes the body of function *F2C*. Function *C2F* is similarly invoked. Possible invocations, together with user input and function output, may look like this:

```
>>> F2C();
Enter degrees in Fahrenheit: -40
-40.0
>>> C2F();
Enter degrees in Celsius: 100
212.0
>>> C2F();
Enter degrees in Celsius: -40
-40.0
```

```
>>> C2F();
Enter degrees in Celsius: 0
32.0
```

Example

The print-statement can be utilized to output several consecutive items. For example, the original *'print Celsius;'* statement from function *F2C* can be replaced by this four-item print-statement:

```
print Fahrenheit, 'Fahrenheit =', Celsius, 'Celsius';
```

The above statement prints the value of the *Fahrenheit* variable, followed by the character string *'Fahrenheit ='*(without the quotes), followed by the value of the *Celsius* variable, followed by the character string *'Celsius'* (without the quotes). The result is an equation that relates the input Fahrenheit value with the calculated Celsius value. A similar change can be made in the *C2F* function. Possible invocations of the enhanced functions may look like this:

```
>>> F2C();
Enter degrees in Fahrenheit: -40
-40 Fahrenheit = -40.0 Celsius
>>> C2F();
Enter degrees in Celsius: 100
100 Celsius = 212.0 Fahrenheit
>>> F2C();
Enter degrees in Fahrenheit: 100
100 Fahrenheit = 37.7777777778 Celsius
```

Writing Readable Programs

Your programs will have at least one important reader – you. They will also be viewed by your instructor. Valuable and useful programs, can be adopted and further developed by others. Your programs should be easy to read and understand. The readability of your programs does not affect the *Python interpreter,* but is important for human readers.

In order to make your programs readable, use appropriate *mnemonic names*. Use names that are descriptive and of appropriate length. Keep in mind that names that are too long may be difficult to work with. Substitute acronyms for excessively long names.

Example

The following function definition is formally correct but unreadable.

```
def f ():
    x = input('Enter data: ');
    y = (5.0 / 9.0) * (x - 32);
    print y;
```

The above function converts degrees measured in Fahrenheit to degrees measured in Celsius. The function uses short, ambiguous names for variables (like *x, y* instead of *Fahrenheit, Celsius*) and communicates with an unclear message ('Enter data' instead of 'Enter degrees in Fahrenheit'). Although the above function will produce correct results, it is unreadable.

Blank lines are ignored by the *Python interpreter*. You can use blank lines to separate logically different components of your programs, such as different function definitions. This contributes to readability.

Attaching plain language comments to your program is another means for enhancing readability. Technically speaking, a *comment* is any part of your program that starts with a hash character, #, and ends with the end of the program file line that contains the hash character. As an exception, the hash character does not start a comment when it appears in a character string. Comments are intended for human readers and are ignored by the *Python interpreter*. Comments have no effect on the program's execution.

Example

The following version of the *Temperature Converter* program has been populated with comments for increased readability. Notice also that the definitions of functions *F2C* and *C2F* are separated by a blank line.

```
# Convert Fahrenheit temperature to Celsius temperature:
def F2C():
    Fahrenheit = input('Enter degrees in Fahrenheit: ');
    Celsius = (5.0 / 9.0) * (Fahrenheit - 32);
    print Fahrenheit, 'Fahrenheit =', Celsius, 'Celsius';
```

```
# Convert Celsius temperature to Fahrenheit temperature:
def C2F():
    Celsius = input('Enter degrees in Celsius: ');
    Fahrenheit = (9.0 / 5.0) * Celsius + 32;
    print Celsius, 'Celsius =', Fahrenheit, 'Fahrenheit';
```

Tokens Matter

A Python program is composed of simple *tokens*, such as names, keywords, operators, numbers, and others. The following table introduces Python language tokens.

Token	Example	Description
Names	Fahrenheit, Celsius, F2C, C2F	Used to identify variables, functions, and other program elements. Chosen by the programmer. May contain only letters, digits, and the underscore character, but cannot start with a digit.
Keywords	def, print	Reserved by the language designer for special purposes, as, for example, starting a function definition or starting a print-statement. Cannot be used as names.
Numeric literals	9.0, 5.0, 32	Represent numeric values that never change during program execution. Values that change can be represented by means of variables.
String literals	'Enter degrees in Celsius: ' 'Enter degrees in Celsius: ' 'Fahrenheit'	Represent sequences of characters that stand for themselves. Enclosed in either double quotes, or single quotes.
Operators	+ - / > >=	Designate arithmetic and logic operations.
Delimiters	: = ; ( )	Serve as punctuation marks. Used to clearly separate constituent parts of compound language structures.

Exercise

Identify all tokens in the following statements:

```
Fahrenheit = 0;
Celsius = (5.0 / 9.0) * (Fahrenheit - 32);
print 'Celsius';
```

Determine the output produced by the print-statement.

Case matters in Python keywords and names. Two Python words are different if they have the same letters but different cases.

> Example
> - The word *Print* is different form the lowercase keyword *print*. *Print* cannot start a print-statement.
> - The word *Def* is different form the lowercase keyword *def*. *Def* cannot start a function definition.
> - The name *celsius* is not the same as the name *Celsius* and cannot be used instead of it.
> - Function *F2C* from the *Temperature Converter* program cannot be referred to as *f2c*.
>
> Exercise
> Search the Web for a list of all Python keywords.

Errors in Programs

The *syntax* of a programming language consists of spelling and grammatical rules. The syntax defines the permissible forms of programs and their parts.

> Example
>
> Python spelling rules mandate that spaces are not allowed within names and within numbers. According to this rule, *x1* is a valid name, while *x 1*, with a space between the 'x' and the '1', in not.

The *semantics* of a programming language defines how programs and their parts are executed.

> Example
>
> The Python semantics defines how various statements are executed.

The syntax and semantics of Python are defined in a document called Language Reference Manual – LRM. This document can be located in the online documentation on the Web or, alternatively, in a *Python system* that has been installed with documentation.

> Exercise
> Search definitions for the following terms on the Web:
> - Syntax
> - Semantics

Coping with various errors is an inherent part of any program development. Programming errors cannot be avoided; they may occur even in the simplest programs. All programmers need to deal with two main categories of errors: syntax errors and run-time errors.

Syntax errors are violations of the spelling and grammatical rules of the language. When a program contains a syntax error, a *syntax error message* is produced by the *Python system*. Programs with syntax errors are never executed.

Example

The following statements exhibit various syntax errors:

```
x1 = 3.14;
Print x1;
x 1 = 3.14;
x1 = 3. 14;
print x1 \ 10;
```

Note that:
- The first statement contains no error – its purpose is to introduce variable *x1* that is needed in the next statements.
- The second statement uses a capital 'P' in *Print* instead of lowercase 'p', as in *print*.
- The third statement is incorrect because there is a space between 'x' and '1' in *x 1* and because spaces are disallowed within names.
- Spaces are disallowed within numbers, too; therefore the space between '3.' and '14' in *3. 14*, in the fourth statement, is an error.
- Finally, the expression *x1 \ 10*, in the fifth statement, is syntactically incorrect because the backslash '\' is not a valid operator.

Runtime errors are violations of the semantics of the language. Most such errors cannot be detected prior to the actual program execution. When the actual execution of a statement results in a runtime error, a *runtime error message* is produced by the *Python system*.

Example

The following statements exhibit a runtime error:

```
x1 = 3.14; x2 = 0;
print x1 / x2;
print X2;
```

Note that:
- The first two statements contain no error – their purpose is to define variables *x1* and *x2* that are needed in the next statements.
- The runtime error in the third statement is caused by a division by zero (because *x2 = 0*).
    - Division by zero is an undefined operation.
- The runtime error in the last statement is caused by the use of a capital 'X' instead of lowercase 'x' in *X2*.
    - Variable X2, with a capital 'X', has not been defined by any of the previous statements.
    - Only variables *x1* and *x2* with lowercase 'x' have been defined.

Working with Numbers

Every value in a Python program has an attribute called *type* that determines the representation scheme of the value in the computer memory. Values of the same type use the same representation scheme in the computer memory, and permit the same operations. For example, values of type integer are whole numbers represented in binary form (including the sign); integer values permit standard arithmetic operations.

Python offers several built-in types for numeric data. Built-in Python types have been given concise names by the language designer, as for example *int* for *integer*. The following table outlines the most important numeric types in Python.

Type Name	Examples of Numbers in Python	Examples in Common Notation	Type Description
Python name: *int* Common name: *integer, plain integer*	-42 100 1	-42 100 1	The plain integer type, *int*, comprises whole numbers. Plain integer numbers can be efficiently processed by most processors, but the size of these numbers is limited, typically to 32 bits.
Python name: *long* Common name: *long integer*	10000000000**L** -9999999999**L**	10,000,000,000 -9,999,999,999	The long integer type, *long*, comprises whole numbers of unlimited size. While long integer numbers can be as large as the whole available computer memory, those numbers are slower to process.
Python name: *float* Common name: *floating point*	3.14 -1000.0 -3**E**2 314**E**-2 2**e**120	3.14 -1000 -3×10^2 314×10^{-2} 2×10^{120}	The floating point type, *float*, comprises numbers with decimal point. These numbers are represented in a special binary scientific notation. While floating point numbers can have very large (yet limited) magnitudes, they often require rounding and can be imprecise.

Note

In addition to integer and floating-point numbers, Python offers built-in *complex* numbers. A self-study of the Python's *complex* type is recommended to the mathematically inclined. Relevant information is provided in the online documentation and supplemented by various sources on the Web.

Python supports standard arithmetic operations. These are outlined in the following table.

x + y	sum of x and y
x - y	difference of x and y
x * y	product of x and y
x / y	quotient of x and y
x % y	remainder of x / y
-x	x negated
+x	x unchanged
x ** y	x to the power y

Python offers useful built-in arithmetic functions. The most important built-in functions are listed in the following table.

abs(x)	absolute value or magnitude of x, | x |
pow(x, y)	x to the power y; same as x**y
int(x)	x converted to integer
float(x)	x converted to floating point
round(x)	x rounded to floating point with 0 fractional digits
round(x, n)	x rounded to floating point with n fractional digits

Example

The following table illustrates possible uses of the built-in functions *float, int*, and *round*.

Statement	Output	Result Type
print float(9);	9.0	float
print int(3.14);	3	int
print int(3.99);	3	int
print round(3.99);	4.0	float

print int(round(3.99));	4	int
print int(9);	9	int
print float(3.14);	3.14	float

When one of the arguments of an arithmetic operation is a floating point number and the other argument is an integer number, the integer argument is automatically converted by the *Python interpreter* to a floating point number. It is necessary to convert arguments to the same type because computer processors cannot perform arithmetic operations on mixed arguments. After the conversion, the *Python interpreter* applies the actual operation and delivers a floating point result.

Example

The following table presents conversion examples:

Mixed Arguments	Converted Arguments	Operation Result	Operation Type
10 + 20	No conversion	30	int
10 + 20.0	float(10) + 20.0	30.0	float
10.0 + 20	10.0 + float(20)	30.0	float
10.0 + 20.0	No conversion	30.0	float

If the programmer does not want to rely on such implicit conversion generated by the *Python interpreter*, she can explicitly use conversion functions in her program.

The quotient operation, x / y, deserves special attention, because its result considerably depends on the types of x and y.
- When both x and y are integer numbers, their quotient is an integer number, too. In Python, as in any other mainstream programming language, the result z of the integer division x / y is the 'floor' of the mathematical quotient x / y.
    - The 'floor' of z is the largest integer less than or equal to z.
- When x and y are floating point numbers, their quotient is a floating point number. The result of a floating point division x / y is an approximation of the exact mathematical quotient x / y.

Example

The following table illustrates possible uses of the built-in quotient operation.

Statement	Output	Result Type
print 9 / 5;	1	int
print float(9) / float(5);	1.8	float
print 9.0 / 5.0;	1.8	float
print float(9 / 5);	1.0	float
print 9 / 10;	0	int
print float(9) / float(10);	0.9	float
print 9.0 / 10.0;	0.9	float

Sample Function: Travel Time Calculator

Consider the following programming problem. Develop a function that can be used to calculate the expected travel *time* for a trip, given the total *distance* of the trip and the average *speed* of the traveler.

The following equations define the travel *time* as a function of the *distance* and the *speed*:

Time = Distance / Speed

The following *time* function can be used to calculate the travel time. The function definition is included in the *Time Calculator* sample program.

```
def time():
    distance = input('Enter distance: ');
    speed    = input('Enter speed: ');
    print 'Travel time =', float(distance) / float(speed);
```

Note that the *distance* and the *speed* are explicitly converted to floating point representations in the quotient *float(distance) / float(speed)*. In the following table, compare values of *float(distance) / float(speed)* to the corresponding values of *distance / speed*. The table shows that simply using *distance / speed*, without conversions to *float*, may produce incorrect travel *time* when the *distance* and the *speed* are whole numbers.

Input for distance	Input for speed	Output from print **float**(distance) / **float**(speed);	Output from print distance / speed;
9.0	10.0	0.9	0.9
9.0	5.0	1.8	1.8
9	10	0.9	0
9	5	1.8	1

Note that explicit conversion to floating point numbers in the quotient *float(distance) / float(speed)* is needed to allow the user to input whole numbers for *distance* and *speed* without harm to the correctness of the calculation of the travel *time*.

Remember that the division of two integer numbers produces the integer floor of the mathematical quotient, without rounding. When you actually need to find the mathematical quotient itself, you should apply the *float* conversion function to the arguments. By doing that you force the *Python interpreter* to always perform floating point division, even if both arguments are integer numbers. As a result, the *Python interpreter* will always deliver the mathematical quotient represented as a floating point number.

It suffices to explicitly convert to *float* only one of the two arguments:

    print 'Travel time =', float(distance) / speed;
    print 'Travel time =', distance / float(speed);

As discussed earlier in this section, the *Python interpreter* will automatically convert the other argument when it happens to be an integer number.

Synonyms

Some terms that have been introduced in this Topic have synonyms. A list of such terms and their corresponding synonyms follows.

Term	Synonym
Program file	Source file; Python module
To execute a program	To run a program
Name	Identifier
Function invocation	Function call

Lab A [Introduction, Optional]

Objective; The Python System; Downloading Python; Installing Python; Creating a Custom Shortcut in Windows

Objective

The objective of this lab is to install the *Python system* on your computer.

The Python System

The *Python system* is a comprehensive Python software package for Windows, Macintosh, and Linux that is freely available from http://www.python.org. The *Python system* includes various components, such as a *Python interpreter*, an *Integrated Development Environment - IDLE*, and documentation. In this course of study, you will use the *Python system* to develop and execute your Python programs.

Downloading Python

Newer releases of the Python system are published periodically on http://www.python.org.

Generally, you should install the latest Python release. Occasionally, the latest Python release may exhibit some new bugs - it may misbehave. If you encounter problems with the latest Python release, you may also install an earlier release and see if the problems disappear.

Use a browser to open http://www.python.org. Go to *Downloads* and download a binary distribution for your particular platform. Follow the download instructions for your specific platform. You do not have to download sources.

For Windows, you should download a Windows installer. The installer is an executable file that installs the *Python system*. For a Macintosh OS, you should download a Macintosh OS installer. In general, download a proper installer for your specific platform.

Installing Python

Follow the platform-specific installation instructions from http://www.python.org. You are advised to accept the default installation parameters for the *Python system*. Make sure your installation includes the documentation that comes with the *Python system* download and the Integrated Development Environment for Python – IDLE.

In order to install the *Python system* on your platform, simply execute the downloaded platform-specific installer.

The *Python system* is used in subsequent labs.

Creating a Custom Shortcut in Windows

This optional step is recommended for Windows installations. You can use your *Python system* even if you do not perform this step.

By default, the Python IDLE runs multiple processes which that communicate with each other. In Windows, this communication may sometimes stall, particularly in the case of some computer graphics programs. Fortunately, you can use IDLE in single-process mode and avoid stalling.

To use IDLE in single-process mode, create a *special shortcut* on your desktop. Perform these steps:
- Use a Windows File Browser to find the file named *idle.pyw* in your Python installation.
  - For example, if you installed Python 2.4 on drive C:\, the *idle.pyw* file will be on this path:

    C:\Python24\Lib\idlelib\idle.pyw

- Right-click on the icon of *idle.pyw* then choose *Send To* create a shortcut to the desktop.
- Go to the desktop, right-click on the shortcut, and select *Properties*.
- In the *Target* field, add a special parameter, -n, that mandates the use of a single-process mode. Your target should be like this:

    C:\Python24\Lib\idlelib\idle.pyw –n

- Click *OK* to save the modified properties.

You can now use this new shortcut to start the Python IDLE. You may delete the original shortcut created by the Windows installer during the previous step.

Lab B [Introduction]

Objective; Overview of the Integrated Development Environment - IDLE; IDLE Windows and Menus; Starting IDLE; Browsing the Documentation; The Master Folder; Creating Your Master Folder; Downloading Sample Programs; Uncompressing Sample Programs; What Are Topic Folders and Labs Folders? Opening a Sample Program; Running a Program; Invoking Functions; Exiting IDLE

Objectives
The objectives of this lab are to:
- Get you acquainted with the Integrated Development Environment for Python – IDLE.
- Browse the documentation provided with IDLE.
- Create a folder for your Python programs.
- Download sample programs from the online study pack.
- Execute in IDLE a sample Python program.

Overview of the Integrated Development Environment - IDLE

The *Integrated Development Environment for Python* – IDLE is part of the *Python system*. You will use Python to create and execute your Python programs.

IDLE provides a uniform graphical user interface to:
- *Python editor*
- *File browser*
- *Python interpreter*
- *Python debugger*

The *Python editor* allows you to type-in and format Python program files.

The *file browser* allows you to navigate your folders and manipulate various files.

The *Python interpreter* executes Python programs.

The *Python debugger* helps you find errors in your Python programs. While the *Python editor* supports standard editing operations, such as copy, cut, paste, and find, it is *Python-specific*. he *Python editor*:
- Automatically suggests proper formatting for Python programs.
- Uses various font colors to make Python programs more understandable and easier to read.

IDLE Windows and Menus

You utilize the *Python editor* through one or more *Python editor windows*. *Python editor windows* are simply referred to as *editors*.

You interact with the *Python interpreter* through one or more *Python shell windows*. Python *shell windows* are simply referred to as *Python shells* or *shells*. They are also known as *interpreter windows*.

IDLE *editors* and *shells* display the same menus, such as *File, Edit, Options,* and *Help* menus.

Starting IDLE

IDLE is distributed for various platforms: Windows, Macintosh, and Linux. You start IDLE on each of them in a platform-specific way. Follow the platform-specific instructions provided with the *Python system* download.

If you are a Windows user, you can start IDLE by using *Start => Programs => Python* (Click the *Start* button, point to *Programs,* point to *Python*, point and then click *IDLE*).
- Start IDLE.
  - Depending on the particular IDLE configuration, IDLE starts with either an *editor window*, or a *shell window*.

Browsing the Documentation

The *Help* menu provides access to valuable documentation on IDLE in particular and Python in general.

First, browse the IDLE documentation:
- Use *Help => About IDLE => README* to open and read the README file for IDLE.
- Use *Help => IDLE Help* to open the IDLE help file.
- Browse the IDLE help and try to locate descriptions of some menus and commands you are familiar with.

Second, browse the Python documentation:
- Use *Help => Python Docs* to open the *document browser*.
- Read the list of available documents.
- Locate and open the *Python Tutorial*.
- Browse the *Python Tutorial*.
- When finished with browsing, close the *document browser*.

The Master Folder

Most *Lab Assignments* for this course require the development of various Python programs. You should keep all Python programs in a single *master* folder. This folder may reside on your preferred medium, such as your laptop's hard drive, a flash memory device, or a diskette. It is always a good idea to keep a backup on another medium as well.

In this course of study, the folder with your Python programs is referred to as the *master* folder. You may keep this name or choose a different name.

Creating Your Master Folder

- Create your *master* folder now.
- Create this folder on your preferred medium.

Downloading Sample Programs

Various Lab Assignments for this course of study are based on ready-to-use sample programs. Such programs are to be downloaded from the online study pack into your *master* folder.

Download sample programs for the current Topic 2 by performing these steps:
- Locate the current *Topic 2* in the online study pack.
- Open the *Lab Assignment* resource.
- Right-click on the *Sample Programs* link.
- Use *Save As* to store the downloaded compressed (zipped) folder, *02.zip,* within your *master* folder.

Uncompressing Sample Programs

- Uncompress the contents of the downloaded compressed (zipped) folder. Depending on your platform, you may use built-in compression support, or compressing utilities.
  - In Windows XP, for example, you can use built-in uncompression support as follows.
    - Use the *file browser* to open your *master* folder.
    - Right-click on the downloaded compressed (zipped) folder.

- Use *Extract All* and extract the contents of the compressed (zipped) folder within the *master* folder.
  - This will create an uncompressed folder, *02*, within the *master* folder. This folder will contain your sample programs.
- Alternatively, you can:
  - *Open* the compressed (zipped) folder.
  - *Cut* folder *02* from within the compressed (zipped) folder, and
  - *Paste* the cut folder *02* outside the compressed (zipped) folder – directly within the *master* folder.
○ Delete the compressed (zipped) folder, *02.zip*, and keep the uncompressed folder, *02*.
○ Open the uncompressed folder *02* and browse its contents.
- Note that Python program files have extension '**.py**'.

What Are Topic Folders and Labs Folders?

Your *master* folder should now contain your current topic folder, *02*. Your topic folder contains downloaded sample programs. It also contains an empty *labs folder, 02Labs*. While working on the *Lab Assignment* for the current topic, you will be saving your programs and other lab results in the *02Labs* folder. After having completed the *Lab Assignment*, you will be instructed to compress the *02Labs* folder and submit it online.

You will keep programs for different topics in different topic folders, all of them residing in the *master* folder. The name of each topic folder is formed by the corresponding *topic number*. Your folders for topics 2, 3, 4, etc will be named *02, 03, 04*, etc. Similarly, your labs folders will be named *02Labs, 03Labs, 04Labs*, etc.

Opening a Sample Program

You can open files from *editor* and *shell windows*. To open the downloaded *Temperature Converter* sample program:
○ Use *File => Open* then navigate to the current topic folder, *02*, within your *master* folder.
○ Locate and open the *TemperatureConverter.py* program file.

The last action displays the *Temperature Converter* sample program in an *editor window*. Do not try to change the program at this time.

Running a Program

Once you have a program in an *editor window*, you can run it.
- Use *Run => Run Module* to run the *Temperature Converter* program.

In response to the *Run Module* command, IDLE does the following:
- Starts the *Python interpreter* and opens a *shell window* for the execution.
- Displays some start-up message followed by the *shell prompt*, **>>>**.
- Executes the statement from the program.

The *Temperature Converter* program contains definition statements for functions *F2C()* and *C2F()*. The execution of these statements defines the functions to the *Python system* but does not invoke them.

Invoking Functions

Once you have functions defined, you can invoke, or call them.
- At the *shell prompt*, **>>>**, type the function invocation *F2C()* and press *Enter*:

  >>> F2C();

- Provide input as requested by the function, one number at a time followed by the Enter key.
- Observe the output produced by the *F2C()* function.
- Use the same method to invoke function *C2F()*:

  >>> C2F();

- Invoke the two functions several more times and experiment with different input data.

Exiting IDLE

- Use *File*, then *Exit* to close all IDLE windows and terminate your IDLE session.
  - Use *File* then *Close* to close an individual window while still keeping IDLE active.

Lab C [Introduction]

Objective; Background; Lab Overview; What to Do Next; Finding Conversion Factors; Designing Conversion Equations; Creating a Program File as a Copy of a Sample Program; Developing a Conversion Function; Running Your Program; Coping with Syntax Errors; Invoking a Function; Coping with Runtime Errors; Testing a Function; Using a Test Table; Coping with Validity Errors; What is Debugging? Developing All Conversion Functions

Objective

The objective of this Lab is to develop a *Converters* program. This program must perform conversions between the following metric and U.S. customary units:
- Centimeters and inches
- Liters and gallons
- Meters and yards
- Kilograms and pounds

Background

The *Temperature Converter* sample program implements conversions between *Fahrenheit* and *Celsius* temperature measurements. This program can be extended to perform conversions between other units, such as centimeters and inches. Such additional conversions can be implemented analogously to temperature conversions.

One inch equals approximately *2.54 centimeters*. This dependency can be expressed with the following *conversion equation*:

   centimeters = 2.54 x inches

The above equation allows the conversion of any measurement in *centimeters* to an equivalent measurement in *inches*. Conversions from *inches to centimeters* are based on a *conversion factor 2.54* because *centimeters = 2.54 x inches*.

All conversions that are to be implemented in this Lab are based on particular conversion factors. All necessary conversion factors can be found on the Web or in library reference resources.

Lab Overview

Note
Read this Lab Overview section, but do not actually perform any of the suggested lab activities at this time. The purpose of this section is to present to you *the big picture* the lab. Once you finish reading, continue with the next section.

To perform this lab, you should:
- Make a copy of the sample *Temperature Converter* program.
- Use the *Temperature Converter's* functions *F2C* and *C2F* as patterns to follow and implement the following new functions:
  - *C2I* and *I2C* for conversions between centimeters and inches
  - *L2G* and *G2L* for conversions between liters and gallons
  - *M2Y* and *Y2M* for conversions between meters and yards
  - *K2P* and *P2K* for conversions between kilograms and pounds
- Thoroughly test your conversion functions with various test data.

What to Do Next
At this time, you are offered these choices:
- Follow the detailed lab instructions below, or
- Try the lab independently, but also peek in the instructions when needed, or
- Perform the lab independently, without looking at instructions at all.

All three approaches can be beneficial for students. Feel free to choose the approach that you believe is most beneficial for you.

Finding Conversion Factors
- Search the Web to find necessary conversion factors. Carefully select your search keywords.

  ### Example
  A search in Google with keywords *'metric conversion factors'* or alternatively, *'measurement conversion'*, should provide all needed conversion factors. For example: 1 gallon [US, liquid] = 3.7854118 liter.

- Instead of searching the Web, you may use library reference resources to find conversion factors.

Designing Conversion Equations
- Use the conversion factors that you found on the Web to design conversion equations.
- Your conversion equations for this lab should be expressed in a similar notation as the already familiar Fahrenheit to Celsius and Celsius to Fahrenheit conversion equations.

  ### Example
  Once you know, for example, that 1 US liquid gallon contains 3.785 liter, you can write down the following conversion equation:

  > litters = 3.785 x gallons
  > gallons = litters / 3.785

- Once you have correct conversion equations, you can transform these equations into a working Python program. Follow the steps outlined in the rest of this Lab.

Creating a Program File as a Copy of a Sample Program
Create this program in your current labs folder, *02Labs*. Folder *02Labs* resides in the current topic folder, *02*. As a part of a previous Lab, you already created these folders. As a part of the same previous Lab, you already downloaded all sample programs, including the *Temperature Converter* sample program.

Perform in sequence the following activities:
- Start IDLE.
- Use *File => Open* browse to find and open the *TemperatureConverter.py* program file.
- Use *File => Save As* and name the saved program file as *Conversions.py*.
  - **Important Note:** You must explicitly supply the file extension '**.py**' when saving from IDLE.

Developing a Conversion Function
- Make sure that the *Conversions.py* program file is open in an IDLE *editor window*.
- Update the beginning comment of the entire program as follows:
  - Replace the original program name, *Temperature Converter*, with the new program name, *Conversions*.
  - Replace the original author name with your own name.
  - Replace the original year with the current date.

- Copy the definition of function *F2C* and paste it at the end of the program.
  - Remember to copy the function explanatory comment that precedes the function definition.
- Convert the copied function *F2C* into a function *I2C* that implements *inches-to-centimeters* conversion. To achieve this, perform the following steps with the pasted copy (not with the original):
  - Replace the copied function name *F2C* with the new function name *I2C*.
  - Replace the copied explanatory comment with a new explanatory comment to adequately describe the *inches-to-centimeters* conversion.
  - Modify the entire copied function body to implement the conversion equation *centimeters = 2.54 x inches*.
- Use *File => Save*.

Running Your Program
- Make sure that your *Conversions.py* program file is still open in an IDLE *editor window*.
- Use *Run => Run Module* to start the execution of your program.

Coping with Syntax Errors
If your program contains a syntax error, IDLE will show you an error message within the *editor window*. You need to find the reason for the error and correct your program. This can be done in the Computer Lab, where you can ask for help.

Perform the following activities:
- Use the *editor window* to correct the syntax error. This requires adequate modifications to your program in the *editor window*.
- Use *File => Save* and then *Run => Run Module*. Repeat this process as needed.

Invoking a Function
If your program does not contain syntax errors, the execution of *Run => Run Module* will show you a *shell window* with a *shell prompt* >>> at its bottom.

Do this:
- At the *shell prompt*, **>>>**, type the function invocation *I2C()* and press *Enter*:

>>> I2C();

Coping with Runtime Errors

If your program contains a runtime error, IDLE will show you an error message within the *shell window*. You need to find the reason for the error message and correct your program. Again, this can be done in the Computer Lab, where you can ask for help.

Perform the following activities:
- Return from the *shell window* to the *editor window* to correct the runtime error. This requires adequate modifications to your program in the *editor window*.
- Use *File => Save* and then *Run => Run Module*. Repeat this process as needed.

Testing a Function

After having corrected all possible syntax and run-time errors, you should test the validity of your *I2C* function. In a *shell window*, invoke the *I2C* function by typing *I2C()*.

Do this:
- Provide various input data and observe the output produced by the *I2C()* invocation.
  - If needed, use a calculator to validate the output of the function.

Using a Test Table

The following *Test Table* contains measurements in inches and their corresponding values in centimeters. Use the table to test your *I2C* function.

Inches	Centimeters
0	0
1	2.54
2	5.08
0.5	1.27

For each inch value from the *Test Table*, invoke the *I2C()* function, supply that inch value, and compare the output to the corresponding centimeter value from the table. The test succeeds if the values are the same; otherwise, it fails. Minor differences due to rounding are acceptable.

Coping with Validity Errors

If your *I2C* function does not produce valid test results, it contains a validity error. You may be using incorrect conversion formula. It is your responsibility to discover and fix validity errors. You need to analyze and explore your program in order to find the reason for the validity errors. As with other errors, this may be done in the Computer Lab where you can ask for help. Once you locate the problem, you need to correct your function definition and retest it. This process should be repeated until the validity of the function is established.

What is Debugging?

The process of locating and correcting various errors is called *debugging*. You should try to debug each function as extensively as possible before proceeding with the development of another function.

Developing All Conversion Functions

Develop all remaining functions that are required for this Lab. These functions are listed in the *Lab Overview* section. Follow a similar approach as with your first developed function, *I2C*.

For each newly developed function, perform these steps:
- Copy the definition of known function, such as *F2C,* that is similar to the function to develop.
- Transform the copied function definition into a definition for the new function.
- Develop a *Test Table* for the new function. Possibly, use a calculator.
- Debug the new function.

Lab D [Introduction]

Objectives; Overview of Interactive Mode; Exploring Interactive Mode; Overview of Error Simulation Experiments; Simulating Syntax Errors; Simulating Runtime Errors; Experimenting on Your Own; Saving Your Interactive Session

Objectives
The objectives of this lab are:
- To introduce interactive programming mode.
- To simulate interactively and gain experience with various syntax and runtime errors.

Overview of Interactive Mode
The *Python interpreter* can be used in two modes: *file input mode* and *interactive mode*. In file input mode, the *Python interpreter* executes entire programs saved in files. In interactive mode, the Interpreter executes statements that are typed interactively without saving them in a file.

In IDLE, you can open a *shell window* then type various Python statements at the *shell prompt*. You immediately observe the results from their execution. The interactive programming mode allows you to experiment with the Python language. If you are not certain how a statement works, test it interactively.

Exploring Interactive Mode
Explore the interactive mode of Python by executing the following steps.
- Start IDLE.
  - If an *editor window* is currently active, use *Run => Python shell* to switch to an *editor window*.
- At the *shell prompt*, >>>, type the statements from the list below.
  - Type one line at a time then hit *Enter* to submit it to the *Python interpreter* for execution.
  - Do not retype the *shell prompt*, >>>, itself.
  - Observe and analyze the execution result before you continue with another statement.

```
>>> x1 = 3.14;
>>> print x1;
>>> print x1 * 2;
>>> x2 = 2;
>>> print x1 * x2;
>>> print x1 + x2;
>>> print x1 - x2;
>>> print x1 / x2;
>>> x3 = x1 * x2;
>>> print x3;
>>> x2 = 10;
>>> print x3;
>>> x3 = x1 * x2;
>>> print x3;
```

The same line can contain a list of simple statements separated by required semicolons. A semicolon at the end of the line is optional, not required Execute the following statement lists in interactive mode:

```
>>> x1 = 3.14; print x1
>>> x2 = x1 * 10; print x2; print x1
>>> x1 = 3.14; print x1; x2 = x1 * 10; print x2; print x1
```

Overview of Error Simulation Experiments

Copying with various errors is an inherent part of any program development. Understanding error messages and fixing errors in Python programs will become easier as you gain programming experience. In the beginning of your study, however, copying with errors is very frustrating. It is a beneficial exercise to simulate some typical programming errors on purpose to observe the corresponding error messages. By making programming errors on purpose and observing the consequences you will gain valuable experience. This experience will make you better prepared to handle errors that appear by accident in your future programming activities.

The interactive programming mode of Python is particularly suited for error simulation experiments. In very few areas of human learning it is possible to safely learn by simulating errors, without paying any penalty for the errors.

In IDLE, you can open a *shell window* then type various incorrect Python statements. You can immediately observe the error messages and how they are related to the actual errors. You can also execute corrected versions of the erroneous statements.

Simulating Syntax Errors

Syntax errors are violations of the syntax rules of the language. When a statement contains a syntax error, a *syntax error message* is produced by the *Python system*. Statements with syntax errors are never executed. The following exercise is intended to simulate syntax errors and observe the corresponding error messages.

At the *shell prompt*, >>>, type the statements from the list below.
- Type one statement at a time on a single line.
- Do not retype the *shell prompt* >>> itself, neither the comment at the end of the statement.
- Observe and analyze syntax error messages.
- Retype a syntactically correct version of each incorrect statement before you continue with another statement.

```
>>> x1 = 3.14;
>>> Print x1;
>>> x 1 = 3.14;
>>> x1 = 3. 14;
>>> print x1 \ 10;
```

Note that:
- The first statement contains no error – its purpose is to introduce the variable *x1* needed in the next statements.
- The second statement uses a capital 'P' in *Print* instead of lowercase 'p', as in *print*.
- The third statement is incorrect because there is a space between 'x' and '1' in *x 1*. Spaces are not allowed in names.
- Spaces invalid within numbers, also. The space between '.' and '1' in *3. 14*, in the fourth statement, is an error.
- Finally, the expression *x1 \ 10*, in the fifth statement, is syntactically incorrect because the backslash '\' is not a valid operator.

Simulating Runtime Errors

Runtime errors are violations of the semantics of the language. Most errors like this cannot be detected prior to the actual program execution. When the execution of a statement results in a runtime error, a *runtime error message* is produced. The following exercise is intended to simulate runtime errors and observe the corresponding error messages.

At the *shell prompt*, **>>>**, type the statements from the list below.
- Type one statement at a time on a single line.
- Do not retype the *shell prompt* >>> itself, or the comment at the end of the statement.
- Observe and analyze runtime error messages.
- Retype a semantically correct version of each incorrect statement before you continue with another statement.

```
>>> x1 = 3.14;
>>> x2 = 0;
>>> print x1 / x2;
>>> print X2;
```

Note that:
- The first two statements contain no error – their purpose is to introduce variables *x1* and *x2* needed in the next statements.
- The runtime error in the third statement is caused by a division by zero.
  - Division by zero is an operation that has an undefined result.
- The runtime error in the last statement is caused by the use of a capital 'X' instead of lowercase 'x' in *x2*.
  - Variable X2, with a capital 'X', has not been introduced by a previous statement and is therefore undefined.
    - Only variables *x1* and *x2* with lowercase 'x' have been defined.

Experimenting on Your Own

Use interactive programming mode to conduct your own experiments with Python.
- Execute statements that you believe are correct.
- Try to simulate syntax and runtime errors and analyze the generated error messages.
  - For example, try to use *Print* instead of *print* and break a string literal between two lines.

Saving Your Interactive Session

- You must save the interactive session with all of your experiments in your current labs folder, *02Labs*.
- From the *shell window*, use *File => Save As*.
- Give the name *Session_2D.txt* to the saved copy.
  - **Important Note:** You must explicitly supply the file extension '**.txt**' when saving from IDLE.

- If you want to perform experiments in two or more interactive sessions, you can save your work in several files. If you choose to do so, use names *Session_2D_1.txt, Session_2D_2.txt*, and so on, for all saved files.
- Your saved file(s) must belong to your Lab Assignment submission.

Lab E [Introduction]

Objective; Background; Lab Overview; What to Do Next; Studying the Sample Program; Creating a Program File; Developing the New Program

Objective

The objective of this lab is to develop a *Seconds Counter* program to:
- Input non-negative numbers for *hours, minutes,* and *seconds*.
- Count the *total number of seconds*.
- Output the *total number of second*.

Background

A sample program named *Cents Counter* counts the total of all pennies in any given collection of coins. In particular, the program:
- Inputs non-negative numbers for *quarters, dimes, nickels,* and *pennies*.
- Counts the *total number of pennies*.
- Outputs the *total number of pennies*.

A *Seconds Counter* program, as required by this Lab, can be developed analogously to the *Cents Counter* sample program.

Lab Overview

Note

Read this Lab Overview section, but do not perform any of the suggested lab activities at this time. The purpose of this section is to present to you *the big picture* the lab. Once you finish reading, continue with the next section.

To perform this lab:
- Study the *Cents Counter* sample program.
- Transform a copy of the *Cents Counter* sample program into a *Seconds Counter* program.
- Design a *Test Table* and debug the *Seconds Counter* program.

What to Do Next
At this time, you are offered these choices:
- Follow the detailed lab instructions below.
- Try the lab independently, but also peek in the instructions when needed.
- Perform the lab independently, with no aid from the instructions.

All three approaches are beneficial to students. Feel free to choose the approach you believe is most beneficial for you.

Studying the Sample Program
- Use IDLE to open and browse the *Cents Counter* sample program.
- Run the program with various input data; observe its output.
- Analyze the program implementation.

Creating a Program File
Create this program in your current lab folder, *02Labs*. Folder *02Labs* resides in the current topic folder, *02*. As part of a previous lab, you already created these folders. As a part of the same previous lab, you already downloaded all sample programs, including the *Cents Counter* sample program.

Perform the following steps:
- Use IDLE to create a copy of the *Cents Counter* program file.
- Give the name *SecondsCounter.py* to the saved copy.
    - **Important Note:** You must explicitly supply the file extension '**.py**' when saving from IDLE.

Developing the New Program
Perform these steps with the newly created *Seconds Counter* program:
- Transform the definition of function *cents* into a definition for function *seconds*.
    - Use the following formula:

    *seconds total = seconds + 60 * minutes + 3600 * hours*

    - Remember to change all comments adequately.
- Develop a *Test Table* for the new function. Possibly, use a calculator.
- Debug the new function.

Lab F [Introduction]

Objective; Background; Lab Overview; What to Do Next; Studying the Sample Program; Creating a Program File; Developing the New Program

Objective

The objective of this lab is to develop an *Order Calculator* program that will:
- Input non-negative numbers for *quantity* of items per order, *item price* and sales *tax rate* (as percentage).
- Calculate the *total price* of the order, the *sales tax*, and the *order total*.
- Output *quantity, item price, sales tax,* and *order total*.

Background

A sample program named *Wage Calculator* calculates *weekly wages* and *tax due*. In particular, the program:
- Inputs non-negative numbers for *hours worked, pay rate,* and *tax rate*.
- Calculates *gross wages, tax due,* and *net wages*.
- Outputs *gross wages, tax due,* and *net wages*.

An *Order Calculator* program, as required by this Lab, can be developed analogously to the *Wage Calculator* sample program.

Lab Overview

Note

Read this Lab Overview section, but do not actually perform any of the suggested lab activities at this time. The purpose of this section is to present to you *the big picture* the lab. Once you finish reading, continue with the next section.

To perform this lab, you should:
- Study the *Wage Calculator* sample program.
- Transform a copy of the *Wage Calculator* sample program into an *Order Calculator* program.
- Design a *Test Table* and debug the *Order Calculator* program.

What to Do Next
At this time, you are offered these choices:
- Follow the detailed lab instructions below.
- Try the lab independently, but also peek in the instructions when needed.
- Perform the lab independently, with no aid from the instructions.

All three approaches are beneficial to students. Feel free to choose the approach you believe is most beneficial for you.

Studying the Sample Program
- Use IDLE to open and browse the *Order Calculator* sample program.
- Run the program with various input data; observe its output.
- Analyze the program implementation.

Creating a Program File
Create this program in your current lab folder, *02Labs*. Folder *02Labs* resides in the current topic folder, *02*. As part of a previous lab, you already created these folders. As a part of the same previous lab, you already downloaded all sample programs, including the *Wage Calculator* sample program.

Perform the following steps:
- Use IDLE to create a copy of the *Wage Calculator* program file.
- Give the name *OrderCalculator.py* to the saved copy.
  - **Important Note:** You must explicitly supply the file extension '**.py**' when saving from IDLE.

Developing the New Program
Perform these steps with the newly created *Order Calculator* program:
- Transform the definition of function *wages* into a definition for function *order*.
  - Use the following formulas:

    total price = *quantity* * *item price*
    sales tax = *total price* * (*tax rate* / 100.0)
    order total = *total price* + *sales tax*

  - Remember to change all comments adequately.
- Develop a *Test Table* for the new function. Possibly, use a calculator.
- Debug the new function.

Lab G [Introduction]

Objective; Background; Lab Overview; What to Do Next; Number Guessing Equation; Creating a Program File; Developing the New Program; Number Guessing Background [Optional]

Objective

The objective of this lab is to develop a *Number Guesser* program that will:
- Ask the user to think of an arbitrary *secret number*.
  - Note the user is supposed to keep the number secret from the program and the program is supposed to guess the user's secret number.
- Ask the user to multiply the secret number by 5, add 6, multiply by 4, add 9, and multiply by 5.
  - Note that it is the user who is supposed to perform those operations with his or her chosen number, not your program.
- Ask the user to enter the *result* of the above operations.
- Guess the secret number.
- Output the guessed secret number.

Background

A possible execution of your Number Guesser program may look like this:

```
>>> guess()
- Think of a secret number.
- Multiply it by 5.
- Add 6 to the result.
- Multiply the previous result by 4.
- Add 9.
- Again, multiply by 5.
- Enter the final result: 4365
Hmmm... I guess you secret number was 42.
>>>
```

Lab Overview

Note
Read this Lab Overview section, but do not actually perform any of the suggested lab activities at this time. The purpose of this section is to present to you *the big picture* the lab. Once you finish reading, continue with the next section.

To perform this lab, you should:
- Study the *number guessing equation* below.
- Use the number guessing equation to write a *Number Guesser* program.
- Design a *Test Table* and debug the *Number Guesser* program.

What to Do Next
At this time, you are offered these choices:
- Follow the detailed lab instructions below.
- Try the lab independently, but also peek in the instructions when needed.
- Perform the lab independently, with no aid from the instructions.

All three approaches are beneficial to students. Feel free to choose the approach you believe is most beneficial for you.

Number Guessing Equation
Remember, the user of the program is asked to think of a secret number, perform several operations, and input the result of the operations into your *Number Guesser* program. The following equation describes how your program can find the *secret number*, given the *result* of the application of all operations:

secret = (result - 165) / 100

If you know the *result* of the above operations, you can easily determine the *secret number* by applying the above equation.

Exercise
Perform number guessing by hand. For example, think of the number 42. Multiply the secret number by 5, add 6, multiply by 4, add 9, and multiply by 5. The result of these operations should be 4365. Subtract the integer number 165 to receive 4200 and divide by the integer number 100 to receive 42.

What to Do Next
At this time, you are offered these choices:
- Follow the detailed lab instructions below.
- Try the lab independently, but also peek in the instructions when needed.
- Perform the lab independently, with no aid from the instructions.

All three approaches are beneficial to students. Feel free to choose the approach you believe is most beneficial for you.

Creating a Program File
Create this program in your current lab folder, *02Labs*. Folder *02Labs* resides in the current topic folder, *02*. As part of a previous lab, you already created these folders.

Perform the following steps:
- Use IDLE to create a new *Number Guesser* program file.
  - Use *File => New Window* to create a new blank file.
- Give the name *NumberGuesser.py* to the file.
  - Use *File => Save As* to save the new file under the name *NumberGuesser.py*.
  - **Important Note:** You must explicitly supply the file extension '**.py**' when saving from IDLE.

Developing the New Program
Perform these steps with the newly created *Number Guesser* program:
- Define a function named *guess*.
- Use six print-statements to tell the user to think of a number and perform required operations with that number.
  - You can make your program output similar messages as these:

    - Think of a secret number.
    - Multiply it by 5.
    - Add 6 to the result.
    - Multiply the previous result by 4.
    - Add 9.
    - Again, multiply by 5.

  - Print all of the above lines at once and do not wait for the user to respond.
- Ask the user to enter the result from the above operations.
  - Use an input statement.

- Transform the number guessing equation into an assignment statement to determine the *secret* number, given the *result*.
- Use a print-statement to output the *secret* number.
- Develop a *Test Table* for the new function. Use a calculator if necessary.
- Debug the new function.

Number Guessing Background [Optional]

Reading this section is optional.

Remember, the user of the program is asked to think of a number, perform several operations, and input the result of the operations into your *Number Guesser* program. The following equation determines the *result* of the application of all operations as a function of the *secret* number:

result = ((secret x 5 + 6) x 4) + 9) x 5

You can simplify the right-hand side by performing all operations:

result = ((secret x 5 + 6) x 4) + 9) x 5
     = ((secret x 5 x 4 + 6 x 4) + 9) x 5
     = ((secret x 20 + 24) + 9) x 5
     = (secret x 20 + 24 + 9) x 5
     = (secret x 20 + 33) x 5
     = secret x 20 x 5 + 33 x 5
     = secret x 100 + 165

Hence, the following equation relates the secret number and the result from the operations:

result = secret x 100 + 165

You can modify that same equation and make it determine the secret, given the result:

secret = (result - 165) / 100

The above number guessing equation is the backbone of the *Number Guesser* program.

Lab H [Introduction, Optional]

Objective; Background; Lab Overview

Objective

The objective of this lab is to develop a *Gas Cost Calculator* program to:
- Input non-negative numbers for *total distance* (in miles) of a trip, *gas mileage* (as miles-per-gallon), and *gas price* (in US currency per gallon).
- Calculate the total *gas cost* of the trip.
- Output the total *gas cost*.

Background

To calculate the *gas cost* of a trip you need to multiple the *gas price* (in US currency per gallon) by the *amount of gas* (in gallons) necessary for the trip. To calculate the *amount of gas* (in gallons), you need to divide the *total distance* (in miles) by the *gas mileage* (as miles-per-gallon).

Lab Overview

- Study sample programs for this topic.
- Design and write formulae for the calculations.
- Design a *Test Table* and check your designed formulae.
- Create a program file in your current labs folder.
- Transform your formulae into a Python program.
- Debug your program; Use your *Test Table*.

Lab I [Introduction, Optional]

Objective; Background; Lab Overview

Objective
The objective of this lab is to develop a *Gas Price Converter* program that will:
- Input the current exchange rate between the *US currency* (the US Dollar) and the *European currency* (the Euro).
- Input non-negative numbers for gas *price per gallon in US currency*.
- Calculate the equivalent *gas price per litter in European currency*.
- Output the two *gas prices*.

Background
Given the gas price *per gallon* in US currency, gas price is calculated *per litter* in US currency. You can then convert the calculated price from *US currency* to *European currency*. On the Web, you can find the current exchange rate between the *US Dollar* and the *Euro*.

Lab Overview
- Study sample programs for this topic.
- Design and write down formulae for the conversions.
- Design a *Test Table* and check your designed formulae.
- Create a program file in your current labs folder.
- Transform your formulae into a Python program.
- Debug your program; Use your *Test Table*.

Program Control: Selection

Sample Programming Problem: Conversion Selection; Sample Program: Conversion Selector; Control Structures; If-Statement Form; If-Statement Execution; If-Statement Layout; Multiple Selection; Two-Way Selection; Repetitive Assignments to the Same Variable; One-Way Selection; Case Study: Quiz Evaluator; Boolean Expressions; Operator Precedence; Parentheses; Nested If-Statements; Redundant Conditions; Synonyms

Sample Programming Problem: Conversion Selection

Consider the following programming problem:
Develop a *Conversion Selector* program that will:
- Display a menu of two possible temperature conversions:
  - Fahrenheit to Celsius conversion
  - Celsius to Fahrenheit conversion
- Ask the user to choose one conversion from the menu.
- Input the user choice
- Perform the conversion chosen by the user.

The menu of possible conversions may look like this:

Temperature Conversions Menu:
(1) Convert Fahrenheit to Celsius
(2) Convert Celsius to Fahrenheit
Enter choice number:

The user choice must be a whole number, 1 or 2, without parentheses. If the user chooses 1, the program will ask the user for a temperature in Fahrenheit, then calculate and display the corresponding temperature in Celsius. If the user chooses 2, the program will ask the user for a temperature in Celsius, then calculate and display the corresponding temperature in Fahrenheit.

Sample Program: Conversion Selector

The following *Conversion Selector* program solves the programming problem proposed in the previous section. The program incorporates a function named *select* to display a menu with the two possible temperature conversions, accept the user choice, and perform the conversion chosen by the user. The program also incorporates additional helper functions that are employed by the *select* function.

Exercise

Run the *Conversion Selector* program. In interactive mode, invoke the *select* function and experiment with various inputs.

The complete *Conversion Selector* program follows.

```python
# Helper function to print all menu items:
def displayMenu():
    print 'Temperature Conversions Menu:';
    print '(1) Convert Fahrenheit to Celsius';
    print '(2) Convert Celsius to Fahrenheit';

# Main function to display menu and invoke
# user-selected conversion:
def select():
    displayMenu();
    choice = input('Enter choice number: ');
    if (choice == 1):
        F2C();
    elif (choice == 2):
        C2F();
    else:
        print 'Invalid choice: ', choice;
    print 'Bye-bye.';

# Convert Fahrenheit temperature to Celsius temperature:
def F2C():
    Fahrenheit = input('Enter degrees in Fahrenheit: ');
    Celsius    = (5.0 / 9.0) * (Fahrenheit - 32);
    print Fahrenheit, 'Fahrenheit =', Celsius, 'Celsius';

# Convert Celsius temperature to Fahrenheit temperature:
def C2F():
    Celsius    = input('Enter degrees in Celsius: ');
    Fahrenheit = (9.0 / 5.0) * Celsius + 32;
    print Celsius, 'Celsius =', Fahrenheit, 'Fahrenheit';
```

The *Conversion Selector* program incorporates the following functions:

Function	Purpose
displayMenu	Displays a menu of two possible temperature conversions: Fahrenheit to Celsius and Celsius to Fahrenheit.
select	Main function in the program invoked in interactive mode. When the function is invoked, it does the following: • Invokes function *displayMenu* to have a menu displayed. • Inputs a user choice. • Tests the user choice and, depending on the choice, selects a conversion function to be invoked (function *F2C* or function *C2F*) or prints an error message when the user choice is invalid. • Prints 'Bye-bye.' at the end.
F2C	Performs a Fahrenheit-to-Celsius conversion.
C2F	Performs a Celsius-to- Fahrenheit conversion.

Note

The definitions of functions *F2C* and *C2F* are the same as those in the *Temperature Converter* program studied in a previous Topic. These definitions have been copied from the *Temperature Converter* program and then pasted into this *Conversion Selector* program. As a matter of fact, a copy of the entire *Temperature Converter* program has been pasted into the *Conversion Selector* program.

The selection of a conversion function to be invoked is implemented by means of an *if-statement*. The following Python-to-English translation provides insight into the meaning of the if-statement from the *Conversion Selector* program.

Python-To-English Translation

Python If-Statement	Common English Meaning
if (choice == 1) :	Step 1. ○ Test if *choice is equal to 1*. • If this is true, continue with the next Step 2; • Otherwise jump over to Step 3. Note: Equality comparisons are denoted by the double token '==', while the single token '=' is reserved for assignment statements.
F2C();	Step 2. ○ Invoke function *F2C()* and wait for the function to complete its execution. ○ After that, jump over to Step 7.
elif (choice == 2) :	Step 3. ○ Test if *choice is equal to 2*. • If this is true, continue with the next Step 4; • Otherwise jump over to Step 5.
C2F();	Step 4. ○ Invoke function *C2F()* and wait for the function to complete its execution. ○ After that, jump over to Step 7.
else :	Step 5. ○ Do not test anything - just continue with the next Step 6.
print 'Invalid choice: ';	Step 6. ○ Execute the print statement. ○ Continue with the next Step 7.
# Immediately after the if-statement: *print 'Bye-bye.';*	Step 7. ○ The execution of the program continues with whichever statement comes after the if-statement (if any). ○ In the *select* function, this is the statement that prints 'Bye-bye'.

Example

The following table presents several invocations of function *select*:

>>> select(); Temperature Conversions Menu: (1) Convert Fahrenheit to Celsius (2) Convert Celsius to Fahrenheit Enter choice number: **1** Enter degrees in Fahrenheit: **32** 32 Fahrenheit = 0.0 Celsius Bye-bye.	>>> select(); Temperature Conversions Menu: (1) Convert Fahrenheit to Celsius (2) Convert Celsius to Fahrenheit Enter choice number: **2** Enter degrees in Celsius: **0** 0 Celsius = 32.0 Fahrenheit Bye-bye.

Control Structures

Computer programs specify actions that are to be executed by computers. The order of execution is specified by means of control structures. All practical programming languages support three basic control structures: sequence, selection, and repetition.

Control Structure	Purpose	Python Example
Sequence	Used to execute several actions in a predetermined order. There is no possibility of skipping an action or branching off to another action. All actions are executed one after the other, in the same order as they appear in the sequence.	Celsius = input('Degrees in Celsius: '); Fahrenheit = (9.0 / 5.0) * Celsius + 32; print Fahrenheit;

Selection	Used to test one or more conditions. Depending on the result of the test, selects one of several possible courses of action.	if (choice == 1):
		    F2C();
		elif (choice == 2):
		    C2F();
		else:
		    print 'Invalid... ';

Repetition	Used to test one condition. If the test succeeds, executes an action. This test-execute process is repeated until the condition test fails.	*Python repetitions are studied in the next Topic.*

In Python, selection is implemented by means of if-statements. Other languages offer additional selection statements, notably the switch-statements in Java and C++, and the case-statements in Pascal.

If-Statement Form

If-statements are compound structures that are built of various sub-structures, such as *conditions* and statement *blocks*. The following table describes allowed forms of if-statements and their sub-structures.

Structure	Description	Example

If-Statement	An if-statement starts with an *if-clause*, optionally followed by one or more *elif-clauses*, optionally followed by one *else-clause*.	if (choice == 1):
		  F2C();
		elif (choice == 2):
		  C2F();
		else:
		  print 'Invalid... ';

Clause	A sequence of a header and a body. The example to the right is an if-clause. The first line is the if-clause header and the second line is the if-clause body.	if (choice == 1): F2C();
If / Elif-clause header	Starts with the keyword 'if'/ 'elif', followed by a condition, followed by a colon.	if (choice == 1):
Else-clause header	Starts with the keyword 'else', without a condition, followed by a colon.	else:
Body	An indented block of statements controlled by a header.	F2C();

Block of statements	A sequence of one, two, three, or more aligned statements.	a = 10;
		b = 20 * a;
		c = a + b;

Condition	An expression that is true or false.	(choice == 2) (18 < age < 21)

If-Statement Execution

The if-statement is used for conditional execution:
- It selects one of the clauses by evaluating the expressions one by one until one is found to be true, then the body of that clause is executed.
  - No other part of the if-statement is executed or evaluated.
- If all expressions are false, the body of the else-clause, if present, is executed.

If-Statement Layout

All headers of a particular if-statement must be vertically aligned, using the same indentation. In each clause, the body must be indented from the corresponding header. Improper clause indentation is a syntax error. It is detected and reported prior to program execution.

Example

The following if-statement is not aligned properly and will trigger syntax error message when execution is attempted:

```
if (choice == 1):
   F2C();
   elif (choice == 2):
   C2F();
      else:
      print 'Invalid choice: ', choice;
```

Multiple Selection

An if-statement starts with an if-clause, optionally followed by one or more elif-clauses, optionally followed by one else-clause. An if-statement that contains at least three clauses is called *multiple selection if-statement*.

The following sample problem requires multiple selection if-statement.

Develop a function to:
- Input taxable annual *income*.
- Determine the applicable tax *rate* and calculate the *tax* due
- Output the *tax* due.

Assume that the following tax rates apply:
- Annual income that is not over $7,150 is taxed at 10%.
- Annual income over $7,150 but less than $29,050 is taxed at 15%.
- Annual income over $29,050 is taxed at 25%.

Given any income, one of the following three calculations must take place:
- tax = 0.10 * income
- tax = 0.15 * income
- tax = 0.25 * income

Before writing a program, it helps to outline the selection process in a design table. The design table for this particular problem will systematically present tax rate limits and the corresponding tax calculation. For example:

Taxable income is over:	But not over:	The tax rate is:	Tax calculation:
	7,150	10%	tax = 0.10 * income
7,150	29,050	15%	tax = 0.15 * income
29,050		25%	tax = 0.25 * income

The above design table can be converted into the following Python function definition:

```
# Multiple selection example:
def taxes():
    income = input('Enter annual income: ');
    if (income <= 7150):
        tax = 0.10 * income;
    elif (income <= 29050):
        tax = 0.15 * income;
    else: # Comment: income is greater than 29,500
        tax = 0.25 * income;
    print 'Tax due =', tax;
```

Exercise

Determine all steps from the execution of the *taxes* function in the following cases:

- Income = 7150
- Income = 29050
- Income = 29051

Two-Way Selection

An if-statement starts with an if-clause, optionally followed by one or more elif-clauses, optionally followed by one else-clause. An if-statement that contains exactly two clauses is called *two-way selection if-statement*, or simply *two-way if-statement*. In two-way if-statement, the following combinations of clauses are possible:

An if-clause followed by an else-clause
or
An if-clause followed by an elif-clause.

The following sample problem can be solved by means of a two-way if-statement.

Develop a function to:
- Input *hours* worked and hourly *pay rate*.
- Calculate *wages* by multiplying *hours* by *rate*.
- Consider hours over 40 as overtime and pay them at *120%*.
- Output *wages*.

As previously mentioned, it helps to outline the selection process in a design table. The design table for this particular problem will systematically present regular and overtime time limits and the corresponding wage calculation. For example:

Hours are over:	But not over:	The pay rate is:	Wage calculation:
0	40	100%	wages = hours * rate
40		120%	wages = 40 * rate + 1.20 * rate * (hours - 40)

The above design table can be converted into the following Python function definition:

```
# Two-way selection example:
def wagesTwoWay():
    hours = input('Enter hours worked: ');
    rate = input('Enter pay rate: ');
    if (hours <= 40):
        wages = hours * rate;
    else:   # hours > 40
        wages = 40 * rate + 1.20 * rate * (hours - 40);
    print 'Wages:', wages;
```

Exercise

Determine all steps from the execution of the *wagesTwoWay* function in the following cases:
- Hours = 40, Rate = 10
- Hours = 41, Rate = 10

Repetitive Assignments to the Same Variable

It is possible to assign values to the same variable multiple times:
- The first assignment to a variable creates the variable and defines its initial value.
- Any subsequent assignment replaces the current value of the variable with the new one.
  - The replaced value is lost.

Example

Consider the following block of statements:

```
wages = 5000;
extraPay = 1000;
wages = wages + extraPay;
print wages;
```

The execution of the above block of statements consists of the following steps:
- The execution of the first statement creates a variable named wages with an initial value 5000.
- The execution of the second statement creates a variable named extraPay with an initial value 1000.
- The execution of the third statement:
  - Evaluates the right-hand side expression *wages + extraPay* by using the current values of the two variables. The expression evaluates to 6000.
  - Assigns the value *6000* of the right-hand side expression to variable *wages*; the old value *5000* of *wages* is lost.
- The last statement prints the current value, *6000*, of variable *wages*.

One-Way Selection

While an if-statement is required to start with an if-clause, elif-clauses and else-clauses are entirely optional. An if-statement that consists of one if-clause and includes no other clauses is called *one-way selection if-statement*, or simply a *one-way if-statement*.

The previous section discusses the problem of wage calculation with overtime and offers a solution based on two-way selection. The same problem can be solved by a one-way if-statement, as illustrated by this function definition:

```
# One-way selection example:
def wagesOneWay():
   hours = input('Enter work hours: ');
   rate  = input('Enter pay rate: ');
   wages = hours * rate;
   if (hours > 40):
      extraPay = 0.20 * rate * (hours - 40);
      # increment the previous value of wages by extraPay:
      wages = wages + extraPay;
   print 'Wages:', wages;
```

The following Python-to-English translation provides insight into the one-way if-statement from function *wagesOneWay*.

Python-To-English Translation

Python If-Statements	Common English Meaning
Immediately before the if-statement: wages = hours * rate;	Calculate all wages at the regular pay rate.
if (hours > 40):	Step 1.<ul><li>Test if *hours are greater than 40*.<ul><li>If this is true, continue with the next Step 2 to calculate overtime and extra pay;</li><li>Otherwise jump over to Step 3.</li></ul></li></ul>
extraPay = 0.20 * rate * (hours - 40); wages = wages + extraPay;	Step 2.<ul><li>Calculate an extra pay of 20% for all hours over 40.</li><li>Add the extra pay to the wages that were previously calculated at the regular rate.</li><li>Replace the previously calculated wages with the newly calculated ones.</li><li>Continue to Step 3.</li></ul>

	Step 3.
Immediately after the if-statement: print 'Wages:', wages;	▫ The execution of the program continues with the statement that comes after the if-statement (if any). ▫ In the *wagesOneWay* function, this is the statement that prints the calculated *wages*.

Exercise

Determine all steps from the execution of the *wagesTwoWay* function in the following cases:
- Hours = 40, Rate = 10
- Hours = 41, Rate = 10

Exercise

Consider the following statements:

```
dollars = input('How many dollars do you have in your wallet? ');
if (dollars > 99):
    print 'Wow! You are rich!';
print 'You have $', dollars, '.';
```

Determine the output of the above statements in the following cases:
- Dollars = 10
- Dollars = 99
- Dollars = 100

Case Study: Quiz Evaluator

Consider the following programming problem.
Develop a *Quiz Evaluator* program to:
- Display one question followed by a menu of four possible answers.
- Ask the user to choose one answer from the menu.
- Input the user choice.
- Evaluate the user choice; provide feedback.

Use the following question and possible answers:
Who was the first U.S. President?
(1) Abraham Lincoln
(2) George Washington
(3) John Lennon
(4) Franklin Roosevelt
Enter choice number:

The user choice must be a whole number, 1, 2, 3, or 4, without parentheses. If the user chooses 2, the program should acknowledge the user answer as correct. If the user chooses 1, 3, or 4, the program should notify the user that the answer is incorrect.

The *Quiz Evaluator* sample program, below, solves the above programming problem.

```
# Display quiz items:
def displayQuiz():
    print 'Who was the first U.S. President?';
    print '(1) Abraham Lincoln';
    print '(2) George Washington';
    print '(3) John Lennon';
    print '(4) Franklin Roosevelt';

# Display the quiz and evaluate user response:
def quiz():
    displayQuiz();
    choice = input('Enter choice number: ');
    if (choice == 1 or choice == 4):
        print 'He was a president, but not the first one.';
    elif (choice == 2):
        print 'That is correct!';
    elif (choice == 3):
        print 'He was not a politician. He was a musician.';
    else:
        print 'Invalid choice: ', choice;
```

The *Quiz Evaluator* program incorporates the following functions:

Function	Purpose
displayQuiz	Helper function displays a quiz question followed by a menu of four possible answers.
quiz	The main function of the program. When invoked in interactive mode: • Invokes function *displayQuiz* to have the quiz question and the menu displayed; • Inputs the user choice. • Tests the user choice and, depending on the choice, displays feedback.

Exercise

Determine all steps from the execution of the *quiz* function for all possible valid choices, 1, 2, 3, and 4. Do the same for choice 5.

Boolean Expressions

In many programming languages, including Python, conditions are called *Boolean expressions*.

Example

The following are valid Boolean expressions:
- choice == 1
- income < 29050
- choice == 1 or choice == 4
- x < 3.14 * r
- b**2 - 4 * a * c > 0

In strict Python terms, to test a condition means to find the value of a Boolean expression. A Boolean expression can have one of two possible logic values: *True* or *False*.

Example

Boolean expressions can be evaluated interactively:

```
>>> income = 1000;
>>> print (income <= 29000);
True
>>> (income <= 29000)
True
>>> (income > 29000)
False
```

Python offers a special built-in type for logic data, the *Boolean type*:

Type Name	Examples of Numbers in Python	Examples in Common Notation	Type Description
Python name: bool Common name: Boolean	True False	true false	The Boolean type, *bool*, consists of two simple logical values *True* and *False*, and some logic operations that relate them - such as *and*, *or* and *not*.

Since everyone has a basic understanding of the concepts of True and False and basic conjunctions, everyone also has a basic understanding of the Boolean type.

Note

The Boolean type is named after George Boole the British mathematician who was the first to represent common logical expressions in a mathematical form.

Exercise

Search the Web for an overview of the work of George Boole.

Python offers a standard set of comparisons that can be used in Boolean expressions. These comparisons are outlined in the following table.

Python notation	Meaning
x == y	x is equal to y
x != y	x is not equal to y
x < y	x is less than y
x <= y	x is less than or equal to y
x > y	x is greater than y
x >= y	x is greater than or equal to y

Note

The following comparisons are denoted by compound two-character tokens: '==', '!=', '<=', and '>='. Remember that spaces are prohibited from all tokens except strings, therefore spaces cannot be present in the above compound comparison tokens.

Python offers several built-in logic operations. The most important built-in logic operations are listed in table below.

Python notation	Evaluation
not A	The expression *(not A)* yields: • True if *A* is *False*. • False if *A* is *True*.
A and B	• The expression *(A and B)* first evaluates *A*. • If *A* is false, its value is returned. • Otherwise, *B* is evaluated and the resulting value is returned.
A or B	• The expression *(A or B)* first evaluates *A*. • If *A* is *True*, its value is returned. • Otherwise, *B* is evaluated and the resulting value is returned.

Example

Consider the following statements:

```
month = input('Enter month number, 1 to 12: ');
if (month < 1 or month > 12):
    print 'Invalid month: ', month;
```

First, evaluate for *month* equals *0*. The evaluation of *(month < 1 or month > 12)* starts with the evaluation of *month < 1*. The value of *month < 1* is *True*, therefore *True* is returned for the whole expression *(month < 1 or month > 12)*, without the evaluation of the other sub-expression, *month > 12*.

Second, evaluate for *month* equals *13*. The evaluation of *(month < 1 or month > 12)* starts with the evaluation of *month < 1*. Because the value of *month < 1* is *False*, the other sub-expression, *month > 12*, is evaluated. The value of *month > 12* is *True*, therefore *True* is returned for the whole expression *(month < 1 or month > 12)*.

Third, evaluate for *month* equals *1*. The evaluation of *(month < 1 or month > 12)* starts with the evaluation of *month < 1*. Because the value of *month < 1* is *False*, the other sub-expression, *month > 12*, is evaluated. The value of *month > 12* is *False*, too, and *False* is returned for the whole expression *(month < 1 or month > 12)*.

Example
Consider the following statements:
```
x = 0; y = 10;
if (x != 0 and y / x > 1):
    print y / x;
```

The evaluation of *(x != 0 and y / x > 1)* starts with the evaluation of *x != 0*. The value of *x != 0* is *False*, and *False* is returned for the whole expression *(x != 0 and y / x > 1)*, without the evaluation of *y / x > 1*. Note that the evaluation of *y / x > 1* would have led to a *division by zero* run-time error. Note also that the argument order is essential: the evaluation of *(y / x > 1 and x != 0)* would have started with the evaluation of *y / x > 1* and that would have caused a *division by zero* run-time error.

The logic values *True* and *False* can be assigned into variables for further use.

Example
Consider the following statements:

```
x = 10; y = 200;
cond = (x != 0 and (y / x > 1 or y / x < -1));
print cond;
if (cond):
    print y / x;
```

The evaluation of *(x != 0 and (y / x > 1 or y / x < -1))* yields *True*. First, the evaluation of *A = (x != 0)* yields *True*; second, the evaluation of *B = (y / x > 1 or y / x < -1)* yields *True*, and lastly, the evaluation of *(A and B)* yields *True*. This value is assigned into variable *cond* and then printed. The if-statement prints the value *20* of *y / x* because *cond* is *True*.

Operator Precedence
In mathematics and in Python, different operators have different precedence. Operator precedence determines the evaluation order of expressions: operators with higher precedence are applied before operators with lower precedence.

Example

Multiplication has higher precedence than subtraction. In an expression that uses both operators, multiplication is applied before subtraction.

```
>>> x = 400; y = 20;
>>> x - y * y
0
```

The following table outlines the precedence of some common operators, from lowest precedence to highest precedence.

Operator	Precedence
or	Lowest (operator is applied after all others)
and	
not	
<, <=, >, >=, <>, !=, ==	
+, -	
*, /, %	Highest (operator is applied before all others)

In Python, operators with the same precedence are applied from left to right.

Example

Multiplication and division have the same precedence. In an expression that uses both operators, they are applied from left to right.

```
>>> x = 9; y = 10;
>>> x / y * 100
0
>>> 100 * x / y
90
```

Parentheses

In common mathematics and Python, parentheses can be used in expressions of any type to impose a desired order of evaluation.

Example

Parentheses can be used to apply a lower-precedence operator, such as subtraction, before a higher-precedence operator, such as multiplication.

```
>>> x = 400; y = 20;
>>> x - y * y
0
>>> (x - y) * y
7600
```

When you are not sure exactly how a complex Python expression will be evaluated, you can study the Python documentation to find out, or use parentheses to clearly state your desired order of evaluation.

Let *E* be an arbitrary expression. The value of *(E)* is the same as the value of *E*. In other words, enclosing an expression in parentheses does not change its value.

Example

Boolean expressions do not change when enclosed in additional parentheses:

```
>>> choice = 2;
>>> choice == 1
False
>>> (choice == 1)
False
```

Recall that an if-clause starts with the keyword 'if', followed by a condition, followed by a colon. In some popular languages, such as Java and C++, this condition must be enclosed in parentheses. In Python, such use of parentheses is allowed but not required.

Example

In a Python if-clause, it is your choice whether to enclose the condition in a pair of parentheses or not. The two if-statements below are equivalent:

```
if (choice == 1):
    F2C();
if choice == 1:
    F2C();
```

In Java and C++, the lack of parentheses around the condition of an if-statement is a syntax error.

In this course of study, we choose the option to parenthesize conditions in conditional control structures. We choose to do so for compatibility with popular languages such as Java and C++, in order to facilitate your possible transition from Python to any of those languages.

Nested If-Statements

Recall that an if-statement incorporates one or more clauses, and each clause consists of a header and a body. Recall also that a body is a block of arbitrary statements, possibly including inner if-statements. Such inner if-statements may contain other inner statements, and so on. The level of nesting statements is unlimited.

The following sample problem can be solved by means of nested if-statements.

Develop a function to:
- Input numeric score.
- Verify whether the score is between 0 and 100 and produce an error message if it is not.
- Otherwise determine a letter grade that corresponds to the numeric score and output the grade due.

Assume that the following grading system applies: the grade is 'A' for score between 90 and 100 (inclusive), 'B' for score between 80 and 89, 'C' for score between 70 and 79, 'D' for score between 60 and 69, and 'F: otherwise.

As a first step towards a solution, two-way selection can be applied to check if the score is a valid number between 0 and 100, and produce an error message if it is not:

```
score = input('Enter numeric score (0..100): ');
if (score < 0 or score > 100):
    print 'Invalid score: ', score;
else:
    # Score is valid;
    # Continue with score to letter grade conversion.
```

As a next step towards a solution, the grading system can be outlined in a design table. The design table for this particular problem will systematically present score limits and the corresponding letter grade calculation.

For example:

Score is less than:	But not less than:	The letter grade is:	Letter grade calculation:
60		'F'	grade = 'F'
70	60	'D'	grade = 'D'
80	70	'C'	grade = 'C'
90	80	'B'	grade = 'B'
	90	'A'	grade = 'A'

The above design table can be converted into the following Python if-statement:

```
if (score < 60):
    grade = 'F';
elif (score < 70):
    grade = 'D';
elif (score < 80):
    grade = 'C';
elif (score < 90):
    grade = 'B';
else: # 90 <= score
    grade = 'A';
```

This if-statement can be combined with the previous score-checking if-statement. The combined statement will first check if the score is a number between 0 and 100 and generate the corresponding letter grade. A complete score-to-grade transformation is implemented by the following function:

```
def grade():
    score = input('Enter numeric score (0..100): ');
    if (score < 0 or score > 100):
        print 'Invalid score: ', score;
    else:
        if (score < 60):
            grade = 'F';
        elif (score < 70):
            grade = 'D';
        elif (score < 80):
            grade = 'C';
        elif (score < 90):
            grade = 'B';
        else: # 90 <= score <= 100
            grade = 'A';
        print 'Grade is', grade, 'for score', score;
```

The above function contains two if-statements. A two-way selection if-statement checks the score correctness; a multiple selection if-statement performs the actual score-to-grade transformation. The latter if-statement is nested in the else-clause of the former if-statement. The outer if-statement performs score checking, while the inner if-statement performs score-to grade transformation.

The following Python-to-English translation provides insight into the outer and inner if-statements from the *grade* function.

Python-To-English Translation

Python If-Statements	Common English Meaning
Immediately before the outer if-statement: *score = input('Enter score (0..100): ');*	Input score from user.
if (score < 0 or score > 100):	Step 1 of the outer if-statement. • Test if *score is less than 0 or greater than 100*. • If this is true, continue to Step 2. • Otherwise jump over to Step 3.

	Step 2.
print 'Invalid score: ', score;	○ Print an error message. ○ Continue to Step 5
else :	Step 3. ○ Do not test anything - just continue to Step 4.

if (score < 60):
   grade = 'F';
elif (score < 70):
   grade = 'D';
elif (score < 80):
   grade = 'C';
elif (score < 90):
   grade = 'B';
else: # 90 <= score <= 100
   grade = 'A';
print 'Grade is', grade;
	Step 4.
	○ Execute the body of the else-clause. This body consists of a multiple selection if-statement, followed by a print statement.
	○ Execute the inner if-statement first. Execution not explained in detail here.
	○ Execute the print statement.

Immediately after the outer if-statement is the end of function body. There are no more statements to be executed.	Step 5 (outer if-statement). ○ This is the end of the execution of the outer if-statement. • In the *grade* function, there are no further statements to be executed.

Exercise

Determine all steps from the execution of the *grade* function in the following cases:
- Score = 80
- Score = 101
- Score = 100
- Score = 0
- Score = -1

Redundant Conditions

Conditions are evaluated during program execution. This involves the application of various operations such as arithmetic, logic, and comparisons. The execution of any operation requires time, and while the time for each individual operation is very small, it may accumulate to a large amount of time in programs that perform repetitive calculations. (Repetitions are to be studied in the next topic.) This is why it is important to minimize the number of operations for any specific calculation.

It is common for beginning programmers to employ redundant operations in selection conditions. Redundancy in conditions (and in all expressions in general) results in an unnecessary increase of the number of operations performed during program execution. For the sake of efficient execution, redundancy should be avoided.

The following table illustrates two common cases of redundancy: (1) testing conditions that are known to be True, or (2) using a sequence of separate if-statements instead of one multiple selection if-statement. The three columns of the table offer statements that deliver correct results. However, notice the statements from the middle and the right columns perform redundant condition tests, as explained below.

Minimal number of tests without redundancy	Unnecessary tests of conditions that are actually known to be *True*	Unnecessary use of a sequence of separate if-statements

if (score < 60):
    grade = 'F';
elif (score < 70):
    grade = 'D';
elif (score < 80):
    grade = 'C';
elif (score < 90):
    grade = 'B';
else:
    grade = 'A';
	if (score < 60):
	    grade = 'F';
	elif (**score >= 60 and** score < 70):
	    grade = 'D';
	elif (**score >= 70 and** score < 80):
	    grade = 'C';
	elif (**score >= 80 and** score < 90):
	    grade = 'B';
	elif (**score >= 90**):
	    grade = 'A';
		if (score < 60):
		    grade = 'F';
		if (score >= 60 and score < 70):
		    grade = 'D';
		if (score >= 70 and score < 80):
		    grade = 'C';
		if (score >= 80 and score < 90):
		    grade = 'B';
		if (score >= 90):
		    grade = 'A';

The left column of the above table offers a multiple selection if-statement that ceases testing once the range of the score is established and the letter grade is determined.

The middle column of the above table depicts a multiple selection if-statement with redundant conditions. The first elif-clause, for example, tests the condition *(score >= 60 and score < 70)*. Note, however, that the execution comes to this elif-clause only when t the condition *(score < 60)* in the leading if-clause yields False, i.e., when *(score >= 60)*. Thus, if the execution comes to the first elif-clause, it is guaranteed that *(score >= 60)*. Likewise, all the other elif-clauses are redundant. Note that the very last elif-clause can be reduced to an else-clause with no condition test, as in the left column.

The right column of the above table depicts a sequence of separate if-statements that perform multiple condition tests. Note how all elif-clauses, and the else-clause from the left column, are reduced in the right column to separate if-clauses. These if-clauses belong to if-statements that are executed in sequence independently from one another. As a result, each if-clause must repeat tests that are already included in earlier yet independent if-clauses. These if-clauses incorporate eight comparisons, comparisons that are always performed regardless of the score. Consider, for example score 50: the corresponding grade is determined by the very first if-statement but the execution continues with redundant tests of all remaining conditions.

The two types of redundancy that are discussed in this section should be avoided.

Synonyms

Some terms that have been introduced in this Topic have synonyms. A list of such terms and their corresponding synonyms follows.

Term	Synonym
Selection structure	Decision structure
Condition	Boolean expression
Boolean expression	Logic expression
Logic value	Boolean value
Logic operation	Boolean operation
To test a condition	To evaluate a Boolean expression

Lab A [Program Control: Selection]

Objective; Background; Lab Overview; What to Do Next; Downloading Sample Programs; Uncompressing Sample Programs; Studying the Sample Program; Creating a Program File; Developing the New Program

Objective

The objective of this lab is to develop a *Multi-Conversion Selector* program that will:
- Display a menu of various conversions.
- Ask the user to choose a conversion form the menu.
- Enter the user choice, and
- Depending on the user choice, invoke a conversion function correspondingly.

Background

- Your menu of various conversions may look like this:

    Conversions Menu:
    (1) Convert Fahrenheit to Celsius
    (2) Convert Celsius to Fahrenheit
    (3) Convert Inches to Centimeters
    (4) Convert Centimeters to Inches
    (5) Convert Gallons to Liters
    (6) Convert Liters to Gallons
    (7) Convert Yards to Meters
    (8) Convert Meters to Yards
    (9) Convert Pounds to Kilograms
    (10) Convert Kilograms to Pounds
    Enter choice number:

- The user choice is a whole number, without parentheses.

Lab Overview

To perform this lab, you should:
- Study the *Conversion Selector* sample program.
- Transform a copy of the *Conversion Selector* sample program into a *Multi-Conversion Selector* program.
- Systematically test the *Multi-Conversion Selector* program.

What to Do Next

At this time, you are offered these choices:
- Follow the detailed lab instructions below, or
- Try the lab independently, but also peek in the instructions when needed, or
- Perform the lab independently, without looking at instructions at all.

All three approaches can be beneficial for students. Feel free to choose the approach that you believe is most beneficial for you.

Downloading Sample Programs

Various Lab Assignments for this course of study are based on ready-to-use sample programs. Such programs are to be downloaded from the online study pack into your *master* folder.

Download sample programs for the current Topic 3 by performing these steps:
- Locate the current *Topic 3* in the online study pack.
- Open the *Lab Assignment* resource.
- Right-click on the *Sample Programs* link.
- Use *Save As* to store the downloaded compressed (zipped) folder, *03.zip*, within your *master* folder.

Uncompressing Sample Programs

- Uncompress the contents of the downloaded compressed (zipped) folder. Depending on your platform, you may use built-in compression support, or compressing utilities.
  - In Windows XP, for example, you can use built-in un-compression support as follows:
    - Use the *File Browser* to open your *master* folder.
    - Right-click on the downloaded compressed (zipped) folder.
    - Use *Extract All* and extract the contents of the compressed (zipped) folder within the *master* folder.

- This will create an uncompressed folder, *03*, within the *master* folder. This folder will contain your sample programs.
  - Alternatively, you can:
    - *Open* the compressed (zipped) folder.
    - *Cut* folder *03* from within the compressed (zipped) folder, and
    - *Paste* the cut folder *03* outside the compressed (zipped) folder – directly within the *master* folder.
- Delete the compressed (zipped) folder, *03.zip*, and keep the uncompressed folder, *03*.
- Open the uncompressed folder *03* and browse its contents.
- Note that Python program files have extension '**.py**'.

Studying the Sample Program
- Use IDLE to open and browse the *Conversion Selector* sample program.
- Run the program with various input data; observe its output.
- Analyze the program implementation.

Creating a Program File
Create this program in your current labs folder, *03Labs*. Perform the following steps:
- Use IDLE to create a copy of the *Conversion Selector* program file.
- Name the saved copy *Multi-ConversionSelector.py*.
  - **Important Note:** You must explicitly supply the file extension '**.py**' when saving from IDLE.

Developing the New Program
Perform these steps with the newly created *Multi-Conversion Selector* program:
- Provide implementations of all necessary conversion functions as follows:
  - Open the *Converters* program that you developed for Topic 02.
  - Copy the definitions of all functions.
  - Paste all definitions in your current *Multi-Conversion Selector* program.
  - Close the *Converters* program.
- Extend the definition of function *displayMenu* to make it display a complete menu for the *Multi-Conversion Selector* program.
  - Follow the menu from the *Background* part of this lab as a sample.

- Extend the definition of function *select* to make it analyze all possible user choices, and invoke corresponding conversion functions.
    - Start with an if-clause for the first conversion from the menu.
    - Use multiple elif-clauses for the remaining conversions.
    - Make sure the function ends with an else-clause to report an invalid menu choice.
- Test the new *select* function. Make sure you select each menu item at least once.

Lab B [Program Control: Selection]

Objective; Background; Lab Overview; What to Do Next; Studying the Sample Program; Creating a Program File; Developing the New Program

Objective
The objective of this lab is to develop a *Tax Calculator* program that:
- Input taxable annual *income*.
- Determine applicable tax bracket and calculate the *tax* due.
- Output *tax* due.

Background
- Implement the *Tax Calculator* in compliance with the following Tax Table:

Taxable income is over:	But not over:	The tax is:	Plus:	Of the amount over:
	7,150	0.00	10%	0
7,150	29,050	715.00	15%	7,150
29,050	70,350	4,000.00	25%	29,050
70,350	146,750	14,325.00	28%	70,350
146,750	319,100	35,717.00	33%	146,750
319,100		92,592.50	35%	319,100

Lab Overview
To perform this lab:
- Study the *Simple Tax Calculator* sample program.
- Transform a copy of the *Simple Tax Calculator* sample program into a *Tax Calculator* program.
- Design a *Test Table*.
- Debug the *Simple Tax Calculator* program.

What to Do Next
At this time, you are offered these choices:
- Follow the detailed lab instructions below, or
- Try the lab independently, but also peek in the instructions when needed, or
- Perform the lab independently, without the aid of the instructions.

All three approaches are beneficial for students. Feel free to choose the approach most beneficial to you.

Studying the Sample Program
- Use IDLE to open and browse the *Simple Tax Calculator* sample program.
- Run the program with various input data and observe its output.
- Analyze the program implementation.

Creating a Program File
To create this program in your current labs folder, *03Labs*, perform the following steps:
- Use IDLE to create a copy of the *Simple Tax Calculator* program file.
- Give the name *TaxCalculator.py* to the saved copy.
  - **Important Note:** You must explicitly supply the file extension '**.py**' when saving from IDLE.

Developing the New Program
Perform these steps with the newly created *Tax Calculator* program:
- Change all comments adequately.
- Transform all existing tax calculation statements to comply with the Tax Table.
  - For example, replace:
    elif (income <= 29050):
        tax = 0.15 * income;
    with:
    elif (income <= 29050):
        tax = 715 + 0.15 * (income - 7150);
- Transform other statements as necessary.
- Add additional 'elif' clauses as required by the Tax Table.

- Test the new function with various input data. Use a calculator if necessary.
  - Start testing with these sample test data:

>>> tax() Enter annual income: **0** Tax due = 0.0	>>> tax() Enter annual income: **146750** Tax due = 35717.0
>>> tax() Enter annual income: **7150** Tax due = 715.0	>>> tax() Enter annual income: **319100** Tax due = 92592.5
>>> tax() Enter annual income: **10000** Tax due = 1142.5	>>> tax() Enter annual income: **1E6** Tax due = 330907.5
>>> tax() Enter annual income: **29050** Tax due = 4000.0	>>> tax() Enter annual income: **1E7** Tax due = 3480907.5
>>> tax() Enter annual income: **70350** Tax due = 14325.0	>>> tax() Enter annual income: **1E8** Tax due = 34980907.5

Lab C [Program Control: Selection]

Objective; Background; Lab Overview; What to Do Next; Studying the Sample Program; Creating a Program File; Developing the New Program

Objective
The objective of this lab is to develop a *Weather Advisor* program that will:
- Input current *temperature* (in Fahrenheit).
- Determine advisable *activity* for the particular temperature.
- Output the advisable *activity*.

Background
- Implement the *Weather Advisor* in compliance with the following Activity Table:

Temperature is below:	But not below:	The advisable activity is:
40		Get some sleep at home
60	40	Browse the Internet
75	60	Take a walk in the park
90	75	Sunbathe on the lawn
	90	Go to the beach

Lab Overview
To perform this lab:
- Study the *Grade Converter* sample program.
- Transform a copy of the *Grade Converter* sample program into a *Weather Advisor* program.
- Design a *Test Table* and debug the *Weather Advisor* program.

What to Do Next
At this time, you are offered these choices:
- Follow the detailed lab instructions below, or
- Try the lab independently, but also peek in the instructions when needed, or

- Perform the lab without the aid of the instructions.

All three approaches are beneficial for students. Feel free to choose the approach most beneficial for you.

Studying the Sample Program
- Use IDLE to open and browse the *Grade Converter* sample program.
- Run the program with various input data; observe its output.
- Analyze the program implementation.

Creating a Program File
To create this program in your current labs folder, *03Labs*, follow these steps:
- Use IDLE to create a copy of the *Grade Converter* program file.
- Give the name *WeatherAdvisor.py* to the saved copy.
  - **Important Note:** You must explicitly supply the file extension '**.py**' when saving from IDLE.

Developing the New Program
Perform these steps with the newly created *Weather Advisor* program:
- Change comments adequately.
- Transform the *grade* function into the *weather* function by performing these steps:
  - Input temperature into a variable called temp.
  - Assume that all temperatures are legitimate, then:
    - Remove the entire two-way selection *'if (0 <= score): ...'* including its *'else:'* part.
    - Align the remaining statements vertically with the *input* statement.
      - Remember, a function body is a block of aligned statements.
    - Implement the entire activity selection in compliance with the Activity Table.
      - For example, replace:
        if (score < 60):
            grade = 'A';
        with:
        if (temp < 40):
            activity = 'Get some sleep at home.';
  - Output activity.

- Test the new function with various input data.
  - You can start testing with these sample test data:

>>> weather(); Enter temperature in Fahrenheit: **39** Get some sleep at home.	>>> weather(); Enter temperature in Fahrenheit: **74** Take a walk in the park.
>>> weather(); Enter temperature in Fahrenheit: **40** Browse the Internet.	>>> weather(); Enter temperature in Fahrenheit: **75** Sunbathe on the lawn.
>>> weather(); Enter temperature in Fahrenheit: **59** Browse the Internet.	>>> weather(); Enter temperature in Fahrenheit: **89** Sunbathe on the lawn.
>>> weather(); Enter temperature in Fahrenheit: **60** Take a walk in the park.	>>> weather(); Enter temperature in Fahrenheit: **90** Go to the beach.

Lab D [Program Control: Selection]

Objective; Background; Lab Overview; What to Do Next; Studying the Sample Program; Creating a Program File; Developing the New Program

Objective
The objective of this lab is to develop a *Multiple Choice* program that will:
- Extend the *Quiz Evaluator* program with at least two more quizzes, and
- Run all quizzes in a sequence.

Background
- You must include at least two additional questions to the *Quiz Evaluator*.
- The new quizzes must be your own design.
- Here are some ideas for easy Quote Quizzes:
    1. Quiz Question:
       Who made this quote famous?
       'I do not know if love proves God's existence, or if love is God Himself.'
       The correct answer is Ingmar Bergman. You need to add several incorrect answers in the quiz.
    2. Quiz Question:
       Who made this quote famous?
       'The slave fights for freedom and the free one for perfection.'
       The correct answer is Yane Sandanski. You need to add several incorrect answers.

Lab Overview
To perform this lab, you should:
- Study the *Quiz Evaluator* sample program.
- Transform a copy of the *Quiz Evaluator* sample program into a *Multiple Choice* program.
- Add two more quizzes after the President Quiz. The three quizzes are processed in sequence, independently from each other.
- Test the *Multiple Choice* program.

What to Do Next
At this time, you are offered these choices:
- Follow the detailed lab instructions below, or
- Try the lab independently, but also peek in the instructions when needed, or
- Perform the lab without the aid of the instructions.

All three approaches can be beneficial for students. Feel free to choose the approach most beneficial for you.

Studying the Sample Program
- Use IDLE to open and browse the *Quiz Evaluator* sample program.
- Run the program with various input data and observe its output.
- Analyze the program implementation.

Creating a Program File
To create this program in your current labs folder, *03Labs*, perform the following steps:
- Use IDLE to create a copy of the *Quiz Evaluator* program file.
- Give the name *MultipleChoice.py* to the saved copy.
    - **Important Note:** You must explicitly supply the file extension '**.py**' when saving from IDLE.

Developing the New Program
Your program should look like a triplicate version of the original Multiple Choice program. It should contain four functions, *displayQuiz1*, *displayQuiz2*, *displayQuiz3*, and a main *quiz* function. The main quiz function can be built according to the following pattern:

```
displayQuiz1();
choice = input('Enter choice number: ');
if ... evaluate user choice for the first quiz;

displayQuiz2();
choice = input('Enter choice number: ');
if ... evaluate user choice for the second quiz;

displayQuiz3();
choice = input('Enter choice number: ');
if ... evaluate user choice for the third quiz;
```

Perform these steps with the newly created *Multiple Choice* program:
- Change all comments adequately.
- Rename the *displayQuiz* to *displayQuiz1*.
- Modify the existing *quiz* function to invoke *displayQuiz1* rather than *displayQuiz*.
- Following *displayQuiz1,* add new display functions, *displayQuiz2, displayQuiz3,* to display your newly designed quizzes.
- Extend the existing *quiz* function to:
  - Invoke *displayQuiz2*.
  - Evaluate the user input using an if-statement.
  - Invoke *displayQuiz3*; evaluate the user input.
  - Evaluate the user input by means of an if-statement.
    - You need to use separate if-statements for the evaluation of each quiz.
- Systematically test the implementation of your new quizzes by running the program multiple times and supplying various input data. It is also a good idea to test the existing implementation of the Quiz Evaluator because it might have been inadvertently changed and made incorrect.

Lab E [Program Control: Selection]

Objective; Background; Lab Overview; What to Do Next; Creating a Program File; Developing the New Program

Objective

The objective of this lab is to develop an *Order Handler* program that will:
- Input non-negative numbers for *quantity* of items per order, *item price*, and sales *tax rate* (as percentage).
- Calculate the *total price* of the order, *sales tax* and *order total*.
- Determine *shipping and handling fee* depending on the *order total*.
- Determine the *order price* as the sum of the *order total* and the *shipping and handling fee*.
- Output the *order total*, *shipping and handling fee*, and *order price*.

Background

Implement the calculation of the *shipping and handling fee* in compliance with the following Fee Schedule:

Order total:	Shipping and handling fee:
Less than $20	$4.99
Less than $40	$5.99
Less than $60	$6.99
$60 or more	$7.99

Lab Overview

To perform this lab, you should:
- Transform a copy of your *Order Calculator* program into an *Order Handler* program.
- Test the *Order Handler* program.

What to Do Next

At this time, you are offered these choices:
- Follow the detailed lab instructions below, or

- Try the lab independently, but also peek in the instructions when needed, or
- Perform the lab independently, without use to any instructions.

All three approaches can be beneficial for students. Feel free to choose the approach most beneficial for you.

Creating a Program File

To create this program in your current labs folder, *03Labs*, perform the following steps:
- Use IDLE to create a copy of the *Order Calculator* program file.
- Open your *Order Calculator* program from folder *02Labs* and use *Save as* to create a copy in folder *03Labs*.
- Give the name *OrderHandler.py* to the saved copy.
  - **Important Note:** You must explicitly supply the file extension '**.py**' when saving from IDLE.

Developing the New Program

Your program should extend the *order* function form your original *Order Calculator* program. An if-statement that calculates the shipping charge must follow the calculation of the *order total*. Your extension can follow this pattern:

…
orderTotal = …;
if … calculate shipping and handling fees;
…
orderPrice = …;
print …;

Perform these steps with the newly created *Order Calculator* program:
- Implement a multiple selection statement to determine the *shipping and handling fee* depending on the *order total*.
  - This multiple selection statement must follow the calculation of the order total.
- Print the *order total*, the *shipping and handling fee*, and the *order price*.
- Develop a *Test Table* for the updated program.
- The design and use of a Test Table is **very essential** for this program. It is recommended to include data that make order cost equal to $19, $20, $39, $40, $59, $60.
- Debug the new function.

Lab F [Program Control: Selection, Optional]

Objective; Background; Lab Overview

Objective
The objective of this lab is to develop a *Dean's List Evaluator* program that will:
- Input the number of *A's, B's, C's, D's,* and *F's* a student earned during a given semester.
- Calculate the student's *grade point average*, GPA for the semester.
- Output the *GPA* with a message if the student made the Dean's list.

Background
- Calculate the *GPA* on a scale of *4.0* for an *A*.
- Assume that a GPA of at least 3.5 is required for making the Dean's list.
- An interaction of your program may look like this:

    Enter number of A's: **2**
    Enter number of B's: **0**
    Enter number of C's: **0**
    Enter number of D's: **1**
    Enter number of F's: **0**

    Grade point average is 3.00
    You cannot make it to the Dean's list.

Lab Overview
To perform this lab, you should:
- Study sample programs for this topic.
- Design and write down formulae for the calculations.
- Design a *Test Table* and check your designed formulae.
- Create a program file in your current labs folder.
- Transform your formulae into a Python program.
- Debug your program using your *Test Table*.

Lab G [Program Control: Selection, Optional]

Objective; Background; Lab Overview

Objective

The objective of this lab is to develop a *Leap Year Evaluator* program that will:
- Input a whole number that represents a *year* in the Gregorian calendar.
  - The Gregorian calendar was introduced in 1582; only years after 1582 should be allowed.
- Evaluate if it is a leap year or a normal year.
- Output its evaluation.

Background

- In the Gregorian calendar, a leap year is any year which number can be divided by 4 without a remainder, and years ending in hundreds are no leap years unless they are divisible by 400.
- An interaction of your program may look like this:

Enter year: **2003**
2003 is not a leap year.
Enter year: **2004**
2004 is a leap year.
Enter year: **1900**
2004 is not a leap year.
Enter year: **2000**
2004 is a leap year.

Lab Overview

To perform this lab:
- Design a leap year evaluation algorithm based on selection and the remainder operation, '%'.
  - The remainder operation, x % y, returns the remainder from the division of x by y.
    - For example:
      - 7 % 4 == 3
      - 2004 % 4 == 0
      - 1900 % 100 == 0
      - 1900 % 400 == 300

- A *year* is divisible by a number *K* if and only if (*year* % *K* == 0).
- A *year* is NOT divisible by a number *K* if and only if (*year* % *K* != 0).
- Note that a *year* in NOT a leap year in two cases:
  - The *year* is not divisible by 4.
  - The *year* is divisible by 4, is divisible by 100, but is not divisible by 400.
- Describe the algorithm in English (or another natural language), rather than a program in Python.
○ Create a program file in your current labs folder.
○ Transform your leap year algorithm into a Python program.
○ Debug your program. Use your *Test Table*.

Lab H [Program Control: Selection, Optional]

Objective; Background; Lab Overview

Objective
The objective of this lab is to develop a *Commission Calculator* program that will:
- Input a salesperson's monthly sales total.
  - Calculate the salesperson's commission.
- Output the commission.

Background
For this lab, the salesperson gets:
- A 5% commission on sales of $1000 or less, and
- A 10% commission on sales in excess of $1000.
  - For example, a sale of $1300 earns the salesperson $80; that is, $50 on the first $1000 of the sale and $30 on the $300 in excess of the first $1000.

Lab Overview
To perform this lab:
- Study sample programs for this topic.
- Design and write down formulae for the calculations.
- Design a *Test Table* and check your designed formulae.
- Create a program file in your current labs folder.
- Transform your formulae into a Python program.
- Debug your program. Use your *Test Table*.

Lab I [Program Control: Selection, Optional]

Objective; Background; Lab Overview

Objective
The objective of this lab is to develop a *Fine Calculator* program that will:
- Input a driver's speed as measured by traffic patrol.
- Determine if a speeding ticket is to be issued and if so, determine the amount of the fine.
  - Assume fine amount 0 when there is no speed violation.
- Output the fine.

Background
For this lab, make the following assumptions:
- The fine for speeding in a 45 MPH zone is $10 for every mile per hour over the speed limit for speeds from 46 to 55 MPH.
- It is $15 for every additional mile per hour between 56 and 65 MPH.
- It is $20 for every additional mile per hour over 65 MPH.
  - For example, the fine for driving 57 MPH is $100 for the fast 10 MPH plus $30 for the 2 MPH in excess of 55 MPH, for a total of $130.

Lab Overview
To perform this lab:
- Study sample programs for this topic.
- Design and write down formulae for the calculations.
- Design a *Test Table* and check your designed formulae.
- Create a program file in your current labs folder.
- Transform your formulae into a Python program.
- Debug your program. Use your *Test Table*.

Program Control: Repetition

Sample Programming Problem: Repetitive Conversions; Sample Program: Conversion Repetitions; While-Statement Form; While-Statement Execution; Loops; The Break-Statement; Conditional, Unconditional, and Hybrid Loops; Sums, Counts, and Averages; Infinite Loops; Stepwise Program Design: Case Study; Input Data Validation; Nested Loops; Random Numbers; Russian Roulette Simulator; Casino Roulette Simulator; String Basics; Binary Search; Synonyms

Sample Programming Problem: Repetitive Conversions

Consider the following programming problem.
Develop a *Conversion Repetitions* program to:
- Display a menu of three choices:
  - Two possible temperature conversions:
    - *Fahrenheit to Celsius* conversion
    - *Celsius to Fahrenheit* conversion
  - Exit the menu choice
- Ask the user to make one choice from the menu.
- Enter the user choice.
- Depending on the particular user choice, do one of the following:
  - Perform the conversion chosen by the user then **repeat** all of the above steps, or
  - Exit the menu repetitions, if that was what the user chose.

The menu of possible conversions may look like this:

Temperature Conversions Menu:
(0) Exit the menu
(1) Convert Fahrenheit to Celsius
(2) Convert Celsius to Fahrenheit
Enter choice number:

The user choice must be a whole number: 0, 1 or 2, without parentheses.
- Should the user chooses 1 or 2, the program will ask the user for a temperature to convert, then calculate and display the corresponding converted temperature.

- The program will then redisplay the menu, ask the user for another choice, and handle the user's choice accordingly.
- If the user chooses 0, the program terminates.

Sample Program: Conversion Repetitions

Below is an examples of the *Conversion Repetitions* program that solves the programming problem posed in the opening of the chapter. The program repeatedly displays a menu with the three possible choices (an exit choice and two temperature conversion choices) and performs chosen temperature conversions. The temperature conversions continue until the user chooses to exit. The program consists of a function named *repeat* and of several helper functions.

Exercise

Run the *Conversion Repetitions* program. In interactive mode, invoke the *repeat* function and experiment with various inputs.

Here is the complete *Conversion Repetitions* program:

```
# Display menu items:
def displayMenu():
    print '...'
    print 'Temperature Conversions Menu:';
    print '(0) Exit the menu';
    print '(1) Convert Fahrenheit to Celsius';
    print '(2) Convert Celsius to Fahrenheit';

# Display menu repeatedly and execute user choice:
def repeat ():
    displayMenu();
    choice = input('Enter choice number: ');
    while (choice != 0):
        if (choice == 1):
            F2C();
        elif (choice == 2):
            C2F();
        else:
            print 'Invalid choice: ', choice;
        displayMenu();
        choice = input('Enter choice number: ');
    print 'Bye-bye.';
```

```
# Convert Fahrenheit temperature to Celsius temperature:
def F2C():
# Convert Celsius temperature to Fahrenheit temperature:
def C2F():
```

The definitions of functions *F2C* and *C2F* are the same as those in the *Conversion Selector* program studied previously.

The main function in program *Conversion Repetitions* is the function *repeat*. When the function is invoked, it does the following:
- Invokes function *displayMenu*, displaying the menu.
- Inputs the user's choice.
- Tests the user's choice and, depending on the choice:
  - Terminates the function execution
  - Selects and invokes a conversion function (either function *F2C* or function *C2F*) before continuing with the first of the above steps
  - Prints an error message when the user choice is invalid, then continues with the first of the above steps.
- Prints 'Bye-bye.' at exit.

The repetitive selection of a conversion function to be invoked is implemented by means of a *while-statement*. The following Python-to-English translation provides insight into the meaning of the while-statement from the *Conversion Repetitions* program.

Python-To-English Translation

Python If-Statement	Common English Meaning
displayMenu(); choice = input('Enter choice..: ');	○ Invoke the *displayMenu* helper function. ○ Enter the **first** user choice.
while (choice != 0):	Step 1. ○ Test if *choice* is different from 0. • If true, continue to Step 2. • Otherwise jump to Step 4.

	Step 2.

if (choice == 1):
    F2C();
elif (choice == 2):
    C2F();
else:
    print 'Invalid choice… ';
	▫ Depending on the user *choice*, either invoke function *F2C*, or invoke function *C2F*, or print an error message. Continue to Step 3.
	• Note that the *choice* is guaranteed to not be *0* at this step. When *choice* is *0*, Step 1 jumps over to Step 4 and thus skips Step 2.

displayMenu(); choice = input('Enter choice… ');	**Step 3.** ▫ Invoke the *displayMenu* helper function. ▫ Enter the **next** user choice. ▫ Jump back to Step 1.
▫ Immediately after the while-statement: print 'Bye-bye.';	**Step 4.** ▫ The execution of the program continues with whichever statement comes after the while-statement (if any). • In the *repeat* function, this is the statement that prints *'Bye-bye'*.

While-Statement Form

While-statements are compound structures that consist of substructures, such as headers and bodies. The following table describes the while-statement and its sub-structures.

Structure	Description	Example

While-Statement	A while-statement has one required *while-clause*, optionally followed by one *else-clause*.
	▫ Using an else-clause in a while-statement is very uncommon and is not covered in this course.
		while (choice != 0):
		  if (choice == 1):
		    F2C();
		  elif (choice == 2):
		    C2F();
		  else:
		    print 'Invalid';
		  displayMenu();
		  choice = input('Enter…');

While-clause	A while-clause is a sequence of a *while-header* and a *body*.	while (choice != 0):
		  if (choice == 1):
		    F2C();
		  elif (choice == 2):
		    C2F();
		  else:
		    print 'Invalid';
		  displayMenu();
		  choice = input('Enter…');

While-header	A while-header starts with the keyword 'while', followed by a condition, followed by a colon.	while (choice != 0):

Body	A body is an indented block of statements controlled by a clause.	if (choice == 1):
		    F2C();
		elif (choice == 2):
		    C2F();
		else:
		    print 'Invalid';
		displayMenu();
		choice = input('Enter...');

Block of statements	A block is a sequence of one or more aligned statements.	a = 10;
		b = 20 * a;
		c = a + b;

Condition	Conditions are boolean expressions that may be true or false.	(choice == 0) (first <= last)

While-statement bodies must be indented from the corresponding headers. All statements of a particular body must be vertically aligned, using the same indentation.

While-Statement Execution

The while-statement is used for repeated execution while a condition is true.
- The condition is repeatedly tested. If true, the body is executed.
- If the condition is false (which it may be the first time it is tested) the while-statement terminates.
- An else-clause, if present in a while-statement, is executed only after the condition evaluates to false and the execution of the while-statement terminates. Using an else-clause in a while-statement is very uncommon and will not be discussed further in this course.

Although while-statements and if-statement may look similar, they serve very different purposes.
- The purpose of an if-statement is to *select* one particular block of statements that is executed once.
- The purpose of a while-statement is to *repeat* a number of times the execution of a block of statements.

Loops

In Python, repetitions are implemented by means of while-statements and for-statements. For-statements will be studied in a later chapter. Other languages offer additional repetition statements, notably the do-while-statements in C++, and the repeat-until statements in Pascal.

In programming lingo, the execution of a repetition statement is called a *loop* because the execution keeps looping back to the start of the statement. The repetition statement itself is also often referred to as a *loop*. The terms *while-loop* and *for-loop* are often used for a particular kind of repetition.

See the Synonyms sections at the end of this topic for a list of usages of the *loop* term.

The Break-Statement

The body of a while-statement is executed repeatedly as long as the while-clause condition is true. The execution of a while-statement terminates when the while-clause condition evaluates as false.

Also, the execution of a while-statement can be terminated from any point of the while-body, by means of a special control statement, the *break-statement*. A break-statement terminates the execution of its immediate enclosing loop.

The table below illustrates two different approaches to repetition termination. Each of the two columns of the table contains a function to repeatedly display a menu of various choices and to perform chosen actions.
- In the left column, repetitions are terminated with the execution of a break-statement.
- In the right column, repetitions are terminated when the condition of a while-clause evaluates to false.
  - Note that the right-column example has been already discussed in details in previous sections.

Using Break-Statement	Using Condition

def repeat():
  while (**True**):
    displayMenu();
    choice = input('Enter choice number: ');
    if (**choice == 0**):
      break;
    elif (choice == 1):
      F2C();
    elif (choice == 2):
      C2F();
    else:
      print 'Invalid choice: ', choice;
  print 'Bye-bye.';
	def repeat():
	  displayMenu();
	  choice = input('Enter choice number: ');
	  while (**choice != 0**):
	    if (choice == 1):
	      F2C();
	    elif (choice == 2):
	      C2F();
	    else:
	      print 'Invalid choice: ', choice;
	    displayMenu();
	    choice = input('Enter choice number: ');
	  print 'Bye-bye.';

The Boolean literal *True* is a legitimate Boolean expression. Of course, this literal always remains true and never becomes false. A while-loop that contains *True* instead of a condition will execute indefinitely unless terminated by a break-statement. The left column in the above table illustrates this type of loop.

The following Python-to-English translations provide insight into how a break-statement can terminate a loop.

Python-To-English Translation

Python While-Statement	Common English Meaning
while (True):	Step 1. ○ Unconditionally continue with the next Step.
displayMenu(); choice = input('Enter choice..: ');	Step 2. ○ Invoke the *displayMenu* helper function. ○ Input user choice.

if (choice == 0):
    break;
	Step 3.
	○ Test if *choice is equal to 0*.
	  • If this is true, jump out of the loop body to Step 5.
	  • Otherwise continue with the next Step 4.

elif (choice == 1):
    F2C();
elif (choice == 2):
    C2F();
else:
    print 'Invalid choice… ';
	Step 4.
	○ Depending on the user choice, either invoke function *F2C*, or invoke function *C2F*, or print an error message.
	○ Jump back to Step 1.

Immediately after the while-statement: print 'Bye-bye.';	Step 5. ○ The execution of the program continues with whichever statement comes after the while-statement (if any). • In the *repeat* function, this is the statement that prints 'Bye-bye'.

Exercise

Determine all steps from the execution of the *repeat* function in the following sequence of input data:

- Choice = 1, Fahrenheit = 32
- Choice = 11
- Choice = 1, Fahrenheit = -40
- Choice = 0

Conditional, Unconditional, and Hybrid Loops

A while-loop can be terminated in different ways, such as:
- When the condition of its while-clause evaluates as false
- With the execution of a break-statement

We distinguish between three kinds of while-loops:
- A *conditional loop* is terminated when the condition of its while-clause evaluates to false.
- An *unconditional loop* is terminated with the execution of a break-statement.
- A *hybrid loop* is a combination of conditional and unconditional loops and can be terminated either way.

A conditional loop incorporates a full while-clause, with a condition that can be true during some stages of execution then turn false during other stages. The table below outlines a general conditional loop pattern with an example.

Conditional Loop Pattern	Example

define condition variables;
 while **(condition)**:
    statement;
    statement;
    ...
    statement;
    update condition variables;
	displayMenu();
	 choice = input('Enter choice number: ');
	 while (**choice != 0**):
	    if (choice == 1): F2C();
	    elif (choice == 2): C2F();
	    else: print 'Invalid choice: ', choice;
	    displayMenu();
	    choice = input('Enter choice number: ');

Example

Consider the conditional loop example in the table above. The condition's only variable, *choice*, is defined before the loop. Initially, the condition may evaluate to *True*. This same variable, *choice*, is updated at the end of each loop body execution. At some step, *choice* will become *0*, the loop condition will evaluate to *False*, and the loop will terminate.

An unconditional loop has a simple while-clause that contains only the Boolean literal *True*, instead of a fully-fledged condition. We refer to such a loop as unconditional, because the Boolean literal *True* is not a 'real' condition. Obviously, such a 'condition' is always valid and never becomes false. This kind of loop is terminated with the execution of a break-statement. The table below outlines a general unconditional loop pattern with an example.

Unconditional Loop Pattern	Example

while *(True)*:
   statement;
   ...
   update condition variables;
   if *(condition)*: **break**;
   statement;
   ...
	while **(True)**:
	   displayMenu();
	   choice = input('Enter choice number: ');
	   if (**choice == 0**): **break**;
	   elif (choice == 1): F2C();
	   elif (choice == 2): C2F();
	   else: print 'Invalid choice: ', choice;

Example

Consider the unconditional loop example in the table above. An if-statement tests the user *choice* and breaks out of the loop when that choice is 0. Variable *choice* is updated each time before being tested with an if-statement. Initially, the if-statement condition may possibly evaluate to *False*. At some loop body execution, *choice* will become *0*, the if-statement condition will evaluate to *True*, the break-statement will be executed, and the loop will terminate.

A hybrid loop is a combination of a conditional loop and unconditional loop. A hybrid loop incorporates:
- A fully-fledged while-clause with a condition that can be initially true for a while then turn false during some stage of the execution, thus terminating the loop, and
- One or more break-statements that also terminate the loop, if executed.

The table below outlines a general hybrid loop pattern.

Hybrid Loop Pattern

define condition variables;
 while *(condition)*:
    statement;
    ...
    update condition variables;
    if *(condition)*: **break**;
    statement;
    ...

Hybrid loops are more complex than conditional and unconditional loops. A hybrid loop is employed in the *Russian Roulette Simulator* sample program discussed in a later section.

Sums, Counts, and Averages

Consider the following score evaluation problem. Develop a function to:

- Input a sequence of non-negative scores terminated by a negative number.
- Accumulate the total of all scores.
- Count all scores.
- Find the average score.
  - The average score is equal to the quotient of the accumulated total of all scores and the number of scores.
- Output the number of all scores along with the average score.

Example

An interaction with the required function may look like this:

```
Enter score (0..100), negative to quit: 80
Enter score (0..100), negative to quit: 90
Enter score (0..100), negative to quit: -1
Scores processed: 2
Average score: 85.0
```

Note that the end of the input data is indicated by an arbitrary negative number. A special value that is used to indicate the end of input data is called a *sentinel*.

The score evaluation problem can be solved by means of either a conditional or unconditional loop. The two types of solutions are discussed in the next two sub-sections.

Conditional Loop

The following function evaluates a sequence of scores.
- The function uses a conditional loop to sum up and count all valid scores.
- After the loop termination, the function calculates the average score.

```
# Sum-up and count with a conditional loop:
def scores():
    total = 0; counter = 0;
    score = input('Enter score (0..100), negative to quit: ');
    while (score >= 0):
        total = total + score;
        counter = counter + 1;
        score = input('Enter score (0..100), negative to quit: ');
    print 'Scores processed:', counter;
    if (counter > 0):
        average = float(total) / counter;
        print 'Average score:', average;
```

The *scores* function above uses a conditional loop. The function repeatedly asks the user to enter either a valid score or any negative number to exit.

The function processes one score at a time. The score currently being processed is held in a variable named *score*.
- The first *score* is input before the loop.
- In the loop body, the current *score* is counted and added to the *score total*, as discussed below. All subsequent scores are input at the bottom of the loop body.

The input statement that precedes the loop initializes the *score* variable, while the input statement at the bottom of the loop body inputs all subsequent scores one at a time.

The loop continues as long as the current *score* is not negative; otherwise, it is terminated. Of course, loop termination is ensured with the while-clause condition *(score >= 0)*.

Scores are counted in a variable named *counter* as follows:
- The *counter* is initialize at *0* before the loop begins:

    counter = 0;

- The *counter* is incremented during each execution of the loop, once for each score:

    counter = counter + 1;

Scores are similarly accumulated in a variable named *total*:
- The *total* is initialized at *0* before the loop begins:

    total = 0;

- The *total* is updated during each execution of the loop by adding each score to the current total:
    total = total + score;

Once the loop has been terminated, the function calculates the *average* score.
- The *average* score is calculated only if at least one valid score has been counted:

    if (counter > 0):
        average = float(total) / counter;

- In the special case when no valid scores are input, *average* is not calculated.

Exercise

Trace a sample score evaluation, as implemented by the conditional *scores* function above. Use the sample input from the left column of the table below, and determine the missing values in the other columns.

Score	Total	Counter	Average
-	0	0	?
80	?	?	?
90	?	?	?
96	?	?	?
100	?	?	?
-1	?	?	?

Exercise

Trace a sample score evaluation, as implemented by the conditional *scores* function above. Use the sample input from the left column of the table below, and determine the missing values in the other columns.

Score	Total	Counter	Average
-	0	0	?
-1	?	?	?

Implementing the following guidelines is vital when using a conditional loop:
- Variables that are used to count and accumulate must (1) be initialized before the loop and (2) be updated in the loop body.
  - Variables *counter* and *total* in the conditional *scores* function above provide valid examples.
- Variables that are used in the loop condition must (1) be initialized before the loop and (2) be updated in the loop body.
  - Variable *score* and the loop condition *(score >= 0)* in the conditional *scores* function above provide good examples.

Exercise

Using a conditional loop, design a function:
- To input a sequence of positive numbers terminated by a negative sentinel.
- To calculate the product of all numbers entered (excluding the sentinel).
- To display the product.

Unconditional Loop

The following function uses an unconditional loop to sum and count all valid scores. After loop termination, the function calculates the average score.

```
# Sum-up and count with an unconditional loop:
def scores ():
    total = 0; counter = 0;
    while (True):
        score = input('Enter score (0..100), negative to quit: ');
        if (score < 0):
            break;
        total = total + score;
        counter = counter + 1;
    print 'Scores processed:', counter;
    if (counter > 0):
        average = float(total) / counter;
        print 'Average score: ', average;
```

The *scores* function above uses an unconditional loop. The *unconditional scores* function serves the same purpose as the previous *conditional scores* function: it repeatedly asks the user to enter either a valid score or any negative number to exit. The key difference between the two functions is the use of an unconditional versus conditional loop.

The loop continues as long as the current *score* is not negative, and is terminated otherwise. Loop termination is implemented with a break-statement in the loop body:

   if (score < 0): break;

One score at a time is processed; the *score* variable stores the value currently being processed.
- In the body of the loop, the current *score* is entered using a singe input statement.

    score = input('Enter score (0..100), negative to quit: ');

- There is no need to initialize the *score* variable before the loop.

Scores are summed and counted in variables named *total* and *counter* respectively.
- Variables *total* and *counter* are initialized at *0* before the loop:

    total = 0; counter = 0;

- Within the loop body, the variables *total* and *counter* are updated each time a score is entered:

    total = total + score;
    counter = counter + 1;

In an unconditional loop:
- Variables that are used to count or sum must (1) be initialized before the loop and (2) be updated in the loop body.
    - The *counter* and *total* variables in the unconditional *scores* function above provide examples.
- Variables that are used in loop break-statements must be updated both in the loop and before the execution of the break-statement. These variables do not need to be initialized before the loop.
    - Variable *score* and the break-statement in the unconditional *scores* function above provide examples.

Exercise

Trace a sample score evaluation, using an implemented of the unconditional *scores* function given above. Use the sample input from the left column of the table below to determine the missing values in the other columns.

Score	Total	Counter	Average
-	0	0	?
80	?	?	?
90	?	?	?
96	?	?	?
100	?	?	?
-1	?	?	?

Exercise

Using an unconditional loop, design a function that will:
- Input a sequence of positive numbers terminated by a negative sentinel.
- Calculate the product of all numbers (excluding the sentinel).
- Display the product.

Infinite Loops

A while-statement is normally expected to repeat the execution of its body for a specified number of times and then terminate. The execution of a while-statement can be terminated:
- When the condition in the while-clause yields false.
- When a break-statement is executed.

If none of the above occurs, the execution of the while-statement continues forever. The term *infinite loop* is applied to any statement that will execute forever. The same term is also used to refer to a particular infinite execution of a while-statement.

Revisiting the score evaluation problem previously discussed, notice the problem calculates an average score by summing and counting all scores entered. The following function, *loop1*, uses the familiar code to correctly sum and count a sequence of scores, terminated by a negative sentinel:

```
def loop1():
    total = 0; counter = 0;
    score = input('Enter score (0..100), negative to quit: ');
    while (score >= 0):
        total = total + score;
        counter = counter + 1;
        score = input('Enter score (0..100), negative to quit: ');
    print 'Total =', total, 'Counter =', counter;
```

Recall that the input statement preceding the loop initializes the *score* variable, while the input statement at the bottom of the loop inputs all subsequent scores, one at a time.

Exercise

Determine which of the two input statements from function *loop1* will input each of the following numbers:

- 80
- 90
- 100
- -1

An improper or missing variable update may yield an infinite loop. For example, an inexperienced programmer may skip an input statement, as illustrated by function *loop2,* resulting in an infinite loop:

```
def loop2():
    total = 0; counter = 0;
    score = input('Enter score (0..100), negative to quit: ');
    while (score >= 0):
        total = total + score;
        counter = counter + 1;
    print 'Total =', total, 'Counter =', counter;
```

In the above case, the loop body contains only two assignment statements that increment the total and counter variables:

```
total = total + score;
counter = counter + 1;
```

In this setup, the loop body does not contain any statements that will alter the condition's logic value. If the very first score (the one that is entered before the loop) is positive, the condition *(score >= 0)* yields *True*. Every condition afterwards will be *True,* and repetitions of the loop body will start. There is no statement in the loop body to trigger a change of the condition's value to *False*, therefore the condition for the while loop will remain true forever, leading to an infinite loop.

Exercise

Assume that the user intends to input the following sequence of numbers:

- 80
- 90
- 100
- -1

Trace the infinite *loop2* above and determine the missing values from the table below.

Score	Total	Counter
-	0	0
80	?	?
?	?	?
?	?	?

Along with missing or improper variable updates, *improper statement alignment* may also yield an infinite loop. For example, an absent-minded programmer may use the improper alignment that is demonstrated here in *loop3*:

```
def loop3():
    total = 0; counter = 0;
    score = input('Enter score (0..100), negative to quit: ');
    while (score >= 0):
        total = total + score;
        counter = counter + 1;
    score = input('Enter score (0..100), negative to quit: ');
    print 'Total =', total, 'Counter =', counter;
```

In the above case, the loop body contains two assignment statements that increment the total and counter variables:

```
total = total + score;
counter = counter + 1;
```

These statements are followed by a statement that is designed to input subsequent scores. However, the input statement is not indented with these two assignment statements. The input statement is aligned with the while-clause, putting the input statement outside the loop body.

In this setup, the loop body does not contain any statements that modify the condition's logic value. If the very first score - the one entered before the loop - is positive, the condition *(score >= 0)* yields *True*. The loop body has no statement that will enter a new score to eventually trigger a change of the condition's value to *False*. As mentioned before, a condition that remains true forever creates an indefinite loop.

Exercise

Assume that the user intends to input the following sequence of numbers:

- 80
- 90
- 100
- -1

Trace the infinite *loop3* above and explain why the second input statement will not be executed.

Once an infinite loop begins, it cannot stop itself. Your only option is to cancel the execution of the program. In the IDLE *shell window*, use *Shell => Restart Shell*. You can also rely on operating system tools. In Windows, for example, the Task Manager can be used to stop the execution of the entire *Python interpreter*.

Exercise

The following function contains an infinite loop. The function body contains a print-statement that displays the current values of all variables.

```
def loop4():
    total = 0; counter = 0;
    score = input('Enter score (0..100), negative to quit: ');
    while (score >= 0):
        total = total + score;
        counter = counter + 1;
        print score, total, counter;
        score = input('Enter score (0..100), negative to quit: ');
    print 'Total =', total, 'Counter =', counter;
```

Invoke the above function and input a non-negative number to start an infinite loop. In IDLE *shell window*, use *Shell => Restart Shell* to cancel the execution. Observe the printed values of the *score* variable.

Stepwise Program Design: Case Study

Consider the following programming problem.
Develop a *Quiz Evaluation* program that will:
- Display one question followed by a menu of four possible answers.
  - Only one of the four answers is correct.
- Ask the user to choose the correct answer from the menu.
- Enter the user choice, evaluate the user choice, and provide feedback.
- Repeat the above steps until:
  - The user chooses the correct answer, or
  - The user makes too many wrong choices.

It is beneficial to approach this problem in two steps.
- First, develop a *simple quiz* function that repeats the quiz until the user enters a correct answer. This simple function does not terminate regardless of how many errors the user makes.

- Second, develop a more complex *counting quiz* function by extending your *simple quiz* with the capacity to count user errors and terminate quiz repetitions after a specified number of user errors.

The *Quiz Evaluation* sample program contains the functions *simpleQuiz* and *countingQuiz*.
These functions are the product of two successive design steps.

Exercise

Run the *Quiz Evaluation* program. In interactive mode, invoke the *simpleQuiz* function and experiment with various inputs. After that, invoke the *countingQuiz* functions and experiment with various inputs. Note any differences.

The stepwise design process of the *Quiz Evaluation* program is outlined in the next two subsections.

First Step: Simple Repetition

The following *simple quiz* function uses an unconditional loop to repeat a quiz until the user selects the correct answer:

```python
# Simple quiz - evaluate user response until correct:
def simpleQuiz():
    while (True):
        displayQuiz();
        choice = input('Enter choice number: ');
        if (choice == 1 or choice == 4):
            print 'He was a president, but not the first one.';
        elif (choice == 2):
            print 'That is correct!';
            break;
        elif (choice == 3):
            print 'He was not a politician. He was a musician.';
        else:
            print 'Invalid choice: ', choice;
```

```
# Display quiz items:
def displayQuiz():
    print '...';
    print 'Who was the first U.S. President?';
    print '(1) Abraham Lincoln';
    print '(2) George Washington';
    print '(3) John Lennon';
    print '(4) Franklin Roosevelt';
```

Note that the *simple quiz* function allows the user an unlimited number of attempts. A methodical user may try all possible answers in order until the correct answer is found. In an improved version of this function, it would be desirable to tally the total of incorrect user choices. Another improvement would be to stop the quiz repetitions if the user gives an excessive amount of incorrect responses.

Second Step: Repetition with Counting

Once the *simple quiz* function is tested and complete, it can be converted into the more sophisticated *counting quiz* function. This enhanced version of the *simple quiz* function not only repeats the quiz questions, but also tallies user errors and terminates the quiz if the user too often enters an incorrect answer. This expansion will require adding additional structures, such as counters and break-statements. Here we see the improved *counting quiz* function.

```
# Counting quiz - evaluate responses while counting user errors:
def countingQuiz():
    incorrect = 0; invalid = 0;
    while (True):
        displayQuiz();
        choice = input('Enter choice number: ');
        if (choice == 1 or choice == 4):
            print 'He was a president, but not the first one.';
            incorrect = incorrect + 1;
        elif (choice == 2):
            print 'That is correct!';
            break;
        elif (choice == 3):
            print 'He was not a politician. He was a musician.';
            incorrect = incorrect + 1;
```

```
        else:
            print 'Invalid choice: ', choice;
            invalid = invalid + 1;
        if (incorrect + invalid >= 4):
            print 'Too many errors, quitting...';
            break;
    if (incorrect > 0):
        print 'Incorrect choices:', incorrect;
    if (invalid > 0):
        print 'Invalid choices: ', invalid;
```

Note that the above function employs two different counters, *incorrect* and *invalid*. The *invalid* counter tallies the number of invalid user responses – responses that do not comply with to the offered quiz answers, such as choice *0* or choice *5*. The *incorrect* counter tallies the number of valid user responses that are incorrect answers, such as choices *1, 3,* or *4*. The function uses two break-statements: one to exit execution upon correct user response, and another to exit execution if the user makes too many errors. Trying to implement the same by means of a conditional loop and without break-statements is an instructive exercise that highlights the benefits of unconditional loops.

Stepwise program design, as illustrated above with the quiz evaluation function, is beneficial to beginners and advanced programmers. It is a step-by-step approach to programming, the breaking down of a complex problem into small, manageable steps. The steps are solved and tested one at a time to reach the solution, instead of trying to create the entire solution at once.

Exercise

Design a function that will:
- Input a sequence of scores terminated by a negative sentinel.
- Calculate the average of all failing scores.
  - Scores below 60 are failing scores.
- Calculate the average of all passing (i.e., non-failing) scores.
- Display the two averages.

You can perform two design steps. First, design a function to simply calculate the average of all scores. Second, modify the function to process failing and passing scores separately.

Note both a conditional function and an unconditional function designed to calculate average scores have already been discussed in earlier sections. You may use these functions as a basis for this exercise, modifying them to process failing and passing scores separately.

Input Data Validation

For a program to be dependable, it must check all input data, rejecting any data that is inaccurate, incomplete, or unreasonable.

Example
- A program that is calculating average student scores on a 100 point scale should ensure that only scores from 0 to 100 are entered.
- A program collecting last names for a database should confirm that only letters are entered and not numbers or other characters.
- A program collecting survey data in the form of 'yes' or 'no' questions should verify that only those responses are accepted.

While the rejection of invalid data is important, the program must not abandon execution upon the detection of such input. An interactive program should attempt to correct invalid data by asking the user for correct input data. A non-interactive program reading input data from file should be capable of recovery after encountering invalid input, continuing as designed with remaining valid input data.

Validation and recovery procedures are typically written into the program code, and are therefore invisible to the user.
A variety of useful validation and recovery procedures are implemented by means of while-loops. The following case study of a wages calculation function will provide an example.

Consider the problem of developing a *single wages* function that will:
- Input an *employee number*, any *hours* worked during a week, and an hourly *pay rate*.
- Validate input data according to the following rules:
    - *Employee number* must be between 1000 and 9999.
    - *Hours* worked must be between 0 and 168.
    - *Pay rate* must be between 10 and 80.
- Calculate *gross wages* (before taxes) by multiplying *hours* by *rate*.
- Provide adequate output.

This problem is solved by the following *single wages*.

```
# Single wages – validate input data then calculate wages once:
def singleWages():
    while (True):
        empNum  = input('Enter employee number (1000..9999) :');
        if (1000 <= empNum <=9999): break;
    while (True):
        hours   = input('Enter hours worked (0..168): ');
        if (0 <= hours <= 168): break;
    while (True):
        payRate = input('Enter pay rate (10..80): ');
        if (10 <= payRate <= 80): break;
    grossWages = hours * payRate;
    print 'Employee number:', empNum;
    print 'Gross wages:', grossWages;
```

The wages function above implements data validation by means of unconditional while-loops. For example, the following loop validates the employee number:

```
while (True):
    empNum  = input('Enter employee number (1000..9999) :');
    if (1000 <= empNum <=9999): break;
```

A correct employee number satisfies the condition *(1000 <= empNum <=9999)*. The loop body is repeated until the user enters a number satisfying this condition. When a valid value is entered, the loop exits by means of a break-statement. For valid input data, the loop body is executed only once.

Exercise

Assume the following employee numbers are input one after the other. Trace the execution of the *single wages* function:
- 900
- -1
- 0
- 10000
- 1000

Nested Loops

The body of a while-statement is a block of arbitrary statements. Consequently, the body of a while-statement may include inner while-statements. Such inner while-statements may contain other inner statements, and so on. The possible level of nesting statements is limitless.

The following sample problem can be solved by means of nested while-statements.

Develop a *multiple wages* function to:
- Input and validate an *employee number*, any *hours* worked during a week, and an hourly *pay rate*.
- Calculate and output *gross wages* by multiplying *hours* by *rate*.
- Repeat the above steps until the user enters 0 for *employee number*.

As stated above, *employee numbers* must be between *1000* and *9999*, *hours* worked must be between *0* and *168*, and *pay rates* must be between *10* and *100*. In this case, the sentinel *0* is also a valid input for an *employee number*.

The *single wages* calculation discussed in the previous section employs while-loops that validate input data. To implement a *multiple wages* calculations, nest *single wages* within a master while-loop. An example of a complete *multiple wages* function is given below.

```
# Multiple wages - validate input and calculate wages repeatedly:
def multipleWages():
   while (True):
      print'...';
      while (True):
         empNum = input(
            'Enter employee number (1000..9999), 0 to quit :');
         if (1000 <= empNum <=9999 or empNum == 0):
            break;
      if (empNum == 0):
         break;
      while (True):
         hours  = input('Enter hours worked (0..168): ');
         if (0 <= hours <= 168): break;
```

```
while (True):
    payRate = input('Enter pay rate (10..80): ');
    if (10 <= payRate <= 80): break;
grossWages = hours * payRate;
print 'Employee number:', empNum;
print 'Gross wages:', grossWages;
```

Note that the *employee number* validity test now admits *0* as a valid input. The inner break-statement exits the inner validity test loop, without exiting the outer loop:

```
if (1000 <= empNum <=9999 or empNum == 0):
    break;
```

A second test will exit the execution of the outer loop when the employee number is *0*:

```
if (empNum == 0):
    break;
```

The inner break-statement in the above example exits only the inner loop, while the outer loop continues. If the outer loop has to be exited, too, a second break-statement, nested directly in the outer loop, is required.

A break-statement exits only the innermost loop containing it.

Exercise

Assume the following employee numbers are input in the following order. Trace the execution of the *multiple wages* function:
- 900
- -1
- 0

Stepwise Program Design Revisited

The design of the *multiple wages* function above is another example of stepwise program design. The function was developed in two steps.

The first step targeted the *single wages* function, designed to validate input data and calculates wages only once. In this step, the programmer concentrated on just one activity: data validation. Focusing on just one goal enhances a programmer's ability to design, implement, and debug an intermediate solution.

The second step built on the results from the first step: a *single wages* function able to validate input data. In this step, the programmer extended the preexisting *single wages* function by concentrating on calculation repetition. . Remember, focusing on just one goal and using a valid intermediate program as a basis enhances a programmer's ability to design, implement, and debug a final solution.

Random Numbers

A "random number" is a number generated entirely by chance. Without a computer, random numbers can be generated by tossing dice, spinning roulettes, drawing cards, etc.. A computer uses a program to generate random numbers. Computer generated random numbers are indispensable for many applications, such as games, modeling and simulation, and scientific computations. Computer games, for example, are made less predictable by randomly choosing actions of various game components.

A function (written in Python or any other language) that produces random numbers is called a *random number generator*.

The *Roulette Simulators* sample program offers two functions that utilize random number generators to simulate games. The first function is a Russian roulette simulator; the second simulates a casino roulette.

> ### Exercise
> Search the Web for possible applications of random numbers. Hint: query a popular search engine with the direct question: *'What are random numbers used for?'*

Russian Roulette Simulator

Russian roulette is a game in which a person (not necessarily a Russian) spins the cylinder of a revolver that is loaded with only one bullet; the person then points the muzzle at his or her head and pulls the trigger. This is a potentially deadly game and everybody is strongly discouraged to even think about thinking about playing the game with a real weapon. Fortunately, simulating the game with a computer program is not only harmless, it is also educational and possibly entertaining.

This section offers a Russian roulette simulator written as a Python function. The function execution behavior is described below:

- The user is asked if he is ready to play.
  - The game continues only when he responds positively; otherwise the game ends.
- A bullet is loaded in a randomly chosen revolver chamber.
- A shot attempt is made using a randomly chosen firing chamber.
- If the randomly chosen firing chamber happens to be loaded, the simulated revolver produces a *shot* and the game is over.
  - Otherwise, the simulated revolver produces a *click*, rather than a *shot*.
- The above steps are repeated until the user decides not to play anymore or the simulated revolver produces a *shot*.

Example

The following table offers two possible interactions with the Russian roulette simulator:

Ready to play? [Yes/No]: **Yes** Click!... Good luck. Play more? [Yes/No]: **Yes** Click!... Good luck. Play more? [Yes/No]: **Yes** Bang!... Bad luck. Dosvidaniya...[So long...]	Ready to play? [Yes/No]: **Yes** Click!... Good luck. Play more? [Yes/No]: **Yes** Click!... Good luck. Play more? [Yes/No]: **No** Dosvidaniya...[So long...]

A complete implementation of the *Russian roulette* simulator function follows.

```python
import random;

# Simulate Russian roulette:
def Russian():
    noChambers = 6;
    chamberWithBullet = random.randint(1, noChambers);
    ans = raw_input('Ready to play? [Yes/No]: ');
```

```
while (ans == 'Yes' or ans == 'yes' or ans == 'Y' or ans == 'y'):
    firingChamber = random.randint(1, noChambers);
    if (firingChamber == chamberWithBullet):
        print 'Bang!... Bad luck.';
        break;
    else:
        print 'Click!... Good luck.';
    ans = raw_input('Play more? [Yes/No]: ');
print 'Dosvidaniya...[So long...]';
```

The *Russian roulette* function randomly chooses two chamber numbers: the number of a chamber where the bullet is loaded, and independently, the number of the chamber used as the current chamber. In doing so, *Russian roulette* relies on a built-in Python module named *random*. The *random* module is a Python program that offers ready-to-use random number generators shaped as Python functions. *Russian roulette* uses one particular number generator, a function called *randint*. Each invocation of the *randint* function returns a random integer from a specified range.

The following Python-to-English translation provides additional insight into the meaning of some new language structures employed in *Russian roulette*. Translations of language structures that have been studied before, such as while-statements and break-statements, are not presented here.

Python-To-English Translation

Python Program Structure	Common English Meaning
import random;	<ul><li>Import a Python module named *random* into the current program.</li><li>The contents of the imported module, *random*, become available in the importing program.<ul><li>Function *randint* that is defined in module random is now used in function *Russian roulette*.</li></ul></li></ul>
random.randint	<ul><li>A reference to the *randint* function, one of the several random number generators defined in module *random*.</li></ul>

random.randint(1, chambers);	◦ An invocation of the *randint* function. The invocation returns an integer number randomly chosen from the range *1, 2, 3, ... chambers.*
raw_input	◦ A built-in function that enters a string of characters. ◦ The *raw_input* function can be used for the input of words and other character sequences, in contrast to the previously studied function *input* that can be used to enter numeric values.
ans = raw_input('Ready? [Yes/No]');	◦ Prompt the user to respond by typing *Yes* or *No* and return a string containing the user response. • The user response must not be enclosed in quotes.

Functions from imported modules can be invoked by means of dot-notation that starts with the module name followed by a dot, ending with the function name. *random.randit* is an example.

The *random* module offers other useful random number generators besides *randint*. Remember, the *randint* function generates random integers. But many applications require randomly generated floating point numbers. To satisfy this need, a function named *random* provides random floating point numbers *f* from the range *(0.0 <= f <1.0)*. Note that the function name is the same as the module name. The function is invoked as *random.random()*. In the invocation, the first *random* stands for the module and the second *random* stands for the function. This dot-notation is commonly used for functions that are imported.

The *Python system* offers a variety of built-in modules. The *random* mode is just one of several important modules. Another important built-in module is the *math* module. The *math* module defines a number of useful mathematical objects, such as pi (*π*) and square root, (√).

Exercise
- Find a description of the *math* module in online documentation.
- Identify the *Python* implementations of *π* and square root, √, and read their descriptions.
- Identify additional mathematical functions and read their description.

Casino Roulette Simulator

Casino roulette is a gambling game in which players bet on which slot of a revolving wheel a small ball will come to rest in. Casino roulette is far less deadly than Russian roulette, but it can still be a painful experience for those who lose substantial amounts of money. As with the Russian roulette, simulating the game with a computer program is not only harmless, it is also educational and possibly entertaining.

This section offers a *casino roulette* simulator shaped written as a Python function. To simplify examples, a small 6-slot roulette is used. Roulette slots are referred to as slot *0*, slot *1*, slot *2*, and so on.

The *casino roulette* simulator behaves as follows:
- The user is asked:
  - How much she wants to bet.
  - On what slot to bet the money.
- A slot where the roulette ball stops is chosen randomly.
- If the randomly chosen slot happens to be the one bet on by the user, the simulated casino roulette pays her 5 times the amount bet.
  - In any other case, she looses her bet.
- The above steps are repeated until the user decides not to play anymore, entering 0 or a negative number as a bet.

Example

The following table offers two possible interactions with the *casino roulette* simulator:

Playing 6-slot roulette. How much do you bet (0 to exit): **10** Choose a slot (0 to 5): **5** Spinning ... Wheel stops at slot **3** You lost $10 You owe the casino $10 How much do you bet (0 to exit): **20** Choose a slot (0 to 5): **5** Spinning ... Wheel stops at slot 5 You won $100 The casino owes you $70	Playing 6-slot roulette. How much do you bet (0 to exit): **1000** Choose a slot (0 to 5): **5** Spinning ... Wheel stops at slot 0 You lost $1000 You owe the casino $1000 How much do you bet (0 to exit): **999999** Choose a slot (0 to 5): **5** Spinning ... Wheel stops at slot 4 You lost $999999 You owe the casino $1000999

| How much do you bet (0 to exit): **0**
So long... Come again | How much do you bet (0 to exit): **0**
So long... Come again |

A complete implementation of the *casino roulette* simulator function follows.

```
import random, time;

# Play casino roulette:
def casino():
    slots = 6; balance = 0;
    print 'Playing ' + \
        str(slots) + '-slot roulette.';
    while (True):
        bet = input('How much do you bet (0 to exit): ');
        if (bet <= 0):
            break;
        balance = balance - bet;
        chosenSlot = input(
            'Choose a slot (0 to ' +
            str(slots-1) + '): ');
        print 'Spinning ... '; time.sleep(2);
        winningSlot = random.randint(0, slots-1);
        print 'Wheel stops at slot ' + str(winningSlot);
        if (chosenSlot != winningSlot):
            print 'You lost $' + str(bet);
        else:
            win = bet * (slots - 1);
            print 'You won $' + str(win);
            balance = balance + win;
        if (balance > 0):
            print 'The casino owes you $' + str(balance);
        elif (balance < 0):
            print 'You owe the casino $' + str(abs(balance));
        else:
            print 'Your balance is $' + str(balance);
    print 'So long... Come again';
```

Notice *casino roulette* uses the *randint* function from module *randoms* to generate the winning roulette slot. Repetition of plays is ensured by an unconditional while-loop. Within the loop, the *sleep* function from the *time* module suspends the execution of the simulator for a short period of time, 2 seconds, to simulate the spinning of a material roulette wheel.

The implementation employs three new language features:
- The backslash line continuation character, \
- The string concatenation operation, +
- The built-in string conversion function, *str*

The following Python-to-English translation provides additional insight into the meaning of the new language structures in the *casino roulette*. The translations of program elements that have been studied before, such as import-statements and random number generators, are not presented here.

Python-To-English Translation

Python Program Structure	Common English Meaning
print 'Playing ' + \ str(slots) + \ '-slot roulette.';	- The physical line that ends in a backslash is joined with the following line forming a single logical line, deleting the backslash and the following end-of-line character. • A backslash cannot continue a comment. • A backslash does not continue a token except for string literals.
str(slots)	- The invocation of the *str* built-in conversion function returns a string containing a nicely printable representation of the argument.
chosenNumber = input('Choose a slot (0 to ' + str(slots-1) + '): ');	- Expressions that are enclosed in parentheses, brackets, and braces, can continue across lines without a backslash (although a backslash is permitted in them, if desired).
'You lost $' + str(bet)	- The string concatenation operator, +, creates a new string by joining the left and the right operands. • Both operands must be strings, therefore ('You lost $' + bet) will be a run-time error when *bet* is a number. • Non-string values must be explicitly converted to strings before concatenation by means of the *str* built-in conversion function.

print 'You lost $' + str(bet);	▫ Convert *bet* to a string, concatenate the result with the string *'You lost $'*, and print the result of the concatenation.
print 'You lost $', bet;	Although the statement on the left is not a part of the casino roulette program, it is worth discussing. ▫ Before printing, the *Python interpreter* concatenates *'You lost $'* with one space, *' '*, and with the string conversion of *bet*, *str(bet)*. ▫ The statement on the left is equivalent to this statement: *print 'You lost $' + ' ' + str(bet);* ▫ Notice the extra space that is inserted in the output when you use comma-separated arguments in a print-statement.

String Basics

Remember, every value in a Python program has an attribute called *type*. Several built-in types have already been discussed, such as the numeric types *int*, *float*, and *long*, and the Boolean type, *bool*. This section outlines some basic features of the string built-in type, *str*. Values of type string, commonly called strings, are sequences of characters.

Strings can represent anything that is text, such as words, names, programs, or an internet address. Strings, however, even when they look like numbers, cannot be added or multiplied by computers directly, unless converted to values of numeric types. Similarly, values of numeric types cannot be presented in human-readable form unless they are converted to strings.

Some basic features of the string type are used in earlier sample programs. Summaries of these and a few additional features are presented in the following table.

String Concept	Example
Literal	'Xena Zucchini' "Xena's name" 'A string with a "double quote" inside' "A string with a 'single quote' inside"
Assignment	name = 'Xena Zucchini';

Concatenation	'Xena' + 'Zucchini' == 'Xena Zucchini'
Repetition	3 * 'Xena' == 'XenaXenaXena'
String input	name = raw_input('What is your name?')
String output	print 'Your name is', name; # comma replaced with one space print 'Your name is ' + name; # name is string
Number output	print 'Your age is', age; # age automatically converted to string print 'Your age is ' + str(age); # age explicitly converted to string
New line control character	print '\n'; # continue on a new line print 'two\nlines'; # split output in two lines

The new line control character, '\n', is used to split a long string onto two or more lines. The *tab* control character, '\t', is applied to indent output strings. The tab control character is useful when printing tables.

Strings have some technically complex features that will be gradually introduced throughout the course. Powerful string processing methods are covered in a future topic.

Binary Search

Imagine the following two-person guessing game. You are supposed to guess another person's birthday. You can start by asking that person how his birthday relates to the middle of the month (say, the 16th day of the month). Is that person's birthday in the middle of the month, the first half of the month, or the second half of the month? If the birthday happens to be in the middle of the month, you would have guessed it with your first question. Otherwise, you will be told that the birthday is either in the first or second half of the month. Let us assume the birthday is in the first half of the month. Now you can apply the same method of interrogation to the first half of the month. You can do it by asking that person how his birthday relates to the middle of the first half of the month (the 8th day of the month). This search process will quickly converge to that person's birthday.

The above birthday guessing method is an informal example of the general problem solving method called binary search. *Binary search* is a dichotomizing search with steps in which the sets of remaining items are partitioned into two equal parts with the search continuing in only one of those parts.

Binary search is useful when searching very large ranges of data, succeeding in a small number of steps. Consider for example the problem of guessing a secret number anywhere between 1 and 1,024. Binary search takes only 10 partitioning steps to reduce a range of 1024 numbers to the single secret number. A range of about one million numbers is reduced to one number in only 20 partitioning steps. In general, if you employ binary search, it will take you not more than N partitioning steps to guess an arbitrary secret number between 1 and 2^N.

Exercise

Determine how many partitioning steps are performed by binary search to guess an arbitrary secret number between *1* and *1073741824*. Note that the number *1073741824* is equal to 2^{30}.

Binary search is easy to implement using a while-loop. A possible implementation is offered in the following *Binary Search* program.

```python
# Display binary search menu:
def displayMenu():
    print '1) Your number is the same.'
    print '2) Your number is smaller.'
    print '3) Your number is larger.'

# Use binary search to guess a number:
def guess():
    first = input('Enter a whole number: ');
    last = input('Enter a much larger whole number: ');
    print 'Think of an arbitrary secret number between', \
        first, 'and', last, '.';
    while (first <= last):
        mid = (first + last) / 2;
        print 'How does your number relate to ', mid, '?';
        displayMenu();
        answer = input('Choose item: ');
        if (answer == 1): # same
            break;
        elif (answer == 2): # before
            last = mid - 1;
        elif (answer == 3): # after
            first = mid + 1;
        else:
            print 'Invalid response.';
    print 'I know your secret number is ', mid, '.';
```

Exercise

Assume the secret number is 12; trace the execution of the *guess* function for the following input data:
- First = 1, Last = 32
- First = 1, Last = 1024
- First = 1, Last = 1048576

Determine the number of partitioning steps in each case.

Synonyms

Some terms that have been introduced in this topic have synonyms. A list of such terms and their corresponding synonyms follows.

Term	Synonym
Repetition structure	Loop
Repetition statement	Loop
Repetition statement execution	Loop
While-statement	While Loop
String control codes	String escape characters
Terminate a loop	Exit a loop

Lab A [Program Control: Repetition]

Objective; Background; Lab Overview; What to Do Next; Downloading Sample Programs; Uncompressing Sample Programs; Studying the Sample Program; Creating a Program File; Developing the New Program

Objective

The objective of this lab is to develop a *Multi-Conversion Repetitions* program that will:
- Display a menu of three choices:
  - A variety of *conversions between metric and US measurements*
  - *Exit the menu* choice
- Ask the user to make one choice from the menu; enter the user choice.
- Depending on the user choice, do one of the following:
  - Perform the conversion chosen by the user then **repeat** all of the above steps, or
  - Exit the menu repetitions, if that was what the user chose.

Background
- Your menu of various conversions may look like this:

   Conversions Menu:
   (0) Exit the menu
   (1) Convert Fahrenheit to Celsius
   (2) Convert Celsius to Fahrenheit
   (3) Convert Inches to Centimeters
   (4) Convert Centimeters to Inches
   (5) Convert Gallons to Liters
   (6) Convert Liters to Gallons
   (7) Convert Yards to Meters
   (8) Convert Meters to Yards
   (9) Convert Pounds to Kilograms
   (10) Convert Kilograms to Pounds
   Enter choice number:

- The user's choice is a whole number, without parentheses.

Lab Overview

To perform this lab:
- Study the *Conversion Repetitions* sample program.
- Transform a copy of the *Conversion Repetitions* sample program into a *Multi-Conversion Repetitions* program by following the detailed instructions that follow in this lab.
- Systematically test the *Multi-Conversion Repetitions* program.

What to Do Next

At this time, you are offered these choices:
- Follow the detailed lab instructions below, or
- Try the lab independently, but also peek in the instructions when needed, or
- Perform the lab without the aid of instructions.

All three approaches can be beneficial for students. Feel free to choose the approach most beneficial for you.

Downloading Sample Programs

Various Lab Assignments for this course of study are based on ready-to-use sample programs. Such programs are to be downloaded from the online study pack into your *master* folder.

Download sample programs for the current Topic 4 by performing these steps:
- Locate the current *Topic 4* in the online study pack.
- Open the *Lab Assignment* resource.
- Right-click on the *Sample Programs* link.
- Use *Save As* to store the downloaded compressed (zipped) folder, *04.zip,* within your *master* folder.

Uncompressing Sample Programs

- Uncompress the contents of the downloaded compressed (zipped) folder. Depending on your platform, you may use built-in compression support, or compressing utilities.
  - In Windows XP, for example, you can use built-in uncompression support as follows:
    - Use the *File Browser* to open your *master* folder.
    - Right-click on the downloaded compressed (zipped) folder.

- Use *Extract All* and extract the contents of the compressed (zipped) folder within the *master* folder.
  - *This* will create an uncompressed folder, *04*, within the *master* folder. This folder will contain your sample programs.
- Alternatively, you can:
  - *Open* the compressed (zipped) folder.
  - *Cut* folder *04* from within the compressed (zipped) folder, and
  - *Paste* the cut folder *04* outside the compressed (zipped) folder – directly within the *master* folder.
- Delete the compressed (zipped) folder, *04.zip*, and keep the uncompressed folder, *04*.
- Open the uncompressed folder *04* and browse its contents.
- Note that Python program files have extension '**.py**'.

Studying the Sample Program

- Use IDLE to open and browse the *Conversion Repetitions* sample program.
- Run the program with various input data and observe its output.
- Analyze the program implementation.

Creating a Program File

Create this program in your current labs folder, *04Labs*.

- Use IDLE to create a copy of the *Conversion Repetitions* program file.
- Give the name *Multi-ConversionRepetitions.py* to the saved copy.
  - **Important Note:** You must explicitly supply the file extension '**.py**' when saving from IDLE.

Developing the New Program

Perform these steps with the newly created *Multi-Conversion Repetitions* program:

Step 1: Developing a *repeat* function

- Provide implementations of all necessary conversion functions as follows:
  - Open the *Multi-Conversion Selector* program that you developed for Topic 03.
  - Copy the definitions of all conversion functions.
  - Paste all definitions at the end of your current *Multi-Conversion Repetitions* program.

- Delete the entire definition of function *displayMenu* inherited form the sample *Conversion Repetitions* program.
- Copy the definition of the *displayMenu* function from your *Multi-Conversion Selector* program into your current *Multi-Conversion Repetitions* program.
- Extend the definition of function *displayMenu* to make it display an *Exit the menu* item.
  - Follow the menu from the *Background* part of this lab as a sample of what the updated menu should look like.
- Extend the definition of function *repeat* to make it analyze all possible user choices, and invoke corresponding conversion functions.
  - Copy the multiple selection if-statement from the *select* function of your *Multi-Conversion Selector* program.
  - Replace the short multiple selection statement inherited from sample *Conversion Repetitions* program with the full if-statement copy.
  - Indent the if-statement so that it becomes a proper member of the while-loop body.
  - Close the *Multi-Conversion Selector* program.
- Test the extended *repeat* function. Make sure you select each menu item at least once.

Step 2: Brushing-Up your program
- Update comments throughout the entire program adequately.
- Supply additional lines of comments if needed to make the program more readable.

Lab B [Program Control: Repetition]

Objective; Background; Lab Overview; What to Do Next; Studying the Sample Program; Creating a Program File; Developing the New Program

Objective

The objective of this lab is to develop a *Weather Advices* program that will:
- Repeatedly perform the following steps:
    - Input current *temperature* (in Fahrenheit).
        - Exit repetitions upon the input of the sentinel value *-9999* for *temperature*.
    - Output advisable *activity* for the particular temperature.
- Determine the *average* of all entered temperatures.
- Implement repetitions in two different ways:
    - By means of a conditional loop
    - By means of an unconditional loop

Background

- Implement these two functions:
    - A function named *weatherConditional* that employs a conditional loop.
    - A function named *weatherUnconditional* that employs an unconditional loop.
- Implement the *Weather Advices* in compliance with the following Activity Table:

Temperature is below:	But not below:	The advisable activity is:
40		Get some sleep at home
60	40	Browse the Internet
75	60	Take a walk in the park
90	75	Go sunbathing on the lawn
	90	Going to the beach

Lab Overview

To perform this lab:
- Study the *Score Evaluation* sample program.
- Transform a copy of the *Score Evaluation* sample program into a *Weather Advices* program.
- Design a *Test Table* and debug the *Weather Advices* program.

What to Do Next

At this time, you are offered these choices:
- Follow the detailed lab instructions below, or
- Try the lab independently, but also peek in the instructions when needed, or
- Perform the lab independently, without looking at instructions at all.

All three approaches can be beneficial for students. Feel free to choose the approach most beneficial for you.

Studying the Sample Program

- Use IDLE to open and browse the *Score Evaluation* sample program.
- Run the program with various input data; observe output.
- Analyze the program implementation.

Creating a Program File

To create this program in your current labs folder, *04Labs,* perform the following steps:
- Use IDLE to create a copy of the *Score Evaluation* program file.
- Name the saved copy *WeatherAdvices.py*.
  - **Important Note:** You must explicitly supply the file extension "**.py**" when saving from IDLE.

Developing the New Program

Step1: Developing a conditional loop

Perform these steps with the newly created *Weather Advices* program:
- Replace the name of function *scoresConditional* with a new name, *weatherConditional*.
- For Step 1, limit your work to function *weatherConditional* only.

- Modify the definition of the newly named function *weatherConditional* to work with temperatures rather than scores.
    - Replace the variable named *score* with a variable named *temp*.
    - Replace the input prompt *"Enter score (0..100), negative to quit: "* - inherited from *scoresConditional* - with a new input prompt, such as *"Enter temperature in Fahrenheit, -9999 to quit: "*.
        - Replace the prompt in the two statements where it appears: before the loop and within the loop body.
    - Use the condition *(temp != -9999)* to test for the temperature sentinel -9999.
        - Do not use a condition like *(temp >= 0)*.
    - In the loop body, use these statements to accumulate and count temperatures:

        total = total + temp;
        counter = counter + 1;

    - Immediately following the while-clause, preceding the above two statements, add a multiple selection if-statement to determine advisable activity depending on the current temperature. Follow the steps below.
        - Open the *Weather Advisor* program developed in Topic 03.
        - Copy the multiple selection if-statement that determines advisable activity AND the print-statement following the if-statement.
            - Close the *Weather Advisor* program.
        - Immediately after the while-clause, paste the multiple selection if-statement and the print-statement.
        - Indent all pasted statements properly so they are members of the loop body.
    - Your conditional while loop should now look like this:

        while (temp != -9999):
            if (temp < 40):
                activity = "Get some sleep at home.";
            elif (temp < 60):
                activity = "Browse the Internet.";
            elif (temp < 75):
                activity = "Take a walk in the park.";
            elif (temp < 90):
                activity = "Sunbathe on the lawn.";

```
        else: # 90 =< temp
            activity = "Go to the beach.";
        print activity;
        total = total + temp;
        counter = counter + 1;
        temp = input("Enter temperature in Fahrenheit, -9999
to quit: ");
    print ...;
```

- In the print-statement immediately following the above loop, replace the prompt *"Scores processed:"* with the prompt *"Temperatures processed:"*.
- In the last print-statement, replace the prompt *"Average score:"* with a prompt *"Average temperature:"*.

○ Extensively test the *weatherConditional* function with various input data.
○ Start testing with this data:

> Enter temperature in Fahrenheit, -9999 to quit: **30**
> Get some sleep at home.
> Enter temperature in Fahrenheit, -9999 to quit: **50**
> Browse the Internet.
> Enter temperature in Fahrenheit, -9999 to quit: **60**
> Take a walk in the park.
> Enter temperature in Fahrenheit, -9999 to quit: **80**
> Sunbathe on the lawn.
> Enter temperature in Fahrenheit, -9999 to quit: **100**
> Go to the beach.
> Enter temperature in Fahrenheit, -9999 to quit: **-9999**
> Temperatures processed: 5
> Average temperature: 64.0

Step2: Developing an unconditional loop

- Proceed as in to the previous part, but work with function *scoresUnconditional*.
  - Start by replacing the function name *scoresUnconditional* with a new name, *weatherUnconditional*.
  - Modify the definition of the newly named function *weatherUnconditional* to make it work with temperatures rather than with scores.
    - At each step, carefully keep proper indentation.
- Extensively test the final version of *weatherConditional* function with various input data.
- Start testing with the same data provided for function *weatherConditional*.

Step3: Brushing-Up your program

- Update comments throughout the entire program as needed.
- Supply additional lines of comments to improve readability.

Lab C [Program Control: Repetition]

Objective; Background; Lab Overview; What to Do Next; Studying the Sample Program; Creating a Program File; Developing the New Program

Objective

The objective of this lab is to develop a *Tax Calculations* program that will:
- Repeatedly perform the following steps:
  - Input taxable annual *income*.
    - Exit repetitions upon the input of any negative *income*.
  - Determine applicable tax bracket, calculate *tax* due, output *tax* due.
- Determine average of all entered *incomes*.
- Determine average of all calculated *taxes*.
- Implement repetitions in two different ways:
  - Using a conditional loop
  - Using an unconditional loop

Background

- Implement the following two functions:
  - A function named *taxesConditional* employing a conditional loop.
  - A function named *taxesUnconditional* employing an unconditional loop.
- Implement the *Tax Calculations* in compliance with the following Tax Table:

Taxable income is over:	But not over:	The tax is:	Plus:	Of the amount over:
0	7,150	0.00	10%	0
7,150	29,050	715.00	15%	7,150
29,050	70,350	4,000.00	25%	29,050
70,350	146,750	14,325.00	28%	70,350
146,750	319,100	35,717.00	33%	146,750
319,100		92,592.50	35%	319,100

Lab Overview

To perform this lab, you should:
- Study the *Score Evaluation* sample program.
- Transform a copy of the *Score Evaluation* sample program into a *Tax Calculations* program.
- Design a *Test Table* and debug the *Tax Calculations* program.

What to Do Next

At this time, you are offered these choices:
- Follow the detailed lab instructions below, or
- Try the lab independently, but also peek in the instructions when needed, or
- Perform the lab independently, without the aid of the instructions.

All three approaches can be beneficial for students. Feel free to choose the approach most beneficial to you.

Studying the Sample Program

- Use IDLE to open and browse the *Score Evaluation* sample program.
- Run the program with various input data; observe its output.
- Analyze the program implementation.

Creating a Program File

To create this program in your current labs folder, *04Labs*, perform the following steps:
- Use IDLE to create a copy of the *Score Evaluation* program file.
- Name the saved copy *TaxCalculations.py*.
  - **Important Note:** You must explicitly supply the file extension '**.py**' when saving from IDLE.

Developing the New Program

Step 1: Developing a conditional loop

Perform these steps with the newly created *Tax Calculations* program:
- Rename function *scoresConditional* to *taxesConditional*.
- For now, limit your work to function *taxesConditional* only.

- Modify the body of newly named function *taxesConditional* to work with taxable incomes rather than scores.
  - Replace the variable named *score* with a variable named *income*.
  - Replace the input prompt *'Enter score (0..100), negative to quit: '* - inherited from *scoresConditional* - with a new input prompt, such as *'Enter annual income, negative to quit: '*.
    - Replace the prompt in the two statements where it appears: before the loop and within the loop body.
  - In the loop body, use these statements to accumulate and count incomes:

    total = total + income;
    counter = counter + 1;

    Be sure to indent the above sequence properly!
  - Immediately following the while-clause, and preceding the above two statements, add a multiple selection if-statement to determine applicable tax bracket and calculate the *tax* due, depending on the current *income*. Follow the steps below.
    - Open the *Tax Calculator* program developed in Topic 03.
    - Copy the multiple selection if-statement determining the *tax* due AND the print-statement that follows the if-statement.
      - Close the *Tax Calculator* program.
    - Immediately after the while-clause, paste the multiple selection if-statement and the print-statement.
    - Indent all pasted statements properly so they are members of the loop body.
  - In function *taxesConditional*, rename variable *total* to *totalIncome*.
  - In the beginning of the body of function *taxesConditional*, add this statement before the while loop:

    totalTax = 0;

- At this time, your conditional while loop should look like this:

    ```
    counter = 0; totalTax = 0;
    while (income >= 0):
        if (income <= 7150):
            tax = 0.10 * income;
        elif (income <= 29050):
            tax = 715 + 0.15 * (income - 7150);
        elif (income <= 70350):
            tax = 4000 + 0.25 * (income - 29050);
        elif (income <= 146750):
            tax = 14325 + 0.28 * (income - 70350);
        elif (income <= 319100):
            tax = 35717 + 0.33 * (income - 146750);
        else:  # income > 319100
            tax = 92592.50 + 0.35 * (income - 319100);
        print 'Tax due =', tax;
        totalIncome = totalIncome + income;
        counter =counter + 1;
        income = input('Enter annual income, negative to quit: ');
    print ...;
    ```

- After the statement:

    totalIncome = totalIncome + income;

  add statement:

    totalTax = totalTax + tax;

- In the print-statement immediately following the loop, replace the prompt *'Scores processed:'* with the prompt *'Incomes processed:'*.
- In the last if-statement, rename variable *average* to *averageIncome*.
- In the last if-statement, add two statements to calculate and print the *average tax*. These are similar to the statements that calculate and print the *average income*.
  ○ Extensively test the *taxesConditional* function with various input data.
  ○ Start testing with this data:

```
Enter annual income, negative to quit: 0
Tax due = 0.0
Enter annual income, negative to quit: 7150
Tax due = 715.0
Enter annual income, negative to quit: 10000
Tax due = 1142.5
Enter annual income, negative to quit: 29050
Tax due = 4000.0
Enter annual income, negative to quit: 70350
Tax due = 14325.0
Enter annual income, negative to quit:
146750

Tax due = 35717.0
Enter annual income, negative to quit: -1
Incomes processed: 6
Average income: 43883.3333333
Average tax: 9316.58333333
```

Step 2: Developing an unconditional loop
- Proceed as in the previous part, but work with function *scoresUnconditional*.
    - Start by replacing the function name *scoresUnconditional* with a new name, *taxesUnconditional*.
    - Modify the definition of the newly named function *taxesUnconditional* to make it work with incomes and taxes rather than with scores.
        - At each step, be careful to use proper indentation.
- Thoroughly test the final version of *taxesUnconditional* function with various input data.
- Start testing with the same data provided for function *taxesConditional*.

Step 3: Brushing-Up your program
- Update comments throughout the program as needed.
- Supply additional lines of comments to improve readability.

Lab D [Program Control: Repetition]

Objective; Background; Lab Overview; What to Do Next; Studying the Sample Program; Creating a Program File; Developing the New Program

Objective

The objective of this lab is to develop a *Wage and Tax Calculations* program that will:
- Repeatedly perform the following steps:
  - Input an *employee number*, any *hours* worked during a week, an hourly *pay rate,* and the *tax rate*.
  - Validate input data.
  - Calculate *taxes due* and *net wages* (after taxes).
- Determine the average of all calculated *taxes due*.
- Determine the average of all calculated *net wages*.

Background

- Verify input data according to the following rules:
  - *Employee number* must be between 1000 and 9999.
    - Repetitions are exited upon the input of 0 for *employee number*.
  - *Hours* worked must be between 0 and 168.
  - *Pay rate* must be between 8 and 100.
  - *Tax rate* must be between 0 and 50.
- Calculate *gross wages* (before taxes) by multiplying *hours* by *rate*.
  - All hours over 40 are paid at 120% of the *pay rate*.
- Calculate *taxes due* by applying *tax rate* to *gross wages*.
- Calculate *net wages* (after taxes) by subtracting *taxes due* from *gross wages*.
- Calculate averages by finding the totals of *net wages* and *taxes due*, and by multiplying these totals by the number of all processed *wages*.

Lab Overview

To perform this lab:
- Study the *Wage Calculations* sample program.
- Transform a copy of the *Wage Calculations* sample program into a *Wage and Tax Calculations* program.
- Extensively test the *Wage and Tax Calculations* program.

What to Do Next

At this time, you are offered these choices:
- Follow the detailed lab instructions below, or
- Try the lab independently, but also peek in the instructions when needed, or
- Perform the lab without the aid of the instructions.

All three approaches are beneficial for students. Feel free to choose the approach most beneficial for you.

Studying the Sample Program

- Use IDLE to open and browse the *Wage Calculations* sample program.
- Run the program with various input data; observe its output.
- Analyze the program implementation.

Creating a Program File

To create this program in your current labs folder, *04Labs*, follow these steps:
- Use IDLE to create a copy of the *Wage Calculations* program file.
- Name the saved copy *WageAndTaxCalculations.py.*
  - **Important Note:** You must explicitly supply the file extension '**.py**' when saving from IDLE.

Developing the New Program

Step 1: Tax Calculations

Perform these steps with the newly created *Wage and Tax Calculations* program:
- Delete the entire definition of function *simpleWages*.
- Rename function *multipleWages* as *taxesAndWages*.

- Modify the body of the newly named function *taxesAndWages* to make it calculate *taxes due* and *net wages* (after taxes).
    - Implement an unconditional loop to input and validate *tax rate*.
        - The tax rate must be between 0 and 50 percent.
        - Place the input loop for the *tax rate* immediately after the input loop for the *pay rate.*
    - Enhance the *gross wages* calculation with overtime *extra pay*.
        - Use a one-way if-statement to pay *hours* over 40 at 120% of the *pay rate*, as studied in a previous topic.
    - Calculate *taxes due* by applying the *tax rate* to the *gross wages*.
        - Place the calculation of *taxes due* immediately after the calculation of *gross wages.*
    - Immediately after the calculation of *taxes due*, calculate *net wages* (after taxes) by subtracting *taxes due* from *gross wages*.
    - At the very end of the function, print *taxes due* and *net wages*.
- Extensively test this intermediate version of the *taxesAndWages* function with various input data.

Step 2: Averages

Perform these steps with the intermediate *Wage and Tax Calculations* program that you created in Part1:
- In the beginning of the body of function *taxesAndWages* and before the outermost loop, initialize the following variables to 0:
    - Variable *counter* to count all processed wages.
    - Variable *totalNetWages* to accumulate all calculated *net wages*.
    - Variable *totalTaxesDue* to accumulate all calculated *taxes due*.
- In the main loop body and immediately after the calculation on *net wages*, insert statements to:
    - Increment the *counter* by 1.
    - Add the calculated *net wages* to the *total net wages*.
    - Add the calculated to *taxes due* the *total taxes due*.
- Outside of the main while loop, calculate the average *net wages* and the average *taxes due*.
- Use a one-way if-statement to test if *(counter > 0)* before dividing the accumulated wage and tax totals by *counter*.
- Carefully indent the calculations of the average wages and taxes to place them outside of he outer loop.
    - Averages are to be calculated only once, after the completion of the repeated wage and tax calculations.

- Extensively test the *taxesAndWages* function with various input data.
- You can start testing with these data:

```
Enter employee number (1000..9999), 0 to quit :2000
Enter hours worked (0..168): 20
Enter pay rate (0..80): 10
Enter tax rate (0..50): 20
Employee number: 2000
Gross wages: 200
Taxes due: 40.0
Net wages: 160.0
...
Enter employee number (1000..9999), 0 to quit :3000
Enter hours worked (0..168): 60
Enter pay rate (0..80): 10
Enter tax rate (0..50): 90
Enter tax rate (0..50): 20
Employee number: 3000
Gross wages: 640.0
Taxes due: 128.0
Net wages: 512.0
...
Enter employee number (1000..9999), 0 to quit :0
Average net wages: 336.0
Average taxes due: 84.0
```

Step 3: Brushing-Up your program
- Update comments throughout the entire program adequately.
- Supply additional lines of comments if needed to make the program more readable.

Lab E [Program Control: Repetition]

Objective; Background; Lab Overview; What to Do Next; Studying the Sample Programs; Creating a Program File; Developing the New Program

Objective
The objective of this lab is to develop a *Seconds Calculations* program that will:
- Repeatedly perform the following steps:
  - Input and validate *hours, minutes,* and *seconds*.
  - Count and output the *total number of seconds*.
- Implement repetitions in two different ways:
  - Using a conditional loop
  - Using an unconditional loop

Background
- Validate input data according to the following rules:
  - *Hours* must be non-negative.
  - *Minutes* must be between 0 and 59.
  - *Seconds* must be between 0 and 59.
- Implement two functions:
  - A function named *secondsConditional* employing a conditional loop.
  - A function named *secondsUnconditional* employing an unconditional loop.

Lab Overview
To perform this lab:
- Study the sample programs for this topic.
- Create a *Seconds Calculations* program by adopting the conditional loop organization from the *Russian* function or the *Roulette Simulators* program, and the input data validation from the *Wage Calculations* program.
- Extensively test the *Seconds Calculations* program.

What to Do Next
At this time, you are offered these choices:
- Follow the detailed lab instructions below, or

- Try the lab independently, but also peek in the instructions when needed, or
- Perform the lab independently, without the aid of the instructions.

All three approaches can be beneficial to students. Feel free to choose the approach most beneficial to you.

Studying the Sample Program
- Use IDLE to open and browse the *Score Evaluation* sample program.
- Run the program with various input data; observe the output.
- Analyze the program implementation.

Creating a Program File
To create this program in your current labs folder, *04Labs*:
- Create a new file for the program, saving it as SecondsCalculations.py.
    - **Important Note:** You must explicitly supply the file extension '**.py**' when saving from IDLE.

Developing the New Program

Step 1: Preparation
- Design formulae for the calculations.
    - This type of conversion, without repetitions, is an optional lab for Topic 02. If you have done that lab, you may reuse that solution for the current lab.

Step 2: Developing a conditional loop without data validation
- Implement function *secondsConditional*.
    - Develop a conditional loop similar to that found in *Russian* or *Roulette Simulators*. Start by copying function *Russian* into your *Seconds Calculations* program. You can then alter the copy to ask for hours, minutes, and seconds, converting all time measurements into seconds.
- Test your function *secondsConditional*.

Step 3: Enhancing the conditional loop with data validation
- Enhance function *secondsConditional* with data validation.
    - Use unconditional while-loops to input valid hours, minutes, and seconds. Follow the approach used in program *Wage Calculations*.

- Thoroughly test your *secondsConditional* function with valid and invalid inputs.

Step 4: Developing an unconditional loop with data validation

- Implement function *secondsUnconditional*.
  - Paste a duplicate of the *secondsConditional* function after the original. Rename it *secondsUnconditional*.
    - If data validation was implemented correctly on the previous step, it will not need to be changed at this step.
  - Convert the copied conditional loop into an unconditional loop. Remove the input preceding the loop, keeping the input at the end of the loop.
- Thoroughly test your *secondsUnconditional* function with valid and invalid inputs.
- Start testing with this provided data:

Interaction with *secondsConditional*	Interaction with *secondsUnconditional*
This program converts time into seconds. Ready to convert? [Yes/No]: **Yes** Enter hours (non-negative): **2** Enter minutes (00..59): **10** Enter seconds (0..59): **10** The total time is 7810 seconds. Convert more? [Yes/No]: **Yes** Enter hours (non-negative): **0** Enter minutes (00..59): **66** Enter minutes (00..59): **56** Enter seconds (0..59): **-2** Enter seconds (0..59): **120** Enter seconds (0..59): **20** The total time is 3380 seconds. Convert more? [Yes/No]: **No** So long...	This program converts time into seconds. Enter hours (non-negative): **2** Enter minutes (00..59): **10** Enter seconds (0..59): **10** The total time is 7810 seconds. Convert more? [Yes/No]: **Yes** Enter hours (non-negative): **0** Enter minutes (00..59): **66** Enter minutes (00..59): **56** Enter seconds (0..59): **-2** Enter seconds (0..59): **120** Enter seconds (0..59): **20** The total time is 3380 seconds. Convert more? [Yes/No]: **No** So long...

Step 5: Brushing-Up your program

- Update comments throughout the program.
- Supply any necessary additional lines of comments to improve readability.

Lab F [Program Control: Repetition, Optional]

Objective; Background; Lab Overview

Objective
The objective of this lab is to develop a *Number Tricks* program that will:
- Repeatedly ask the user to think of an arbitrary *secret number*, perform several operations with that secret number, then input the *result* from those operations.
- Guess and output the secret number.
    - Implement repetitions in two different ways:
        - Using a conditional loop
        - Using an unconditional loop

Background
- Ask the user to multiply the secret number by 5, add 6, multiply by 4, add 9, and multiply by 5.
    - Note that it is the user who is expected to perform these operations with the chosen number, not your program.
- Use the following equation in your program to find the *secret number* once the program is given the *result* of the application of all of the above operations:

    $secret = (result - 165) / 100$

Lab Overview
To perform this lab:
- Study sample programs for this topic.
- Create a program file in your current labs folder.
- Design two functions:
    - One function to use a conditional loop.
    - A second function to use an unconditional loop.
- Test both functions. Design and use a *Test Table*.

Lab G [Program Control: Repetition, Optional]

Objective; Background; Lab Overview

Objective

The objective of this lab is to develop a *Leap Year Evaluations* program that will:
- Repeatedly input and validate a whole number representing a *year* in the Gregorian calendar.
  - Evaluate if it is a leap year or a normal year, outputting the evaluation.
- Implement repetitions in two different ways:
  - Using a conditional loop
  - Using an unconditional loop

Background

- Validate input data according to the following rule:
  - The Gregorian calendar was introduced in 1582; only years **after** 1582 are allowed.

Lab Overview

To perform this lab:
- Study sample programs for this topic.
- Create a program file in your current labs folder.
- Design two functions:
  - One function using a conditional loop.
  - A second function using unconditional loop.
- Test both functions. Design and use a *Test Table*.

Lab H - Challenge [Program Control: Repetition, Optional]

Objective; Background; Lab Overview

Objective
The objective of this lab is to implement a program to play the game of *Craps*.

Background
- *Craps* is a gambling game using two dice. A *Craps* program should repeatedly throw the dice, evaluating the result according to the rules of the game.

Lab Overview
To perform this lab:
- Research the game of *Craps* on the Web and/or in the Library.
- Implement a program to play the chosen game.
  - Implement the program file in your current labs folder.
- Post in the General Forum:
  - A brief description of the rules of the game.
  - A brief description of the program implementation of the game.

Lab I - Challenge [Program Control: Repetition, Optional]

Objective; Background; Lab Overview

Objective

The objective of this lab is to implement a program to play the game of *Nim*.

Background

- *Nim* is a game in which matchsticks are arranged in rows, while players alternately remove one or more of them. In some versions the object is to take the last remaining matchstick on the table; in other versions the object is to avoid taking the last remaining matchstick on the table. A *Nim* program is to play one or more *Nim* games against the user.

Lab Overview

To perform this lab:
- Research the game of *Nim* on the Web or in the Library.
- Implement a program to play the chosen game.
  - Implement the program file in your current labs folder.
- Post in the General Forum:
  - A brief description of the rules of the game.
  - A brief description of the program implementation of the game.

Functions

Sample Programming Problem: Switch Function; Sample Program: Conversion Manager; Program Design with Functions: Lottery Odds; Case Study: Input Validation Function; Functions for Code Reuse; Keyword Arguments and Positional Arguments; Function Definition Form; Function Definition Execution; Parameters and Local Variables; Program Design with Functions: Score Transformations; Program Design with Functions: Quiz Evaluation; Function Invocations; Return Statements; Function-to-Function Communication; The None Value; Synonyms

Sample Programming Problem: Switch Function

Consider the following programming problem.
Develop a *Conversion Manager* program that will:
- Offer the user a menu of two temperature conversion choices.
- Employ a special *switch* function to:
  - Analyze the user choice, and
  - Switch the execution to a conversion function that implements the particular user choice.
- Repeat the above steps until the user chooses to exit.

The menu of possible conversions might look like this:

Temperature Conversions Menu:
(0) Exit the menu
(1) Convert Fahrenheit to Celsius
(2) Convert Celsius to Fahrenheit
Enter choice number:

From the user's perspective, the output of this program is the same as the output of the *Conversion Repetitions* program studied in a previous topic. The difference between the two programs is in their implementations. The *Conversion Manager* program must introduce an additional *switch* function to manage the user choice by switching to the appropriate conversion function. The earlier *Conversion Repetitions* program did not use any switch.

Sample Program: Conversion Manager

A sample program named *Conversion Manager* solves the programming problem formulated above. The program uses a function named *repeat* to repeatedly display a menu with possible choices (an exit choice and two temperature conversion choices), and perform the chosen temperature conversions. The program introduces a special function named *switch* to analyze the user *choice* and switch the execution to a relevant conversion function.

Exercise

Run the *Conversion Manager* program. In interactive mode, invoke the *repeat* function and experiment with various inputs.

The main parts of the *Conversion Manager* program follow.

```python
# Manage choice by switching to appropriate conversion function:
def switch(choice):
    if (choice == 1):
        F2C();
    elif (choice == 2):
        C2F();
    else:
        print 'Invalid choice: ', choice;

# Display menu and implement user choice repeatedly:
def repeat():
    displayMenu();
    currentChoice = input('Enter choice number: ');
    while (currentChoice != 0):
        switch ( choice = currentChoice );
        displayMenu();
        currentChoice = input('Enter choice number: ');
    print 'Bye-bye.';

# Display menu items:
def displayMenu():
# Convert Fahrenheit temperature to Celsius temperature:
def F2C():
# Convert Celsius temperature to Fahrenheit temperature:
def C2F():
```

The definitions of functions *displayMenu, F2C* and *C2F* are the same as those in the *Conversion Repetitions* program studied in a previous topic.

The main function in program *Conversion Repetitions* is the function *repeat. When repeat* is executed, it does the following:
- Invokes function *displayMenu* to display the menu.
- Inputs the current user choice.
- Repeatedly tests the current user choice.
  - Invokes the switch function and passes the current user choice to the function chosen.
    - The *switch* function analyses the user's choice, and
    - Invokes a conversion function (function *F2C* or function *C2F*) to implement that choice.
  - Exits the execution when the user chooses to do so.

The user choice is managed by means of a custom *switch* function.

The following Python-to-English translations provide insight into the definition and invocation of the *switch* function from the *Conversion Manager* program.

Python-To-English Translation

Python Statement	Common English Meaning
○ Run program *Conversion Manager*.	○ Execute all function definitions from the program. ○ The execution of a function definition makes the corresponding function available for invocations.

def switch(choice):
   if (choice == 1):
      F2C();
   elif (choice == 2):
      C2F();
   else:
      print 'Invalid choice: ', choice;
	○ Define function named *switch* with one parameter named *choice*.
	  • The programmer is free to choose names for his/her functions and their parameters.
	○ The *choice* parameter can be used like a variable in function *switch*.
	○ The *choice* parameter is **local** to the *switch* function:
	  • The *choice* parameter can be used inside its defining function *(switch)* but not outside of that function.

▫ Invoke function *repeat* in interactive mode: `>>> repeat();`	▫ Execute the statements from the body of function *repeat*.

▫ In function *repeat*, before the while-loop:
`def repeatl():`
   `displayMenu();`
   `currentChoice = input('Choice: ');`
	▫ Invoke the *displayMenu* helper function.
	▫ Input the current user *choice*.
	▫ The *currentChoice* variable is **local** to the *repeat* function:
	   • The *currentChoice* variable can be used only inside its defining function *(repeat)* but not outside of that function.

`while ( currentChoice != 0 );`	▫ While *currentChoice* is not *0*, execute the loop body, as specified below. • When *currentChoice* becomes *0*, terminate the loop and continue with the print-statement that follows the loop.

`switch ( choice = currentChoice );`	Step 1 – function invocation:
	▫ Suspend the execution of function *repeat* and invoke function *switch*.
	▫ The invocation is executed in two steps:
	   • *Parameter assignment*, and
	   • *Execution* of the function body.
	▫ These two steps are detailed below.

`switch ( choice = currentChoice );`	Step 1.1 – parameter assignment: ▫ Assign the *argument, currentChoice,* into the *parameter, choice:* `choice = currentChoice;`.

`if (choice == 1):`
   `F2C();`
`elif (choice == 2):`
   `C2F();`
`else:`
   `print 'Invalid choice... ';`
	Step 1.2 – function body execution:
	▫ Execute the body of the invoked *switch* function.
	   • Use the function parameter, *choice*, as a local variable.
	   • Remember that in Step 1, the *choice* parameter has been already assigned the value of the argument, *currentChoice*.

▫ In function *repeat*:
   `switch(choice = currentChoice);`
   `displayMenu();`
   `currentChoice = input('Choice: ');`
	Step 2 – statements after the function invocation:
	▫ The execution of the suspended invoking function, repeat, is now resumed.
	   • In the *repeat* function, the statement that displays the menu will be executed next.

▫ In function *repeat*, after the while-loop: `print 'Bye-bye.';`	Print *'Bye-bye'*, thus completing the invocation: `>>> repeat().`

Example

Function *switch* can be invoked in interactive mode. Each such invocation must provide an argument to be passed to the function, as illustrated in the sample invocations below.

```
>>> switch(choice = 1);
Enter degrees in Fahrenheit: 32
32 Fahrenheit = 0.0 Celsius

>>> switch(choice = 2);
Enter degrees in Celsius: 0
0 Celsius = 32.0 Fahrenheit

>>> switch(choice = 3);
Invalid choice:  3
```

Exercise

Run the *Conversion Manager* program. In interactive mode, invoke the *switch* function and experiment with various arguments.

Program Design with Functions: Lottery Odds

Stepwise Design with Functions

Stepwise program design, as we have already learned, is programming by making small and manageable steps towards a final solution rather than trying to develop a complete solution at once. In stepwise program design, each step towards the final solution is thoroughly tested before attempting the next step.

Solving an entire programming problem at once is often impossible. Instead, a solution can be found by breaking a complex problem into smaller sub-problems, solving those problems one at a time, and integrating the sub-solutions into a complete solution of the original problem. Even some sub-problems are complex and difficult to tackle. Fortunately, the stepwise approach can and should be applied to complex sub-problems, breaking them down to sub-sub-problems, and so on - until you end up with sub-problems that are simple enough to be easily solved.

Functions provide valuable support to stepwise program design. Indeed, the solution of a simple sub-problem may be shaped as a function, with or without parameters. In stepwise program design, the result from each individual design step can be a function, and various functions can be composed to obtain a final solution. This approach will be demonstrated with the following lottery problem.

Background

A lottery is a game of chance based upon the random selection of numbers. The lottery operator periodically draws a set of random numbers from a given field of numbers. Before a drawing, lottery players make bets on what numbers will be drawn next. Lottery players who guess correctly all drawn numbers wins a large prize called the jackpot.

In any practical lottery, the *draw* size is significantly smaller than the *field* size, in order to make the chances of winning the jackpot very small. This give the jackpot ample opportunity to become enormous. For example, a lottery called *Fantasy 5* operated by the state of California draws 5 numbers from a field of 39. The *Fantasy 5* jackpot as of this writing is $110,000. Another lottery that is available in California, the *Super Lotto,* draws 6 numbers from a field of 49. The current *Super Lotto* jackpot is $7,000,000.

It is possible to systematically win large amounts of money from a lottery. Lottery operators do just that. Regular players, on the other hand, win only by extreme luck. Before playing a lottery, it may help a player to know the odds of winning the jackpot of that lottery. A simple formula that determines these odds is presented below.

Assume that a lottery draws k numbers out of a field of size n. For the *Fantasy 5* lottery the *draw* size is *5* and the *field* size is *39*. For the *Super Lotto*, the *draw* size is *6* and the *field* size is *49*. The total number of possible drawings determines the *odds* of winning the jackpot with a single bet. The odds are calculated with:

odds = N / D

where:

D = 1 * 2 * 3* ... draw
N = (field – draw + 1) *(field – draw + 2) * ... * field

For the *Fantasy 5* lottery *draw* = 5, *field* = 39, and:

D = 1 * 2 * 3 * 4 * 5 = 120;
N = (39 − 5 + 1) *(39 − 5 + 2) * ... * 39 = 35 * 36 * ... * 39 = 69090840;
odds = 69090840 / 120 = 575757

Consider the following programming problem. Develop a *Lottery Odds* program that will:
- Input arbitrary *draw* and *field* sizes, such that $1 \leq draw \leq field$.
- Evaluate the *odds* of winning the lottery jackpot with a single ticket.

The rest of this section presents the design of a *Lottery Odds* program in a three-step process. First, design a function to calculate *products*, such as the products *N* and *D* in the formula *odds* = *N* / *D*. Second, design a function to calculate *odds* using the *product* function from the first step. Finally, design a *lottery* evaluation function to input lottery *draw* and *field* sizes, *k* and *n*, to calculate the *odds*, and print them.

First Step: Product Calculation

The following *product* function calculates the product $a*(a+1)*(a+2)*...*b$, given any two whole numbers *a*, *b*, $a \leq b$. The function accepts *a*, *b* as parameters and returns the corresponding product.

```
# Multiply numbers a, a+1, a+2,... , up to b:
def product(a, b):
    theProduct = 1;
    while (a <= b):
        theProduct = theProduct * a;
        a = a + 1;
    return theProduct;
```

Note function *product* does not check the validity of any supplied arguments. The function assumes it is always invoked with correct argument values for *a* and *b*.

Simply writing the above function, *product*, does not complete this design step. The function must be tested. Individual functions are easily tested using the interactive mode of the *Python interpreter*.

Example

Function *product* can be invoked in interactive mode for the purpose of testing. Each invocation must provide arguments to be assigned into parameters *a*, *b*. The return-value from each invocation is conveniently displayed after the invocation, as illustrated in the samples below.

```
>>> product(a = 1, b = 1)
1
>>> product(a = 1, b = 4)
24
>>> product(a = 10, b = 11)
110
>>> product(a = 35, b = 39)
69090840
```

Exercise

Run the *Lottery Odds* program. In interactive mode, invoke function *product* and experiment with various arguments. Observe and check each displayed return-value.

Second Step: Odds Calculation

The following function evaluates the *odds* of winning the lottery jackpot with a single ticket. The function:
- Accepts the *draw* and *filed* sizes as parameters.
- Uses the *product* function to calculate:
  - D = 1 * 2 * 3* ... draw
  - N = (field − draw + 1) *(field − draw + 2) * ... * field
- Returns the ratio N / D, which represents the lottery *odds*, as discussed earlier in this section.

```
# Calculate the odds of winning the jackpot:
def odds(draw, field):
    N = product(a = field - draw + 1, b = field);
    D = product(1, draw);
    return N / D;
```

Again, merely writing a function does not complete a design step. The function must be tested.

Example

Function *odds* can be tested in interactive mode by invocations with various arguments. Sample invocations are shown below.

```
>>> odds(draw = 1, field = 1)
1
>>> odds(draw = 5, field = 39)
575757
>>> odds(draw = 6, field = 49)
13983816L
```

Exercise

Run the *Lottery Odds* program. In interactive mode, invoke function *odds* and experiment with various arguments.

Third Step: Input, Calculation, and Output

This final step produces a *lottery* function that will:
- Input lottery *draw* and *field* sizes.
- Calculate the lottery *odds*.
- Print the *odds*.

The definition of the *lottery* function follows.

```
# Evaluate and print arbitrary lottery odds:
def lottery():
    print 'This program evaluates lottery odds.'
    while (True):
        fieldSize = input('Lottery field size: ');
        drawSize = input('Lottery draw size: ');
        theOdds = odds(draw = drawSize, field = fieldSize);
        print 'Field size:', fieldSize, 'Draw size:', drawSize;
        print 'Odds: 1 to', theOdds;
        ans = raw_input('Evaluate more? [Yes/No]: ');
        if(ans == 'No' or ans == 'no'): break;
    print 'Good luck with the jackpot :-)';
```

Note that the *lottery* function invokes the *odds* function to calculate the odds. Remember that the *odds* function invokes the *product* function.

It is important to test the overall integration of all functions in a working solution. A function that was tested individually and behaved at a previous step may not behave when integrated into a final solution. Functions must to be reworked and retested at each step until a working solution is reached. Program development is often an iterative process, alternating testing and design.

Example

Program *Lottery Odds* as a whole, and function *lottery* in particular, can be tested in interactive mode by invocations of function *lottery* with various inputs. Sample invocations are shown below.

```
>>> lottery();
This program evaluates lottery odds.
Lottery filed size: 39
Lottery draw size: 5
Field size: 39 Draw size: 5
Odds: 1 to 575757
Evaluate more? [Yes/No]: Yes
Lottery filed size: 49
Lottery draw size: 6
Field size: 49 Draw size: 6
Odds: 1 to 13983816
Evaluate more? [Yes/No]: No
Good luck with the jackpot :-)
```

Exercise

Run the *Lottery Odds* program. In interactive mode, invoke function *lottery* and experiment with various input data.

Case Study: Input Validation Function

For a program to be dependable, it must verify all input data, rejecting any data that is inaccurate, incomplete, or unreasonable.. As discussed in a previous topic, input data may easily be validated with while loops.

Consider for example a simple *wages* function that validates its input data according to the following rules:
- Employee number must be between 1000 and 9999.
- Hours worked must be between 0 and 168.
- Pay rate must be between 10 and 80.

The simple *wages* function can validate input data by means of three while-loops, as shown below.

```
# Validate input data and calculate wages:
def wages():
    while (True):
        empNum = input('Enter employee number (1000..9999) :');
        if (1000 <= empNum <=9999): break;
    while (True):
        hours  = input('Enter hours worked (0..168): ');
        if (0 <= hours <= 168): break;
    while (True):
        payRate = input('Enter pay rate (10..80): ');
        if (10 <= payRate <= 80): break;
    grossWages = hours * payRate;
    print 'Employee number:', empNum;
    print 'Gross wages:', grossWages;
```

The three data validation loops above are very similar to one another. Each loop inputs a *value* and tests if that *value* is between certain *low* and *high* bounds. The following table outlines all values with their bounds.

Input value	Low bound	High bound
Employee number	1000	9999
Hours worked	0	168
Pay rate	10	80

It is possible to define a single function to replace similar input validation loops. Such a function can receive *low* and *high* bounds as arguments, and return an input *value* that are within the *low* and *high* bounds. This opportunity is demonstrated in a case study of a user-defined input function.

Consider the following programming problem:
- Define a *custom input* validation function that will:
  - Output a *prompt* to the user.
  - Wait for the user to input a *value*.
  - Verify if the input *value* is within some specified *low* and *high* bounds.
  - Repeat the above steps until the user enters an acceptable *value*.

- Use the *custom input* validation function in the *wages* calculation function.
  - Instead of various input validation loops, use invocations of the *custom input* function to input valid employee numbers, hours worked, and pay rate.

A sample program named *Wage Manager* solves the above programming problem. The program defines a *custom input* validation function and a *wages* function. The *wages* function invokes the *custom input* function three times to input valid *employee number, hours worked,* and *pay rate*.

Exercise

Run the *Wage Manager* program. In interactive mode, invoke the *wages* function and experiment with various inputs.

The most important parts of the *Wage Manager* program follow.

```
# Input value, low <= value <= high:
def inputLoHi(prompt, low, high):
    while (True):
        value = input(prompt);
        if (low <= value <= high):
            return value;
        else:
            print 'Invalid input:', value;

# Validate input data and calculate wages:
def wages ():
    empNum  = inputLoHi(
          prompt = 'Enter employee number (1000..9999): ',
          low = 1000, high = 9999);
    hours = inputLoHi(prompt = 'Enter hours (0..168): ',
          low = 0, high = 168);
    payRate = inputLoHi(prompt = 'Enter rate (10..80): ',
          low = 10, high = 80);
    grossWages = hours * payRate;
    grossWages = hours * payRate;
    print 'Employee number:', empNum;
    print 'Gross wages:', grossWages;
```

The *Wage Manager* program defines a custom input function named *inputLoHi*. The purpose of this function is to display a *prompt* and repeatedly ask the user to input a value until the input value falls within specified *low* and *high* bounds. The particular *prompt* to be displayed and particular bounds, *low* and *high*, to be used by the function, are supplied as arguments in each invocation of function *inputLoHi*.

Function *wages* invokes *inputHiLo* three times. For each invocation, *wages* assigns specific arguments into the prompt and the *low,* and *high* parameters for function *inputLoHi*. For any specific invocation, the body of function *inputLoHi* executes with the specifically assigned argument values. For example, the first invocation assigns the string *'Enter employee number (1000..9999): '* into the *prompt* parameter, and the numbers 1000 and 9999 into parameters *low* and *high*. Once argument values are assigned into the parameters, the function body is executed. In the body of function *inputLoHi*, the *prompt 'Enter employee number (1000..9999): '* is passed to the *input* function, which displays that same prompt to the user. The values *low =1000* and *high = 9999* are used to validate the input data for this particular invocation. The next two invocations assign different values into the *prompt, low,* and *high* parameters of function *inputLoHi*. Each invocation is executed with specific argument values, and the argument values may change completely from one invocation to the next.

Example

Function *inputLoHi* can be invoked in interactive mode. Each such invocation must provide argument values to be assigned into each of the three parameters, as illustrated in the sample invocations below.

```
>>> hours = inputLoHi(prompt = 'Enter hours (0..168): ',
           low = 0, high = 168);
Enter hours (0..168): 200
Invalid input: 200
Enter hours (0..168): 20
>>> print 'Hours:', hours;
Hours: 20
```

Exercise

Run the *Wage Manager* program. In interactive mode, invoke the *inputLoHi* function and experiment with various arguments.

Functions for Code Reuse

Functions are a very convenient way to encapsulate statements that may be needed more than once. For example, a *custom input* function can be used in a wages program for the input of valid employee numbers, hours worked, and pay rates. The same custom input function can be used equally well in other programs requiring similar input validation.

Functions support *code reuse* because they allow packaged code to be used multiple times.

Functions may be used to provide *generic solutions* in various programs. For example, many programs will be able to utilize the same ready-to-use random number generator, *randint*, shaped as a function and included in the *random* module. This opportunity relieves programmers from developing a program generator from scratch, a task that is complex and time consuming.

Keyword Arguments and Positional Arguments

A *keyword argument* is similar to an assignment statement – it consists of a parameter name followed by an assignment operator, followed by an expression. For a function invocation, the expression value is assigned into the corresponding parameter. Keyword arguments may appear in a function invocation in any order.

Example
This invocation uses three keyword arguments:

```
hours   = inputLoHi(high = 168, low = 0,
                    prompt = 'Enter hours (0..168): ');
```

A *positional argument* is an *expression* without an associated parameter name. For a function invocation, the argument position determines its receiving parameter: the first positional argument is assigned into the first parameter, the second positional argument is assigned into the second parameter, and so on. Positional arguments must appear in a function invocation in the same order as their receiving parameters.

Example
This invocation uses three positional arguments:

```
hours   = inputLoHi('Enter hours (0..168): ', 0, 168);
```

It is possible to mix positional and keyword arguments in the same function invocation. However, the positional arguments <u>must</u> precede the keyword arguments.

Example

This invocation uses one positional argument and two keyword arguments:

```
hours  = inputLoHi('Enter hours (0..168): ',
                   high = 168, low = 0);
```

Function Definition Form

Function definitions are statements, referred to as *def-statements*. They are compound structures that incorporate headers and bodies. The following table describes the form of the def-statement and its sub-structures.

Structure	Description	Example

Def-Statement	A def-statement consists of one *def-clause*.	def switch(choice):
		  if (choice == 1): F2C();
		  elif (choice == 2):C2F();
		  else: print 'Invalid...;

Def-clause	A def-clause is a sequence of a *def-header* and a function *body*.	Same example as above

Def-header	Starts with the keyword 'def', followed by a list of zero, one, two, or more *parameters* (all enclosed in parentheses), and followed by a colon.	def displayMenu():
		def switch(choice):
		def odds(draw, field):
		def inputLoHi(prompt, low, high):

Body	A block of statements controlled by a clause.	if (choice == 1): F2C();
		elif (choice == 2):C2F();
		else: print 'Invalid...;

Block of statements	A indented sequence of one, two, three, or more aligned statements.	a = 10;
		def f(x): print 'Blah', x;
		f(a);

List of parameters	Parameters separated by commas.	prompt, low, high
Parameter	A name optionally followed by a default-value. ◦ A parameter with a default value is a special case that is not used in this course.	prompt, low, high

Function bodies must be indented from the corresponding function headers. All statements of a particular body must be vertically aligned, using the same indentation.

A function body may contain any statements, including def-statements. This allows for nested function definitions. Nested functions are complex but relatively unimportant. This course does not further discuss nested functions.

Function Definition Execution

The execution of a function definition, i.e., a def-statement, makes the function available for invocations but does not execute the function body. The function body may then be executed through a function invocation. Running a program executes that program's function definitions. The defined functions are then available for invocation.

A function definition is like an assignment statement: it defines a name and assigns a function to that name. If you define two functions with the same name in the same program, the second definition will override the first definition; you will be unable to use the original function.

Example

The second function definition below overrides the first. The first definition becomes unavailable.

```
>>> def function(x, y): return x + y;
>>> function (2, 100)
102
>>> def function (x, y): return x ** y;
>>> function (2, 100)
1267650600228229401496703205376L
```

You must be careful not to redefine existing functions; careless redefining can easily make your program erroneous. In particular, defining a function with the same name as a built-in function can lead to infinite function invocations.

Example

Remember that *input* is the name of a built-in function. The following function definition gives the same name *input* to a new user-defined function and makes the built-in *input* function unavailable:

```
def input (low):
    while (True):
        value = input('Enter value:');
        if (low <= value): return value;
        else: print 'Invalid value';
```

Inside the above function body, the name *input* refers to the newly defined function and not to the built-in *input* function. Therefore, the statement *value = input('Enter value:')* triggers an infinite chain of invocations of this same user-defined function.

Exercise

In interactive mode, enter the above function definition then make the invocation *input(100)* to observe an infinite chain of invocations.

In Python, using unique names in new function definitions is good programming practice, and strongly recommended.

Parameters and Local Variables

Variables that are defined in a function are *local* for that function. Local variables cannot be accessed outside of their defining function.

All parameters are local and cannot be accessed outside of their defining function. There is one exception concerning parameters: they may be used outside of their defining function to form keyword function arguments in function invocations.

Example

The following *product* function below returns the *product* of its parameters, *a*, and *b*:

```
def product(a, b):
    theProduct = 1;
```

```
    while (a <= b):
        theProduct = theProduct * a;
        a = a + 1;
    return theProduct;
```

Variable *theProduct* and parameters *a, b* are local for the product function and cannot be accessed from outside of the function. An attempt to use any of them results in a run-time error.

```
>>> print product(a = 1, b = 6);
720
>>> print a;
...
NameError: name 'a' is not defined

>>> print theProduct;
...
NameError: name 'theProduct' is not defined
```

Any parameter may be used as a local variable in its defining function. In particular, a parameter name may be assigned values in the function body. Such assignments, however, affect only the parameter and <u>not</u> the corresponding argument.

Example

Consider again the *product* function from the previous example. Parameter *a* is repeatedly modified during invocation by means of the statement *a = a + 1*. This assignment into *a*, however, does not affect the argument that is assigned into parameter *a* for an invocation of function *product*. An illustrative example follows.

```
>>> argument = 1;
>>> print product(a = argument, b = 6);
720
>>> print argument;
1
```

Notice that the *argument* assigned into parameter *a* in the invocation *product(a=argument, b=6)* retains its value after the invocation, despite parameter *a* changing several times during the execution of the *product* body.

Local variables and parameters do not exist before, after, and between function invocations.

Program Design with Functions: Score Transformations

Stepwise program design is making small and manageable steps towards a final solution, rather than trying to develop a complete solution at once. As discussed in a previous section, functions provide adequate support to stepwise program design. The result from each design step can be a function or functions. Various functions are composed to obtain a final solution. This approach is used in this section to solve a sample score transformation problem.

Consider the following sample problem. Develop a *Score Transformer* program that will:
- Input a sequence of non-negative scores terminated by a negative number.
  - Identify numbers over 100 as invalid scores.
- For each valid score, determine and output its corresponding letter grade.
- Calculate and output, at the end, the average of all scores.

The rest of this section outlines the design of a *Score Transformer* program in a three-step process. First, design a function to transform scores into letter grades. Second, design a function to provide valid input. Finally, design a function to integrate the previous two functions and calculate the average score.

First Step: Score to Grade Transformation

The following function transforms an individual valid score into the corresponding letter grade. The function accepts *score* as a parameter and returns the letter grade.

```
# Transform score into a letter grade:
def theGrade(score):
    if (score < 60): grade = 'F';
    elif (score < 70): grade = 'D';
    elif (score < 80): grade = 'C';
    elif (score < 90): grade = 'B';
    else: grade = 'A';
    return grade;
```

Note that function *theGrade* does not check the validity of any supplied scores. The function assumes that it is always invoked with correct scores.

Just writing the above function, *theGrade*, does not complete this first design step. The function must be tested. Individual functions can be easily tested using the interactive mode of the *Python interpreter*.

Example

Function *theGrade* can be invoked in interactive mode for the purpose of testing. Each invocation must provide an argument value to be assigned into the *score* parameter. The return-value from each invocation is conveniently displayed after the invocation, as illustrated in the samples below.

```
>>> theGrade(100)
'A'
>>> theGrade(89)
'B'
>>> theGrade(59)
'F'
```

Exercise

Run the *Score Transformer* program. In interactive mode, invoke function *theGrade* and experiment with various arguments. Observe and check each displayed return-value.

Second Step: Input Validation

The goal at this step is to design a function that inputs valid scores. A valid score is never above 100. The input validation function should allow negative input as sentinel in the score processing loop.

It pays to develop an input validation function that is more general that this particular problem requires. The benefit of function generalization is code reuse: a general function can eventually be applied to other problems as well. With functions, generalization is achieved by using parameters.

Instead of just designing a function that is specialized for score input, consider the following generalized problem. Design a general input validation function that will:
- Output a *prompt* to the user.
- Wait for the user to input a *value*.

- Verify that the input *value* is less than some specified *high* bound.
  - For valid score input, the *high* bound is 100.
- Repeat the above steps until the user enters an acceptable *value*.

The following function is a solution to the above problem.

```
# Input value, 'low' <= value:
def inputHi(prompt, high):
    while (True):
        value = input(prompt);
        if (value <= high):
            return value;
        else:
            print 'Invalid input:', value;
```

Again, merely writing a function does not complete a design step. The function must be tested. Testing individual functions is easy in the interactive mode of the *Python interpreter*.

Example

Function *inputHi* can be tested in interactive mode by invocations with various arguments. Sample invocations are shown below.

>>> inputHi(high = 100, prompt = 'Enter score (0..100), negative to quit: ');
Enter score: **120**
Invalid input: 120
Enter score: **99**
99
>>> inputHi(high = 100, prompt = 'Enter score (0..100), negative to quit: ');
Enter score: **-1**
-1

Exercise

Run the *Score Transformer* program. In interactive mode, invoke function *inputHi* and experiment with various arguments.

Note

Function *inputHi* is similar to the *inputLoHi* function. Both functions can be replaced by a single Python function that supports both kinds of input validation. Such a function is not discussed here because it requires some advanced knowledge of the Python language.

Third Step: Input, Calculation, and Output

The goal of this final step is:
- To input valid scores by means of function *inputHi* from a previous design step.
- Transform valid scores into letter grades by means of function *theGrade* from a previous design step and output those letter grades.
- Calculate and output the average of all scores.

This step produces a final and complete solution for the *Score Transformation* problem.

```
# Find average score with a conditional loop:
def scoresConditional():
    total = 0; counter = 0;
    currentScore = inputHi(high = 100,
        prompt = 'Enter score (0..100), negative to quit: ');
    while (currentScore >= 0):
        total = total + currentScore;
        counter = counter + 1;
        print 'Grade:', theGrade(score = currentScore);
        currentScore = inputHi(high = 100,
            prompt = 'Enter score (0..100), negative to quit: ');
    print 'Scores processed:', counter;
    summarize(total, counter);

# Display average score:
def summarize(total, counter):
    if (counter > 0):
        average = float(total) / counter;
        print 'Average score:', average;
```

Note the main function, *scoresConditional*, uses a helper function, *summarize*, to calculate and print the average score. This helper function makes the main *scores* function more concise and easier to read.

The *summarize* helper function should be tested individually, as should be the *scores* main function.

> Exercise
>
> Run the *Score Transformer* program. In interactive mode, invoke function *summarize* and experiment with various arguments. After that, invoke function *scores* and experiment with various input data, valid and invalid.

It is important to test the overall integration of all functions in a working solution. A function that was tested individually and behaved at a previous step may not behave when integrated into a final solution. Such functions need to be reworked and retested. Thus, program development is often an iterative process that alternates testing and design.

Program Design with Functions: Quiz Evaluation

You may be aware of the benefits from stepwise program design. You may also be aware that functions are a natural structure to use in a stepwise program design. The result from each design step can be one or more new functions. New functions can and should be tested at each step interactively. All new functions can be composed to obtain a final solution. This approach is used in this section to solve a sample quiz evaluation problem.

Consider the following programming problem. Develop a *Quiz Manager* program to:
- Display a sequence of multiple-choice and Yes/No questions.
  - For each question, input and evaluate user response.
- After the evaluation of all questions, display a quiz summary that presents the total number of questions and attempts along with the final score.

The design of a *Quiz Manager* program is a three-step process. First, design a function to evaluate a single multiple-choice question. Second, design a function to evaluate a single Yes/No question. Finally, design a function tp manage a complete quiz by using the previous two functions and a function to display a quiz summary.

First Step: Multiple Choice Question Evaluation

In this first step, we design a function that evaluates an arbitrary multiple choice question. We choose the name *evaluateMultipleChoice* for this function. The function is defined with three parameters:

- *question* to be displayed
- correct question *answer* (one of several possible answers)
- *limit* of answer attempts to produce the correct answer

The *evaluateMultipleChoice* function displays the quiz *question*, then inputs and evaluates the user *choice*. This process continues until the user chooses correct *answer* or reaches the specified *limit* of attempts. All answer *attempts* are counted. A final *mark* of 1 or 0 is assigned, depending whether the user gave the correct answer. This function returns two values at once: the *mark* and the number of *attempts*. The quiz itself is displayed by means of a simple *displayQuestion* helper function. The definitions of the *evaluateMultipleChoice* and *displayQuestion* functions follow.

```
# Evaluate multiple choice question responses up to a limit:
def evaluateMultipleChoice(question, answer, limit):
    mark = 0; attempts = 0;
    while (attempts < limit):
        displayQuestion(question);
        choice = raw_input('Enter choice: ');
        attempts = attempts + 1;
        if (choice == str(answer)):
            print 'That is correct!';
            mark = 1; break;
        else:
            print 'Incorrect choice: ', choice;
    return mark, attempts;

# Display single question:
def displayQuestion(question):
    print '...';
    print question;
```

Note that function *evaluateMultipleChoice* does not check the validity of any user choice. Such validity check can certainly be implemented by a custom input function.

Example

Function *evaluateMultipleChoice* should be invoked in interactive mode for the purpose of testing. Each invocation must provide argument values to be assigned into the three function parameters. The two return-values from each invocation are assigned into two variables, *mark* and *attempts* respectively. The values are conveniently displayed after the invocation by means of a print-statement, as illustrated in the samples below.

```
>>> newLine = '\n';
>>> question1 = \
    'Who was the first U.S. President?' + newLine + \
    '(1) Abraham Lincoln' + newLine + \
    '(2) George Washington' + newLine + \
    '(3) John Lennon' + newLine + \
    '(4) Franklin Roosevelt';
>>> mark, attempts = evaluateMultipleChoice(question1, answer = 2, limit = 3);
...
Who was the first U.S. President?
(1) Abraham Lincoln
(2) George Washington
(3) John Lennon
(4) Franklin Roosevelt
Enter choice: 2
That is correct!
>>> print 'Mark:', mark, 'Attempts:', attempts;
Mark: 1 Attempts: 1
```

Exercise

Run the *Quiz Manager* program. In interactive mode, invoke function *evaluateMultipleChoice* similarly to the above example. Observe the displayed return-values.

Second Step: Yes/No Question Evaluation

In the second step, we design a function that evaluates an arbitrary Yes/No question. We choose the name *evaluateYesNo* for this function. The function is defined with two parameters:
- *question* to be displayed
- correct question *answer,* either 'Yes' or 'No'

Because this is a Yes/No question, the user is always limited to one attempt. The *evaluateYesNo* function displays the quiz *question* and evaluates a single user *answer*. A final *mark* of 1 or 0 is assigned, depending on if the user gave the right *answer*. Although the number of attempts is always one, this function returns two values as well, like the earlier *evaluateMultipleChoice* function. In this way, both functions return uniform results and are invoked in the same way. A valid user response must be either 'Yes', or 'No'. Input validity is ensured with a custom input function named *inputYesNo*. The definitions of the *evaluateYesNo* and *inputYesNo* functions follow.

```python
# Evaluate Yes/No question once:
def evaluateYesNo(question, answer):
   displayQuestion(question);
   response = inputYesNo();
   if (response == str(answer)):
      print 'That is correct!';
      mark = 1;
   else:
      print 'Incorrect response: ', response;
      mark = 0;
   attempts = 1;
   return mark, attempts;

# Input valid answer for a Yes/No question:
def inputYesNo():
   response = raw_input('Enter response [Yes/No]: ');
   while (response != 'Yes' and response != 'No'):
      print 'Invalid response: ', response;
      response = raw_input('Enter response [Yes/No]: ');
   return response;
```

Note that function *evaluateYesNo* reuses function *displayQuestion*, originally developed to display a multiple choice question. This reuse is possible because the text to display is a parameter of function *displayQuestion*.

Example

Function *inputYesNo* can be tested in interactive mode. Sample invocations are shown below.

```
>>> response = inputYesNo();
Enter response [Yes/No]: Yes
>>> print 'Response:', response;
Response: Yes
>>> response = inputYesNo();
Enter response [Yes/No]: Nooooo
Invalid response:  Nooooo
Enter response [Yes/No]: No
```

```
>>> print 'Response:', response;
Response: No
```

Function *evaluateYesNo* should be tested in interactive mode by invocations with various arguments. Sample invocations are shown below.

```
>>> question2 = 'Does the adult platypus have teeth?';
>>> mark, attempts = evaluateYesNo(
        question = question2, answer = 'No');
...
Does the adult platypus have teeth?
Enter response [Yes/No]: Yes
Incorrect response:  Yes
>>> print 'Mark:', mark;
Mark: 0
```

Exercise

Run the *Score Transformer* program. In interactive mode, invoke functions *inputYesNo* and *evaluateYesNo* and experiment with various arguments.

Third Step: Quiz Management

The goal of this final step is to develop a *manageQuiz* function that will:
- Evaluate a multiple choice question by means of function *evaluateMultipleChoice* from a previous design step.
- Evaluate a Yes/No question by means of function *evaluateYesNo* from a previous design step.
- Accumulate the total number of *marks* received from all questions and the total number of *attempts* for all questions.
- Display a quiz summary presenting the total number of questions, attempts, and score.

This step leads to a complete solution for the *Score Transformation* problem.

```
# Ask questions, collect answers, count attempts,
# and determine marks:
def manageQuiz():
    marksTotal = 0; questions = 0; attemptsTotal = 0;
    newLine = '\n';
```

```
question1 = \
'Who was the first U.S. President?' + newLine + \
'(1) Abraham Lincoln' + newLine + \
'(2) George Washington' + newLine + \
'(3) John Lennon' + newLine + \
'(4) Franklin Roosevelt';
mark, attempts = evaluateMultipleChoice(
    question = question1, answer = 2, limit = 3);
questions = questions + 1;
marksTotal = marksTotal + mark;
attemptsTotal = attemptsTotal + attempts;

question2 = 'Does the adult platypus have teeth?';
mark, attempts = evaluateYesNo(
    question = question2, answer = 'No');
questions = questions + 1;
marksTotal = marksTotal + mark;
attemptsTotal = attemptsTotal + attempts;

summarizeQuiz(marksTotal, questions, attemptsTotal);

# Print number of questions and score:
def summarizeQuiz(marksTotal, questions, attemptsTotal):
    print 'Number of questions attempted:', questions;
    if (questions > 0):
        print 'Total attempts:', attemptsTotal;
        print 'Total marks:', marksTotal;
        decimal = float(marksTotal) / questions;
        score = round(100 * decimal);
        print 'Score on a 100 points scale:', score;
```

Note that the main function, *manageQuiz*, uses a helper function, *summarizeQuiz*, to calculate and print the average score. This helper function makes the main *manageQuiz* function more concise and easier to read. The *summarizeQuiz* helper function should be tested individually, and so should the *manageQuiz* main function. The *manageQuiz* function should be tested to ensure that all used functions integrate well in a correct final solution.

Function Invocations

A function invocation is a function name followed by a list of zero, one or more arguments enclosed in parentheses. Two kinds of arguments are permitted: keyword arguments and positional arguments. In a mixed-argument invocation, positional arguments must precede keyword arguments.

For the execution of a function invocation, an argument value is assigned into each parameter and then the function body is executed. During the execution of the invoked function, the invoking function is suspended.

Function invocations can be used to assign return-values from the invoked functions into variables of the invoking functions.

> Example
> The following function, *f*, returns the *sum* of its parameters, *x*, and *y*:
>
> ```
> def f(x, y):
>     return x + y;
>
> def test():
>     x0 = 10; y0 = 20;
>     sum = f(x0, y0);
> ```

Return Statements

A return-statement starts with the keyword 'return'. This keyword can be followed by return-value expressions.

The execution of a return-statement:
- Specifies the return-values of the current function invocation.
- Ends the execution of the current invocation and resumes the execution of the invoking function.

In most cases, a return-statement contains just one expression that specifies one return-value. However, a list of two, or more expressions, separated by commas, may be employed to return a list of values when necessary. The invoking function may assign a list of return-values into a list of corresponding variables.

> Example
> The following function, *g*, returns the *sum* and the *product* of its parameters, *x*, and *y*:

```
def g(x, y):
    return x + y, x * y;
def test():
    x0 = 10; y0 = 20;
    sum, product = g(x0, y0);
```

In this example, the two values returned from the invocation of *g* are assigned into two different variables in the invoking *test* function.

Function-to-Function Communication

Functions communicate with other functions by means of parameters, arguments, and return-statements. Functions communicate with human users by means of input and output.

Example

The following functions, *odds and product*, communicate using parameters and return-statement.

```
# Calculate the odds of winning the jackpot:
def odds(draw, field):
    N = product(a = field - draw + 1, b = field);
    D = product(1, draw);
    return N / D;

# Multiply numbers a, a+1, a+2,... , up to b:
def product(a, b):
    theProduct = 1;
    while (a <= b):
        theProduct = theProduct * a;
        a = a + 1;
    return theProduct;
```

Note that the *product* function does not input its arguments from the keyboard. Instead, the function is provided with arguments by the invoking function, *odds*. In function invocations, these arguments are assigned into the functions parameters.

Also, the *product* function does not print the calculated result to the screen. Instead the *product* function uses a return-statement to supply the result to its invoking function, *odds*.

The None Value

It is possible to use functions that do not contain a return-statement. In this case, a default return-statement is inserted at the end of the function body. This default statement returns a special built-in value named *None*. The *None* value can be tested, printed, passed as an argument, and processed just like any other value. The type of the *None* value is *None*.

Example

The following function, *f*, contains no explicit return-statement. In this case, the statement *return None* is inserted at the very end of the function body. Thus, the function always returns the *None* built-in value. A definition of function *f* and invocations of *f* follow in interactive mode.

```
>>> def f(): print 'Hello';
>>> f();
Hello
>>> result = f();
Hello
>>> print result;
None
```

It is also possible to use a return-statement without a return expression. This can be useful in cases when no actual return-value is expected from a function invocation. The purpose of a return-statement without an expression is to end the current invocation and resume the execution of the invoking function. A return-statement without an expression always returns the built-in value *None*.

Example

The following function, *g*, contains a return-statement without an expression. This statement returns the built-in value *None*. The definition of function *g* and one invocation of *g* in interactive mode follow:

```
>>> def g():
        print 'Bye'; return;
>>> g();
Bye
>>> result = g();
Bye
>>> print result;
None
```

Exercise

Design a function named *ratio* that returns the ratio *a / b* of its arguments *a, b*. When the ratio *a / b* is undefined (because *b* = 0), the *ratio* function must return the *None* value. Sample invocations of the *ratio* function follow.

```
>>> print ratio(100, 2);
50
>>> result = ratio(100, 0);
>>> print result;
None
>>> result == None
True
```

Synonyms

Some terms that have been introduced in this topic have synonyms. A list of such terms and their corresponding synonyms follows.

Term	Synonym
Function invocation	Function call
Invoking function	Caller
Invoked function	Callee
Parameter	Formal parameter
Argument	Actual parameter
Parameter assignment	Parameter passing
Function	Subroutine
Function	Procedure

Lab A [Functions]

Objective; Background; Lab Overview; What to Do Next; Downloading Sample Programs; Uncompressing Sample Programs; Studying the Sample Program; Creating a Program File; Developing the New Program

Objective

The objective of this lab is to develop a *Multi-Conversion Manager* program that will:
- Offer the user a menu of various conversions choices.
- Use a special *switch* function to:
  - Analyze user choice.
  - *Switch* execution to a conversion function implementing that choice.
- Repeat the above steps until the user chooses to exit.
- Implement conversion *repetitions* in two different ways:
  - Using a conditional loop
  - Using of an unconditional loop

Background

- Your menu of conversions may look like this:

  Conversions Menu:
  (0) Exit the menu
  (1) Convert Fahrenheit to Celsius
  (2) Convert Celsius to Fahrenheit
  (3) Convert Inches to Centimeters
  (4) Convert Centimeters to Inches
  (5) Convert Gallons to Liters
  (6) Convert Liters to Gallons
  (7) Convert Yards to Meters
  (8) Convert Meters to Yards
  (9) Convert Pounds to Kilograms
  (10) Convert Kilograms to Pounds
  Enter choice number:

- The user choice is a whole number, without parentheses.

- Implement two functions:
  - A function named *repeatConditional* employing a conditional loop.
  - A function named *repeatUnconditional* employing an unconditional loop.
- Each of the implementations will invoke the same *switch* function.

Lab Overview

To perform this lab:
- Study the *Conversion Manager* sample program.
- Transform a copy of the sample program *Conversion Manager* into a *Multi-Conversion Manager* program by following the detailed instructions that follow.
- Systematically test the *Multi-Conversion Manager* program.

What to Do Next

At this time, you are offered these choices:
- Follow the detailed lab instructions below, or
- Try the lab independently, but also peek in the instructions when needed, or
- Perform the lab independently, without the aid of the instructions.

All three approaches can be beneficial to students. Feel free to choose the approach most beneficial to you.

Downloading Sample Programs

Various Lab Assignments for this course are based on ready-to-use sample programs. These programs are downloaded from the online study pack into your *master* folder.

Download sample programs for the current Topic 5 by performing these steps:
- Locate the current *Topic 5* in the online study pack.
- Open the *Lab Assignment* resource.
- Right-click on the *Sample Programs* link.
- Use *Save As* to store the downloaded compressed (zipped) folder, *05.zip,* within your *master* folder.

Uncompressing Sample Programs
- Uncompress the contents of the downloaded compressed (zipped) folder. Depending on your platform, you may use built-in compression support, or compressing utilities.
- In Windows XP, use the built-in un-compression support as follows:
  - Open your *master* folder using the *File Browser*.
  - Right-click on the downloaded compressed (zipped) folder.
  - Use *Extract All* to extract the contents of the compressed (zipped) folder.
    - A new, uncompressed folder, *05*, will be created within the *master* folder. This folder will contain your sample programs.
  - Alternatively, you can:
    1. *Open* the compressed (zipped) folder.
    2. *Cut* folder *05* from within the compressed (zipped) folder.
    3. *Paste* the cut folder *05* outside the compressed (zipped) folder – directly within the *master* folder.
- Delete the compressed (zipped) folder, *05.zip*. Keep the uncompressed folder, *05*.
- Open the uncompressed folder *05* and browse its contents.
- Note the Python program files have extension '**.py**'.

Studying the Sample Program
- Use IDLE to open and browse the *Conversion Manager* sample program.
- Run the program with various input data; observe the output.
- Analyze the program implementation.

Creating a Program File
To create this program in your current labs folder, *05Labs*:
- Create a copy of the *Conversion Repetitions* program file using IDLE.
- Name the copy *Multi-ConversionManager.py*.
  - **Important Note:** You must explicitly supply the file extension '**.py**' when saving from IDLE.

Developing the New Program

Perform the following steps with the newly created *Multi-Conversion Manager* program.

Step 1: Copying existing code to reuse
- Provide implementations of all necessary conversion functions as follows:
  - Open the *Multi-Conversion Repetitions* program developed for Topic 04.
  - Copy the definitions of the *displayMenu* function; paste it at the end of your current *Multi-Conversion Manager* program.
  - Copy the definitions of all conversion functions; paste them at the end of your current *Multi-Conversion Manager* program.
- Copy the definition of the *switch* function from the *Conversion Manager* sample program into your current *Multi-Conversion Manager* program.

Step 2: Redesigning the sample *switch* function
- Extend the definition of function *switch* to invoke, depending on the user choice, any of the ten possible conversions.
- Test the *switch* function by:
  - Running the *Multi-Conversion Manager* program.
  - Testing function *switch* in interactive mode with all possible valid arguments and with some invalid arguments.

Step 3: Designing a *repeatConditional* function
- Rename function *repeat* as *repeatConditional*.
- Modify the definition of function *repeatConditional* to invoke the newly created *switch* function.
- Remove the long if-statement from the original *repeatConditional* function utilized to invoke a proper conversion function.
  - Use just one simple invocation of the *switch* function instead.
- Run program *Multi-Conversion Manager*.
- In interactive mode, test function *repeatConditional* by performing various conversions.

Step 4: Designing a *repeatUnconditional* function
- Create a copy of function *repeatConditional*; rename the copy *repeatUnconditional*.
  - Remember to keep also function *repeatConditional*.
- Replace the condition in the while-loop header with the literal *True*.

- Remove any display and input statements found before the while-loop.
- Remove any display and input statements at the bottom of the while-loop body.
- In the very beginning of the loop body, insert statements that will:
  - Display a menu.
  - Input user's choice.
- Test the redesigned *repeatUnconditional* function. Make sure you select various menu items.

Step 5: Updating comments
- Update all existing comments as necessary.

Lab B [Functions]

Objective; Background; Lab Overview; What to Do Next; Studying the Sample Programs; Creating a Program File; Developing the New Program

Objective

The objective of this lab is to develop a *Sum Evaluations* program that will:
- Input a pair of numbers *a, b* where *a* ≤ *b*.
- Calculate the *sum total* of the numbers *a, a+1, a+2, ,,,,,* up to *b*.
- Display the *sum total*.
- Repeat the above with various pairs of numbers until the user wishes to quite.

Background
- The *Lottery Odds* sample program defines a function named *product*. Given a pair of numbers *a,b* where *a* ≤ *b*, that function calculates and returns the product of the numbers *a, a+1, a+2, ...*up to *b*.
- The implementation of a sum total calculation is similar to that of a product calculation.
  - The variable used to accumulate the sum total is initialized at *0*.
  - A variable used to accumulate a product is initialized at *1*.

Lab Overview

To perform this lab:
- Study the *Lottery Odds* sample program.
- Transform a copy of the *Lottery Odds* sample program into a *Sum Evaluations* program by following the detailed instructions that follow in this lab.
- Systematically test the *Sum Evaluations* program.

What to Do Next

You are now offered the following choices:
- Follow the detailed lab instructions below.
- Try the lab independently, using the instructions when you require help.

- Perform the lab independently, without any aid from the instructions.

All three approaches are beneficial to students. Choose the approach most beneficial to you.

Studying the Sample Program
- Using IDLE, open and browse the *Lottery Odds* sample program.
- Run the program with various input data; observe the output.
- Analyze the program implementation.

Creating a Program File
Create this program in your current labs folder, *05Labs*.
- Create a copy of the *Lottery Odds* program file using IDLE.
- Name the saved copy *SumEvaluations.py* .
  - **Important Note:** You must explicitly supply the file extension '**.py**' when saving from IDLE.

Developing the New Program
Perform the following steps with the newly created *Sum Evaluations* program.

Step 1: Design a function to sum up a sequence of numbers
- In the new *Sum Evaluations* program, delete the definition of function *odds*. Keep all other function definitions.
- Transform the definition of function *product* into a definition of the function *sumTotal*:
  - Change the name of the defined function from *product* to *sumTotal*.
  - Initialize variable *theSum* at 0 to accumulate the sum total.
    - Remember, a variable to accumulate a product is initialized with *1*.
  - Use addition instead of multiplication in the sum total evaluation loop.
- In interactive mode, test function *sumTotal:*
  - Invoke the *sumTotal* function with various arguments.

Step 2: Design a function to repeat sum total evaluations
- Convert the definition of function *lottery* into function *repeat*.
  - Program *repeat* to invoke the new *sumTotal* function instead of the *odds* function.
  - Adjust all prompts and variable names to reflect the changes.
  - Run the *Sum Evaluations* program.

- In interactive mode, test function *repeat*:
  - Supply various input data; check the validity of the evaluated sums.

Step 3: Update comments
- Update all existing comments.

Test Data Sample
- Interactions with the two functions, *sumTotal* and *repeat,* may look like this:

```
>>> sumTotal(a = 1, b = 10)
55
>>> sumTotal(-10, 10)
0
>>> repeat();
This program sums up sequences of numbers.
Enter sequence bottom: 1
Enter sequence top: 10
Bottom: 1 Top: 10
Sum: 55
Sum up more? [Yes/No]: Yes
Enter sequence bottom: -10
Enter sequence top: 10
Bottom: -10 Top: 10
Sum: 0
Sum up more? [Yes/No]: No
Bye.
>>>
```

Lab C [Functions]

Objective; Background; Lab Overview; What to Do Next; Studying the Sample Programs; Creating a Program File; Developing the New Program

Objective

The objective of this lab is to develop a *Seconds Producer* program that will:
- Repeatedly input *hours, minutes,* and *seconds*.
- Count and output the *total number of seconds*.
- Validate input data by means of custom input functions.
- Implement repetitions in two different ways:
  - Using a conditional loop
  - Using of an unconditional loop

Background

- Validate input data according to the following rules:
  - *Hours* must be non-negative.
  - *Minutes* must be between 0 and 59.
  - *Seconds* must be between 0 and 59.
- Provide two *custom input* functions:
  - A function named *inputLo* used for the input of *hours*.
    - This function takes a prompt and a *low* bound as parameters, returning an input *value* such that *low* <= *value*.
  - A function named *inputLoHi* used for the input of *minutes* and *seconds*.
    - This function can be readily borrowed from the sample program *Wage Manager*.
- Two main functions must be implemented:
  - Function named *secondsConditional* and *secondsUnconditional*, employing a conditional loop and unconditional loop respectively.
    - Initial versions of these functions may be borrowed from the *Seconds Calculations* program created for a previous topic.
    - These initial versions can be redesigned to utilize your *custom input* validation functions instead of the built-in *input* function.

Lab Overview

To perform this lab:
- Study the *Wage Manager* sample program.
- Transform a copy of the sample program *Wage Manager* into a *Seconds Producer* program by following the detailed instructions that follow.
- Systematically test the *Seconds Producer* program.

What to Do Next

You are now offered the following choices:
- Follow the detailed lab instructions below.
- Try the lab independently, using the instructions when you require help.
- Perform the lab independently, without any aid from the instructions.

All three approaches are beneficial to students. Choose the approach most beneficial to you.

Studying the Sample Program

- Using IDLE, open and browse the *Wage Manager* sample program.
- Run the program with various input data; observe the output.
- Analyze the program implementation.

Creating a Program File

Create this program in your current labs folder, *05Labs*.
- Create a copy of the *Wage Manager* program file using IDLE.
- Give the name *SecondsProducer.py* to the saved copy.
  - **Important Note:** You must explicitly supply the file extension '**.py**' when saving from IDLE.

Developing the New Program

Perform the following steps with the newly created *Seconds Producer* program.

Step 1: Copy existing functions to reuse
- In the newly created *Seconds Producer* program, keep only the definition of function *inputLoHi*; delete all other function definitions.
- From the *Seconds Calculations* program created for a previous topic, copy the definitions of functions *secondsConditional* and *secondsUnconditional*; paste these definitions at the end of the *Seconds Producer* program.

Step 2: Design a custom *inputLo* function
- In the newly created *Seconds Producer* program, copy the entire definition of function *inputLoHi*; paste it before the original definition.
- Transform the copy into a definition for function *inputLo*:
  - Change the name of the copy.
  - Remove the *high* parameter from the function heading and function body.
  - Run the *Seconds Producer* program.
  - In interactive mode, test function *inputLo*:
    - Invoke the *inputLo* function with *prompt* = 'Enter hours (non-negative): ' and *low* = 0.

Step 3: Redesign the *secondsConditional* function
- Modify the definition of function *secondsConditional* so it will invoke, depending on the input data, any of the two custom input functions, *inputLo* or *inputLoHi*.
- Test the *secondsConditional* function by:
  - Running the *Seconds Producer* program.
  - Testing function *secondsConditional* in interactive mode.
    - Supply various valid and invalid input data, checking the validity of the results.

Step 4: Redesign the *secondsUnconditional* function
- Proceed as in the previous step, this time working with function *secondsUnconditional*.
- Test the redesigned *secondsUnconditional* function. Supply various valid and invalid input data, checking the validity of the results.

Step 5: Update comments

- Update all existing comments as necessary.

Test Data Sample

- Possible interactions with the two functions, *secondsConditional* and *secondsUnconditional,* may look like this:

Interaction with *secondsConditional*	Interaction with *secondsUnconditional*
This program converts time into seconds. Ready to convert? [Yes/No]: **Yes** Enter hours (non-negative): **-1** Invalid input: -1 Enter hours (non-negative): **2** Enter minutes (00..59): **60** Invalid input: 60 Enter minutes (00..59): **-1** Invalid input: -1 Enter minutes (00..59): **10** Enter seconds (0..59): **100** Invalid input: 100 Enter seconds (0..59): **-100** Invalid input: -100 Enter seconds (0..59): **0** The total time is 7800 seconds. Convert more? [Yes/No]: **No** So long...	This program converts time into seconds. Enter hours (non-negative): **-1** Invalid input: -1 Enter hours (non-negative): **2** Enter minutes (00..59): 60 Invalid input: 60 Enter minutes (00..59): **-1** Invalid input: -1 Enter minutes (00..59): **10** Enter seconds (0..59): **100** Invalid input: 100 Enter seconds (0..59): **-100** Invalid input: -100 Enter seconds (0..59): **0** The total time is 7800 seconds. Convert more? [Yes/No]: **No** So long...

Lab D [Functions]

Objective; Background; Lab Overview; What to Do Next; Studying the Sample Program; Creating A Program File; Developing the New Program

Objective

The objective of this lab is to develop an *Activity Manager* program that will:
- Enter a sequence of *temperatures* (in Fahrenheit) terminated by a negative number.
  - Exit repetitions upon the input of the sentinel value *-9999* for *temperature*.
- For each temperature, determine an advisable *activity*.
- Calculate and print, at the end, the *average* of all temperatures.
- Implement repetitions in two different ways:
  - Using a conditional loop
  - Using an unconditional loop
- Implement your program as a set of functions, each function performing a well-defined single task.
  - For example, design a special function to receive a *temperature* and return the corresponding *activity*.

Background
- Implement the *Activity Manager* in compliance with the following Activity Table:

Temperature is below:	But not below:	The advisable activity is:
40		Getting some sleep at home
60	40	Browsing the Internet
75	60	Taking a walk in the park
90	75	Sunbathing on the lawn
	90	Going to the beach

Lab Overview

To perform this lab, you:
- Study the *Score Transformer* sample program.
- Study your *Score Calculations* sample program from the topic on Repetition.
- Convert a copy of the *Score Transformer* sample program into an Activity *Manager* program.
- Extensively test the *Activity Manager* program.

What to Do Next

You are now offered the following choices:
- Follow the detailed lab instructions below.
- Try the lab independently, using the instructions when you require help.
- Perform the lab independently, without any aid from the instructions.

All three approaches are beneficial to students. Choose the approach most beneficial to you.

Studying the Sample Program

- Using IDLE, open and browse the *Score Transformer* sample program.
- Run the program with various input data; observe the output.
- Analyze the program implementation.

Creating A Program File

Create this program in your current labs folder, *05Labs*.
- Create a copy of the *Score Transformer* program file using IDLE.
- Name the saved copy *ActivityManager.py*.
  - **Important Note:** You must explicitly supply the file extension '**.py**' when saving from IDLE.

Developing the New Program

Perform these steps with the newly created *Activity Manager* program:
- In the newly created *Activity Manager* program, delete the definition of function *inputHi*.
- Transform the definition of function *theGrade* (with parameter *score*) into a definition for function *theActivity* (with parameter *temperature*). Make the new function return an activity as a string value. This function must not print anything.

- In interactive mode, extensively test *theActivity* function. Provide a variety of arguments to test the implementation of all condition checks.
- Rename function *scoresConditional* to *weatherConditional*; modify it to work with temperatures rather than with scores. Be sure to call *theActivity* function instead of *theGrade* function.
- Modify the definition of function *summarize* to work with temperatures instead of scores.
- In interactive mode, extensively test the *weatherConditional* function.
- Rename function *scoresUnconditional* to *weatherUnconditional*; modify it to work with temperatures instead of scores. Remember to call *theActivity* function instead of *theGrade* function.
- In interactive mode, extensively test the *weatherUnconditional* function.
- Update comments throughout the entire program.
- Supply additional lines of comments to improve readability.

Lab E [Functions]

Objective; Background; Lab Overview; What to Do Next; Studying the Sample Program; Creating a Program File; Developing the New Program

Objective

The objective of this lab is to develop a *Tax Manager* program that will:
- Repeatedly input taxable annual *income*.
  - Exit repetitions upon the input of any negative *income*.
- For each *income*, determine tax bracket, calculate the *tax* due, and output the *tax* due.
- Finally, calculate and print:
  - The *average* of all entered *incomes*
  - The average of all calculated *taxes*
- Implement repetitions in two different ways:
  - Using a conditional loop
  - Using an unconditional loop
- Implement your program as a set of functions, each function performing a well-defined single task.
  - For example, design a special function to receive an *income* and return its corresponding *tax*.

Background

- Implement the *Tax Manager* according to the following Tax Table:

Taxable income is over:	But not over:	The tax is:	Plus:	Of the amount over:
	7,150	0.00	10%	0
7,150	29,050	715.00	15%	7,150
29,050	70,350	4,000.00	25%	29,050
70,350	146,750	14,325.00	28%	70,350
146,750	319,100	35,717.00	33%	146,750
319,100		92,592.50	35%	319,100

Lab Overview

To perform this lab:
- Study the *Score Transformer* sample program.
- Study your *Tax Calculations* program designed for the topic on Repetition.
- Transform a copy of the *Score Transformer* sample program into a Tax *Manager* program.
- Extensively test the *Tax Manager* program.

What to Do Next

You are now offered the following choices:
- Follow the detailed lab instructions below.
- Try the lab independently, using the instructions when you require help.
- Perform the lab independently, without any aid from the instructions.

All three approaches are beneficial to students. Choose the approach most beneficial to you.

Studying the Sample Program

- Using IDLE, open and browse the *Score Transformer* sample program.
- Run the program with various input data; observe the output.
- Analyze the program implementation.

Creating a Program File

You have to create this program in your current labs folder, *05Labs*.
- Use IDLE to create a copy of the *Score Transformer* program file.
- Give the name *TaxManager.py* to the saved copy.
  - **Important Note:** You must explicitly supply the file extension '**.py**' when saving from IDLE.

Developing the New Program

Perform these steps with the newly created *Tax Manager* program:
- In the new *Tax Manager* program, delete the definition of function *inputHi*.
- Transform the definition of function *theGrade* (with parameter *score*) into a definition for function *theTax* (with parameter *income*). Make the new function determine and return the *tax*. This function does not print anything.

- In interactive mode, extensively test *theTax* function. Provide a variety of arguments to test the implementation of all condition checks.
- Rename function *scoresConditional* to *taxesConditional*, modifying it to work with incomes rather instead of scores. Remember, call *theTax* function instead of *theGrade* function.
- Modify the definition of function *summarize* to work with incomes and taxes instead of scores.
- In interactive mode, extensively test the *taxesConditional* function.
- Rename function *scoresUnconditional* to *taxesUnconditional*, modifying it to work with incomes instead of scores. Remember to call *theTax* function instead of *theGrade* function.
- In interactive mode, extensively test the *taxesUnconditional* function.
- Update comments throughout the program.
- Supply additional lines of comments to improve readability.
- Test your program. Start testing with this data:

```
Enter annual income, negative to quit: 0
Tax due = 0.0
Enter annual income, negative to quit: 7150
Tax due = 715.0
Enter annual income, negative to quit: 10000
Tax due = 1142.5
Enter annual income, negative to quit: 29050
Tax due = 4000.0
Enter annual income, negative to quit: 70350
Tax due = 14325.0
Enter annual income, negative to quit: 146750
Tax due = 35717.0
Enter annual income, negative to quit: -1
Incomes processed: 6
Average income: 43883.3333333
Average tax: 9316.58333333
```

Lab F [Functions, Optional]

Objective; Background; Lab Overview; What to Do Next; Studying the Sample Program; Creating A Program File; Developing the New Program

Objective
The objective of this lab is to extend the sample *Quiz Manager* program with several additional elements. The extended program, *Quiz Manager 2* should incorporate:
- At least one additional multiple choice question.
- At least one additional Yes/No question.
- A new function to evaluate fill-in question.
- At least two concrete fill-in questions.

Background
- A fill-in question requires one correct answer. For example, the question 'What is the most populous state in the USA?' has one correct answer, 'California'. Of course, a correct answer may have several forms. For example, an alternative form of the above correct answer is 'CA'. For this lab, however, consider juts one allowed form for a correct fill-in answer.

Lab Overview
To perform this lab:
- Study the *Quiz Manager* sample program.
- Transform a copy of the *Quiz Manager* sample program into a *Quiz Manager 2* program.
- Extensively test the *Quiz Manager 2* program.

What to Do Next
You are now offered the following choices:
- Follow the detailed lab instructions below.
- Try the lab independently, using the instructions when you require help.
- Perform the lab independently, without any aid from the instructions.

All three approaches are beneficial to students. Choose the approach most beneficial to you.

Studying the Sample Program
- Using IDLE, open and browse the *QuizManager* sample program.
- Run the program with various input data; observe the output.
- Analyze the program implementation.

Creating A Program File
Create this program in your current labs folder, *05Labs*.
- Create a copy of the *Quiz Manager* program file using IDLE.
- Name the saved copy *QuizManager2.py*.
  - **Important Note:** You must explicitly supply the file extension '**.py**' when saving from IDLE.

Developing the New Program
Perform these steps with the newly created *Quiz Manager 2* program:
- Design an arbitrary new multiple choice question; add it to the *manageQuiz* function.
- Test the *manageQuiz 2* function. Be sure marks and scores are calculated correctly.
- Design an arbitrary Yes/No question; add it to the *manageQuiz* function.
- Test the *manageQuiz 2* function. Be sure marks and scores are calculated correctly.
- In program *Quiz Manager 2*, add a new function to evaluate an arbitrary fill-in question.
  - Name the function *evaluateFillIn*.
  - Include the following parameters:
    - *question* to be displayed
    - the expected correct *answer*
    - *limit* of user attempts at producing the correct answer
  - The function must display the fill-in *question* and evaluate the user *choice*. This process is continued until the user chooses the correct *answer* or reaches the specified *limit* of attempts. All *attempts* are counted. A final *mark* of 1 or 0 is assigned, depending on whether the user gave the right answer or not. This function returns two values at once: the *mark* and the number of *attempts*.
    - Use the built-in function *raw_input* to enter the user response to fill-in questions.
- In interactive mode, extensively test the *evaluateFillIn* function.

- Design at least two arbitrary fill-in questions; include them in the *manageQuiz 2* function.
- Test the *manageQuiz 2* function. Be sure marks and scores are calculated correctly.
- Update comments throughout the program.
- Supply additional lines of comments to improve readability.

Lab G [Functions, Optional]

Objective; Background; Lab Overview

Objective

The objective of this lab is to develop a *Leap Year Evaluations* program that will:
- Input a whole number representing a *year* in the Gregorian calendar, evaluate if it is a leap year or not, and output the evaluation.
  - The Gregorian calendar was introduced in 1582; only years after 1582 should be allowed.
- Repeat the above step with various pairs of numbers until the user desires to quite.
- Utilize two new functions: one function to evaluate if the given *year* is a leap, and a second that will provide the input of a *year*, evaluate that *year*, and display the evaluation.

Background
- In the Gregorian calendar, a leap year is any year divisible by 4 with no remainder. Years ending in hundreds are <u>not</u> leap years unless they are divisible by 400.
- An interaction of your program may look like this:

    Enter year: **2003**
    2003 is not a leap year.
    Enter year: **2004**
    2004 is a leap year.
    Enter year: **1900**
    2004 is not a leap year.
    Enter year: **2000**
    2004 is a leap year.

Lab Overview

To perform this lab:
- Design a leap year evaluation algorithm based on selection and the remainder operation, '%'.
  - The remainder operation, x % y, returns the remainder from the division of x by y. For example, (7 % 4 == 3),(2004 % 4 == 0), (1900 % 100 == 0), (1900 % 400 == 300). A *year* is divisible by 4 if (*year* % 4 == 0). In general, a *year* is divisible by a number *K* if and only if (*year* % *K* == 0).
  - Note that a *year* is NOT a leap year in two cases:
    1. The *year* is not divisible by 4
    2. The *year* is divisible by 4, is divisible by 100, but is not divisible by 400
  - Describe the algorithm in English (or another natural language), rather than a program in Python.
- Transform your leap year algorithm into a function *leap* with one parameter, *year*, which returns True or False depending on whether the year is a leap. Create the program file in your current labs folder.
  - The *leap* function must not print anything.
- In interactive mode, extensively test your *leap* function.
- Implement a function *repeat* to repeatedly input a *year*, invoke function *leap* to test the year, and output an evaluation of the *year*.
- Test the *repeat* function.

Lab H [Functions, Optional]

Objective; Background; Lab Overview

Objective
- The objective of this lab is to convert the sample *Roulette Simulators* program from the topic on Repetition into an equivalent program, *Parameterized Roulettes,* which utilizes functions with parameters.

Background
You may convert the original monolithic *Russian* and *casino* functions into several parameterized functions:
- Function *Russian* with one parameter representing the *number of chambers*.
- A helper function *tryShot* used in the *Russian* function.
- Function *casino* with one parameter representing the *number of roulette positions*.
- Helper functions *inputLo, inputLoHi, play,* and *displayBalance* used in the *casino* function.

Lab Overview
To perform this lab:
- Study the *Roulette Simulators* sample program from the topic on Repetition.
- Transform a copy of the *Roulette Simulators* sample program into a *Parameterized Roulettes* program by breaking the existing monolithic functions into smaller parameterized functions.
  - Implement the program file in your current labs folder.
- Extensively test the *Parameterized Roulettes* program.

Lab I [Functions, Optional]

Objective; Background; Lab Overview;

Objective
- The objective of this lab is to develop a *Prime Test* program that will repeatedly input an arbitrary whole number n, $n > 2$, and determine if n is a prime number.

Background
- A whole number n, $n > 2$, is prime if n in not divisible by any whole number k, $2 \leq k \leq \sqrt{n}$.

Lab Overview
To perform this lab:
- Implement a function *isPrime* with one parameter, n, testing if n is prime. Return True or False upon the result.
  - Use a loop to generate all values of k such that $2 \leq k \leq \sqrt{n}$.
  - If a value k is generated such as $n \% k$ is 0, break out of the loop to return False. Otherwise, return True.
- Implement a function named *repeat* that will repeatedly input a whole number n, $n > 2$, invoke *isPrime* to evaluate if n is prime, and output the evaluation. Create the program file in your current labs folder.
  - Use a function *inputLo* to ensure that the input value for n satisfies the condition $n > 2$.
- Extensively test the *Prime Test* program.

Lab K [Functions, Optional]

Objective; Background; Lab Overview

Objective
The objective of this lab is to:
- Define a *safe input* validation function that will:
  - Output a *prompt* to the user.
  - Input a *value* from the user.
  - Verify if the input *value* is within some specified *low* and *high* bounds.
  - Never crash, even if the user provides illegal input (such as a word instead of a decimal number).
  - Repeat the above steps until the user enters a valid *value*.
- Employ the *safe input* validation function in a *wages* calculation function.
- Integrate both functions in a *Safe Wages* program.

Background
- Even if a program is syntactically correct, it may cause a run-time error when execution is attempted.
  - Run-time errors are also called *exceptions.*
- Illegal input for the built-in *input* function triggers an exception. For example:

  >>> input('Enter a number: ')
  Enter a number: **100**
  100
  >>> input('Enter a number: ')
  Enter a number: **hundred**
  ...
  NameError: name 'hundred' is not defined
  >>>

- An exception not recognized and handled by a program is fatal to the program.
- Programs can recognize and handle exceptions by means of try-statements.

- A *safe input* function can utilize a try-statement to catch and handle input exceptions without crashing.
    For example:

    >>> safeInput('Enter a number: ', low = 0, high = 100);
    Enter a number: **hundred**
    Illegal input.
    Enter a number: **110**
    Invalid input: 110 .
    Enter a number: **100**
    100
    >>>

Lab Overview

To perform this:
- Self-study errors and exceptions.
    - In IDLE window, use *Help -> Python Docs* then locate and study the chapter on Errors and Exceptions in the Python Tutorial.
- Transform the *Wage Manager* sample program into a *Safe Wages* program.
    - Replace the *inputLoHi* function from the *Wage Manager* program with a *safe input* function.
        - In the *safe input* function, use an appropriate try-statement to catch all possible exceptions.
- Test your program.
- Supply adequate comments.

Lists and Dictionaries

Sample Programming Problem: Processing Months; Sample Program: List Processor; What is a List? List Operations and Functions; Introduction to Objects and Methods; List Methods; The For-Statement; Embedded Lists; List Subscriptions as Variables; Variables as References; Sample List Programs; Sample Program: Interactive Dictionary; What is a Dictionary? Dictionary Operations, Functions, and Methods; Sample Program: Dictionary Processor; Dictionary and List Embedding; Dictionary Subscriptions; Sample Dictionary Programs; Introduction to Tuples; Synonyms

Sample Programming Problem: Processing Months

Consider the following simple programming problem. Develop a program that will:
- Input the name of any month and output the number of days in that month.
- Repeat the above steps until the user chooses to exit.

For this problem, we use only three-letter abbreviations for month names. Using abbreviations contributes to a cleaner, more readable program. For the sake of simplicity, leap years are excluded from consideration.

Sample Program: List Processor

A simple program named *List Processor* solves the programming problem formulated in the previous section. The program is based on the *list* built-in data type. The name *List Processor* is a convenient abbreviated version of *Simple List-Based Month Processor*. The *List Processor* program is composed of a function named *months* that prints a list of twelve month names, repeatedly ask the user for a month name and responds with that month's number of days. In this section, we discuss a simple initial version of the program. A more sophisticated second version of the program, named *Enhanced List Processor,* is available for further self-study.

Exercise

Run the *List Processor* program. In interactive mode, invoke the *months* function and experiment with various inputs.

Example

An interaction with function *months* may look like this:

>>> months()
This program determines the number of days in a month.
List of all months: ['Jan', 'Mar', 'May', 'Jul', 'Aug', 'Oct', 'Dec', 'Apr', 'Jun', 'Sep', 'Nov', 'Feb']
Enter month name (unquoted) : **Jan**
Month: Jan Days: **31**
Process more? [Yes/No]: **Yes**
Enter month name (unquoted) : **Sep**
Month: Sep Days: **30**
Process more? [Yes/No]: **Yes**
Enter month name (unquoted) **: Okt**
Month: Incorrect Month Name Days**:** 0
Process more? [Yes/No]: **Yes**
Enter month name (unquoted) **: Oct**
Month: Oct Days: **31**
Process more? [Yes/No]: **No**
So long...

The entire *List Processor* program follows.

```
# Input month name and output number of days:
def months ():
    print 'This program determines the number of days in a month.'
    list31 = ['Jan', 'Mar', 'May', 'Jul', 'Aug', 'Oct', 'Dec'];
    list30 = ['Apr', 'Jun', 'Sep', 'Nov'];
    list28 = ['Feb'];
    listOfAllMonths = list31 + list30 + list28;
    print 'List of all months: ', listOfAllMonths;
    while (True):
        month = raw_input('Enter month name (unquoted): ');
        if (month in list31): days = 31;
        elif (month in list30): days = 30;
        elif (month in list28): days = 28;
        else: days = 0;
        print 'Month:', month, 'Days:', days;
```

```
        ans = inputYesNo('Process more? [Yes/No]: ');
        if (ans == 'No'): break;
    print 'So long...';

# Input valid answer for a Yes/No question:
def inputYesNo(prompt):
    response = raw_input(prompt);
    while (response != 'Yes' and response != 'No'):
        print 'Invalid response: ', response;
        response = raw_input(prompt);
    return response;
```

The main function in program *List Processor* is function *months*. When the function is invoked, it does the following:
- Creates four lists of month names. Three of the lists contain all months with 31, 30, and 28 days correspondingly and a fourth list incorporates all twelve months.
- Repeatedly inputs a month name, tests which list the month name belongs to, and depending on that, determines the number of days in the month.
- Exits the execution when the user chooses to do so.

The following Python-to-English translation provides insight into list creation and list membership tests.

Python-To-English Translation

Python Statement	Common English Meaning

list31 = ['Jan', 'Mar', 'May', 'Jul', 'Aug', 'Oct', 'Dec'];
list30 = ['Apr', 'Jun', 'Sep', 'Nov'];
list28 = ['Feb'];
	○ Assign a list of seven string items into variable *list31*. The seven string items represent all months that have *31* days.
	• The list is formed by placing comma separated items in square brackets.
	• All list items in this particular case are strings.
	○ Assign a list of four string items into variable *list30*. The four string items represent all months that have *30* days.
	○ Assign a list of just one string item into variable *list28*. This string item represents the only month that has *28* days.

listOfAllMonths = list31 + list30 + list28;	▫ Concatenate the three lists, *list31*, *list30*, and *list28*, and assign the resulting list into variable *listOfAllMonths*. • The concatenation consists of all items of *list31*, followed by all items of *list30*, followed by all items of *list28*.
print 'List...', listOfAllMonths;	▫ Print the result of the concatenation, the *listOfAllMonths*.

while (True):
    month = raw_input('Enter month...');
    ....
	▫ Repeatedly enter a *month* name...

if (month in list31): days = 31;
elif (month in list30): days = 30;
elif (month in list28): days = 28;
	▫ Test if the current *month* is a member of *list31*. If so, *days* become 31. Proceed with additional list membership tests if necessary.

print month, days;
ans = inputYesNo('More?');
if (ans == 'No'): break;
	▫ Print the current month name and its number of days.
	▫ Test if the user wishes to continue with another month.

What is a List?

A Python *list* is a finite sequence of items. Placing comma-separated expressions within square brackets forms a list.

Example

```
>>> weekday = ['Mon', 'Tue', 'Wed', 'Thu', 'Fri'];
>>> weekend = ['Sat', 'Sun'];

>>> x = 10; y = 20;
>>> operations = [x + y, x - y, x * y, x / y];
>>> print operations;
[30, -10, 200, 0]
```

Items that belong to the same list can possibly be of different types.

Example

```
>>> mixed = [3.0, True, 123];
>>> print mixed;
[3.0, True, 123]
>>> address = ['Orange', 'California', 92866, 'USA'];
```

```
>>> print address;
['Orange', 'California', 92866, 'USA']
```

The *empty list* contains zero items and is denoted by two square brackets, [ ].

Example

```
>>> print 'Empty list:', [];
Empty list: []

>>> print [] + [] + [];
[]
```

Note that in Python, expressions in parentheses, square brackets or curly braces can be split over two or more lines without using backslashes. Consequently, lists may also be split over several lines without explicit backslashes.

List Operations and Functions

This section introduces the principal operations and functions that construct and process lists. As you read, try to run the examples and experiment on your own.

The built-in function *len* returns the number of items of list.

Example

```
>>> weekday = ['Mon', 'Tue', 'Wed', 'Thu', 'Fri'];
>>> weekend = ['Sat', 'Sun'];

>>> print len(weekday);
5
>>> len(weekend);
2
>>> print len([]);
0
```

List items are indexed with non-negative numbers: *0, 1, 2,...* The first list item has index *0*, the second has index *1*, the third has index *2*, and so on.

Item *i* of list *a* is referred to as *a[i]*. The first item of a list is *a[0]*, and the last one is *a[n-1]*. The *index set* of a list of *n* items includes the numbers *0, 1, ..., n-1*.

Example

```
>>> print weekday[0];
Mon
>>> print weekday[4];
Fri
```

Negative indexes are used to refer to list items backwards. Note that negative indexes are an unusual feature of the Python language that most languages do not support. When the length of a list is *n*, the negative numbers *-1, -2,..., -n* are valid indexes. The last item of list *a* can be referred to as *a[-1]*, the one before the last one as *a[-2]*, etc., and the first item can be referred to as *a[-n]*.

Example

```
>>> print weekday[-1], weekday[-2], weekday[-3];
Fri Thu Wed
>>> print weekday[0], weekday[1], weekday[2];
Mon Tue Wed
```

If the length of a list is *n*, the entire index set of the list consists of the numbers *0, 1, 2, ... n-1* and *-1, -2,..., -n*. Attempts to use indexes outside of the index set result in run-time errors.

Example

```
>>> print len(weekday);
5
>>> print weekday[5];
...
IndexError: list index out of range
```

The *membership test* (*X* in *L*) returns True if *X* is an item of *L*. Otherwise, False is returned. The test (*X* not in *L*) is the same as (not (*X* in *L*)). Like other operators and functions, membership tests apply to various sequences, such as lists and strings, not just to lists.

Example

```
>>> test = 'Mon' in weekday;
>>> print test;
True
>>> print 'Mon' in weekend;
False
>>> print 'Mon' not in weekend;
True
```

The *concatenation* P + Q of lists P and Q is a list that contains copies of all items of P followed by copies of all items of Q. The repetition L * n is a list that repeats n times copies of the items of L.

Example

```
>>> week = weekday + weekend;
>>> print week;
['Mon', 'Tue', 'Wed', 'Thu', 'Fri', 'Sat', 'Sun']
>>> reverseWeek = weekend + weekday;
>>> print reverseWeek;
['Sat', 'Sun', 'Mon', 'Tue', 'Wed', 'Thu', 'Fri']
>>> print weekend * 3;
['Sat', 'Sun', 'Sat', 'Sun', 'Sat', 'Sun']
>>> print [0] * 10;
[0, 0, 0, 0, 0, 0, 0, 0, 0, 0]
```

The *min* and *max* built-in functions return the smallest and the largest items of a list. These operations are useful when applied to homogenous lists consisting of same-type items.

Example

```
>>> score = [80, 75, 100, 65, 90];
>>> print min(score), max(score);
65 100
```

Some useful lists of integer numbers are created with the *range* built-in function. The invocation *range(n)* generates the list *[0, 1, 2, 3, ... n-1]*. The invocation *range(m, n)* generates the list *[m, m+1, m+2, ... n-1]*.

Example

```
>>> print range(10);
[0, 1, 2, 3, 4, 5, 6, 7, 8, 9]
>>> print range(10, 15);
[10, 11, 12, 13, 14]
>>> print range(-5, 5);
[-5, -4, -3, -2, -1, 0, 1, 2, 3, 4]
>>> print len(range (-100, 100));
200
```

The *slicing* operation allows you to copy a part of an existing list and create a new list with that copy. If *a* is a list, *a[i:k]* selects all items with index j such that $i <= j < k$. The index set of the slice is renumbered so it starts at 0.

Example

```
>>> year = ['Jan', 'Feb', 'Mar', 'Apr', 'May', 'Jun', 'Jul', 'Aug', 'Sep', 'Oct', 'Nov', 'Dec'];
>>> spring = year[2:5];
>>> print spring;
['Mar', 'Apr', 'May']
```

List items may be deleted by means of the *delete statement*. The delete statement consists of the reserved word *del* followed by the deletion target[s]. Various deletion targets are permitted, such as individual list items or list slices.

Example

```
>>> spring = year[1:5];
>>> print spring;
['Feb', 'Mar', 'Apr', 'May']
>>> del spring[0];
>>> print spring;
['Mar', 'Apr', 'May']
```

The *map* built-in function is used to apply any function *f* to every item of *list* and return a list of the results. To illustrate the use of the *map* function, consider again the problem of finding a letter grade for a given score. Suppose you have a function, *theGrade* that is applied to one score to determine one letter grade. You can *map* the *theGrade* function to a list of scores and receive the list of corresponding letter grades at once.

Example

```
# Transform score into a letter grade:
def theGrade(score):
    if (score < 60): grade = 'F';
    elif (score < 70): grade = 'D';
    elif (score < 80): grade = 'C';
    elif (score < 90): grade = 'B';
    else: grade = 'A';
    return grade;

>>> oneGrade = theGrade(90);
>>> print oneGrade;
A
>>> scoreList = [80, 75, 100, 65, 90];
>>> gradeList = map(theGrade, scoreList);
>>> print gradeList;
['B', 'C', 'A', 'D', 'A']
```

Similar to the map function, there are other functions that apply functions to sequences such as *filter* and *reduce*. These functions require more advanced programming knowledge and will not be further covered in this introductory course.

A summary of list operations and functions is presented in the following table.

Operation or Function	Description
[ ]	Empty list.
[$item_0$, $item_1$, ...$item_{n-1}$]	List of *n* items (at positions *0, 1, ... n-1*).
len(*list*)	The number of items in *list*.
list[*i*]	*List* item at position *i*.
item in *list*; *item* not in *list*	Test if *item* is a member of *list*.
del *list*[*i*]	Delete *list* item at position *i*.
P + Q	Concatenate copies of the items of *P* and *Q*.
n * L	Repeat *n* times copies of the items of *L*.

range(n)	[0, 1, 2, ... n-1].
range(m, n)	[m, m+1, m+2, ... n-1].
min(list)	The smallest item of list.
max (list)	The larges item of list.
list[i:j]	A list slice: [list[i], list[i+1], ... list[j-1]].
map(f, [it_0, it_1, ...it_{n-1}])	The list [$f(it_0)$, $f(it_1)$, ... $f(it_{n-1})$].

Introduction to Objects and Methods

Programs are written because to be executed and produce useful results. Only when programs run do they do what they are supposed to.

When a program does not run, it is normally saved as a file on some media. When a program runs, all of its structures – numbers, strings, lists, functions, etc - are represented in the computer memory in binary form, as sequences of 0s and 1s. The different program structures use different binary representation schemes.

In widespread terminology, the memory representation of any program structure at run-time is called an *object*. This is a very general yet useful concept. There are various types of objects: a *numeric objects* represent a number while a *string object* represents a sequence of characters. An object can also represent executable code, like a function. A *list object* is the run-time memory representation of a list.

Generally speaking, the term "object" stands for anything that can be assigned a name: a number, a string, a function, a list, and much more.

Objects usually have functions attached to them. For example, a set of useful built-in functions is attached to every list object. This means that every list is like a module carrying its own functions with all lists carrying the same functions. The most notable examples of such list functions are *sort, append,* and *reverse*. These are always invoked through a list, using a dot-notation, as illustrated by the examples below.

Example

```
>>> score = [80, 75, 100, 65, 90];
>>> print score;
[80, 75, 100, 65, 90]
>>> score.append(99);
```

```
>>> print score;
[80, 75, 100, 65, 90, 99]

>>> score.sort();
>>> print score;
[65, 75, 80, 90, 99, 100]

>>> score.reverse();
>>> print score;
[100, 99, 90, 80, 75, 65]
```

Note that functions from imported modules, such as the *randint* function from module *random*, are invoked by means of a similar dot-notation, like *random.randint*.

Functions attached to objects are invoked by means of dot-notation and are commonly referred to as *methods*.

List Methods

Once created, list objects can be queried or modified by a number of list methods. A summary of list methods is presented in the following table. It is important to remember that some of these methods actually change the lists they are attached to.

Method	Description
list.count(*item*)	Return the number of times *item* occurs in *list*.
list.index(*item*)	Return the position of the first occurrence of *item* in *list*.
list.index(*item, i*)	Return the position of the first occurrence, after position *i*, of *item* in *list*.
list.sort()	Sort the items of *list*.
list.reverse()	Reverse the items of *list*.
list.append(*item*)	Append *item* to *list*.
list.insert(*i, item*)	Insert *item* into *list* before position *i*.
list.pop()	Delete and return the last *item* of *list*.
list.remove(*item*)	Delete the first occurrence of *item* in *list*.

Exercise

In interactive mode, create some lists and apply the above list methods to them. Print lists to observe how these methods modify them.

The For-Statement

The for-statement is indispensable when you need to iterate the elements of a sequence, such as in a list or string.

Example

In interactive mode, the following for-statement iterates over the list of all spring moths.

```
>>> spring = ['Apr', 'May', 'Jun'];
>>> for month in spring:
        print month;
Apr
May
Jun
>>> for char in 'May':
        print char;
M
a
y
```

The for-statement is used frequently in combination with the *range* built-in function.

Example

In interactive mode, the following for-statements iterate over lists of integer numbers, as generated by the *range* function.

```
>>> print range(3);
[0, 1, 2]
>>> for i in range(3):
        print i;
0
1
2
>>> for i in range(3):
        print i+4, ':', spring[i];
4 : Apr
5 : May
6 : Jun
```

For-statements are compound structures that consist of sub-structures, such as headers and bodies. The following table describes the for-statement and its sub-structures.

Structure	Description	Example

For-Statement	A for-statement consists of one required *for-clause*, optionally followed by one *else-clause*. Using an else-clause in a for-statement is uncommon.	for month in spring:
		    print month;
		else:
		    print 'End of repetitions';

For-clause	A for-clause is a sequence of a *for-header* and a *body*.	for month in spring: print month;
For-header	A for-header starts with the keyword 'for', followed by a *target variable*, followed by the keyword 'in', followed by a sequence, such as list, string, and more.	for month in spring:
Body	A body is an indented block of statements controlled by a clause.	print month;

For-statement bodies must be indented from the corresponding headers. All statements of a particular body must be vertically aligned, using the same indentation.

We focus on the execution the for-statement as seen here in its most common form:

    for *target variable* in *sequence*:
        body

The body of the for-statement is executed once for each item in the sequence. Each item from the sequence is assigned to the target variable, then the body is executed. Items are assigned to the target variable in order of ascending indices. When the items are exhausted , the execution of the for-statement terminates. Note that when the sequence is empty, the body is not executed at all.

Remember, a break statement terminates the execution of the immediately enclosing repetition statement. This rule applies to both while-statements and for-statements.

The *range* function is used to generate a list of successive integer numbers to be assigned to a target variable in a for-statement. The target variable in this kind of loop is called *counter*, and the loop itself is called *counter loop*.

Embedded Lists

A Python list is a finite sequence of items of any type. Consequently, lists can be embedded as items in other lists. The level of list embedding is limitless.

Example

```
>>> weekday = ['Mon', 'Tue', 'Wed', 'Thu', 'Fri'];
>>> weekend = ['Sat', 'Sun'];
>>> week = [weekday, weekend];
>>> print week;
[['Mon', 'Tue', 'Wed', 'Thu', 'Fri'], ['Sat', 'Sun']]
>>> print week[0];
['Mon', 'Tue', 'Wed', 'Thu', 'Fri']
>>> print week[1];
['Sat', 'Sun']
```

List Subscriptions as Variables

A list item is a list followed by an index in square brackets: *list[index]*. In Python, such an expressions is called a *list subscription*.

List subscriptions are variables. This means:
- List subscriptions are assigned items using assignment statements.
- List subscriptions may participate in expressions.
- List subscriptions may be used as arguments in function invocations.

Until now we have used variables that have simple names only. Now we will also be using lists subscriptions as variables.

Example

```
>>> score = [80, 75, 100, 65, 90];
>>> # increment all scores by 10 but keep them
>>> # from exceeding 100:
for i in range(len(score)):
    score[i] = min(100, score[i] + 10);
>>> print score;
[90, 85, 100, 75, 100]
```

In a list subscription *list[index]*, the *list* and the *index* may be determined by arbitrary expressions. In particular, the *list* itself may be specified by means of a list subscription. This leads to complex list subscriptions that incorporate two or more indexes.

Example

```
>>> weekday = ['Mon', 'Tue', 'Wed', 'Thu', 'Fri'];
>>> weekend = ['Sat', 'Sun'];
>>> week = [weekday, weekend];
>>> print week;
[['Mon', 'Tue', 'Wed', 'Thu', 'Fri'], ['Sat', 'Sun']]
>>> print week[0][0], week[0][4], week[1][0], week[1][1];
Mon Fri Sat Sun
```

In this example, *week[0]* is a list subscription that is actually a list. By adding the index *4* (enclosed in square brackets) to the list *week[0]*, we receive the list subscription *week[0][4]*.

Variables as References

An assignment statement defines a variable as a *reference* to a specific object. This reference may be changed to a different object by a subsequent assignment into the same variable. At any time, the *value* of the variable is represented by the object referred to by the variable.

Example

```
>>> V = [65, 95, 100];
>>> print V;
[65, 95, 100]
```

The above assignment statement defines variable *V* as a reference to the list *[65, 95, 100]*. The reference is visualized by means of an arrow in the following figure.

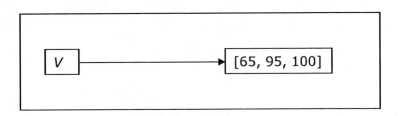

A list assignment statement $V = [i_0, i_1, ...i_{n-1}]$ defines variable V as a reference to the list $[i_0, i_1, ...i_{n-1}]$. After the assignment, V is used to access that list. A subsequent assignment $V = [j_0, j_1, ...j_{k-1}]$ redefines V as a reference to a different list, $[j_0, j_1, ...j_{k-1}]$. V now ceases to refer to the original list, $[i_0, i_1, ...i_{n-1}]$.

Example

```
>>> V = [65, 95, 100];
>>> print V;
[65, 95, 100]
>>> V = [100, 95, 80, 75];
>>> print V;
[100, 95, 80, 75]
```

The above assignment statement defines variable V as a reference to the list $[65, 95, 100]$. The reference change is depicted in the following figure.

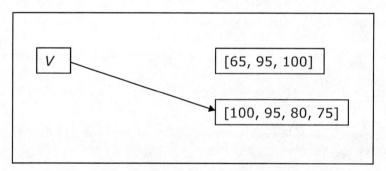

Note that two or more variable may refer to the same object. Consider a sequence of two assignments:

$V = [i_0, i_1, ...i_{n-1}]$; $W = V$;

The first assignment, $V = [i_0, i_1, ...i_{n-1}]$, defines variable V as a reference to the list $[i_0, i_1, ...i_{n-1}]$. The next assignment, $W = V$, defines variable W as a second reference to the same list, $[i_0, i_1, ...i_{n-1}]$. The assignment copies the reference only; it does not create a copy of the entire list.

Example

```
>>> V = [65, 95, 100];
>>> print V;
[65, 95, 100]
>>> W = V;
>>> print W;
[65, 95, 100]
```

The first two assignments define variables V and W as references to the same list, *[65, 95, 100]*. These references are depicted with the following figure.

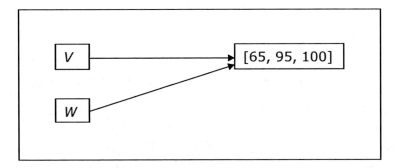

When two variables refer to the same list object, each of them may modify the object. Any modifications of list items made through one of the variables will be visible through the other variable as well.

Example

```
>>> V = [65, 95, 100];
>>> W = V;
>>> print V, W;
[65, 95, 100] [65, 95, 100]
>>> V[0] = 99;
>>> print V, W;
[99, 95, 100] [99, 95, 100]
```

The first two assignments define variables V and W as references to the same list, *[65, 95, 100]*. The assignment *V[0] = 99* affects both variables V and W. The update is depicted in the following figure.

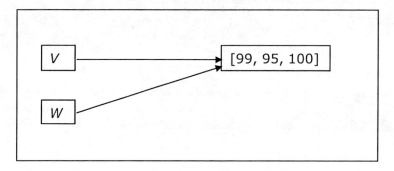

A subsequent assignment can redefine V as a reference to a separate list:

```
>>> V = [0, 0, 0, 0, 0];
>>> print V, W;
[0, 0, 0, 0, 0] [99, 95, 100]
```

The above reference change is depicted with the following figure.

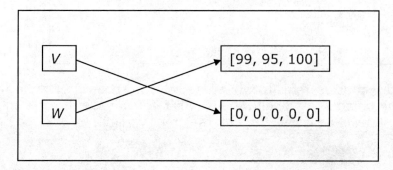

Consider a list variable $V = [i_0, i_1, ...i_{n-1}]$. Variable V is embedded in another list $A = [V, ...]$. After that, variables A[0] and V refer to the same list, $[i_0, i_1, ...i_{n-1}]$. Modifications of list items made through either of the variables, A[0] or V, are visible through the other variable as well.

Example

Weekday and *weekend* lists are embedded in a *week* list:

```
>>> weekday = ['Mon', 'Tue', 'Wed', 'Thu', 'Fri'];
>>> weekend = ['Sat', 'Sun'];
>>> week = [weekday, weekend]; print week;
[['Mon', 'Tue', 'Wed', 'Thu', 'Fri'], ['Sat', 'Sun']]
```

The following statements demonstrate how changes of the *weekend* list affect the embedding *week* list.

```
>>> weekend[0] = 'SAT'; weekend[1] = 'SUN';
>>> print weekend;
['SAT', 'SUN']
>>> print week;
[['Mon', 'Tue', 'Wed', 'Thu', 'Fri'], ['SAT', 'SUN']]
```

Consider a list variable $V = [i_0, i_1, ...i_{n-1}]$ and a function invocation $g(W = V)$. The argument-to-parameter assignment, $W = V$, defines the parameter W as a *reference to the argument* $V = [i_0, i_1, ...i_{n-1}]$. Recall that a list assignment creates a reference to the assigned list but does not create a copy of the original list. Through parameter W, function g can update individual items of the argument $V = [i_0, i_1, ...i_{n-1}]$. This is because parameter W refers to the same list as argument V. Although function g can change individual items of the original list V, the function cannot make V refer to new list.

Example

The following statements demonstrate how a function can change individual items of a list argument. At the same time, the function is unable to change or replace a list argument.

```
def g(W):
   W[0] = 99;
   W = [0, 0, 0, 0, 0];
   return;

>>> V = [65, 95, 100];
>>> g(W = V);
>>> print V;
[99, 95, 100]
```

First, the function invocation $g(W = V)$ assigns V into W. This makes both V and W refer to the argument list, *[65, 95, 100],* as depicted in the following figure.

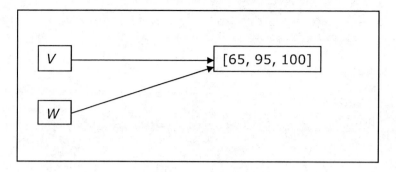

Second, the function invocation *g(W = V)* executes the body of function *g*.

A. The function body executes the statement *W[0] = 99*, which updates the list referred to by *W*. The change affects *V* because it refers to the same list, as depicted in the following figure.

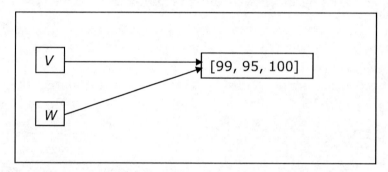

B. The function body executes the statement *W = [0, 0, 0, 0, 0]* and thus redefines the parameter *W* as a reference to a new list, *[0, 0, 0, 0, 0]*. This change does not affect the argument *V*, as illustrated in the figure below.

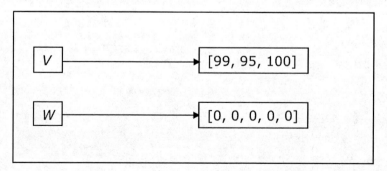

The function invocation *g(W = V)* changes an individual item of the argument, *V*, but does not assign an entire new object into *V*. As a result of the invocation, *V* is updated. After the invocation the parameter, *W*, is lost, as depicted in the following figure.

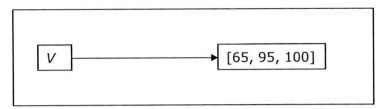

It is very important to understand that list assignment and list embedding do not create new copies of the assigned lists. Instead, list assignments and list embeddings use list references only.

Sample List Programs

Several complete list-based sample programs are provided with this topic. You are advised to study, analyze and enhance these programs. Your independent work with sample programs will help you master your knowledge of lists and your capability to use lists in program design. Brief descriptions of these list-based sample programs follow.

Enhanced List Processor

A program named *List Processor* is discussed in the beginning of this topic. This program offers a function called *months* that inputs the name of a month then outputs the number of days in that month. The function continues doing so as long as the user wishes.

Program *Enhanced List Processor* improves the *List Processor* with two interesting functions: a string input function and a list output function. (The name *Enhanced List Processor* is an abbreviated version of *Enhanced List-Based Month Processor*.)

The string input function provides a valid user response from a given list of valid inputs. In the *Enhanced List Processor*, the function is used for two purposes: to input month names and Yes/No responses. A complete implementation of the function follows:

```
# Input a valid response from a given list of valid inputs:
def inputResponse(prompt, validInputs):
    response = raw_input(prompt);
    while (response not in validInputs):
```

```
        print 'Invalid input: ', response;
        print 'List of valid inputs:';
        printList(validInputs, lineLimit = 30);
        response = raw_input(prompt);
    return response;
```

When the above function is given a list of all months, it inputs a valid month name:

```
month = inputResponse(
    prompt = 'Enter month name (unquoted): ',
    validInputs = listOfAllMonths);
```

The same function can also be used to input a valid Yes/No response of several different forms:

```
ans = inputResponse(prompt = 'Process more? [Yes/No]: ',
                    validInputs = ['Yes', 'Y', 'y', 'No', 'N', 'n']);
```

The list output function uses tabs to vertically align all displayed list items. A list with vertically aligned items is more pleasant visually than a list produced with a plain print statement.

A sample execution in interactive mode of the enhanced *months* function follows.

```
>>> months();
This program determines the number of days in a month.
    Jan   Mar   May   Jul Aug   Oct   Dec   Apr
    Jun   Sep   Nov   Feb
Enter month name (unquoted) : Jan
    Month: Jan Days: 31
Process more? [Yes/No]: Yes
Enter month name (unquoted): Okt
Invalid input: Okt
List of valid inputs:
    Jan   Mar   May   Jul Aug   Oct   Dec   Apr
    Jun   Sep   Nov   Feb
Enter month name (unquoted): Oct
    Month: May    Days: 31
Process more? [Yes/No]: No
So long...
```

Score Processor

The *Score Processor* sample program inputs an entire sequence of non-negative scores terminated by a negative number while identifying numbers over 100 as invalid scores. The program then sorts all scores in ascending order. For each score from the sorted list of valid scores, the program determines and prints its corresponding letter grade. At the end, the program calculates and prints the average of all scores.

The *Score Processor* uses some functions that have been introduced in previous topics, such as a function to transform a score into a letter grade. In addition to known functions, several new list processing functions appear in the *Score Processor*. Most important are a function to input a list of numbers and a function to find the average of a list of numbers. A sample execution in interactive mode of the main function, *scores*, follows.

```
>>> scores();
Enter score (0..100), negative to quit: 90
Enter score (0..100), negative to quit: 1000
Invalid input: 1000
Enter score (0..100), negative to quit: 100
Enter score (0..100), negative to quit: 80
Enter score (0..100), negative to quit: -1
Scores, Grades
80   B
90   A
100  A
Scores processed: 3
Average score: 90.0
```

Binary List Search

Binary search is a general problem solving method introduced in a previous topic. It is a dichotomizing search with steps in which the sets of remaining items are partitioned into two equal parts with the search continuing in only one of those parts. Binary search is used to efficiently look up an item in a list and return its index if found. The *Binary List Search* sample program does exactly this.

The *Binary List Search* program consists of a single function named *find*. This function takes two arguments: a *list* of items and an *item* to search in that list. The *list* of items must be sorted in ascending order. The *find* method looks for the *item* in the *list*. If the *item* is found, a corresponding list *index* is returned, 0 <= index < len(list). If the *item* is not found, the number *len(list)* is returned. Sample invocations in interactive mode of the *find* function follow.

```
>>> aList = [80, 75, 100, 65, 90];
>>> aList.sort();
>>> print aList;
[65, 75, 80, 90, 100]
>>> print find(aList, item = 80);
2
>>> print find(aList, item = 65);
0
>>> print find(aList, item = 100);
4
>>> print find(aList, item = 10);
5
>>> if (find(aList, item = 10) == len(aList)):
    print 'Not found.';
Not found.
```

Raffle Operator

The purpose of the R*affle Operator* sample program is to randomly distribute raffle prizes among raffle participants. This program offers two functions to invoke. The main *raffle* function inputs a list of prizes and a list of participants. The function then distributes prizes among randomly selected raffle participants. At the end, the function displays the name of each participant and a prize, if won. The *simpleRaffle* function does not input lists of prizes and participants but has them created by assignment statement instead.

The *Raffle Operator* relies on one powerful function from module *random* to distribute prizes to winners. The name of this function is *sample*, and in the *Raffle Operator* the function is referred to in dot-notation as *random.sample*. In order to understand the *Raffle Operator*, you must study this function from the Python online documentation.

Sample invocations in interactive mode of the two main raffle functions follow.

```
>>> simpleRaffle();
This program randomly selects raffle winners.
PARTICIPANT ==> PRIZE
Anna ==> Porsche
Elliot
Jose ==> A+ in programming
```

Oliver ==> Hawaii vacation
Travis
Xena
Congratulations to all winners.

>>> raffle();
This program randomly selects raffle winners.
Enter a list of prizes: **['Porsche', 'A+ in programming', 'Hawaii vacation']**
Enter a list of participants: **['Anna', 'Jose', 'Elliot', 'Xena', 'Oliver', 'Travis']**
PARTICIPANT ==> PRIZE
Anna
Elliot ==> A+ in programming
Jose
Oliver
Travis ==> Hawaii vacation
Xena ==> Porsche

Gift Assignment

The purpose of the *Gift Assignment* sample program is to randomly determine gift exchange among party participants. To do so, the program inputs a *participant* list. The program creates a *recipient* list as a randomly shuffled copy of the original *participant* list. The idea is to have *participant[i]* provide a gift to *recipient[i]*. It is necessary, however, to avoid situations when *participant[i]* is the same as *recipient[i]*, because it makes sense to have everybody provide a gift for someone else, and not for themselves. The *Gift Assignment* program uses a special function to test if each *participant[i]* is different from *recipient[i]*. If necessary, the program continues shuffling *participants* into *recipients* until it produces an acceptable recipient list. Shuffling is implemented by the *random.sample* function is used and discussed in the *Raffle Operator* program. In order to understand the *Gift Assignment* program, you should study this function from the Python online documentation. A sample execution in interactive mode of the main *gifts* function follows.

>>> gifts();
This program generates party gift exchange.
Enter list of 2 or more people: **['Kellie', 'Luis', 'Tore', 'Brian', 'Jenny']**
FROM ==> TO
Kellie ==> Tore
Luis ==> Kellie

```
Tore ==> Luis
Brian ==> Jenny
Jenny ==> Brian
Handle another raffle? [Yes/No]: **No**
Have a happy party.
```

Russian List Logger

Note first that the word *logger* has two meanings. The first meaning is 'an individual whose profession is cutting timber', and the second meaning is 'a process that adds entries to a log'. We use the word *logger* in its second meaning here.

As a part of a previous topic, a sample *Roulette Simulator* program has been studied. The program contains a function named *Russian* to simulate Russian roulette games. In this topic, the *Russian List Logger* sample program offers an enhanced version of the *Russian* function that not only simulates Russian roulette games, but at the same time records information about all games in a special log. At the end, the *Russian* function returns the log. A separate *display* function is provided to print the log.

The log that is created and maintained by the *Russian List Logger* is a list that starts with the number of chambers used in the game and the randomly chosen chamber with bullet. The list uses an embedded sublist for each game to represent the randomly chosen shot chamber and the outcome from the game. Please refer to the original description of the *Roulette Simulator* for details of the Russian roulette game itself. A sample execution in interactive mode of the *Russian* function follows.

```
>>> log = Russian();
Ready to play? [Yes/No]: **Yes**
Click!... Good luck.
Play more? [Yes/No]: **Yes**
Bang!... Bad luck.
Dosvidaniya...[So long...]

>>> displayRussian(log);
Russian roulette log
Number of chambers: 6
Chamber with bullet: 2
Shot chamber: 6 Outcome: Click!... Good luck.
Shot chamber: 2 Outcome: Bang!... Bad luck.
Games  played: 2
```

Sample Program: Interactive Dictionary

Consider the following simple programming problem:
- Create a dictionary of several keywords, such as *peace*, *love*, and *beauty*, with a description of the meaning of each keyword.
- Interactively look up the meaning of any keyword from the dictionary.

We solve this problem by means of the *dictionary* built-in data type. The following interactive program creates a dictionary object and looks up various words:

```
>>> dictionary = {
   'Peace' : 'Absence of war or other hostilities.',
   'Love' : 'Warm, tender feeling toward a person.',
   'Beauty' : 'Quality that gives pleasure to the mind or senses.'
};
>>> dictionary['Peace'];
'The absence of war or other hostilities.'
>>> dictionary['Love'];
'A deep, tender feeling of affection toward a person.'
>>> dictionary['Beauty'];
' Quality that gives pleasure to the mind or senses.'
```

The above dictionary is a collection of three items. Each item is a keyword/meaning pair. Syntactically, keywords and their meanings are separated by colons; all dictionary items are enclosed in curly braces and separated by commas. The application of a keyword, in square brackets, to the dictionary looks up the keyword meaning.

What is a Dictionary?

A Python *dictionary* is a finite set of key/item pairs.
- Two expressions separated by a colon create a *key/item pair*.
- Placing comma separated key/item pairs in curly braces forms a dictionary.

Dictionary *items* can be of any type, including lists and dictionaries.

Dictionary *keys* must be objects that never change, such as strings and numbers. Because lists and dictionaries may change, they cannot be used as keys.

Example

The following dictionary contains student scores. The dictionary consists of *key-item* pairs of the following kind: Each *key* is a student name and each *item* is the student's numeric score.

```
>>> score = {'Johnny' : 85, 'Xena' : 95 };
>>> print score;
{'Johnny': 85, 'Xena': 95}
```

The *empty dictionary* contains zero key/item pairs; it is made up of two curly braces, { }.

Remember that in Python, expressions in parentheses, square brackets or curly braces can be split over two or more lines without using backslashes. Consequently, dictionaries can be split over several lines without explicit backslashes.

Dictionary Operations, Functions, and Methods

This section introduces the principal operations and functions that construct and process dictionaries. As you read, run the examples and to experiment on your own.

The built-in function *len* returns the number of key/item pairs in a dictionary.

Example

```
>>> score = {'Johnny' : 85, 'Xena' : 95 };
>>> print len(score);
2
>>> print len({});
0
```

Items stored in a dictionary are looked up by means of keys. If a *dictionary* contains a particular *key/item* pair, the *item* is referred to as *dictionary[key]*.

Example

```
>>> score = {'Johnny' : 85, 'Xena' : 95 };
>>> print score['Johnny'], score['Xena'];
85 95
```

Attempts to use keys that do not belong to the dictionary result in run-time errors. Note that string keys are case sensitive.

Example

```
>>> print score['Alex'];
...
KeyError: 'Alex'
```

The *membership test* (*key* in *dictionary*) returns *True* or *False* depending on whether the dictionary contains a *key-item* pair with this particular *key*. The test (*key* not in *dictionary*) is the same as not (*key* in *dictionary*).

Example

```
>>> score = {'Xena' : 95, 'Johnny' : 85};
>>> if ('Xena' in score): print score['Xena'];
95
>>> if ('Alex' in score): print score['Alex'];
>>> print 'Alex' in score;
False
>>> print 'Alex' not in score;
True
```

The list of all keys in a *dictionary* is returned by the *dictionary.keys()* method. This list can be used to look up all items in the dictionary.

Example

```
>>> score = {'Xena' : 95, 'Johnny' : 85};
>>> listOfAllStudents = score.keys();
>>> listOfAllStudents.sort();
>>> print listOfAllStudents;
['Johnny', 'Xena']
>>> for student in listOfAllStudents:
        print student, score[student];
Johnny 85
Xena 95
```

A summary of the most common dictionary operations, functions, and methods, is presented in the following table; many more can be found in the Python online documentation.

Operation, Function, or Method	Description
{ }	Empty dictionary.
{ $k_0 : v_0, k_1 : v_1, \ldots k_{n-1} : v_{n-1}$ }	Dictionary of *n* key-item pairs, $k_i : v_i$.
len(*dictionary*)	The number of key-item pairs in *dictionary*.
dictionary[*key*]	*Look-up dictionary* item for this *key*.
del *dictionary*[*key*]	Delete the *key-item* pair for this particular *key*.
key in *dictionary* *key* not in *dictionary*	Test if *dictionary* contains a *key-item* pair for this particular *key*.
dictionary.keys()	List of all keys in this *dictionary*.
dictionary.values()	List of all items in this *dictionary*.
dictionary.copy()	A copy of this *dictionary*.

A dictionary assignment, such as *score* = {'Xena' : 95, 'Johnny' : 85} creates a *dictionary variable*. A dictionary variable is a reference to a dictionary object. Once a dictionary variable is assigned into another dictionary variable, both variables refer to the same dictionary object. You can change the dictionary through any variable that refers to the dictionary. Essentially, the same dictionary object is shared between variables that refer to it. To avoid dictionary sharing, use the *copy* method to create a new instance of an existing dictionary.

Sample Program: Dictionary Processor

Consider again the simple programming problem from the beginning of this topic: develop a program to repeatedly input any month name and output the number of days in that month. This section presents a simple program named *Dictionary Processor* that solves this problem based on the *dictionary* built-in data type. The name *Dictionary Processor* is an abbreviated version of *Simple Dictionary-Based Month Processor*. A more sophisticated second version of the *Dictionary Processor* program, the *Enhanced Dictionary Processor,* is available for further self-study.

Exercise

Run the *Dictionary Processor* program. In interactive mode, invoke the *months* function and experiment with various inputs.

The complete *Dictionary Processor* program follows below.

```
# Input month name and output number of days:
def months ():
    print 'This program determines the number of days in a month.'
    dictionaryOfAllMonths =
        {'Jan' : 31, 'Feb' : 28, 'Mar' : 31, 'Apr' : 30,
         'May' : 31, 'Jun' : 30, 'Jul' : 31, 'Aug' : 31,
         'Sep' : 30, 'Oct' : 31, 'Nov' : 30, 'Dec' : 31};
    listOfAllMonths = dictionaryOfAllMonths.keys();
    print 'List of all months: ', listOfAllMonths;

    while (True):
        month = raw_input('Enter month name (unquoted): ');
        if (month in listOfAllMonths):
            days = dictionaryOfAllMonths[month];
        else: days = 0;
        print 'Month:', month, 'Days:', days;
        ans = inputYesNo('Process more? [Yes/No]: ');
        if (ans == 'No'): break;
    print 'So long...';
```

The main function in program *Dictionary Processor* is function *months*. The function creates a dictionary of twelve items. Each of the twelve dictionary items is a pair of month name and number of days - 31, 30, or 28 - in that month. The function inputs a month name and tests if the name is in the dictionary. If the name is in the dictionary, the number of days in that month is extracted from the dictionary. This process is repeated if the user chooses to exit.

Dictionary and List Embedding

A Python dictionary is a finite set of key/item pairs.

It has been already stated that dictionary *keys* are typically strings; they may also be numbers or other objects that are not studied in this course. It has been also said that lists and dictionaries cannot be used as keys.

Recall that dictionary *items* can be of any type. Therefore, dictionary items can be dictionaries or entire lists. Also, list items can be dictionaries or lists.

In summary, lists and dictionaries alike can be embedded as items in other lists and dictionaries. The level of list and dictionary embedding is limitless.

Example

A fill-in-the-blank quiz question can easily be represented as a dictionary. Such a dictionary may include three items: question *type*, question *text*, and correct question *answer*. A sample question represented as a dictionary follows:

```
question =
    {
        'type' : 'fill-in',
        'text' : 'What is the most populous state in the USA?',
        'answer' : 'California'
    };
```

A complete quiz is a list of dictionaries, with each dictionary representing one question. A sample quiz follows:

```
quiz =
    [
        {   #question 1
            'type' : 'fill-in',
            'text' : 'What is the most populous state in the USA?',
            'answer' : 'California'
        },

        {   #question 2
            'type' : 'yes/no',
            'text' : 'Does the adult platypus have teeth?',
            'answer' : 'No'
        }

        {   #question 3
            'type' : 'multiple-choice',
            'text' :
                'Who was the first U.S. President?\n' +
                '(1) Abraham Lincoln\n' +
                '(2) George Washington\n' +
                '(3) John Lennon\n' +
```

```
            '(4) Franklin Roosevelt',
        'answer' : 2
    },

];
```

A quiz represented as a list of dictionaries may easily include more than one question of each kind: fill-in, multiple choice or yes/no.

Dictionary Subscriptions

A dictionary item is a *dictionary* followed by a *key* in square brackets: *dictionary[key]*. In Python, such a structure is called a *dictionary subscription*.

Dictionary subscriptions evaluate to dictionary items. Because dictionary subscriptions have items, they can participate in expressions. Dictionary subscriptions may also be used as arguments in function invocations.

Dictionary subscriptions are assigned items by means of assignment statements. Assignments to dictionary subscriptions change the dictionary in one of two possible ways. When a *dictionary* does not contain a given *key*, the assignment *dictionary[key] = item* inserts a new key/item pair into the dictionary. The dictionary position of a key/item pair is unpredictable. Once the *key* is in the *dictionary*, any subsequent assignment simply updates the *item*.

Example

```
>>> score = {'Johnny' : 85, 'Xena' : 95 };
>>> score['Xena'] = score['Xena'] - 5;
>>> print score;
{'Xena': 90, 'Johnny': 85}
>>> score['Alex'] = 100;
>>> print score;
{'Alex': 100, 'Xena': 90, 'Johnny': 85}
```

In a list subscription *dictionary[key]*, the *dictionary* and the *key* may be determined by arbitrary expressions. In particular, the *dictionary* itself may be specified as another dictionary subscription, or as a list subscription. This leads to complex subscriptions that incorporate various indexes and keys.

Example

Consider again the list of quiz questions from the previous example. The following assignment states that both 'California' and 'CA' are correct answers to the first question, 'What is the most populous state in the USA?':

```
>>> question1 = { 'type' : 'fill-in',
        'text' : 'What is the most populous state in the USA?',
        'answer' : 'California' };
>>> question2 = { 'type' : 'yes/no',
        'text' : 'Does the adult platypus have any teeth?',
        'answer' : 'No' };
>>> quiz = [ question1, question2];
>>> print quiz[0];
{'answer': ['California', 'CA'], 'text': 'What is the most populous state in the USA?', 'type': 'fill-in'}
>>> quiz[0]['answer'] = ['California', 'CA'];
>>> print quiz[0]['answer'];
['California', 'CA']
```

Example

Consider again the problem of building a dictionary of keywords and their meanings. Most keywords have more than one meaning. Multiple meanings of each keyword may be represented as lists, as shown below.

```
dictionary = {
  'Peace' :
      [ 'Absence of war or other hostilities.',
        'Inner contentment; serenity.'
      ],
  'Love' :
      [ 'Warm, tender feeling toward a person.',
        'To have a feeling of intense desire and attraction.'
      ],
  'Beauty' :
      [ 'Quality that gives pleasure to the mind or senses.'
      ]
};
```

Example

A complex dictionary with embedded lists can be printed with nested for-statements:

```
keywordList = dictionary.keys();
for keyword in keywordList:
    print keyword;
    meaningList = dictionary[keyword];
    for meaning in meaningList:
        print '\t', meaning;
```

The dictionary from the previous example would produce the following output using the above nested loops:

> Peace
>   Absence of war or other hostilities.
>   Inner contentment; serenity.
> Love
>   Warm, tender feeling toward a person.
>   To have a feeling of intense desire and attraction.
> Beauty
>   Quality that gives pleasure to the mind or senses.

Sample Dictionary Programs

Enhanced Dictionary Processor

A program named *Dictionary Processor* is discussed earlier in this topic. This dictionary based program offers a function named *months* that inputs the name of a month and outputs the number of days in that month. The function continues doing so as long as the user wishes.

Program *Enhanced Dictionary Processor* improves the *Dictionary Processor* with two functions that have been borrowed from another sample program, the *Enhanced List Processor*. The functions are a string input function and a list output function. The description of the *Enhanced List Processor* that is available earlier in this topic offers more details on the two functions.

The user interaction with the *Enhanced Dictionary Processor* is similar to the user interaction with the *Enhanced List Processor,* as described in an earlier section.

Russian Dictionary Logger

A program named *Russian List Logger* is discussed earlier in the section of Sample List Programs. The program contains a function named *Russian* to simulate Russian roulette games and at the same time records information about all games in a special log. A separate *display* function is provided to print the log. The log in the *Russian List Logger* is organized by means of embedded lists.

In contrast to the *Russian List Logger*, the *Russian Dictionary Logger* program uses dictionaries instead of lists to represent individual games. All individual game dictionaries are embedded in a master game list. This master game list is incorporated in a master dictionary that represents the entire log. Study the dictionary based log and compare it to the list based log. You will see the benefits and advantages of dictionaries, especially when it comes to the representation of heterogeneous data structures like logs.

The user interaction with the *Russian Dictionary Logger* is similar to the user interaction with the *Russian List Logger,* as described in an earlier section.

Quiz Processor

The purpose of the *Quiz Processor* sample program is to administer a quiz that consists of multiple-choice, Yes/No, and fill-in questions. This program represents a quiz as a list of questions, where individual questions are represented as dictionaries. The main function to invoke is named *processQuiz.* This function asks questions (in random order), collects answers, counts attempts, and determines marks. At the end, this function prints a quiz summary. Various helper functions are involved in quiz administration, such as functions to evaluate various types of questions.

A sample invocation in interactive mode of the *processQuiz* function is partially presented below.

```
>>> processQuiz();
...
Does the adult platypus have teeth?
Enter response [Yes/No]: No
That is correct!
...
What is the most populous state in the USA?
Enter response: California
That is correct!
...
Who was the first U.S. President? ...
...
Who made this quote famous? ...
...
```

Number of questions attempted: 4
Total attempts: 6
Total marks: 4
Score on a 100 points scale: 100.0

Introduction to Tuples

Python *tuples* are similar to lists; they are finite sequence of items. A tuple item may be of any type. There is just one difference between tuples and lists: While lists can be modified, tuples, once created, never change.

Placing comma-separated expressions in parenthesis forms a tuple. Parentheses may be omitted from any tuple with two or more items.

Example

```
>>> t1 = (10, 20, 30);
>>> t2 = 10, 20, 30;
>>> print t1, t2;
print t1, t2;
(1, 2, 3) (1, 2, 3)
>>> print t1 == t2;
True
```

Because tuples never change, they permit more efficient memory representation and faster operations. If speed is important for your program, you should consider using tuples instead of lists. Of course, any sequence that needs to be changed in your program must be represented as a list because tuples cannot be modified.

Recall that dictionary keys must be objects that never change, such as strings or numbers. Because tuples can never change, they can be used as dictionary keys, too.

Example

Recall that Python offers several built-in logic operations, such as *and, or, not*. Additional logic operations can be conveniently defined as dictionaries. Consider for example the *'exclusive or'* logic operation which is usually abbreviated as *'xor'*. The *xor* operation returns *True* when its Boolean arguments are different; it is *False* otherwise. This definition is given in the table below.

A	B	A xor B
False	False	False
False	True	True
True	False	True
True	True	False

The *xor* operation, as defined above, may be implemented with a dictionary:

```
>>> xor =
  {(False, False): False, (False, True): True,
   (True, False): True, (True, True): False};
>>> xor[(True, True)]
False
```

When a tuple is used as a dictionary key, its parenthesis can be omitted:

```
>>> xor[True, True]
False
```

Summaries of some tuple operations and functions are presented in the table below. Note that there are no tuple methods.

Operation or Function	Description
( )	Empty tuple.
(i_0, i_1, ...i_{n-1})	Tuple of *n* items (at positions 0, 1, ... *n-1*).
len(*tuple*)	The number of items in *tuple*.
tuple[*i*]	*Tuple* item at position *i*.
item in *tuple*; *item* not in *tuple*	Test if *item* is a member of *tuple*.
P + Q	Concatenate tuples *P* and *Q*.
n * L	Repeat *n* times the items of *L*.
min(*tuple*)	The smallest item of *tuple*.
max (*tuple*)	The largest item of *tuple*.
tuple(*i:j*)	A tuple slice: (*tuple*(i),*tuple*(i+1) ... *tuple*(j-1)).
tuple(*list*)	Copy the list into a tuple.
list(*tuple*)	Copy the tuple into a list.

Synonyms

Some terms that have been introduced in this topic have synonyms. A list of such terms and their corresponding synonyms follows.

Term	Synonym
Function invocation	Function call
Function	Method
Index	Subscript
List	Array
Dictionary	Hash Table

Lab A [Lists and Dictionaries]

Objective; Background; Lab Overview; What to Do Next; Downloading Sample Programs; Uncompressing Sample Programs; Interactive Exploration of Lists; Saving Your Interactive Session; Studying the Sample Program; Creating a Program File; Developing the New Program

Objective

The objective of this lab is to develop a *Singer Advisor* program that will:
- Display a list of several popular singers.
- Repeatedly input a singer's name; if that particular singer is known to the program, it will output the rating of that singer.

Background

- A possible interaction of a *Singer Advisor* program may look like this:

```
>>> singers();
This program rates singers.
List of known singers:
    Elvis Presley
    Enrico Caruso
    John Lennon
    Johnny Pancake
    Willie Nelson
    Xena Zucchini
Enter singer (unquoted) name: Elvis Presley
Singer: Elvis Presley Rating: Excellent
Rate more? [Yes/No]: Yes
Enter singer (unquoted) name: Madonna
Singer: Madonna Rating: Unknown
Rate more? [Yes/No]: Yes
Enter singer (unquoted) name: Xena Zucchini
Singer: Xena Zucchini Rating: So-so
Rate more? [Yes/No]: Yes
Enter singer (unquoted) name: John Lennon
```

```
Singer: John Lennon Rating: Good
Rate more? [Yes/No]: Yes
Enter singer (unquoted) name: Enrico Caruso
Singer: Enrico Caruso Rating: Excellent
Rate more? [Yes/No]: No
So long...
>>>
```

- The choice of singers rated in your program and their specific ratings is left up to you.
- Implement at least four different ratings, with at least two singers with any particular rating.

Lab Overview

To perform this lab:
- Study the *List Processor* sample program.
- Transform a copy of the sample program *List Processor* into a *Singer Advisor* program by following the detailed instructions that follow.
- Systematically test the *Singer Advisor* program.
- For this lab, you may choose to work with the *Enhanced List Processor* rather than with the *List Processor*. This option offers a more challenging lab.

What to Do Next

You are now offered the following choices:
- Follow the detailed lab instructions below.
- Try the lab independently, using the instructions when you require help.
- Perform the lab independently, without any aid from the instructions.

All three approaches are beneficial to students. Choose the approach most beneficial to you.

Downloading Sample Programs

Various Lab Assignments for this course of study are based on ready-to-use sample programs. Such programs should be downloaded from the online study pack into your *master* folder.

Download sample programs for the current Topic 6 by performing these steps:
- Locate the current *Topic 6* in the online study pack.

- Open the *Lab Assignment* resource.
- Right-click on the *Sample Programs* link.
- Use *Save As* to store the downloaded compressed (zipped) folder, *06.zip,* within your *master* folder.

Uncompressing Sample Programs
- Uncompress the contents of the downloaded compressed (zipped) folder. Depending on your platform, you may use built-in compression support, or compressing utilities.
  - In Windows XP, use built-in un-compression support as follows:
    - Open your *master* folder using the *File Browser*.
    - Right-click on the downloaded compressed (zipped) folder.
    - Use *Extract All* to extract the contents of the compressed (zipped) folder within the *master* folder.
      - This will create an uncompressed folder, *06*, within the *master* folder. This folder contains your sample programs.
  - Alternatively, you can:
    - *Open* the compressed (zipped) folder.
    - *Cut* folder *06* from within the compressed (zipped) folder.
    - *Paste* the cut folder *06* outside the compressed (zipped) folder – directly within the *master* folder.
- Delete the compressed (zipped) folder, *06.zip.* Keep the uncompressed folder, *06*.
- Open the uncompressed folder *06* and browse its contents.
- Note that Python program files have extension '**.py**'.

Interactive Exploration of Lists
Explore list operations and functions by executing the following steps in interactive mode.
- Feel free to choose your preferred singers in the sample statements below.

```
>>> excellentList = ["Enrico Caruso", "Elvis Presley"];
>>> goodList = ["John Lennon", "Willie Nelson"];
>>> soSoList = ["Xena Zucchini"];
>>> poorList = ["Johnny Pancake"];
>>> listOfSingers = excellentList + goodList + soSoList + poorList;
>>> print listOfSingers;
>>> len(listOfSingers)
>>> listOfSingers[0]
>>> listOfSingers[len(listOfSingers)-1]
```

```
>>> # This will cause a run-time error:
>>> listOfSingers[len(listOfSingers)]
>>> "Elvis Presley" in excellentList
>>> "Elvis Presley" in soSoList

>>> listOfMinutes = range(60);
>>> print listOfMinutes;
>>> listOfMonths = range(1, 13);
>>> print listOfMonths;
>>> temp = [82, 65, 100, 65, -20];
>>> print min(temp), max(temp);
```

Explore list methods by executing the following steps in interactive mode.

```
>>> listOfSingers.sort();
>>> print listOfSingers;
>>> goodList.reverse();
>>> print goodList;
>>> goodList.append('John Doe');
>>> print goodList;
>>> last = goodList.pop();
>>> print last;
>>> print goodList;
```

Explore a simple technique to display a list, one indented item per line, by executing the following steps in interactive mode.

```
>>> aList = listOfSingers;
>>> print aList;
>>> print '\t', aList[0];
>>> print '\t', aList[1];
>>> print '\t', aList[5];
>>> i = 0;
>>> while (i < len(aList)):
        print '\t' + str(aList[i]);
        i = i + 1;
>>> print i;
```

Saving Your Interactive Session

- You must save the interactive sessions from all of your experiments in your current labs folder, *06Labs*.
- From the *shell window*, use File => Save As.

- Give the name *Session_6A.txt* to the saved copy.
  - **Important Note:** You must explicitly supply the file extension '**.txt**' when saving from IDLE.
- If you want to perform experiments in two or more interactive sessions, save your work in several files. If you choose to do so, use names *Session_6A_1.txt, Session_6A_2.txt*, and so on, for all saved files.
- Your saved file(s) must be included in you Lab Assignment submission.

Studying the Sample Program
- Open and browse the *List Processor* sample program using IDLE.
- Run the program with various input data; observe the output.
- Analyze the program implementation.

Creating a Program File
Create this program in your current labs folder, *06Labs*.
- Use IDLE to create a copy of the *List Processor* program file.
- Name the saved copy *SingerAdvisor.py*.
  - **Important Note:** You must explicitly supply the file extension '**.py**' when saving from IDLE.

Developing the New Program
Perform the following steps with the newly created *Singer Advisor* program.

Step 1: Adapting the sample program to work with singers in place of months
- Rename the *months* function to *singers*.
- Eliminate lists of months, introducing lists of singers instead. Create one list for each singer rating category; assign singer names into their corresponding rating list.
  - For example:
    - excellentList = ['Enrico Caruso', 'Elvis Presley'];
    - goodList = ...; soSoList = ...; poorList = ...;
  - You are encouraged to use your own ratings.
- Modify the while-loop to:
  - Input singer names instead of month names.
  - Test the membership of the current singer name in all possible rating lists.
  - Provide corresponding singer rating.
- Test you program with various names.

- Use at least one name for each rating category and at least one name that is not present in any rating category.

Step 2: Designing a custom *displayList* function
- Define a function to display a list, one indented item per line.
  - Apply the list display technique offered in the Interactive Exploration of Lists section above. Start with the pattern below.

    ```
    def displayList(aList):
        i = 0;
        while ... # Recall your interactive experiments.
    ```

- Test your completed *displayList* function interactively.
- For example, use invocations such as this:

    ```
    >>> testList = ["Enrico Caruso", "Elvis Presley", "John Lennon"];
    >>> displayList(testList);
        Enrico Caruso
        Elvis Presley
        John Lennon
    ```

- Employ your *displayList* function in the *singers* function to display the list of all singers.
- Again, test you program with various names to double check that *displayList* function works properly within the *singers* function.

Step 3: Brushing-up your program
- Update all existing comments. Add new comments if necessary.

Lab B [Lists and Dictionaries]

Objective; Background; Lab Overview; What to Do Next; Studying the Sample Program; Creating a Program File; Developing the New Program

Objective

The objective of this lab is to develop a *Tax Processor* program that will:
- Input a sequence of non-negative *incomes* terminated by any negative number.
- Sort all *incomes* in ascending order.
- For each income, calculate and output the *tax* due.
- Lastly, calculate and output the *averages* of all entered *incomes* and calculated *taxes*.

Background

- The objective of this lab is similar to that of an earlier topic. The difference is the sorted income list. This requires inputting the entire list of scores instead of inputting one score at a time.
- Implement the *Tax Processor* in compliance with the following Tax Table:

Taxable income is over:	But not over:	The tax is:	Plus:	Of the amount over:
	7,150	0.00	10%	0
7,150	29,050	715.00	15%	7,150
29,050	70,350	4,000.00	25%	29,050
70,350	146,750	14,325.00	28%	70,350
146,750	319,100	35,717.00	33%	146,750
319,100		92,592.50	35%	319,100

Lab Overview

To perform this lab:
- Study the *Score Processor* sample program.
- Study your *Tax Processor* program designed for the topic on Functions.
- Transform a copy of the *Score Processor* sample program into a *Tax Processor* program.
- Extensively test the *Tax Processor* program.

What to Do Next

You are now offered the following choices:
- Follow the detailed lab instructions below.
- Try the lab independently, using the instructions when you require help.
- Perform the lab independently, without any aid from the instructions.

All three approaches are beneficial to students. Choose the approach most beneficial to you.

Studying the Sample Program

- Using IDLE, open and browse the *Score Processor* sample program.
- Run the program with various input data; observe the output.
- Analyze the program implementation.

Creating a Program File

Create this program in your current labs folder, *06Labs*.
- Create a copy of the *Score Processor* program file using IDLE.
- Name the saved copy *TaxProcessor.py*.
  - **Important Note:** You must explicitly supply the file extension '**.py**' when saving from IDLE.

Developing the New Program

Perform these steps with the newly created *Tax Processor* program:
- In the newly created *Tax Processor* program, transform the definition of function *inputListOfScores* into a definition for function *inputListOfIncomes*. The new function must input non-negative incomes, returning them all in a list.
- In interactive mode, test *inputListOfIncomes* function. Input various incomes terminated by a negative number.

- Delete the definition of function *inputHi* from the *Tax Processor* program.
- Replace the definition of function *theGrade* (with parameter *score*) with the definition of function *theTax* (with parameter *income*). You can copy this function from your *Tax Processor* program designed for the topic on Functions.
- Convert the function used to display *listOfScores* and *listOfGrades* into a function that will display a *listOfIncomes* and *listOfTaxes*.
- In interactive mode, thoroughly test the new *display* function. Provide a lists of arbitrary positive numbers for *listOfIncomes* and an equally long list of arbitrary positive numbers for *listOfTaxes*. These lists are to be used for testing purposes only: they do not have to contain actual incomes and correct taxes.
- Preserve the *displayAverage* function as it is. This function is capable of finding the average of any numeric list, regardless of it being a list of scores, incomes or taxes.
- Modify the definition of function *summarize* to work with *listOfIncomes* and *listOfTaxes*.
- In interactive mode, test the *summarize* function. Again, provide artificially constructed lists.
- Transform function *scores* into function *incomes*.
- In interactive mode, extensively test the *incomes* function.
- Update comments throughout the program.
- Supply additional lines of comments to improve readability.
- Test your complete program. You can start testing with this data:

```
Enter annual income, negative to quit: 0
Enter annual income, negative to quit: 7150
Enter annual income, negative to quit: 10000
Enter annual income, negative to quit: 29050
Enter annual income, negative to quit: 70350
Enter annual income, negative to quit: 146750
Enter annual income, negative to quit: -1

Income  Tax
0       0.0
7150    715.0
10000   1142.5
29050   4000.0
70350   14325.0
146750  35717.0
```

```
Incomes processed: 6
Average income: 43883.0
Average Tax: 9317.0
```

Lab C [Lists and Dictionaries]

Objective; Background; Lab Overview; What to Do Next; Studying the Sample Program; Creating a Program File; Developing the New Program

Objective
The objective of this lab is to develop a *Trip Advisor* program that will:
- Display a list of several popular travel destinations.
- Repeatedly input any destination name; if that destination is known to the program, output travel advice.

Background
- The purpose of this program is similar to the *Singer Advisor* program from an earlier lab.
  - The differences are you must advise about travel destinations instead of rating singers and you must use dictionaries rather than lists.
- The choice of the travel destinations used in your program and the specific travel advice is left up to you.
- Implement at least four travel destinations, supplying travel advice for each of them. You may have more than one destination for which you give the same travel advice.

Lab Overview
To perform this lab:
- Study the *Dictionary Processor* sample program.
- Transform a copy of the sample program *Dictionary Processor* into a *Trip Advisor* program by following the detailed instructions that follow.
- Systematically test the *Trip Advisor* program.
- For this lab, you may choose to work with the *Enhanced Dictionary Processor* rather than with the *Dictionary Processor*. This option will make the lab more challenging.

What to Do Next
You are now offered the following choices:
- Follow the detailed lab instructions below.
- Try the lab independently, using the instructions when you require help.
- Perform the lab independently, without any aid from the instructions.

All three approaches are beneficial to students. Choose the approach most beneficial to you.

Studying the Sample Program
- Using IDLE, open and browse the *Dictionary Processor* sample program.
- Run the program with various input data; observe the output.
- Analyze the program implementation.

Creating a Program File
Create this program in your current labs folder, *06Labs*.
- Create a copy of the *Dictionary Processor* program file using IDLE.
- Give the name *TripAdvisor.py* to the saved copy.
  - **Important Note:** You must explicitly supply the file extension '**.py**' when saving from IDLE.

Developing the New Program
Perform the following steps with the newly created *Trip Advisor* program.
- Create a dictionary of travel destinations.
  - Each key-item in the dictionary should be a travel destination and its rating. For example:
    - 'Orange' : 'This is a great town to go to college and even live permanently.'
    - 'Paris' : 'Once you see Paris, you want to return again and again.'
  - You are encouraged to use your own travel destinations and corresponding travel advice.
- Modify the while loop to:
  - Input travel destinations instead of months.
  - Provide adequate destination advice.
- Test you program with various destination names.
  - Use all of your destination names at least once.
- Update all existing comments.

Lab D [Lists and Dictionaries]

Objective; Background; Lab Overview; Saving Your Interactive Session

Objectives
- The objective of this lab is to study and get hands-on experience with all sample programs for the current topic.

Background
- A number of sample programs are available to help you learn lists and dictionaries.
- The following sample **list-based** programs are available for study:
  - *List Processor*
  - *Enhanced List Processor*
  - *Score Processor*
  - *Binary List Search*
  - *Raffle Operator*
  - *Gift Assignment*
  - *Russian List Logger*
- The following sample **dictionary-based** programs are also available for study:
  - *Dictionary Processor*
  - *Enhanced Dictionary Processor*
  - *Russian Dictionary Logger*
  - *Quiz Processor*
- The E-text offers descriptions of all sample programs. Two of the programs, *List Processor* and *Dictionary Processor*, are described in detail. The descriptions of all other programs are overviews. Your task is to analyze these programs and experiment with them.

Lab Overview
To perform this lab:
- For each sample program from the above two lists:
  - Read the description of the sample program in the E-Text.
  - Open and browse the sample program using IDLE.

- Run the program with various input data; observe output.
 - Analyze the program implementation.
- Finally, save your IDLE interactive session in a text file.

Saving Your Interactive Session

- Save the interactive session with all of your experiments in your current labs folder, *06Labs*.
- From the Shell Window, use *File → Save As*.
- Give the name *Session_6D.txt* to the saved copy.
  - **Important Note:** You must explicitly supply the file extension '**.txt**' when saving from IDLE.
- If you want to perform experiments in two or more interactive sessions, save your work in several files. Use names *Session_6D_1.txt, Session_6D_2.txt*, and so on, for all saved files.
- Your saved file(s) must be included in your Lab Assignment submission.

Lab E [Lists and Dictionaries, Optional]

Objective; Background; Lab Overview

Objective
The objective of this lab is to develop a program *List Logger* that will:
- Simulate *casino* roulette games, recording all information about the games in a special log.
- Create the log using **lists**.

Background
Note that the sample *Russian List Logger* program:
- Already contains an enhanced function *Russian* simulating Russian roulette games while recording information about all games in a list-based log.
- Contains a valid *casino* simulator function that does not create a log but can easily be enhanced to do so by following the *Russian* function as a pattern.

You may convert the original sample program *Russian List Logger* into a *List Logger* program as explained in the Lab Overview below.

Lab Overview
To perform this lab:
- Study the *Russian List Logger* sample program.
- Save a copy of the *Russian List Logger* sample program in your current labs folder. To transform the copy into a *List Logger* program:
  - Extend the *casino* function with game logging statements.
    - Follow function *Russian* as a sample; use lists to represent the log.
  - Develop a casino log display function, *displayCasino*.
    - Follow function *displayRussian* as a sample.
- Update all comments adequately.
- A possible interaction with a *List Logger* program is presented below. Use it as a testing guideline for your version of the *List Logger* program.

```
>>> log = casino();
Playing 6-position roulette.
How much do you bet (0 to exit): **100**
Choose a position (0 to 5): **2**
Spinning ...
Wheel stops at position 3
You lost $100
You owe the casino $100
How much do you bet (0 to exit): **100**
Choose a position (0 to 5): **2**
Spinning ...
Wheel stops at position 3
You lost $100
You owe the casino $200
How much do you bet (0 to exit): **100**
Choose a position (0 to 5): **2**
Spinning ...
Wheel stops at position 2
You won $500
The casino owes you $200
How much do you bet (0 to exit): **0**
So long... Come again
>>> displayCasino(log);
Casino roulette log
Number of positions: 6
Bet: $100 Chosen number: 2 Winning number: 3 Outcome: You lost $100
        Player balance: $-100
Bet: $100 Chosen number: 2 Winning number: 3 Outcome: You lost $100
        Player balance: $-200
Bet: $100 Chosen number: 2 Winning number: 2 Outcome: You won $500
        Player balance: $200
Games  played: 3
>>>
```

Lab F [Lists and Dictionaries, Optional]

Objective; Background; Lab Overview

Objective

The objective of this lab is to develop a program *Dictionary Logger* that will:
- Simulate *casino* roulette games while recording information about all games in a special log.
- Create the log using **dictionaries and lists**.

Background

Note that the sample *Russian Dictionary Logger* program:
- Already contains an enhanced function *Russian* to simulate Russian roulette games while recording information about all games in a dictionary-based log.
- Contains a valid *casino* simulator function that does not create a log but can be easily enhanced to do so by following the *Russian* function as a pattern.

You may convert the original sample program *Russian Dictionary Logger* into a *Dictionary Logger* program as explained in the Lab Overview below.

Lab Overview

To perform this lab:
- Study the *Russian Dictionary Logger* sample program.
- Save a copy of the *Russian Dictionary Logger* sample program in your current labs folder. Transform the copy into a *Dictionary Logger* program:
    - Extend the *casino* function with game logging statements.
        - Follow function *Russian* as a sample, using dictionaries and lists to represent the log.
    - Develop a casino log display function, *displayCasino*.
        - Follow function *displayRussian* as a sample.
- Update all comments adequately.
- A possible interaction with a *Dictionary Logger* program is presented below. Use it as a testing guideline for your version of the *Dictionary Logger* program.

```
>>> log = casino();
Playing 6-position roulette.
How much do you bet (0 to exit): **100**
Choose a position (0 to 5): **2**
Spinning ...
Wheel stops at position 3
You lost $100
You owe the casino $100
How much do you bet (0 to exit): **100**
Choose a position (0 to 5): **2**
Spinning ...
Wheel stops at position 3
You lost $100
You owe the casino $200
How much do you bet (0 to exit): **100**
Choose a position (0 to 5): **2**
Spinning ...
Wheel stops at position 2
You won $500
The casino owes you $200
How much do you bet (0 to exit): **0**
So long... Come again
>>> displayCasino(log);
Casino roulette log
Number of positions: 6
Bet: $100 Chosen number: 2 Winning number: 3 Outcome: You lost $100
        Player balance: $-100
Bet: $100 Chosen number: 2 Winning number: 3 Outcome: You lost $100
        Player balance: $-200
Bet: $100 Chosen number: 2 Winning number: 2 Outcome: You won $500
        Player balance: $200
Games  played: 3
>>>
```

Lab G [Lists and Dictionaries, Optional]

Objective; Background; Lab Overview

Objective

The objective of this lab is to develop a *Lottery Operator* program that will:
- Input a number of prizes.
- Input a range of participating ticket numbers.
- Define the range of tickets by the smallest and largest ticket numbers.
- Draw a winning ticket number for each prize.
- Display all winning tickets with their corresponding prize numbers.

Background

Note that the *Raffle Operator* sample program randomly distributes raffle prizes among known participants. The *Lottery Operator* program is somewhat similar to the *Raffle Operator*. These are the main differences between the two programs:
- In the *Raffle Operator*, both prizes and participants are given specific names (represented as strings).
  - The *Lottery Operator* must use ticket and prize numbers instead of participant and prize names.
- The *Raffle Operator* displays all participants, winner or not.
  - The *Lottery Operator* must display only winning ticket numbers, because the ticket number range is presumably too large to be entirely displayed.

Lab Overview

To perform this lab:
- Study the *Raffle Operator* sample program.
- Save a copy of the *Raffle Operator* sample program in your current labs folder. Transform the copy into a *Lottery Operator* program:
  - Transform the *raffle* function into analogous *lottery* function.
  - Transform the *displayAll* function into analogous *displayWinners* function.
- Update all comments as needed.

- A possible interaction with a *Lottery Operator* program is presented below. Use it as a testing guideline for your version of the *Lottery Operator* program.

```
>>> lottery();
This program randomly selects lottery winners.
First ticket number: 1000
Last ticket number: 9999
Number of prizes to be given: 10
Ticket and prize numbers:
1233    1
4236    2
4969    3
4996    4
5767    5
6205    6
6537    7
7374    8
9300    9
9658    10
Handle another raffle? [Yes/No]: No
Congratulations to all winners.
>>>
```

Lab H [Lists and Dictionaries, Optional]

Objective; Background; Lab Overview; Shakespearean Words

Objective

The objective of this lab is to develop a program that will randomly generate *Shakespearean insults*.

Background

- Genuine Shakespearean insults are expressions used in Shakespearean works, such as plays and sonnets.
- Examples of traditional Shakespearean insults are:
  - *Thou art a very ragged Wart!* [Henry IV]
  - *Idol of idiot-worshippers!* [Troilus and Cressida]
- Computer generated *Shakespearean insults* are randomly generated sentences that:
  - Start with 'Thou', and
  - Continue with three words from three independent lists of *Shakespearean words*.
- Examples of computer-generated Shakespearean insults are:
  - *Thou spleeny dizzy-eyed clack-dish!*
  - *Thou spongy scurvy-valiant blind-worm!*
- A *Shakespearean Insults* program should repeatedly generate Shakespearean insults as long as the user is interested in reading them.

Lab Overview

To perform this lab:
- Implement a program in your current lab to:
  - Incorporate three Shakespearean word lists containing ten or more words each.
  - Randomly choose three Shakespearean words, one word from each of the three lists.
  - Preface the three randomly generated Shakespearean words with 'Thou' to generate a Shakespearean insult.
  - Output the insult.
- Before generating the very first Shakespearean insult, the program should confirm if the user wants to proceed.

- The program should repeatedly generate insults as long as the user is interested in reading them.
- Use the Shakespearean words table below as a word resource.

Shakespearean Words

One	Two	Three
artless	base-court	apple-john
bawdy	bat-fowling	baggage
bootless	beetle-headed	bladder
churlish	boil-brained	boar-pig
clouted	clay-brained	bum-bailey
craven	common-kissing	canker-blossom
dissembling	dizzy-eyed	coxcomb
errant	dread-bolted	death-token
fawning	earth-vexing	dewberry
fobbing	elf-skinned	flap-dragon
frothy	fen-sucked	flirt-gill
impertinent	fool-born	gudgeon
infectious	full-gorged	haggard
jarring	guts-griping	harpy
loggerheaded	half-faced	hedge-pig
lumpish	hasty-witted	horn-beast
paunchy	ill-breeding	lout
rank	onion-eyed	minnow
saucy	reeling-ripe	nut-hook
spleeny	rough-hewn	pigeon-egg
spongy	rude-growing	pignut
villainous	tardy-gaited	strumpet
wayward	toad-spotted	vassal
yeasty	weather-bitten	wagtail

Lab I - Challenge [Lists and Dictionaries, Optional]

Objective; Background; Lab Overview

Objective

The objective of this lab is to develop a program to play *Tic-Tac-Toe*.

Background

- *Tic-Tac-Toe* is a game in which two players alternately put crosses and circles in one of the compartments of a 3-by-3 board. The game objective is to gain a winging sequence of crosses (X's) or circles (O's) before your opponent does. A winning sequence consists of three adjacent crosses or three adjacent circles in a row, column or diagonal.
- Develop a programmatic version of the Tic-Tac-Toe game. The human player is challenged to get three crosses in a row before the program gets three circles in a row.

Lab Overview

To perform this lab:
- Research different strategies for *Tic-Tac-Toe* on the Web and/or in the Library.
- In your current labs folder, implement a program to play the game.
- Post in the General Forum a brief description of:
  - The rules of the game.
  - Your chosen strategy.
  - Your program implementation of the game.

Strings, Files, and the Web

Strings Revisited; Escape Sequences; String Operations and Functions; String Methods; Sample String Functions; Sample Programming Problem: Filing Scores; Sample Program: Score Filer; File Objects, Functions, and Methods; Sample File Functions; Working with Directories; Mutable and Immutable Sequences; Sample Program: Hangman; Web Resources and URLs; Web Resource Input; Sample Programming Problem: Tracking Stocks; Sample Program: Stock Tracker; Direct Data Input; Synonyms

Strings Revisited

Strings are sequences of characters that represent anything text-like; examples are words, names, programs, and internet addresses. During program execution, strings are represented as string objects. Python offers a variety of operations, functions, and methods to process string objects.

Some basic properties of strings were studied in earlier topics. Various strings have already been used in sample programs. A concise summary of previously discussed string concepts is presented in the following table.

String Concept	Example
Literal	'Xena Zucchini', "Xena's name", 'A string with a "quote" inside'
Assignment	name = 'Xena Zucchini';
Concatenation	'Xena' + 'Zucchini' == 'Xena Zucchini'
Repetition	3 * 'Xena' == 'XenaXenaXena'
Input	name = raw_input('What is your name? ')

Number to string conversion	age = input('Enter your age: '); print 'Your age is ' + str(age);
String to number conversion	a = '12'; b = '3.14'; i = int(a); f = float(b);
Control characters	print '\n'; print 'column1\tcolumn2';

Exercise

In interactive mode, execute all example operations and statements from the above table. Experiment with your own examples as well.

Escape Sequences

Recall that a *string literal* is a finite sequence of characters enclosed in matching single or double quotes. The *empty string* contains no characters and is represented with a pair of matching quotes.

Example

'' - empty string with two single quotes and nothing in between
"" - empty string with two double quotes

String literals may include control characters, such as the new line character, '\n', or the tab character, '\t'. The backslash character itself can become a member of a string literal if preceded by another backslash character, '\\'. Character sequences that start with the backslash character are termed *escape sequences*.

Example

```
>>> path = 'C:\\Python24';
>>> print path;
C:\Python24
```

Single or double quotes can also be prefixed by a backslash character to form escape sequences. In this way, a single or double quote can become a part of a string literal when necessary.

String Operations and Functions

This section introduces the principal operations and functions that construct and process strings. As you read, run the examples and experiment on your own.

Many string operations and functions mirror list operations and functions. This is because strings and lists are sequences of items. The difference is that lists can comprise items of any type while strings comprise only characters.

The built-in function *len* returns the number of characters in a string.

> Example
>
> ```
> >>> print len('Orange');
> 6
> >>> print len('');
> 0
> >>> print len('\n');
> 1
> ```

The built-in function *list* is used to convert a string of characters to a list of those same characters.

> Example
>
> ```
> >>> characterList = list('Orange');
> >>> print characterList;
> ['O', 'r', 'a', 'n', 'g', 'e']
> ```

String characters are indexed by non-negative numbers: 0, 1, 2,... The first character in a string has index 0, the second has index 1, the third has index 2, and so on.

When the length of a string is *n*, the index set of the string contains the numbers *0, 1, ..., n-1*. Item *i* of string *a* is referred to as *a[i]*. The first item of a string is *a[0]*, and the last is *a[n-1]*.

> Example
>
> ```
> >>> path = 'C:\\Python24';
> >>> print path[0], path[1], path[2], path[3], path[4];
> C : \ P y
> ```

Negative indexes can be used to refer to string characters backwards. When the length of a string is *n*, the negative index set of the string contains the numbers *-1, -2,..., -n*. The last tem of string *a* is referred to as *a[-1]*, the one before the last one is *a[-2]*, etc., to the first item *a[-n]*.

Example

```
>>> path = 'C:\\Python24';
>>> print path[-2], path[-1];
>>> 2 3
```

When the length of a string is *n*, the entire index set of the string consists of the numbers *0, 1, 2, ... n-1* and *-1, -2,..., -n*. Attempts to use indexes outside of the index set result in run-time errors.

Example

```
>>> path = 'C:\\Python24';
>>> print len(path);
11
>>> print path[11];
...
IndexError: string index out of range
```

The *membership test* (*X* in *S*) returns *True* if *X* is a substring of *S* and *False* otherwise. The test (*X* not in *S*) is the same as (not (*X* in *S*)).

Example

```
>>> path = 'C:\\Python24';
>>> test = 'Py' in path;
>>> print test;
True
>>> print 'pY' in path;
False
```

The *slicing* operation permits you to copy part of an existing string, creating a new string with the copy. If *a* is a string, *a[i:k]* selects all items with index *j* such that *i <= j < k*. The index set of the slice is renumbered so that it starts at 0.

Example

```
>>> path = 'C:\\Python24';
>>> drive = path[0:3];
>>> print drive;
C:\
```

A summary of string operations and functions is presented in the following table.

Operation or Function	Description
len(string)	The number of characters in string.
list(string)	A list of characters in string.
string[i]	String character at position i.
substring in string; substring not in string	Test if substring belongs to a string.
string[i:j]	A string slice: [string[i], string[i+1], ... string[j-1]].

String Methods

A string *method* is a function attached to a *string* object. Some string methods require arguments while others do not. These are the patterns of string method invocation:

string.method()
string.method(arguments)

Example

```
>>> string = 'Banana';
>>> string.upper(), string.lower()
('BANANA', 'banana')
>>> string.count('a')
3
```

Methods are invoked through variables, literals and, in general, expressions.

Example

```
>>> 'Banana'.count('a')
3
>>> 'Banana'.upper(), 'Banana'.lower()
('BANANA', 'banana')
```

```
>>> string = 'Banana';
>>> string[1:4].upper()
ANA
>>> ('Ban' + 'ana').count('na')
2
```

There are four principal groups of string methods:
- Methods that test string contents.
- Methods that search substrings in strings.
- Methods that produce changed copies of strings.
- Methods that transform strings into lists and lists into strings.

Methods That Test String Contents

The following table summarizes principal methods that test string contents.

Method	Description
string.isalpha()	Return true if all characters in the *string* are alphabetic and there is at least one character, false otherwise.
string.isdigit()	Return true if all characters in the *string* are digits and there is at least one character, false otherwise.
string.isalnum()	Return true if all characters in the *string* are alphanumeric (alphabetic and numeric) and there is at least one character, false otherwise.

Example

```
>>> '123'.isdigit()
True
>>> '3.14'.isdigit()
False
>>> 'Orange'.isalpha(), 'Python24'.isalpha()
(True, False)
>>> 'Python24'.isalnum()
True
>>> 'C:\\Python24'.isalnum()
False
```

Methods That Search Substrings in Strings

The following table summarizes principal methods that search substrings in strings.

Method	Description
string.count(*substring*)	Return the number of non-overlapping occurrences of *substring* in *string*.
string.find(*substring*)	Return the lowest index in the *string* where *substring* is found. Return -1 if *substring* is not found.
string.find(*substring, start*)	Return the lowest index in the *string* where substring *sub* is found, such that *sub* is contained at or after the start index. Return -1 if *substring* is not found.

Example

Method *count* returns the number of non-overlapping occurrences of a substring in a string:

```
>>> 'ananas'.count('a');
3
>>> 'ananas'.count('ana');
1
```

Example

Method *find* searches a substring in a string:

```
>>> # Find the index of the first occurrence of 'na' in 'ananas':
>>> first = 'ananas'.find('na');
>>> print first;
1
>>> # Search for 'na' in 'ananas' past the first 'na':
>>> second = 'ananas'.find('na', first+1);
>>> print second;
3
>>> # Search for 'na' in 'ananas' past the second 'na':
>>> third = 'ananas'.find('na', second+1);
>>> print third;
-1
```

Methods That Produce Updated Copies of Strings

The following table summarizes methods that produce updated copies of strings.

Method	Description
string.lower()	Return a copy of the *string* converted to lowercase.
string.upper()	Return a copy of the *string* converted to uppercase.
string.replace(*old, new*)	Return a copy of the *string* with all occurrences of substring *old* replaced by *new*
string.lstrip(*characters*)	Return a copy of the *string* with any leading *characters* removed (lstrip = left-strip).
string.rstrip(*characters*)	Return a copy of the *string* with any trailing *characters* removed (rstrip = right-strip).

Example

Methods *upper* and *lower* copy strings into all uppercase or all lowercase strings:

```
>>> response = 'Yes';
>>> response.upper();
'YES'
>>> response.lower();
'yes'
```

Example

Method *replace* returns an updated copy of a string:

```
>>> 'ananas'.replace('ana', 'bana');
'bananas'
```

Example

Methods *lstrip* and *rstrip* copy strings while removing all leading or trailing characters:

```
>>> 'ananas'.lstrip('a');
'nanas'
>>> 'ananas'.lstrip('an');
's'
>>> # Repeatedly left-strip any character of 'na' from 'ananas':
>>> 'ananas'.lstrip('nas');
''
```

```
>>> 'ananas\n'.rstrip('\n');
'ananas'
>>> 'C:\\Python24'.lstrip('C:\\');
'Python24'
```

Methods That Transform Strings into Lists and Lists into Strings

The following table summarizes methods that transform strings into lists and lists into strings.

Method	Description
string.split(*separator*)	Return a list of the words in the *string*, using *separator* as the delimiter string.
separator.join(*list*)	Return a string by concatenating all items of a *list* of strings, with intervening occurrences of a *separator*.

Example

When the *split* method is applied to a string, it returns a list. When that same list is submitted to the *join* method, the original string is returned:

```
>>> string = 'Zucchini, Xena, 95';
>>> string
'Zucchini, Xena, 95'
>>> lst = string.split(',');
>>> lst
['Zucchini', ' Xena', ' 95']
>>> string = ','.join(lst);
>>> string
'Zucchini, Xena, 95'
```

Exercise

In interactive mode, create some strings and apply the above string methods to them. Print and observe results. Start by repeating all examples in this section.

Sample String Functions

The *String Functions* sample program offers several string-processing functions. Analyze, experiment with, and possibly use these sample functions. Your independent work with sample string functions will help you master the use of strings in program design.

Brief descriptions of string-processing sample functions follow.

Function *alphabet* generates a string with all letters from the English alphabet:

```
def alphabet():
    result = 'abcdefghijklmnopqrstuvwxyz';
    return result + result.upper();
```

Example

```
>>> alphabet()
'abcdefghijklmnopqrstuvwxyzABCDEFGHIJKLMNOPQRSTUVWXYZ'
```

Function *scramble* generates a randomly scrambled version of a string:

```
import random;
def scramble(string):
    characterList = list(string);
    random.shuffle(characterList);
    return ''.join(characterList);
```

Example

```
>>> scramble('Atanas')
'santaA'
>>> scramble('real fun')
' fuel ran'
```

Function *fpToString* converts a floating point value to a string with specified decimal positions:

```
def fpToString(value, decimalPositions):
    string = str(round(value, decimalPositions));
    periodPosition = string.find('.');
    if (periodPosition >= 0):
        string = string[0: periodPosition + decimalPositions + 1];
    return string;
```

Example

```
>>> print fpToString(value = 3.14159, decimalPositions = 2);
3.14
>>> print 10.0 / 6;
1.66666666667
>>> print fpToString(value = 10.0 / 6, decimalPositions = 2);
1.67
```

A palindrome is a string that reads the same backward and forward. For example, strings '2002' and 'racecar' are palindromes, while strings '2000' and 'racecars' are not palindromes. Function *palindrome* returns *True* if a string is a palindrome; the function returns *False* otherwise:

```
def isPalindrome(word):
    characterList = list(word);
    characterList.reverse();
    backword = ''.join(characterList);
    return (word == backword);
```

Example

```
>>> isPalindrome('ananas'), isPalindrome('ANANA')
(False, True)
>>> isPalindrome('Dot saw I was Tod'.lower())
True
```

Functions *encode* and *decode* use simple ciphers to encode and decode arbitrary text messages.

A cipher is represented by two strings, *old* and *new*. To encode a message, the characters are replaced according to the following rule: character *old[0]* is replaced with character *new[0]*, character *old[1]* is replaced with character *new[1]*, etc.. The same method is used to decode an encoded message.

Example

```
>>> old = alphabet();
>>> new = scramble(old);
>>> print new;
oUQFMAxhtGmauqVKyNIcXspbOJPRSZlrjEiTYLBkfCgnHWevdDwz
```

```
>>> message = ...;
>>> secret = encode(message, old, new);
>>> print secret;
WhM rtqoa lbou tI htFFMq XqFMN chM KtaaVp!
>>> print decode(secret, old, new);
The Final Exam is hidden under the pillow!
```

The *encode* function converts the original message to a list of characters before applying an *old -> new* cipher to this list to generate an encoded list. Finally, the encode function converts the encoded list into a string and returns that string:

```
def encode(message, old, new):
    result = [];
    for char in message:
        pos = old.find(char);
        if(pos >= 0):
            char = new[pos];
        result.append(char);
    return ''.join(result);
```

To decode a message, characters are replaced according to the following rule: character *new[0]* is replaced with character *old[0]*, character *new[1]* is replaced with character *old[1]*, etc.. To decipher a message, the *decode* function simply invokes the *encode* function with the *old* and *new* arguments exchanged:

```
def decode(message, old, new):
    return encode(message, new, old);
```

Sample Programming Problem: Filing Scores

Consider the following simple programming problem. Develop a *Score Filer* program that will:
- Input student records from an existing external file (such as a disk file).
  - Each student record contains a *last name*, *first name*, and numeric *score*.
- Sort all student records alphabetically.
- Extend each student record with the letter grade for that student's score.
- Output all records in a new external file.
- Display a summary of all student records by providing the lowest, highest, and average scores.

Until now we have only designed programs to directly interact with the user to input data and provide results. At this time we will discuss a *non-interactive* program that inputs and outputs data from and into external files without direct interaction from the user.

There are valuable benefits gained from non-interactive file input-output programs. Non-interactive file input-output programs:
- Process significantly larger amounts of data at a much faster rate than programs requiring data to be hand entered by the user.
- Input data that have been stored in files by other programs.
- Output data into files to be further processed by other programs.

Sample Program: Score Filer

A simple program named *Score Filer* solves the programming problem that is formulated in the previous section. The present section outlines the main steps from the design of the *Score Filer* program. These steps focus on the following issues:
- How to represent data in a file
- How to input data from a file
- How to output data into a file
- How to integrate input, sorting, processing, and output
- How to summarize file records

How to Represent Data in a File

As a first step of the *Score Filer* design, we represent all student data in text files. One benefit of this choice is text files are easy to create and edit using any word processor. Text files also provide a high degree of interoperability between programs. For example, a program written in Python can easily use a text file created by a C++ program.

There are some widespread text file formats that are specially designed for file exchange between applications. Many applications support the *comma-separated-values (CSV)* format in which each line is composed of values separated by commas. Spreadsheet programs, such as Microsoft Office Excel, export and import worksheets as CSV files. Of course, CSV files can be also imported and exported by any word processing program, such as Notepad or Microsoft Office Word.

Because CSV files are common and easy to work with, they are used with the *Score Filer* program as well. The program inputs one CSV file and eventually outputs one CSV file. In the CSV files, each student record is represented in a single line, as a sequence of comma-separated values. As stated earlier in this topic, each student record in the input file has a last name, first name, and score. In addition, each record in the output file includes a letter grade.

Example

The following table outlines the contents of two sample CSV files. The left column outlines a CSV file input by the *Score Filer* program. The right column outlines the CSV file output by the program.

Input File	Output File
Zucchini,Xena,95	Kingsley,Bob,83,B
Pancake,Johnny,59	Pancake,Johnny,59,F
Kingsley,Bob,83	Zucchini,Xena,95,A

Exercise

A sample input file named *scores.csv* accompanies the *Score Filer* program. Use a word processor, such as Notepad, to open the *scores.csv* file. Observe the file format and content. Open the file in a spreadsheet program, such as Microsoft Office Excel, to open and observe the same file.

Exercise

Use a word processor, such as Notepad, to create a CSV file named *friends.csv* containing data for your friends such as first name, last name, nickname, favorite food, and phone number.

Use a spreadsheet program, such as Microsoft Office Excel, to open and observe the same file. Use the spreadsheet program to update the file by adding new records and modifying existing ones. Save the modified file.

Use a word processor, such as Notepad, to open the modified *friends.csv* file.

Exercise

Run the *Score Filer* program. In interactive mode, invoke the *scores* function. Enter *scores.csv* as input file name and *grades.csv* as output file name.

Example

An interaction with function *scores* may look like this:

```
>>> scores();
Enter name of file to read from: scores.csv
Enter name of file to write into: grades.csv
Students processed: 14
```

Exercise

Use a word processor, such as Notepad, to open the *grades.csv* file. Observe the file format and content.

Use a spreadsheet program, such as Microsoft Office Excel, to open and observe the same file.

How to Input Data from a File

Data that is input from a file can be converted into a list for further processing. Function *read* from the *Score Filer* program is designed to do exactly this: It inputs student records from a file and returns a list of records.

Example

Function *read* produces lists as the one shown below.

```
>>> listOfStudents = read(fileName='scores.csv');
>>> print listOfStudents;
[['Zucchini', 'Xena', '95'], ['Pancake', 'Johnny', '59'], ['Kingsley', 'Bob', '83']]
```

The complete definition of function *read* follows.

```
# Input student records from a file and return a list of records:
def read(fileName):
The following function is designed to input student records from a file and return a list of records
    listOfStudents = [ ];
    inFile = open(fileName, 'r');
```

```
    for line in inFile:
        # Strip unnecessary '\n' from right end:
        line = line.rstrip('\n');
        student = line.split(comma);
        # student = ['last-name', 'first-name', 'score']
        listOfStudents.append(student);
    inFile.close();
    return listOfStudents;
```

The following Python-to-English translation provides insight into Function *read*.

Python Statement	Common English Meaning
def read(fileName):	▫ Function *read* is defined with a *fileName* as a parameter.
listOfStudents = [];	▫ Initialize an empty *listOfStudents*.

inFile = open(fileName, 'r');	▫ Create a file object that represents, in the computer memory, an external file with the specified file name.
	  • The file object is a sequence of lines.
	  • Each line is a string terminated with the '\n' character.
	▫ The file object is created in *reading mode*, as specified by the 'r' parameter.
	  • Besides in *reading mode*, 'r', files can be created in *writing mode*, 'w', or in *appending mode*, 'a' (to be discussed later).

for line in inFile:
   ...
	▫ Process each *line* from the file object, as described bellow.
	  • Each *line* ends with a new line character, '\n'.

line = line.rstrip('\n');	▫ Remove the trailing new line character, '\n'.

student = line.split(',');	▫ Split each *line* into a *student* list of comma-separated items.
	  • Remember that each line represents one student record in CSV format.
	  • For example, line *'Zucchini,Xena,95'* will be split into list *['Zucchini', 'Xena', '95']*.

listOfStudents.append(student);	o Append the current student to the entire *listOfStudents*.
inFile.close();	o Once all lines from the file have been processed, close the file. This terminates the program's connection to the external file.
return listOfStudents;	o Return the *listOfStudsents* and end this invocation.

To better understand the file input function, recall that the *rstript* method returns a copy of a *string* with trailing characters removed.

Example

```
>>> line = 'Zucchini,Xena,95\n';
>>> line = line.rstrip('\n');> print line;
Zucchini,Xena,95
```

As already studied, the *split* method converts a *string* into a list of substrings determined by intervening occurrences of a *separator*.

Example

```
>>> string = 'Pancake,Johny,59';
>>> string;
'Pancake,Johny,59'
>>> separator = ',';
>>> list = string.split(separator); print list;
['Pancake', 'Johnny', '59']
```

How to Output Data into a File

Results produced by a program can be output into a file. Function *write* from the *Score Filer* program is designed to do exactly this. It accepts a list of student records as an argument and outputs them into a file.

Example

Function *write* can be invoked to save a list of student records into a file as shown below. Note that student records already contain letter grades.

```
>>> listOfStudents = [['Zucchini', 'Xena', '95', 'A'], ['Pancake', 'Johnny', '59', 'F'], ['Kingsley', 'Bob', '83', 'B']];
>>> save(listOfStudents, fileName = 'grades.csv');
```

The complete definition of the *write* function follows.

```
# Output a list of student records into a file:
def write(listOfStudents, fileName):
    outFile = open(fileName, 'w');
    for student in listOfStudents:
        string = ','.join(student);
        print >> outFile, string;
    outFile.close();
```

The following Python-to-English translation provides insight into Function *write*.

Python Statement	Common English Meaning
def write(listOfStudents, fileName):	○ Function *write* is defined with a *listOfStudents* and a *fileName* as parameters.
outFile = open(fileName, 'w');	○ Create a file object that represents an external file with the specified file name. ○ The file object is created in *writing mode*, as specified by the 'w' parameter.
for student in listOfStudents: ...	○ Process each *student* from the *listOfStudents*, as described bellow. • Each *student* record is represented as a dictionary object.
string = ','.join(student);	○ Use the *join* method to convert a *student* into a CSV string. • In this case, the *join* method concatenates all items of the *student* list with intervening occurrences of the comma. • This creates a student string in CSV format. • The *join* method can only be applied to lists of strings.
print >> outFile, string;	○ Output the current *student* string into o*utFile*. • Remember that the print statement automatically end a trailing new line character, '\n'.

outFile.close();	○ Once all *student* records have been processed, close the file. This terminates the program's connection to the external file.

Recall that the *join* method converts a *list* of strings into a single string by concatenating all items of the list with intervening occurrences of a *separator*.

Example

It is important to remember that the *join* method can work with lists of strings only. An attempt to concatenate a list that contains non-string items results in a run-time error.

```
>>> ## List of strings:
>>> student = ['Zucchini', 'Xena', '95', 'A'];
>>> print student;
['Zucchini', 'Xena', '95','A']
>>> comma = ',';
>>> string = comma.join(student); print string;
Zucchini,Xena,95,A
>>> # List of strings and integers:
>>> student = ['Pancake', 'Johnny', 100, 'A'];
>>> string = comma.join(student);
...
TypeError: sequence item 2: expected string, int found
```

How to Integrate Input, Sorting, Processing, and Output

The main function of the *Score Filer* program is named *scores*. This function reads all student records from a file, sorts all records, extends each student's record with a letter grade as determined by the student's score, then writes all extended records into a file. A complete implementation of the *scores* function follows.

```
# Input student records, add letter grades, and output records:
def scores():
    inFileName = raw_input('Enter name of file to read from: ');
    listOfStudents = read(inFileName);
    listOfStudents.sort();
```

```python
    for student in listOfStudents:
        # student == ['last-name', 'first-name', 'score']
        score = int(student[2]); # Convert score string into int score
        student.append(theGrade(score));
    outFileName = raw_input('Enter name of file to write into: ');
    write(listOfStudents, outFileName);
    print 'Students processed:', len(listOfStudents);

# Transform score into a letter grade:
def theGrade(score):
    if (score < 60):    grade = 'F';
    elif (score < 70):  grade = 'D';
    elif (score < 80):  grade = 'C';
    elif (score < 90):  grade = 'B';
    else:               grade = 'A';
    return grade;
```

How to Summarize File Records

The *Score Filer* program offers a function to summarize a file of student records. The *summary* function reads all student records from a file and calculates the average score. The function also tests each score to determine the lowest and the highest scores. At the end, the function displays the average, lowest, and highest scores.

Example

Function *summary* is invoked to summarize a file of student records.
```
>>> summary();
Enter name of file to read from: grades.csv
Students processed: 14
Average score: 84.0
Lowest score: 59
Highest score: 100
```

A complete implementation of the *summary* function follows.

```python
# Input student records from a file; determine and output
# min, max, and average scores:
def summary():
    inFileName = raw_input('Enter name of file to read from: ');
    listOfStudents = read(inFileName);
    counter = len(listOfStudents);
```

```
    print 'Students processed:', counter;
    if (counter > 0):
        total = 0;
        firstStudent = listOfStudents[0];
        firstScore = firstStudent[2];
        min = int(firstScore); max = int(firstScore);
        for student in listOfStudents:
            score = int(student[2]);
            total = total + score;
            if (score < min): min = score;
            if (max < score): max = score;
        print 'Average score:', round(total / float(counter));
        print 'Lowest score:', min;
        print 'Highest score:', max;
```

File Objects, Functions, and Methods

An *external file* is a collection of records stored on disk or in other media. An external file can be created by one program and later used by another program.

A *Python file* is an object that is connected to an external file. The connection between a file object and an external file is established when the file object is created.

In Python, a file object can be created by means of built-in functions, such as the *open* function. The following is a common pattern of use for the *open* function:

fileObject = open(externalFileName, fileMode);

External file names and file modes are passed to the *open* function as strings. The two principal file modes are the *reading mode*, abbreviated as 'r', and the *writing mode*, abbreviated as 'w'. A file that is open in reading mode can only be read from, and a file that is open in writing mode can only be written into. Note that opening a file in writing mode erases existing data in the corresponding external file. The *append mode*, 'a', allows appending data to an existing file without erasing it.

Example

```
>>> inFile = open('scores.csv', 'r');
>>> outFile = open('grades.csv', 'w');
```

A Python file object contains a sequence of lines. A line is a string that is normally terminated by a new line character, '\n'. All lines from a file that has been open in reading mode can be processed by a for-loop. An empty file contains no lines.

Example

```
>>> for line in inFile:
        print line;
```

When a for-loop needs to be repeated, the *seek* method has to be used to reset the file position to the beginning of the file.

Example

The following statements copy an input file into an output file. The current position of the input file is then reset to the beginning of the file for the file to be printed:

```
>>> for line in inFile:
        print >> outFile, line;
>>> inFile.seek(0);
>>> for line in inFile:
        print line;
```

A summary of principal file functions and methods is presented in the following table.

Functions and Methods	Description
open(*fileName*, 'r')	Create a file object in reading mode and connect it to the external file *fileName*.
open(*fileName*, 'w')	Create a file object in writing mode and connect it to the external file *fileName*.
file(*fileName, mode*)	Same as open(*fileName, mode*).
file.read()	Return entire *file* as a single string.
file.readline()	Return next line, as a string, from *file*.
file.readlines()	Return entire *file* as a list of line strings.

file.seek(*position*)	Set the *file*'s current *position*.
file.write(*string*)	Write *string* into *file*.
print >> file, string	Same as *file*.write(*string* + '\n')
file.close()	If the *file* is in writing mode, save it before that. Terminate the connection to the external file.

Sample File Functions

The *File Functions* sample program offers a couple of file-processing functions. Analyze, experiment with and use these sample functions. Your independent work with sample file functions will help you master your knowledge and ability to program successfully using files.

Brief descriptions of sample file-processing functions follow.

Function *fileCopy* creates a copy of a text file:

```
def fileCopy(sourceName, targetName):
    inFile = open(sourceName, 'r');
    localData = inFile.read();
    outFile = open(targetName, 'w');
    print >> outFile, localData;
    inFile.close(); outFile.close();
```

Example
Function *fileCopy* creates a copy of a file of scores in CSV format and a copy of any Python source program:

```
>>> fileCopy(sourceName = 'scores.csv', targetName = 'scoresCopy.csv');
>>> fileCopy(sourceName = 'FileFunctions.py', targetName = 'CopyOfFileFunctions.py');
```

Function *countChars* counts the number of occurrences of each character in a text file:

```
def countChars(fileName):
    inFile = open(fileName, 'r');
    text = inFile.read();
    count = {}
```

```
    for char in text:
        char = char.upper();
        if (char not in count.keys()): count[char] = 1;
        else: count[char] = count[char] + 1;
    return count;
```

Example

Function *countChars* can count the characters in any Python source program, such as the program that contains the function itself:

```
>>> countChars(fileName = 'FileFunctions.py');
{'\n': 20, ' ': 132, '#': 3, '"': 6, ')': 12, '(': 12, '+': 1, '-': 1, ',': 6, '.': 7, '1': 2, '0': 2, '2': 1, '5': 1, '4': 1, ';': 12, ':': 7, '=': 9, '>': 2, 'A': 36, 'C': 33, 'B': 2, 'E': 53, 'D': 7, 'G': 3, 'F': 22, 'I': 27, 'H': 11, 'K': 2, 'M': 8, 'L': 22, 'O': 30, 'N': 35, 'P': 10, 'S': 14, 'R': 29, 'U': 18, 'T': 33, 'W': 1, 'Y': 4, 'X': 4, '[': 3, ']': 3, '{': 1, '}': 1}
```

Working with Directories

The *operating system* module, in short the *os*, offers a variety of functions to provide interface to the operating system where Python is running.

The *os* module is not standardized, and some of its functions differ in Windows, Unix, and Macintosh. Complete descriptions of all available *os* functions are found in the Python's online documentation.

In this course, we limit the use of the *os* module to a few useful functions that allow you to work with folders (in Windows and Macintosh) and directories (in Unix). Note that Python uses the term *directory* synonymously with the term *folder*. The following table introduces basic folder-related functions.

Function	Purpose
getcwd()	Return a string representing the current working directory (folder).
listdir(*path*)	Return a list containing the names of the entries in the directory (folder) specified by *path*.
chdir(*path*)	Change the current working directory (folder) to *path*.

Example
These statements provide the pathname of the current working directory (folder):
```
>>> import os;
>>> cwd = os.getcwd();
>>> print cwd;
C:\Python24
```

Example
These statements provide a listing of all files in the current working directory (folder):
```
>>> cwd = os.getcwd();
>>> fileList = os.listdir(cwd);
>>> print fileList;
...
```

Example
These statements change the current working directory (folder):
```
>>> myPrograms = 'A:\\Labs\\ 07\\Scores ';
>>> os.chdir(myPrograms);
>>> print os.getcwd();
A:\Labs\07\Scores
```

Mutable and Immutable Sequences

A *sequence* is an ordered set of items indexed by non-negative numbers. Item i of sequence s is denoted by a *sequence subscription*, $s[i]$. Sequences also support slicing: $s[i:k]$ is a copy of all items of s with index j such that $i <= j < k$. Sequence subscriptions and slices can be used in expressions; this includes using them as arguments in function invocations.

Lists are called *mutable sequences* because list items may be changed after lists are created. Subscriptions and slices may be used as targets in assignment and delete statements.

Example

```
>>> lst = ['Zucchini', 'Xena', '95'];
>>> lst[2] = '100'; print lst;
['Zucchini', ' Xena', '100']
```

Strings and tuples are called *immutable sequences* because their items cannot be changed. String and tuple subscriptions cannot be used as targets in assignment and delete statements. (String and tuple subscriptions may still be used in expressions.)

Example

```
>>> string = 'ananas';
>>> string[0] = 'A';
...
TypeError: object doesn't support item assignment
>>>
```

When a string method is intended to change a string, the method actually produces a changed copy of the original string without changing the original string.

Example

```
>>> string = 'ananas';
>>> word = string.replace('ana', 'bana');
>>> print string, word;
ananas bananas
```

Sample Program: Hangman

Hangman is a game in which one player chooses a secret word and the other player tries to guess the word by supplying one or more letters at a time. The number of guesses is limited.

Consider the following programming problem: Develop a program to act as the first player in a game of hangman, with the user taking the part of the second player (the one who tries to guess). A solution to this problem is offered with the *Hangman* sample program.

The *Hangman* program inputs a file of words and randomly chooses one of those words, which the program keeps secret. The user is repeatedly invited to guess one or more consecutive letters from the secret word. The result of each guess is communicated to the user. This is repeated until either the user guesses the entire secret word, or the user reaches a predefined number of allowed attempts.

The *Hangman* sample program is accompanied by a small sample file of possible secret words. The sample file that comes with the program contains student names. You can replace the contents of this file with any words you prefer.

Example

A possible interaction of the Hangman program may look like this:

```
>>> play();
```
This program plays the game of Hangman.
You are to guess a secret word by typing one or more adjacent letters.
You can make at most 8 attempts.

(1):	_ _ _ _	Your guess: **A**
(2):	_ _ _ _	Your guess: **O**
(3):	_ _ _ _	Your guess: **E**
(4):	_ _ _ _	Your guess: **U**
(5):	_ U _ _	Your guess: **S**
(6):	_ U _ S	Your guess: **LUIS**
(6):	L U I S	You won!

Play more? [Yes/No]: Yes

(1):	_ _ _ _ _ _	Your guess: **E**
(2):	E _ _ _ _ _	Your guess: **I**
(3):	E _ _ I _ _	Your guess: **U**
(4):	E _ _ I _ _	Your guess: **A**
(5):	E _ _ I _ _	Your guess: **Y**
(6):	E _ _ I _ _	Your guess: **C**
(7):	E _ _ I _ _	Your guess: **B**
(8):	E _ _ I _ _	Your guess: **M**
(8):	E _ _ I _ _	You lost. It is ELLIOT.

Play more? [Yes/No]: **No**
So long...

Exercise

Run the *Hangman* sample program, invoke the *play* function, and play a few games.

In the Hangman program, the *secret word* and the user *guess* are strings of characters. In the course of the game, the program must keep track of all letters the user has guessed. The program uses a special list that represents all characters of the word. In this list, all characters that have not been guessed so far are represented by underscore, '_'.

Example

>   secretWord = 'LUIS'; lettersGuessedSoFar = ['_', '_', '_', '_'];

When the user makes a correct guess, the list of letters guessed so far is adequately updated.

Example

>   secretWord = 'LUIS';
>   guess = 'U'; lettersGuessedSoFar = ['_', 'U', '_', '_'];
>   guess = 'S'; lettersGuessedSoFar = ['_', 'U', '_', 'S'];

If the list of letters guessed so far contains zero underscores, the user wins.

Example

```
if (lettersGuessedSoFar.count('_') == 0):
    print 'You won!';
```

The main function in the *Hangman* program is named *play*. This function displays the rules then plays individual games for as long as the user wishes. The implementation of the *play* function follows.

```
# Repeatedly play the game of Hangman:
def play():
    maxAllowedAttempts = 8;
    print rulesDisplay(maxAllowedAttempts);
    listOfWords = inputListOfWords('words.txt');
    while (True):
        playOneGame(maxAllowedAttempts, listOfWords);
        ans = inputYesNo('\nPlay more? [Yes/No]: ');
        if(ans.lower() == 'no'): break;
    print 'So long...';
```

```
# Return the rules for the Hangman game:
def rulesDisplay(maxAllowedAttempts):
    return \
        'This program plays the game of Hangman.\n' + \
        'You are to guess a secret word by typing one or more adjacent letters.\n' + \
        'You can make at most ' + str(maxAllowedAttempts) + ' attempts.\n';
```

The *inputListOfWords* function provides to *play* function with a list of possible secret words. The implementation of the *inputListOfWords* function follows.

```
# Input words from file and return a list of all words:
def inputListOfWords(fileName):
    inFile = open(fileName, 'r');
    listOfWords = [];
    for line in inFile:
        # Strip unnecessary '\n' from right end:
        line = line.rstrip('\n');
        if (len(line) > 0 and line.isalpha()):
            listOfWords.append(line);
    inFile.close();
    return listOfWords;
```

The *inputYesNo* function is designed to provide a valid Yes/No response for the *play* function. It converts the user response to lowercase and then compares it to 'yes' and 'no'. In this way, the case of the user response does not matter. The implementation of the *inputYesNo* function follows.

```
# Input valid answer for a Yes/No question while ignoring case:
def inputYesNo(prompt):
    response = raw_input(prompt);
    while (response.lower() != 'yes' and response.lower() != 'no'):
        print 'Invalid response: ', response;
        response = raw_input(prompt);
    return response;
```

Example

```
>>> response = 'YEs'; print response.lower();
Yes
>>> response.lower() == 'yes';
True
```

When the user makes a guess, the program must check if the guess belongs to the secret word, and if so, properly update the list of guessed letters. This is implemented by a function named *update*. The implementation of the *update* function follows.

```
# Update the letters guessed so far with the current guess:
def update(lettersGuessedSoFar, guess, secretWord):
    position = secretWord.find(guess);
    while (position >=0):
        for char in guess:
            lettersGuessedSoFar[position] = char;
            position = position + 1;
        position = secretWord.find(guess, position);
```

Example

```
>>> secretWord = 'ANANAS';
>>> lettersGuessedSoFar = ['_', '_', '_', '_', '_', 'S'];
>>> guess = 'A';
>>> update(lettersGuessedSoFar, guess, secretWord);
>>> lettersGuessedSoFar;
['A', '_', 'A', '_', 'A', 'S']
```

A single game is played by a function named *playOneGame*. This function uses three helper functions. First, function *chooseSecretWord* selects a random word from a list of words and returns it in uppercase. Second, function *inputGuess* inputs the player's guess and returns it in uppercase. Third, function *gameDisplay* returns a string that includes the current attempt number and all letters guessed so far. The implementation of function *playOneGame* and the three helper functions follows.

```
# Play a single game of Hangman:
def playOneGame(maxAllowedAttempts, listOfWords):
    secretWord = chooseSecretWord(listOfWords);
    attempt = 1;
    unknownLetter = '_';
    lettersGuessedSoFar = len(secretWord) * [unknownLetter];
    for attempt in range(1, maxAllowedAttempts + 1):
        display = gameDisplay(attempt, lettersGuessedSoFar);
        guess = inputGuess(display);
        update(lettersGuessedSoFar, guess, secretWord);
        if (lettersGuessedSoFar.count(unknownLetter) == 0):
            print gameDisplay(attempt, lettersGuessedSoFar) + \
                '\tYou won!'; return;
    print gameDisplay(attempt, lettersGuessedSoFar) + \
        '\tYou lost. It is ' + secretWord + '.';

# Select a random word from a list of words
# and return it in uppercase:
def chooseSecretWord(listOfWords):
    secretWord = random.choice(listOfWords);
    return secretWord.upper();
# Input player's guess and return it in uppercase:
def inputGuess(display):
    guess = raw_input(display + '\tYour guess: ');
    return guess.upper();

# Return, as a string, the current attempt number
# and letters guessed so far:
def gameDisplay(attempt, lettersGuessedSoFar):
    space = ' ';
    string = '('+str(attempt)+')' + \
        ':\t' + space.join(lettersGuessedSoFar);
    return string;
```

Web Resources and URLs

The Web is a network of *host* computers that provides various *resources*, such as web pages, video files, and audio files. A web page can be a static file residing permanently on the web host, but usually a web page is a file dynamically generated by the host upon user request. All data that must be included in a dynamically generated web page is extracted from a database.

Exercise

Access a search host, such as www.google.com or www.yahoo.com, to search and locate a web host that provides weather information. The web page you are going to find in response to your search request will be dynamically generated by the search host. Current data in this dynamic web page will be extracted from the search host databases.

Access a weather information host to find the current weather forecast for your current location. The web page that you are going to receive in response to your weather forecast request will be dynamically generated by the weather host. Current data in this dynamic web page will be extracted from the weather host databases.

A *transfer protocol* is a set of rules that governs the access to resources on the Web. The Hyper-Text Transfer Protocol (HTTP) is the most common protocol used on the Web. The File Transfer Protocol (FTP) is used for file downloads, while Telnet protocol is used to connect to your account in a remote computer.

Any web resource is identified by means of a *Universal Resource Locator* (URL).

A URL is a character string that typically consists of the following parts:
- The *transfer protocol* used when accessing the resource (typically http)
- The *name of the web host* providing the resource
- A *pathname* that specifies the location of the resource on the web host
- A *query* that tells the web host what exactly you want included in the provided resource

A typical web resource URL has the form:

> http://host-name/path-name?query

The URL section preceding the query is called the URL *location*.

Exercise

Use a browser to connect to the website of this course and open the course's main page. Observe the URL in the browser's address toolbar. Identify which of the following parts are present in the URL:

transfer protocol, host name, path name, and query. Identify the location section of the URL. Open the E-Text for this topic and observe its URL in the same way.

Web Resource Input

In Python, input of files or other resources provided by remote hosts is as easy as input of files located on your computer. In either case, a Python program *opens* a file object then uses some file method, such as *read*, to obtain the data from the file object.

Recall the *open* function which is used to create a file object connected to a local external file. The *open* function expects the file name as a parameter. The *read* method returns a string that contains all data from the file.

Example

These statements create a copy of a local file:

```
>>> inFile = open('scores.csv', 'r');
>>> localData = inFile.read();
>>> outFile = open('scoresCopy.csv', 'w');
>>> print >> outFile, localData;
>>> inFile.close(); outFile.close();
```

The saved *scoresCopy.csv* file can be open and checked with a word processor or spreadsheet program.

A Python program can *open* a web resource as a file and use standard file methods, such as *read*, to obtain the data from the file object. A URL library module, *urllib,* offers a function named *urlopen* that is used to create a file object connected to a web resource. The *urlopen* function expects a URL string as a parameter.

Example

These statements download a web resource and save a copy as a local file:

```
>>> import urllib;
>>> inFile = urllib.urlopen('http://www.yahoo.com');
>>> webData = inFile.read();
>>> outFile = open('webData.html', 'w');
>>> print >> outFile, webData;
>>> inFile.close(); outFile.close();
```

The locally saved *webData.html* file is opened and checked using a web browser. Note the saved resource may contain links to other resources, such as image files. Such linked resources are not saved automatically by the above statements and are not displayed when you open the saved file with a browser.

Sample Programming Problem: Tracking Stocks

Sample Problem Summary

Consider the following problem: design a program to download real-time stock data from the Web. Some basic stock-related concepts are needed to discuss the above problem and its solution in concrete technical terms. Such concepts are introduced in the following section.

Stocks-Related Concepts

An *investor* is someone who commits capital to gain financial return. For example, some investors buy real estate in hopes of selling it at a higher price. Others invest money in long term certificates of deposit that give a guaranteed yield.

A substantial group of investors buy *shares* of ownership in publicly traded companies. Their expectation is that the company's assets and earnings will increase, thus increasing the value of the owned shares.

Stock is the general term for an ownership investment in a corporation, represented by shares that are a claim on the company's assets and earnings. Common stocks give investors voting rights in the company, entitling them to vote on the election of directors and other issues.

Trade is a transaction involving one party buying stock or other investments from another party. A *stock exchange* is an institution where stocks are traded. The three major stock exchanges in the USA are the New York Stock Exchange, the NASDAQ, and the American Stock Exchange. Stock exchanges are also called stock markets.

Stock symbol is an abbreviated stock name that is used to uniquely identify the stock in any trade.

Example
- YHOO is the symbol for the stock of the company named Yahoo! Inc.
- GOOG is the symbol for the company named Google Inc.
- MSFT is the symbol for the company named Microsoft Corp.

> Exercise
>
> Symbol lookup is available at finance.yahoo.com/. Retrieve the symbol of two or more companies of your choice.

A *trader* is an investor who buys and sells stocks and other investments to take advantage of small price changes within a short period of time--sometimes days or hours. A *trader* may also be an employee of a financial firm who buys and sells securities for the firm's accounts or clients.

Stock quote is the price at which the last trade of a particular stock took place. It is important for traders to track *stock quotes* in real time, as trades occur, and to plan their trades accordingly.

Stocks are traded in real time, over computer networks, therefore stock quotes must be known in real time, as trades occur. Many web hosts offer free or paid stock quotes in real time or with a small delay.

As of the writing of this text, free stock quotes are available, with a delay of about 15-20 minutes, at finance.yahoo.com/. The stock quotes are dynamically generated resource that is represented in CSV format.

> Exercise
>
> Retrieve quotes for two or more stock symbols on your choice. Find the last trade price. Observe the trade time, compare it to the actual time when the quote was provided, and determine the quote delay.

Real-time stock tracking is vital for traders who want to make profit by frequently buying and selling stock as stock price fluctuate.

Sample Program: Stock Tracker

A sample program named *Stock Tracker* downloads and displays stock quotes from the Web. The program uses stock-related resources freely available at finance.yahoo.com/.

For a particular stock symbol, the *Stock Tracker* program performs several functions, as specified below.
- Stock *checkup*: downloads and displays a stock quote.
- Investment *evaluation*: given a number of shares, calculates the current value of investment.

- Stock *watch*: repeatedly downloads and displays stock quotes within specified time intervals.

The *Stock Tracker* program has main and helper functions. All functions are described in the following two sections.

Main Functions

Functions *checkup, evaluate,* and *watch* are the main functions in the program. These functions provide stock quotes, investment evaluation, and stock tracking.

The *checkup* function downloads and displays a stock quote. The *checkup* function takes a stock *symbol* as an argument. The function then downloads and displays a stock quote for that symbol.

Example

An interaction with function *checkup* may look like this:

```
>>> checkup(symbol = 'YHOO');
{Symbol: YHOO, Volume: 6905353, Time: 1:25pm, Date: 11/4/2005, Open: 37.60, Price: 37.65}
```

The above quote shows the last price for the YHOO stock was recorded at $37.65. The first trade for the day, at the opening of the market, was at $37.60. The YHOO stock has gained value over the course of the day. The trading volume from the market opening and until the quoted last trade has amounted to 6,905,353 shares.

Exercise

Run the *Stock Tracker* program. In interactive mode, invoke the *checkup* function using your preferred symbol.

The *evaluate* function calculates the value of an investment of a given number of shares. The *evaluate* function expects, as arguments, a stock *symbol* and a number of *shares*. The function then downloads the current stock price for that symbol and calculates the current value of all shares in the investment.

Example

An interaction with function *evaluate* may look like this:

>>> evaluate(symbol = 'YHOO', shares = 50);
{Symbol: YHOO, Shares: 50, Value: 1891.0, Time: 2:27pm, Date: 11/4/2005, Price: 37.82}

The above evaluation shows that the value of 50 shares of the YHOO stock is $1891.00.

Exercise

In interactive mode, invoke the *evaluate* function using your preferred symbol and with some sample numbers of shares.

The *watch* function repeatedly downloads and displays stock quotes within specified time intervals. The *watch* function expects as arguments a stock *symbol*, a number of seconds between consecutive stock checks, and a total number of *checks*. The function then downloads the current stock price for that symbol and calculates the current value of all shares in the investment.

Example

An interaction with function *watch* may look like this:

>>> watch(symbol = 'YHOO', seconds = 30, checks = 6);
{Date: 11/4/2005, Symbol: YHOO, Open: 37.60, Price: 37.85, Time: 2:30pm}
{Price: 37.84, Change: -0.01, Time: 2:31pm}
{Price: 37.82, Change: -0.03, Time: 2:32pm}
{Price: 37.82, Change: -0.03, Time: 2:32pm}
{Price: 37.82, Change: -0.03, Time: 2:33pm}
{Price: 37.81, Change: -0.04, Time: 2:33pm}
First price: 37.85 Most recent price: 37.81

The above execution performs 6 consecutive checks of the YHOO stock with 30 second intervals between checks. Subsequent checks display the change of the current price from the price obtained at the first check.

Exercise

In interactive mode, invoke the *watch* function with your preferred symbol, waiting time between checks in seconds, and number of checks. Remember, stock prices only change when the stock market is open.

All of the above functions, *checkup, evaluate,* and *watch*, rely on a helper function named *getStock*. The *getStock* function expects a symbol and a list of keywords to determine exactly what data needs to be downloaded for the stock quote. The *getStock* function returns a quote as a dictionary, combining keywords with corresponding downloaded values. The list of all possible keywords supported by the *Stock Tracker* program is ['Symbol', 'Price', 'Open', 'Date', 'Time', 'Volume'].

Example

An interaction with function *getStock* may look like this:

```
getStock(symbol = 'YHOO', keywords = ['Symbol', 'Price', 'Date', 'Time']);
{'Date': '11/4/2005', 'Symbol': 'YHOO', 'Price': '37.78', 'Time': '3:05pm'}
```

Exercise

In interactive mode, invoke the *getStock* function with your preferred symbol and keyword list.

The implementations of the *checkup* and *evaluate* functions follow.

```
# Stock checkup - Download and display a stock quote:
def checkup(symbol):
    keywords = ['Symbol', 'Price', 'Open', 'Date', 'Time', 'Volume'];
    stock = getStock(symbol, keywords);
    display(stock);

# Display stock quote from a dictionary:
def display(stock):
    string = str(stock);
    # Strip single quotes from output:
    singleQuote = "'"; emptyString = '';
    text = string.replace(singleQuote, emptyString);
    print text;
```

```
# Evaluate investment - Download a quote and evaluate shares:
def evaluate(symbol, shares):
    keywords = ['Symbol', 'Price', 'Date', 'Time'];
    stock = getStock(symbol, keywords);
    price = float(stock['Price']);
    value = shares * price;
    investment = stock.copy();
    investment['Value'] = fpToString(value, 2);
    investment['Shares'] = str(shares);
    display(investment);
```

Recall that function *watch* repeatedly downloads and displays stock quotes within specified time intervals. For example, the invocation *watch(symbol = 'YHOO', seconds = 30, checks = 6)* performs six consecutive check and waits for 30 seconds between each check. In the *watch* function, waiting is implemented by means of the *sleep* function provided by module *time*. An invocation *time.sleep(seconds)* suspends the execution of the invoking program for the specified amount of seconds.

Exercise

In interactive mode, experiment with function *sleep*. First import module *time,* then invoke the *sleep* function with your preferred wait time. For example:

```
>>> import time;
>>> time.sleep(2.5);
```

The implementation of the *watch* function follows below.

```
def watch(symbol, seconds, checks):
    stock = getStock(symbol,
            keywords = ['Symbol', 'Price', 'Date', 'Time', 'Open']);
    display(stock);
    firstPrice = currentPrice = float(stock['Price']);
    for check in range(checks - 1):
        time.sleep(seconds);
        stock = getStock(symbol, keywords = ['Time', 'Price']);
        currentPrice = float(stock['Price']);
        change = currentPrice - firstPrice;
        stock['Change'] = fpToString(change, 2);
```

```
            display(stock);
    print 'First price:', firstPrice, 'Most recent price:', currentPrice;
```

Helper Functions

The *Stock Tracker* sample program consists of a number of functions. The main functions of the program, *checkup, evaluate,* and *watch*, are discussed in the previous section. The main functions are implemented by means of various helper functions. A summary of all functions is presented in the following table.

Function	Provides	Employs
checkup	Stock quotes	*getStock*
evaluate	Investment evaluation	*getStock*
watch	Stock tracking	*getStock*
getStock	Stock quote as a dictionary	*getList*
getList	Stock quote as a list	*getText*
getText	Stock quote as a CSV string	URL
URL	URL for stock quote	query, location
query	Query part of URL	format
format	Keywords to query translation	
location	Location part of URL	

The *Stock Tracker* sample program relies on stock-related resources freely available at the finance.yahoo.com/ host. The site requires cryptic abbreviations to specify what data is to be included in any stock resource. In the *Stock Tracker* program, cryptic queries are conveniently constructed by the *query* function. The query function uses a *format* helper function which transforms readable keywords into the correct abbreviations required by the host, finance.yahoo.com/. The implementations of functions *query* and *format* follow bellow.

```
# Form a query for specific data on a selected symbol:
def query(symbol, keywords):
    return 's=' + symbol + '&' + format(keywords) + '&e=.csv';
    # Example: 's=YAHOO&f=sl1d1t1o&e=.csv';

# Format a list of keywords into an abbreviated query:
def format(keywords):
    abbreviation = {
```

```
    'Symbol' : 's', 'Price' : 'l1', 'Open' : 'o',
    'Date' : 'd1', 'Time' : 't1', 'Volume' : 'v'
};
format = 'f='
for keyword in keywords:
    format = format + abbreviation[keyword];
return format;
# Example:
#   keywords = ['symbol', 'price', 'date', 'time', 'open'];
#   format(keywords) = 'f=sl1d1t1o&e=.csv';
```

Exercise

In interactive mode, invoke functions *query* and *format*. Supply stock symbols and lists of keywords of your choice. Observe the results.

Recall that a typical web resource URL has the form *http://hostname/path-name?query*. Also, recall that the entire URL section preceding the query is called the URL *location*. The *URL* function follows this pattern to build a URL for a stock quote by invoking two helper functions, *location* and *query*, and concatenating their results in a complete stock URL. The implementations of functions *URL* and *location* follow below. The *query* function is discussed later in this section.

```
# Form a URL for financial data:
def URL(symbol, keywords):
    url = location() + '?' + query(symbol, keywords);
    return url;
    # Example:
    #    http://finance.yahoo.com/d/quotes.csv?
    #       s=YHOO&f=sl1d1t1o&e=.csv';
# Return a yahoo location for financial data:
def location():
    return 'http://finance.yahoo.com/d/quotes.csv';
    # location = protocol + '://' + site + path;
    # protocol = 'http';
    # site = 'finance.yahoo.com';
    # path = '/d/quotes.csv';
```

Exercise

In interactive mode, invoke functions *location* and *URL*. Supply stock symbols and lists of keywords of your choice to function *URL*; the *location* function does not require an argument. Observe the results.

It has already been said that the *getText* helper function provides a stock quote as a string of comma-separated values. The implementation of function *getText* is below.

```
# Download a stock quote as a string:
def getText(symbol, keywords):
   url = URL(symbol, keywords);
   webData = urllib.urlopen(url);
   text = webData.read();
   # Example: "YHOO',36.47,'10/28/2004','2:26pm',35.83\r\n';
   webData.close();
   # Strip unnecessary characters:
   for char in ['\n', '\r', "'", '"']:
      text = text.replace(char, '');
   return text;
   # Example: 'YHOO,36.47,10/28/2004,2:26pm,35.83';
```

Exercise

In interactive mode, invoke function *getText*. Supply stock symbols and lists of keywords of your choice. Observe the results.

The *getStock* helper function provides a stock quote represented as a dictionary. The *getStock* function uses a function *getList* that provides a stock quote as a list. The implementations of functions *getStock* and *getList are* below.

```
# Download a stock quote as a dictionary:
def getStock(symbol, keywords):
   values = getList(symbol, keywords);
   dictionary = {};
   for keyword, value in zip(keywords, values):
      dictionary[keyword] = value;
   # You can also use: dictionary = dict(zip(keywords, list));
   return dictionary;
```

```
# Download a stock quote as a list:
def getList(symbol, keywords):
    text = getText(symbol, keywords);
    list = text.split(',');
    return list;
    # Example: ['YHOO','36.49','10/28/2004','2:28pm','35.83'];
```

Exercise

In interactive mode, invoke functions *getStock* and *getList*. Supply stock symbols and lists of keywords of your choice. Observe the results.

The *getStock* function is the backbone of the *Stock Tracker* sample program. Functions *checkup, evaluate* and *watch* provide a convenient interface for users. A number of helper functions implement various supplemental tasks, such as URL formation and stock quote download in CSV format.

Direct Data Input

It is possible to construct valid Python expressions on the fly in a running program, and to dynamically evaluate such expressions. This process is supported by a special built in function named *eval*. In a typical usage pattern, the *eval* function takes one string argument – a presumably valid Python expression. The function then interprets the string as a Python expression and returns its value.

Example

```
>>> # String assignment:
>>> E = '10 + 20';
>>> E
'10 + 20'
>>> # Evaluation of an expression represented as string:
>>> eval(E)
30
>>> 10 * eval(E)
300
>>> # String concatenation:
>>> '(' + E + ') * 100'
'(10 + 20) * 100'
```

```
>>> # Construction and evaluation of an expression:
>>> eval('(' + E + ') * 100')
3000
```

The *eval* function can evaluate any type of expression, including complex expressions that contain lists and dictionaries.

Example

```
>>> P = '[10 * 20, ';
>>> Q = '[300, 400';
>>> R = ']]';
>>> P + Q + R;
'[10 * 20, [300, 400]]'
>>> eval (P + Q + R)
[200, [300, 400]]
```

Strings submitted for evaluation may be input from an external file.

Example

Consider two data files named DataFile1.txt and DataFile2.txt. The files contain these lines:

DataFile1.txt	DataFile2.txt
(10 +	[10 * 20,
20	[300, 400
) * 10	]]

A program can input either of the files as strings and evaluate them, converting those files into non-string values:

```
>>> inFile = open('DataFile1.txt', 'r');
>>> string = inFile.read(); inFile.close();
>>> string
'(10 +\n 20\n ) * 10\n'
>>> value = eval(string1);
>>> value
300
>>> inFile = open('DataFile2.txt', 'r');
>>> string = inFile.read(); inFile.close();
```

```
>>> string
'[10 * 20, \n[300, 400\n]]\n'
>>> value = eval(string);
>>> value
[200, [300, 400]]
```

In a general setup, let us assume that some data file contains a valid *list* of data: $[i_0, i_1, ...i_{n-1}]$. A Python program can directly input an arbitrary valid Python *list* by means of the following statements:

inFile = open('DataFile.txt', 'r');
string = inFile.read(); inFile.close();
list = eval(string);
... process list ...

The *Quiz Handler* sample program uses direct data input, as outlined by the above pattern, to input an arbitrary quiz from an external file. The program then administers the quiz. A quiz file contains a list of quiz questions where each question is represented as a dictionary.

Exercise

Open the *Quiz1.py* and *Quiz2.py* files that accompany the *Quiz Handler* sample program and observe their contents.

Exercise

Run the *Quiz Handler* program.

Invoke function *handleQuiz,* supply *Quiz1.py* as a quiz file and answer quiz questions.

Invoke function *handleQuiz* again, supply *Quiz2.py* as a quiz file, and answer quiz questions.

Synonyms

Some terms that have been introduced in this topic have synonyms. A list of such terms and their corresponding synonyms follows.

Term	Synonym
File in reading mode	Input file
File in writing mode	Output file
Folder	Directory
Web host	Web server

Lab A [Strings, Files, and the Web]

Objective; Background; Lab Overview; Downloading Sample Programs; Uncompressing Sample Programs; Interactive Experiments with Strings; Saving Your Interactive Session

Objectives
- The objective of this lab is to study and interactively experiment with:
  - Built-in string operations, functions, and methods.
  - Sample string-processing functions.

Background
- A number of built-in string operations, functions, and methods are described in the E-text and Slides.
- The following string-processing functions are incorporated in the *String Functions* sample program:
  - Function *alphabet* generates a string with all the letters from the English alphabet.
  - Function *scramble* generates a randomly scrambled version of a string.
  - Function *fpToString* converts a floating point value to a string with specified decimal positions.
  - Function *palindrome* checks if a string is a palindrome.
  - Functions *encode* and *decode* use simple ciphers to encode and decode arbitrary text messages.
- Your task is to study string-processing sample functions and perform interactive experiments as specified in the Interactive Experiments section below.

Lab Overview
To perform this lab:
- Study built-in string operations, functions, and methods from the E-text or Slides concerning Strings.
- Perform interactive experiments as specified in the Interactive Experiments section.
- Study the *String Functions* sample program from the E-text or Slides.

- Perform interactive experiments as specified in Interactive Experiments section with Strings.
- Save your IDLE interactive session in a text file.

Downloading Sample Programs

Various Lab Assignments for this course of study are based on ready-to-use sample programs. Such programs are downloadable from the online study pack. Save these files into your *master* folder.

Download sample programs for the current Topic 7 by performing these steps:
- Locate *Topic 7* in the online study pack.
- Open the *Lab Assignment* resource.
- Right-click on the *Sample Programs* link.
- Use *Save As* to store the downloaded compressed (zipped) folder, *07.zip*, within your *master* folder.

Uncompressing Sample Programs

- Uncompress the contents of the downloaded compressed (zipped) folder. Depending on your platform, you may use built-in compression support, or compressing utilities.
  - In Windows XP, use built-in un-compression support as follows:
    - Open your *master* folder using the *File Browser*.
    - Right-click on the downloaded compressed (zipped) folder.
    - Use *Extract All* to extract the contents of the compressed (zipped) folder within the *master* folder.
      - This will create an uncompressed folder, *07*, within the *master* folder. This folder contains your sample programs.
    - Alternatively, you can:
      - *Open* the compressed (zipped) folder.
      - *Cut* folder *07* from within the compressed (zipped) folder, and
      - *Paste* the cut folder *07* outside the compressed (zipped) folder – directly within the *master* folder.
- Delete the compressed (zipped) folder, *07.zip*; keep the uncompressed folder, *07*.
- Open the uncompressed folder *07* and browse its contents.
- Note that Python program files have extension '**.py**'.

Interactive Experiments with Strings

Start IDLE. At the interactive prompt, type all expressions and statements listed below. Also experiment with your own expressions and statements. Observe and analyze the results.

Exploration of built-in string operations and functions

```
>>> print 'A string with a "quote" inside';

>>> a = "-100";
>>> b = "-3.1415";
>>> c = int(a) * float(b);
>>> print c;

>>> print a + '\t\t' + b;
>>> print 'C:\\';
>>> path = 'C:\\Python24';
>>> print path;

>>> print len('Lemon');
>>> print len('');
>>> print len('\t\t');

>>> characterList = list('Lemon');
>>> print characterList;

>>> path = 'C:\\Python24';
>>> print path[0], path[1], path[2], path[3], path[4];
>>> print path[-2], path[-1];
>>> print len(path);
>>> print path[11];

>>> 'Py' in path, 'Py' not in path
>>> 'pY' in path

>>> drive = path[0:3];
>>> print drive;
```

Exploration of built-in string methods

```
>>> string = 'Banana';
>>> string.upper(), string.lower()
>>> string.count('a')
```

```
>>> 'Banana'.upper().count('A')
>>> 'Banana'.upper(), 'Banana'.lower()
>>> string[1:4].upper()
>>> ('Ban' + 'ana').upper().count('NA')

>>> for ch in string: print ch.upper();

>>> '123'.isdigit()
>>> 'digit'.isdigit()
>>> '3.14'.isdigit()
>>> 'Lemon'.isalpha(), 'Python24'.isalpha()
>>> 'Python24'.isalnum()
>>> 'C:\\Python24'.isalnum()

>>> 'ananas'.count('a');
>>> 'ananas'.count('an');
>>> 'ananas'.count('ana');

>>> # Find the index of the first 'na' in 'ananas':
>>> first = 'ananas'.find('na');
>>> print first;
>>> # Search for 'na' in 'ananas' past the first 'na':
>>> second = 'ananas'.find('na', first+1);
>>> print second;
>>> # Search for 'na' in 'ananas' past the second 'na':
>>> third = 'ananas'.find('na', second+1);
>>> print third;

>>> response = 'Yes';
>>> response.upper(), response.lower()
>>> response.lower() in ['yes','y']
>>> 'Yes'.lower() in ('yes','y')

>>> 'ananas'.replace('ana', 'bana');

>>> 'ananas'.lstrip('a');
>>> 'ananas'.lstrip('an');
>>> # Repeatedly left-strip any character of 'na' from 'ananas':
>>> 'ananas'.lstrip('nas');
>>> 'ananas\n'.rstrip('\n');
>>> 'C:\\Python24'.lstrip('C:\\');

>>> string = 'Zucchini, Xena, 95';
>>> string
```

```
>>> lst = string.split(',');
>>> lst
>>> string = ','.join(lst);
>>> string
```

Interactive Experiments with Sample String-Processing Functions

Open and run the *String Functions* sample program. At the interactive prompt, type all the expressions and statements listed below. You may also experiment with your own expressions and statements. Observe and analyze the results.

```
>>> alphabet()

>>> scramble('Your Name')
>>> scramble('real fun')

>>> print fpToString(value = 3.14159, decimalPositions = 3);
>>> print 100.0 / 6;
>>> print fpToString(value = 100.0 / 6, decimalPositions = 3);

>>> isPalindrome('ananas')
>>> isPalindrome('ANANA')
>>> isPalindrome('Anana')
>>> isPalindrome('Anana'.upper())
>>> isPalindrome('Dot saw I was Tod'.lower())

>>> old = alphabet();
>>> new = scramble(old);
>>> print old; print new;
>>> message = 'Type your own message here.';
>>> secret = encode(message, old, new);
>>> print secret;
>>> print decode(secret, old, new);
```

Saving Your Interactive Session

- Save the interactive session with all of your experiments in your current labs folder, *07Labs*.
- From the Shell Window, use *File → Save As*.
- Name the saved copy *Session_7A.txt*.
  - **Important Note:** You must explicitly supply the file extension '**.txt**' when saving from IDLE.

- If you want to perform experiments in two or more interactive sessions, save your work in several files. If you choose to do so, use names *Session_7A_1.txt, Session_7A_2.txt*, and so on, for all saved files.
- Your saved file(s) must be included in your Lab Assignment submission.

Lab B [Strings, Files, and the Web]

Objective; Background; Lab Overview; What to Do Next; Studying the Sample Program; Creating a Program File; Developing the New Program

Objective

The objective of this lab is to develop a *Tax Filer* program that will:
- Input taxpayer records from an external storage file (such as a disk file).
  - Assume that each taxpayer record contains a *last name*, *first name*, and numeric *income*.
- Sort all taxpayer records alphabetically.
- Extend each taxpayer record with the taxes due for each taxpayer's income.
- Output all records in an external storage file.
- Summarize the records by providing the lowest, highest, and average taxes.

Background

- The objective of this lab is similar to that of an earlier topic. The difference is the use of the external file for input and output.
- Base your program on text files in *comma-separated-values (CSV)* format. Refer to the E-Text for an introduction to CSV files.

Example

The following table presents two sample CSV files. The left column represents a CSV file that can be input by your *Tax Filer* program. The right column presents the CSV file that would be output by the program. Note the lack of spaces in the CSV files.

Input File	Output File
Zucchini,Xena,146750 Pancake,Johnny,70350 Holden,Mary,0 Norris,Anna,29050 Kingsley,Bob,7150 Norris,Alex,10000	Holden,Mary,0.0,0.0 Kingsley,Bob,7150.0,715.0 Norris,Alex,10000.0,1142.5 Norris,Anna,29050.0,4000.0 Pancake,Johnny,70350.0,14325.0 Zucchini,Xena,146750.0,35717.0

- Implement the *Tax Filer* program in compliance with the following Tax Table:

Taxable income is over:	But not over:	The tax is:	Plus:	Of the amount over:
	7,150	0.00	10%	0
7,150	29,050	715.00	15%	7,150
29,050	70,350	4,000.00	25%	29,050
70,350	146,750	14,325.00	28%	70,350
146,750	319,100	35,717.00	33%	146,750
319,100		92,592.50	35%	319,100

Lab Overview
To perform this lab:
- Study the *Score Filer* sample program.
- Study your *Tax Processor* program designed for the Functions topic.
- Create a sample input CSV file with a few sample taxpayer records.
- Transform a copy of the *Score Filer* sample program into a *Tax Filer* program.
- Extensively test the *Tax Filer* program.

What to Do Next
You are now offered the following choices:
- Follow the detailed lab instructions below.
- Try the lab independently, using the instructions when you require help.
- Perform the lab independently, without any aid from the instructions.

All three approaches are beneficial to students. Choose the approach most beneficial to you.

Studying the Sample Program
- Open and browse the *Score Filer* sample program using IDLE.
- Invoke function *scores* with the provided input CSV file, *scores.csv*. Save the output to an output file named *grades.csv*; observe the output file contents.

- Invoke function *summary* with the provided input CSV file, *scores.csv*.
- Analyze the program implementation.

Creating a Program File

Create this program in your current labs folder, *07Labs*.
- Create a copy of the entire *Scores* folder; rename the copy to *Taxes*.
  - From this point, continue your work with the *Taxes* folder.
- In the *Taxes* folder, rename the *ScoreFiler.py* file as *TaxFiler.py*.
  - This will be the program file for your *Tax Filer* program.

Developing the New Program

Step 1: Creating a sample input file
- To create a sample CSV input file, you can either use a spreadsheet program, such as Microsoft Office Excel, or a simple word processor, such as Notepad. Choose the program you are most comfortable with; there is no need to use both. Create one CSV input file.
- If you decided to create a sample CSV input file using Microsoft Office Excel, follow these instructions:
  - Open a new spreadsheet; add at least ten sample taxpayer records.
  - Every taxpayer record should contain last name, first name, and income.
  - You can use all sample records presented earlier in the Background section of this lab and add a few made-up records on your own.
    - Do not explicitly input commas when you create a CSV file with Microsoft Office Excel.
- Use *File* → *Save As* and then *Save As type* → *CSV*. Give the name *incomes* to the saved file. Microsoft Office Excel will add the file extension '.csv'.
- If you decided to create a sample CSV input file using Notepad, follow these instructions:
  - Open a new file; add at least ten sample taxpayer records.
  - Every taxpayer record should contain last name, first name, and income.
    - You can use all sample records presented earlier in the Background section of this lab and add a few made-up records on your own.

- Separate all values with commas when you create a CSV file with Notepad.
- Do not include any spaces.
• Use *File → Save As* and then *Save As type → All Files*. Give the name *incomes.csv* to the saved file. In this case, you must include the extension '.csv'.

Step 2: Converting the *Score Filer* program into a *Tax Filer* Program

Follow these general guidelines; replace students with taxpayers, scores with incomes, and grades with taxes. Modify one function at a time, testing each modified function in interactive mode.

- Start with function *read*; transform it to work with taxpayers, incomes, and taxes.
  - In interactive mode, test the updated *read* function.
    - Use the *incomes.csv* sample input file.
- Continue with function *write*, transforming it to work with taxpayers, incomes, and taxes.
  - In interactive mode, test the updated *write* function.
    - Create a simple list of taxpayers and save it in file *taxes.csv*.
      - Verify that the output file *taxes.csv* is correct.
- Continue with the definition of function *scores*; transform it into a definition for function *taxes*.
  - Convert string-represented incomes to *float* and not *int*.
  - When you append a tax value to a taxpayer's record, make sure that the tax value is converted into a string by means of the *str* built-in function.
    - Note that *write* function joins all elements of a taxpayer record into a *csv* string and then writes the *csv* string onto a *csv* file. The write function uses the *join* method. Keep in mind that the *join* method only operates on lists of stings and not on lists that contain numeric items.
  - In interactive mode, test *taxes* function.
    - Use the *incomes.csv* sample input file as input for the *taxes* function.
    - Direct the output to a file named *taxes.csv*.
    - Open the *taxes.csv* with Microsoft Office Excel or with Notepad to observe it.
    - Compare your output file to the sample output file from the Background section above.
- Continue with the definition of function *summary*.

- Remember, the original *summary* function works with scores. You need to make this function summarize taxes instead of scores.
- Your transformed *summary* function must input taxpayer records from the *taxes.csv* file.
- Be sure to convert string-represented taxes to *float* and not *int*.
- In interactive mode, test the transformed *summary* function.
  - Use file *taxes.csv* as input for the *summary* function.
  - Use a calculator if necessary to verify the output of your *summary* function.
- Update comments throughout the program.
- Supply additional lines of comments to improve readability.

Lab C [Strings, Files, and the Web]

Objective; Background; Lab Overview; What to Do Next; Studying the Sample Program; Creating a Program File; Developing the New Program

Objective
- The objective of this lab is to develop a *Mixed-Up Words* program that takes the part of the first player in a game of mixed-up words. The user takes the part of the second player (the one who guesses).

Background
- *Mixed-Up Words* is a game in which one player chooses a secret word, mixes-up the letters of the secret word, then tells the mixed-up word to another player. The other player then tries to guess the word the secret word. The number of guesses is limited.
- An interaction with a *Mixed-Up Words* program may look like this:

>>> play();
This program plays the game of Mixed-Up Words.
You are to guess a mixed word.
You can make at most 4 attempts.

(1):   A N B Y R   Your guess: BYRNA
(2):   A N B Y R   Your guess: BRYAN
(2):   B R Y A N   You won!

Play more? [Yes/No]: **Yes**
(1):   I B N R A A Your guess: **BRIANA**
(1):   B R I A N A You won!

Play more? [Yes/No]: Yes
(1):   U S J A H O Your guess: ...
...
Play more? [Yes/No]: **No**
So long...
>>>

- A program to play the game of mixed-up words can be designed through modifications of the *Hangman* sample program.

Lab Overview

To perform this lab:
- Study the *Hangman* sample program.
- Transform a copy of the *Hangman* sample program into a *Mixed-Up Words* program.
- Extensively test the *Mixed-Up Words* program.
- Replace the sample names file associated with the *Hangman* program with a file containing your own secret words; test your program with the new file.

What to Do Next

You are now offered the following choices:
- Follow the detailed lab instructions below.
- Try the lab independently, using the instructions when you require help.
- Perform the lab independently, without any aid from the instructions.

All three approaches are beneficial to students. Choose the approach most beneficial to you.

Studying the Sample Program

- Use IDLE to open and browse the *Hangman* sample program.
- Invoke function *play* with the provided input file, *words.txt* and observe the program input and output.
- Analyze the program implementation.

Creating a Program File

Create this program in your current labs folder, *07Labs*.
- Create a copy of the entire *Hangman* folder; rename the copy *MixedUpWords*.
  - From this point, continue your work with the *MixedUpWords* folder.
- In the *MixedUpWords* folder, rename the Hangman.*py* file as *MixedUpWords.py*.
  - This will be the program file for your *MixedUpWords* program.

Developing the New Program

Perform the following steps with your newly created *Mixed-Up Words* program.

- Remove function *update* and its invocation from the program.
  - The *update* function is needed in the *Hangman* program to keep track of successive user guesses. In the *Mixed-Up Words* program, the user tries to guess the entire word, therefore user attempts do not successively build up.
- Design a new function named *mixWord* to receive a word as a string argument and return a list of that word's characters randomly shuffled. For example:

  ```
  >>> mixWord('LUIS');
  ['S', 'I', 'U', 'L']
  >>> mixWord('OLIVER');
  ['O', 'V', 'L', 'E', 'R', 'I']
  >>>
  ```

- Your *mixWord* function can be based on the built-in functions *list* and *shuffle*. This function should have one parameter named word: def mixWord(word):... The following interactive session is intended to give you some ideas as of how to use those functions in the implementation of the *mixWord* function:

  ```
  >>> word = 'ORANGE';
  >>> # Convert a string into a character list:
  >>> characterList = list(word);
  >>> # Observe character list:
  >>> print characterList;
  ['O', 'R', 'A', 'N', 'G', 'E']
  >>> import random;
  >>> # Randomly shuffle the list elements:
  >>> random.shuffle(characterList);
  >>> # Observe shuffled character list:
  >>> print characterList;
  ['O', 'N', 'E', 'R', 'A', 'G']
  # Join the shuffled character list into a shuffled word
  # using the empty string '' as separator:
  >>> shuffledWord = ''.join(characterList);
  # The shuffledWord must be returned (not printed)
  # by the mixWord function:
  >>> print shuffledWord;
  ```

Study the *shuffle* function from the online documentation if necessary. Use the above examples as ideas for the design of your *mixWord* function. Do not include print-statements in the mixWord function; use a return-statement instead.
- In function *playOneGame*:
  - Remove unknownLetter = '_'.
  - Replace:
      lettersGuessedSoFar = len(secretWord) * [unknownLetter]
    with
      mixedUpWord = mixWord(secretWord).
  - Replace lettersGuessedSoFar with mixedUpWord.
  - Replace the condition (lettersGuessedSoFar.count(unknownLetter) == 0) with (guess == secretWord).
- In the *play* function, change the number of max attempts to fewer (4 is a good number).
- Overall, replace 'Hangman' with 'Mixed-Up Words'.
- Update comments throughout the program.
- Supply additional comments to improve readability.
- Test the entire program.
- Replace the original sample names file with a file containing your own secret words; test your program with the new file.

Lab D [Strings, Files, and the Web]

Objective; Background; Lab Overview; What to Do Next; Studying the Sample Program; Creating a Program File; Developing the New Program

Objective

The objective of this lab is to develop a *Stock Analyzer* program that will:
- Download and display stock quotes repeatedly within specified time intervals.
- Determine the lowest, highest, and average stock prices from all downloaded stock quotes.

Background

- The E-text provides basic stock-related background needed for this lab.
- The *Stock Analyzer* program can be designed as an extension of the *Stock Tracker* program.

Lab Overview

To perform this lab:
- Study the E-Text description of the *Stock Tracker* sample program.
- In interactive mode, experiment with the *Stock Tracker* sample program by invoking all of its functions.
- Transform a copy of the *Stock Tracker* sample program into a *Stock Analyzer* program.
- Extensively test the *Stock Analyzer* program.

What to Do Next

You are now offered the following choices:
- Follow the detailed lab instructions below.
- Try the lab independently, using the instructions when you require help.
- Perform the lab independently, without any aid from the instructions.

All three approaches are beneficial to students. Choose the approach most beneficial to you.

Studying the Sample Program
- Use the E-Text to read the description of the *Stock Tracker* sample program.
- Use IDLE to open and browse the *Stock Tracker* sample program.
- Invoke all functions from the *Stock Tracker* sample program.
  - Follow the exercises from the E-Text description of the *Stock Tracker* sample program.
- Analyze the program implementation.

Creating a Program File
Create this program in your current labs folder, *07Labs*.
- Create a copy of the entire *Stocks* folder; rename the copy *StockAnalysis*.
  - From this point, continue your work in the *StockAnalysis* folder.
- In the *Stocks* folder, rename the *StockTracker.py* file as *StockAnalyzer.py*.
  - This will be the program file for your *Stock Analyzer* program.

Developing the New Program
Perform the following steps with your newly created *Stock Analyzer* program.
- Create a copy of the definition of function *watch;* rename the copy *analyze*.
- Extend the newly created function *analyze* with statements to find the minimum, maximum, and average stock prices.
  - Before the stock quote loop, define variables *minimum, maximum,* and *total*. Insert assignment statements to make *minimum, maximum,* and *total* equal to the *first stock price*.
  - At the end of the loop body, insert if-else statements to test and eventually update the *minimum* and *maximum* variables.
  - At the end of the loop body, insert an assignment statement to add the *current stock price* to the *total*.
  - After the stock quote loop, insert statements that calculate and print the *average* stock price. Remember, the total number of stock quotes is the same as the number of stock *checks*. In addition, print the *minimum* and *maximum* stock prices.
- Test the entire program with a stock symbol on your choice.

- Test the program during normal market hours for the market where your chosen symbol is traded.
- Note that US stock markets open at 9:30AM Eastern time and close at 4:00PM Eastern time. Few stocks are traded online after hours, therefore most stock prices should not be expected to change when the markets are closed. You can choose symbols of active stocks to explore from the following table.

Stock Symbol	Company	Stock Exchange
YHOO	Yahoo! Inc.	NASDAQ
GOOG	Google Inc.	NASDAQ
^KS11	KOSPI Composite Index	South Korea
NWS.AX	News Corporation, Inc.	Sydney
ANZ.AX	Australia and New Zealand Banking Group Ltd.	Sydney
BMWG.F	Bayerische Motoren-Werke AG	Frankfurt
LHAG.F	Deutsche Lufthansa AG	Frankfurt

- A possible interaction with the *analyze* function may look like this:

  ```
  >>> analyze(symbol = 'YHOO', seconds = 30, checks = 6);
  {Date: 11/5/2004, Symbol: YHOO, Open: 37.60, Price: 35.96, Time: 2:36pm}
  {Price: 35.98, Change: 0.02, Time: 2:36pm}
  {Price: 35.98, Change: 0.02, Time: 2:37pm}
  {Price: 35.98, Change: 0.02, Time: 2:37pm}
  {Price: 35.96, Change: 0.0, Time: 2:38pm}
  {Price: 35.97, Change: 0.01, Time: 2:38pm}
  First price: 35.96 Most recent price: 35.97
  Average: 35.97 Minimum: 35.96 Maximum: 35.98
  >>>
  ```

- Update all existing comments. Supply additional comments if needed.

Lab E [Strings, Files, and the Web, Optional]

Objective; Background; Lab Overview

Objective

The objective of this lab is to develop a program *Gift Handler* that will:
- Input a party participant list from an external text file.
- Randomly determine gift exchange among party participants.
- Save the gift exchange into an external file in comma-separated values (CSV) format.

Background

Note that the *Gift Assignment* sample program from the topic on *Lists and Dictionaries* already determines a random gift exchange. The *Gift Assignment* program, however, inputs and outputs data interactively. The *Gift Handler* program must input all names of party participants from an external file and output the gift exchange in an external file in comma-separated values (CSV) format.

Lab Overview

To perform this lab:
- Study the *Gift Assignment* sample program from the topic on *Lists and Dictionaries.*
- Create a copy of the *Gift Assignment* sample program in your current labs folder. Transform the copy into a *Gift Handler* program.
- Create a test file with the names of party participants; test your program. Observe the output file.
- A possible interaction with a *Gift Handler* program is presented below.

```
>>> gifts();
This program generates party gift exchange.
Enter name of file to read from: names.csv
Enter name of file to save in: exchange.csv
Names processed: 5
>>>
```

- Possible input and output file contents are presented below:

Input File	Output File
Kellie	Kellie,Tore
Luis	Luis,Kellie
Tore	Tore,Luis
Brian	Brian,Jenny
Jenny	Jenny,Brian

Graphics and Interfaces

Introduction to Turtle Graphics; Sample Program: Pattern Designer; Turtle Graphics Methods; Modules and Program Execution; Global Variables; Introduction to Graphical User Interfaces; Stepwise GUI Design; Widgets and Their Properties; Import Patterns; The Global-Statement; The Pass-Statement; Sample GUI Programs; Synonyms

Introduction to Turtle Graphics

Computer graphics is a general term embracing the creation, manipulation and display of images with the aid of a computer. Computer images are generated by graphics applications and displayed by graphics devices. Color displays and printers are well-known examples of graphics devices. Typical examples of popular graphics applications are photo editors, digital movie players, and computer games. Even common applications such as web browsers and word processors include considerable graphics components that allow them to generate and display images.

An easy way to get started with graphics programming in Python is to use a custom module named *turtle*. This module allows you to use a *pen* object that can draw on a *window* object. Pen movements along the screen can be likened to the movements of a little turtle, hence the module name *turtle*. This type of computer graphics is often referred to as *turtle graphics*.

> Note
>
> The Python system is distributed with a built-in *turtle* module. Regretfully, the built-in *turtle* module is not bug-free. Our custom *turtle* module is a debugged version of a built-in *turtle* module, originally distributed with the Python 2.4 series. This custom *turtle* module is intended to behave uniformly with different Python releases. We recommend using our custom turtle module instead of a built-in *turtle* module.

> Note
>
> The custom *turtle* module is part of the *Turtle Demo* sample program. The easiest way to start using *turtle* in interactive mode is to

open the *turtle.py* file and then run it. Then you can type various turtle statements in the corresponding shell window. You do not need to keep *turtle.py* open.

Example
>>> # Open the *turtle.py* file from *Turtle Demo*;
>>> # Run the *turtle.py* file (you may then close this file);
>>> # Type statements in the corresponding shell window;

The statements below create a pen object with an associated drawing window. The drawing window is shown in reduced size. The pen is visualized as a little triangle in the middle of the window:

>>> pen = Pen();
>>> pen.reset();

Note
The title bar of the drawing window contains the abbreviation *tk*. This is the name of a general purpose graphics toolkit that is used to implement the *turtle* module.

Note
Before you draw:
- Close all unnecessary windows.
- Minimize completely or at least reduce partially the size of all remaining widows.

Make sure the drawing window is uncovered at all times.

The pen can be programmed to move forward and backward, and to make left and right turns. As the pen moves, it draws lines on the window. In this way, the task of drawing a shape on the window is reduced to the task of programming pen movements.

Example

Some of the statements below move the pen forward while others make it turn left. As the pen moves across the window, it draws a triangle.

```
>>> pen.forward(distance = 100);
>>> pen.left(angle = 120);
>>> pen.forward(distance = 100);
>>> pen.left(angle = 120);
>>> pen.forward(distance = 100);
```

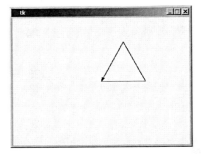

Note

When you need to close the drawing window, close the *Shell Window*. Use the *File -> Exit* command. This should safely close the drawing window as well. Avoid closing the drawing window directly.

When you do not see the pen on the drawing window, or when the drawing window is not responding, invoke the reset method on the pen: *pen.reset()*. Note, however, that this will erase everything from the drawing window.

A coordinate system is associated with the drawing window. The origin (0,0) of the coordinate system is in the center of the window. A point in the drawing window is defined by a horizontal coordinate, *x*, and a vertical coordinate, *y*.

The window *width* determines the minimal and the maximal horizontal coordinates:

x_{min} = - width / 2.0; x_{max} = +width / 2.0.

Likewise, the window *height* determines minimal and the maximal vertical coordinates:

$y_{min} = -\ height\ /\ 2.0;\quad y_{max} = +\ height\ /\ 2.0.$

Example

The following statements print the width and the height of a drawing window, x_{min} and x_{max}, and y_{min} and y_{max}:

```
>>> w = pen.window_width();
>>> h = pen.window_height();
>>> print w, h;
382 269
>>> print -w/2.0, +w/2.0
-191.0 191.0
>>> print -h/2.0, +h/2.0
-134.5 134.5
```

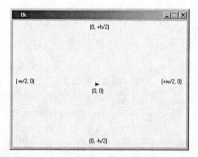

Several simple pen methods can be employed to produce various images. These methods are named *up, down, goto,* and *circle*.

The *up* method lifts the pen above the drawing window, which stops drawing. The *down* method puts the pen back to the drawing window, which resumes drawing.

The *goto* method moves the pen to a new location on the drawing window. If the pen is down, it draws a line while moving. If the pen is up, it does not draw a line, but moves directly to the new location.

The *circle* method draws a circle with a specified radius. The circle is drawn on top of the starting pen position. The circle is drawn only when the pen is down.

Example

```
>>> pen.up();
>>> pen.goto(75, 100);
>>> pen.down();
>>> pen.goto(0, -100);
>>> pen.goto(-75, 100);
>>> pen.up();
>>> pen.goto(0, 0);
>>> pen.down();
>>> pen.circle(20);
```

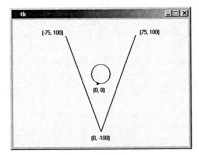

There are three primary colors, red, green and blue. When combined, the primary colors produce secondary colors such as yellow, cyan, magenta, and white. The color white is achieved by combining the three primary colors together in equal amounts. The color black is the absence of any color.

Any imaginable color is some combination of the three primary colors, and any such color combination can be specified by a triple of numbers:

(R, G, B), where $0 \leq R, G, B \leq 1$.

The numbers R, G, and B determine the amounts of red, green, and blue that make up the combination.

Example
Secondary colors are combinations of primary colors:

```
>>> # yellow = red + green:
>>> yellow = (1, 1, 0);
>>> # cyan = green + blue:
>>> cyan = (0, 1, 1);
```

```
>>> # magenta = red + blue:
>>> magenta = (1, 0, 1);
>>> # white = red + green + blue:
>>> white = (1, 1, 1);
>>> # black = no colors:
>>> black = (0, 0, 0);
```

Primary colors can also be represented as *(R, G, B)* triples:

```
>>> red = (1, 0, 0); green = (0, 1, 0); blue = (0, 0, 1);
```

We use the term *RGB color* for any combination *(R, G, B)* of the three primary colors, $0 \leq R, G, B \leq 1$.

Exercise

Search the Web for introductory articles on RGB colors. Use 'RGB' or 'RGB world' as search queries.

The color black is the default drawing color in the *turtle* module.

The drawing color can be changed at any moment by means of the pen's *color* method. This method expects a valid RGB color as an argument.

Exercise

Execute the following statements in interactive mode and observe the changes of the drawing color:

```
>>> pen = Pen(); pen.reset()
>>> # draw with the default black color:
>>> pen.goto(100, 0);
>>> # draw in yellow:
>>> pen.color(1, 1, 0); pen.goto(100, 100);
>>> # draw in cyan:
>>> pen.color(0, 1, 1); pen.goto (0, 0);
>>> # draw in magenta:
>>> pen.color(1, 0, 1); pen.goto (-100, -100);
>>> # draw in darker magenta:
>>> pen.color(0.5, 0, 0.5); pen.goto (-100, 0);
>>> # draw in black:
>>> pen.color(0, 0, 0); pen.goto (0, 0);
>>> # draw in white:
>>> pen.color(1, 1, 1); pen.goto (100, 0);
```

Displays and other graphics devices are viewed as rectangular arrays of primitive graphic elements known as *pixels*. Pixels are horizontally arranged on *rows* and vertically arranged in *columns*. Note that row and column numbers are whole numbers. This means when a drawing window is displayed by a device, any fractional coordinates are rounded to whole pixel coordinates.

Sample Program: Pattern Designer

Consider the following programming problem. Develop a program to produce various original computer graphics patterns. Imagine a human designer wants to use unusual programmatically generated patterns as inspiration for the design of wallpaper, tablecloth, coffee mugs, and other household products.

A sample program named *Pattern Designer* offers a simple solution for the programming problem posed in the previous paragraph. The main function of the *Pattern Designer* program is called *pattern*. The *pattern* function takes a *number* as an argument and produces a design for that number.

Example
The invocation:

>>> pattern(number = 5);

produces this pattern:

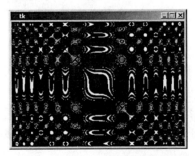

The *Pattern Designer* sample program consists of the *pattern* main function and two helper functions, *init* and *draw*. All three functions are discussed in details in the rest of this section.

The purpose of the *init* function is to create a pen object with an associated drawing window, to set the current drawing color to blue, and to extract the default width and height of the drawing window. Note that you can only use pen objects that are created with this default width and height.

The implementation of the *init* function follows.

```
# Create a blue pen and determine the window's width and height:
def init():
    pen = Pen();
    pen.color(0, 0, 1); # blue
    width = pen.window_width();
    height = pen.window_height();
    return pen, width, height;
```

The *pattern* function invokes the *init* function to obtain a pen object and the *width* and the *height* of the drawing screen. The *pattern* function then uses two nested for-loops to generate a rectangular matrix of points. For each point, the *pattern* function invokes the *draw* function that decides whether and what to draw at this point.

A programmer who uses the *turtle* module can control the speed of line drawing by a special *tracing flag*.

When the tracing flag is set to "true," lines are drawn slower, with an animation of an arrow along the line. This drawing mode makes it easier to follow the drawing process.

When the tracing flag is set to "false," lines are drawn at maximum speed. This drawing mode provides faster execution of graphics programs because parts of the image are composed in memory and displayed at once.

A pen method named *tracer* is used to set the tracing flag: *tracer(True)* switches to the slow drawing speed, while *tracer(False)* switches to the fast drawing speed.

The *pattern* function uses the *tracer* method to start at the higher drawing speed. In the process of drawing, the *pattern* function switches to the slower speed, then back to higher. This flushes any newly composed pieces of the image onto the drawing window. This "off-on-off" approach provides a higher execution speed than possible with the tracing being *on* continuously, and an opportunity to view several different stages of the drawing progress.

The implementation of the *pattern* function follows.

```
# Given a number, design a pattern:
def pattern(number):
    pen, w, h = init();
    # Switch off tracing for higher speed:
    pen.tracer(False);
    for x in range(-w/2, +w/2):
        for y in range (-h/2, +h/2):
            draw(pen, number, x, y);
        # Temporarily switch on tracing to observe drawing:
        if (x % 100 == 0):
            pen.tracer(True); pen.tracer(False);
    pen.tracer(True);
```

The *draw* function takes the coordinates *(x, y)* for any point in the drawing window, transforming those coordinates into an integer value, *ez*. If *ez* is even, the draw function draws a circle with radius 1 on top of point *(x, y)*. Because this circle is small, it simply appears as a tiny dot. If *ez* is odd, no circle is produced and the area on top of point (x, y) remains unchanged.

The implementation of the *draw* function follows.

```
# Draw a pattern element at point (x, y):
def draw(pen, number, x, y):
    a = y * (number / 100.0);
    b = x * (number / 100.0);
    ez = int(a*a*a + b*b*b);
    if (ez % 2 == 0):
        pen.up(); pen.goto(x, y); pen.down();
        pen.circle(1);
```

Note the final graphic is formed by tiny circles produced by the *draw* function.

New designs are created by supplying different numbers to the *pattern* function. If you conduct a few experiments, you will notice many patterns appear similar, and many more seem boring. Never fear. By making some changes in the *draw* function, you will significantly increase the number of interesting graphics patterns. Here is a list of possible changes to explore:

- Use alternative expressions to defined the *ez* variable in terms of *a* and *b*.
- Change the *ez*-tests; in place of *(ez % 2)*, put *(ez % 3)*.
- Use new drawing methods. Replace *circle* with *forward* or *backward*, methods that will be described in the next section. Use multiple selection *ez*-tests to choose colors for each point.

Example

The statement *ez = int(a*a + b*b)* can replace the statement *ez = int(a*a*a + b*b*b)* in the draw function. After this replacement, the invocation:

```
>>> pattern(number = 5);
```

produces this pattern:

Turtle Graphics Methods

The *turtle* module provides easy-to-use turtle graphics primitives. As demonstrated in the previous sections, the *turtle* module allows you to create and use a *pen* object to draw on a *window* object. A pen object comes with several methods that facilitate graphics programming. The following methods are defined and used in the previous sections: *goto, circle, color, up, down, tracer*.

The *turtle* module provides a variety of useful methods. For example, the *left* and *right* methods turn the pen at a specified angle to change its direction. The *forward* method moves the pen a specified distance in its current direction. The *fill* method paints the inside of a shape with the current color.

The following table outlines principal graphics methods from the *turtle* module.

Method	Description
pen.reset();	Clear the screen, re-center the pen, and restore default values.
pen.clear();	Clear the screen.
pen.tracer(*flag*);	Set tracing to *True* or *False*. Tracing implies line drawing is slower, with an animation of an arrow along the line.
pen.forward(*distance*); *pen*.backward(*distance*);	Go forward / backward *distance* steps.
pen.degrees(*degrees*); *pen*.radians(*radians*);	Set angle measurement units to *degrees/radians*.
pen.left(*angle*); *pen*.right(*angle*);	Turn left/right *angle* units. Units default to degrees, but are set via the *degrees* and *radians* methods.
pen.up();	Move the pen up and stop drawing.
pen.down();	Move the pen down and draw when moving.
pen.width(*width*);	Set the line width to *width* units.
pen.color(*R, G, B*)	Set the pen color to *(R, G, B)*.
pen.write(*text*)	Write *text* at the current pen position.
pen.fill(*flag*)	The complete specification is rather complex, but the recommended usage is: use *pen*.fill(True) before drawing a path you want to fill, and *pen*.fill(False) when you finish to draw the path.
pen.circle(*radius*)	Draw a circle with given *radius* on top of the current pen position. This method can also draw arches; see the online documentation for details.
pen.goto(*x, y*)	Go to coordinates *x, y*.

Exercise

The *Turtle Demo* sample program employs most turtle graphics methods. Study the program, run it and invoke the *demo* function to observe its behavior.

Modules and Program Execution

A Python program is a sequence of Python statements.
Python programs are executed by the *Python interpreter* in two modes: *file input mode* and *interactive mode*. In file input mode, the *Python interpreter* runs a program saved previously in a program file. In interactive mode, the *Python Interpreter* executes statements that are typed interactively without saving them to a file.

In Python, program files are referred to as *modules*. The term module is synonymous with program file.

So far we have studied modules that consist exclusively of function definition statements. However, a module may contain <u>any</u> statements, not just function definitions. In particular, a module may start with one or more function definitions and end with a statement to invoke one of the defined functions. The execution of such a module defines all functions then continues with the execution of the invoked function.

Example
The following statements belong to the *Simple Wages* sample program.

```
# Given hours worked and pay rate, calculate wages:
def wages():
    hours    = input('Enter hours worked: ');
    payRate = input('Enter pay rate: ');
    grossWages = hours * payRate;
    print 'Gross wages: ', grossWages;

# Invoke the wages function:
wages();
```

When executed, the above program defines a function named *wages* then automatically invokes the *wages* function. The *wages* function then asks the user to enter data, calculates and outputs the wages.

The user who runs the *Simple Wages* program need not explicitly invoke the *wages* function to achieve this result.

In Windows, the *Python Interpreter* automatically registers itself as the program that opens Python program files. In systems other than Windows, you can arrange similar registration for the *Python Interpreter*.

Note

In Unix-like systems, a Python program can be made directly executable by means of a first-line comment pointing to the exact location of the Python interpreter. For example:

#! /usr/bin/env python

Unix-related specifics are found in the Python documentations.

When the *Python Interpreter* opens a program file, it simply executes its statements.

You open files by clicking (or double clicking) on their icons. By clicking on the icon of a Python program file, you trigger its execution by the *Python Interpreter*.

In Windows, the following events occur when you click (or double click) on the icon of a Python program file:
- Windows invokes the *Python Interpreter* to open the file.
- The interpreter automatically launches a pop-up *shell window* to support the program's input and output operations.
- The interpreter executes the program.
- At the end of program execution, the interpreter immediately closes the pop-up *shell window* and exits.

Exercise

Click (double click) on the icon for the *Pattern Designer* program and observe the opening and closing of a pop-up *shell window*.

In summary, when you launch a Python program in Windows by clicking on the program's icon, the program executes in a pop-up *shell window* that is immediately closed upon completion of the last statement. Other windows that have been opened by your program, such as drawing windows, will also be closed. This may cause a problem because you may not be able to fully observe the program's output.

Fortunately, it is easy to solve this problem by adding an extra input statement to the end of your program. You can use the *raw_input* built-in function, which will ask the user to press the Enter key. The program will wait for the input before closing the pop-up *shell window*.

You will be able to observe your program's output. When ready, provide the requested input and the program will exit.

Example

The complete version of the *Simple Wages* sample program ends with an extra input statement. The statement waits for the user to press the Enter key, thus preventing the immediate closing of the pop-up shell.

```python
# Given hours worked and pay rate, calculate wages:
def wages():
    hours   = input('Enter hours worked: ');
    payRate = input('Enter pay rate: ');
    grossWages  = hours * payRate;
    print 'Gross wages:', grossWages;

# Invoke the wages function:
wages();

# Ask the user to confirm program exit:
ans = raw_input('Press Enter to exit.');
```

The execution of the above program will end after the user presses the Enter key (in response to the prompt displayed by the *raw_input* function). Thus, the pop-up *shell window* will not close before the user presses the Enter key.

Note finally that in this case, you do not need to assign the value returned by the *raw_input* function. The following simple invocation sequence will suffice:

```python
# Invoke the wages function:
wages();

# Ask the user to confirm program exit:
raw_input('Press Enter to exit.');
```

Exercise

Use a *file browser* to retrieve the icon of the *Simple Wages* sample program. Click (or double click) on the program icon to execute the program. Input all required data and observe the program's behavior.

Exercise

Choose one of your favorite programs. Create an enhanced version of that program that can be launched directly with mouse clicks. Use the program pattern described in this section and illustrated by the *Simple Wages* program.

Note

Optionally, you can use the if-pattern below to create a module that is either directly executed as a main program, or imported in other modules.

```
def wages():
    hours  = input('Enter hours worked: ');
    ... wages definition continued ...
if (__name__ == '__main__'):
    wages();
```

In the above module:
- Function *wages* is invoked only when the module is directly executed as a main program
- Function *wages* is not executed when the module is imported

This above if-pattern is not further used in this course. The pattern is left for optional self-study from the Python online documentation.

Global Variables

Modules that we have discussed in previous topics consist exclusively of function definitions in the form of def-statements. However, a Python module may be comprised of any kind of statements, not just def-statements. In particular, a module may contain assignment statements that define variables.

A variable that is defined outside of a function, at the module level, is referred to as *global*. A function that needs to access a global variable must list the global variable in a global-statement. The global-statement consists of the keyword *global*, followed by one or more comma-separated names.

Example

The following module defines a global variable named *g*. The value of the global variable is updated in function *producer* and used in function *consumer*.

```
# Module start
g = 1; # defines global variable g
def producer():
    global g;
    g = 100;
def consumer():
    global g;
    print 10 * g;
producer();
consumer();
# Module end
```

A global variable does not have to be created by a module-level assignment. Instead, a global variable can be produced from within a function, provided the variable is listed in a global-statement. A consumer function that uses a global variable but does not assign into it is not required to list the global variable in a global-statement.

Example

The following module contains a *producer* function that defines a global variable named *g*. The value of the global variable is used in a *consumer* function.

```
# Module start
def producer():
    global g; # defines global variable g
    g = 100;
def consumer():
    print 10 * g;
producer();
consumer();
# Module end
```

A global variable is accessible to the entire module, even across function boundaries. Remember, a function that assigns into a global variable must list the variable in a global-statement. A function that uses a global variable can list the global variable in a global-statement, but it is not required.

Introduction to Graphical User Interfaces

"User interface" is a general term referring to the communication channel between a program and the human user. There are two widespread types of user interfaces:
- Text-only interfaces
- Graphical user interfaces

Programs that employ *text-only interfaces* typically output text to the screen and input text from the keyboard. In Python, text-only interfaces are implemented by means of simple statements and functions, such as the print-statement and the input function. Note that all Python programs we have studied in this course employ text-only interfaces.

Example

The sample program named *Simple Wages* employs a simple text-only interface. When the program is executed in IDLE, it uses the Python *shell window* for input-output. As recently explained, this program can launch independently from IDLE as a standalone program. In this case, the program uses a pop-up *shell window* for input and output. Either way, the two-way communication between the user and the program consists of a sequence of text lines. A sample execution of this program in a pop-up DOS window is shown below to illustrate a text-only interface.

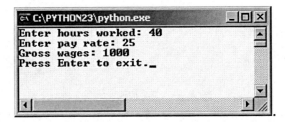

Programs employing *graphical user interfaces (GUIs)* take advantage of the computer's graphics capabilities to facilitate the interaction with the user. Such programs display various widgets on the screen, such as buttons, menus, scroll bars and text areas, positioned within windows. Typical GUIs involve graphics displays, keyboards, and pointing devices (example: mouse).

Commercial applications predominantly use GUIs. Communication with most of the components of the Windows operating system is based on GUIs. However, GUIs are complex and difficult to program while text-only interfaces are simple and easy to program. Many programmers prefer text-only interfaces. Perhaps for this reason communication with most of the components of the Linux operating system uses text-only interfaces.

The popular module *Tkinter* will get us started with GUI programming in Python. This module allows you to compose GUIs out of basic widgets, such as buttons, menus, scroll bars, text areas, frames, windows, and others.

GUI programming in Python and *Tkinter* is simpler than GUI programming in most known platforms. Nevertheless, an in-depth study of GUI programming requires a considerable amount of time and effort. GUIs are the subject of many textbooks and courses; it is unreasonable to attempt comprehensive study of a complex subject such as GUI in an introductory course. This course of study employs *Tkinter*, together with several smaller modules derived from *Tkinter*, to introduce basic GUI programming concepts.

Instead of a comprehensive study of all possible GUIs, we introduce by means of sample programs some of the easier to use GUI concepts and techniques. Your study of the sample GUI programs in the next sections will lead you to the following worthy results:
- Understanding how GUIs work.
- Knowing how to develop simple GUIs for your own programs.

The next section presents a stepwise design process to produce a sample GUI program. Studying a program by following its design steps enhances your understanding of the program and prepares you for applying stepwise design to your next programs.

Stepwise GUI Design

Consider the following sample problem: develop a wage calculation program with a GUI. The program must use its GUI to input hours worked and hourly rate, calculate the wages, and use the GUI to output the calculated wages.

A sample program named *Wage Calculator* solves this problem. A snapshot of the *Wage Calculator* GUI is shown below.

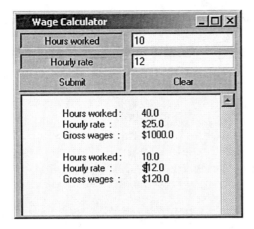

Exercise

Launch the *Wage Calculator* sample program by clicking on its icon or running it from IDLE. Input various numbers and submit them for wage calculation. Exit the program by clicking on the *Close* button on the *shell window*'s right upper corner.

The *Wage Calculator* GUI consists of the following types of widgets: labels, entries, buttons, a scrolled text, and a main window.
- *Entries* are the white-colored widgets containing numbers, such as *10* and *12*. Entries are typically used for data input.
- *Labels* are the widgets marked as *Hours worked* and *Hourly rate*. Labels are used to output prompts and other messages. Labels can change during program execution.
- *Buttons* are the widgets marked as *Submit* and *Clear*. Buttons are used to trigger computations. Buttons can be programmed to invoke functions.
- *Scrolled Text* is the large white widget with a scrollbar containing columns of hours, rates, and calculated wages. A scrolled text can be used for output of large amounts of data. This widget can also be used for data input. The edit pane of a word processor is a scrollable text widget.
- The *Main window* is the frame that embeds all other widgets.

It is beneficial to use stepwise program design to reduce a complex program design task to smaller, easy to solve tasks. Stepwise design is particularly beneficial in GUI programming because of the inherent complexity of GUI development.

The rest of this section describes a possible stepwise design of the *Wage Calculator* sample program.

First, design a function to configure and display the main GUI window.

Second, design a function to create various widget objects.

Third, design a function to position the widgets within the main window.

Fourth, design a function to configure each widget by specifying various widget properties, such as size, relief, borders. Through widget configuration we specify what text is displayed in the widget. For buttons, we specify what action functions are to be executed upon button clicks.

Finally, define particular action functions to be invoked upon clicks on the *Submit* and *Clear* buttons. The action function for the *Submit* button gets *hours* and *rate* values from the corresponding entry widgets, calculates the *wages*, and inserts the *wages* to the scrolled text widget. The action function for the *Clear* button zeroes the hours and rate entries and erases any text that has been inserted to the scrolled text widget.

Note that each step produces an intermediate program to be executed and tested.

First Step: Main Window Initialization

The goal of this step is to create, configure, and display the main GUI window. In the *Wage Calculator* program, this is implemented by a function named *init*. The function definition is listed and defined below. Review the function definition before you acquaint yourself with the *init* function with careful study of the subsequent Python-to-English translation.

```
from Tkinter import *;
from ScrolledText import *;

# Initialize program components:
def init():
    # Create and configure the main window:
    global window;
    window = Tk();
    window.title('Wage Calculator');
    createWidgets();
    positionWidgets();
```

```
    configureWidgets();
    # Display the window:
    window.mainloop();

def createWidgets(): pass;
def positionWidgets(): pass;
def configureWidgets(): pass;

# Start execution:
init();
```

The *init* function invokes three other functions that will embed in the main window all necessary widgets, such as buttons, labels, entries, and scrolled text. Those functions are defined at subsequent steps.

The following Python-to-English translation provides insight into the definition and invocation of the *init* function.

Python Statement	Common English Meaning
from Tkinter import *; from ScrolledText import *;	○ Import all names defined at the top level of modules *Tkinter* and *ScrolledText*. This includes functions, global variables, and other entities defined in the two modules. • All imported names may be further used without prefixes. For example, instead of writing *window = Tkinter.Tk()*, skip the *Tkinter* prefix and simply write *window = Tk()*.
def init(): global window;	○ Start the definition of function named *init*. ○ Declare the *window* variable as global. • The global *window* variable can be assigned a value in the *init* function and then accessed in any function in the *Wage Calculator* program.
window = Tk();	○ Create a main window widget. ○ The window widget is represented by an object in memory but not displayed yet.
window.title('Wage Calculator');	○ Define the text to be displayed in the main window title bar: *Wage Calculator*.

createWidgets();
positionWidgets();
configureWidgets();
	○ Invoke these functions to create all embedded widgets, position them in the main window, and configure them properly.

	▫ These invocations are intended to compose all widgets that are embedded in the main window: buttons, entries, labels, and scrolled text.
window.mainloop();	▫ Invoke the *mainloop* method. ▫ This method displays the main window and starts listening for various events, such as button clicks. • One such event is a click on the *close button* that is in the upper right corner of virtually any GUI. The *mainloop* method provides a response to this event.

def createWidgets(): pass;
def positionWidgets(): pass;
def configureWidgets(): pass;
	▫ Define three functions that can be invoked but actually do nothing.
	 • These functions need to be available for invocation in the init function but are developed at subsequent steps.
	 • The *pass-statement* fills-in for a missing body. Its execution has no effect.

init();	▫ Invoke the *init* function to start the execution of the entire program. • This invocation comes after all function definitions. ▫ The *init* invocation creates and displays the GUI, letting users enter data, click buttons, and observe result.

Example

The intermediate program produced in this first design step can be executed. When executed, the program produces the GUI depicted below. Actual widgets will appear in the main window after the completion of subsequent design steps.

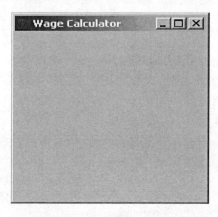

Second Step: Widget Creation

The goal of this step is to create all widgets that need to be embedded in the main window. Widgets are created by special constructor invocations. Widget constructor invocations return widget objects that can be assigned into widget variables.

Example

The following statements create a button widget:

```
global submitButton;
submitButton = Button(window);
```

The first statement declares a global widget variable named *submitButton*. This variable can be accessed in all other functions of the *Wage Calculator* program.

The second statement implements the actual button. A button is created by the invocation *Button(window).* The button is created with a reference to its *master* widget, which in this case is the main *window*. As a result, the button knows its master at the time of its creation.

In the *Wage Calculator* program, a function named *createWidgets* creates all widgets to be embedded in the main window. The function creates two labels, two entries, two buttons, and one scrolled text.

```
# Create widget objects:
def createWidgets():
    global hoursLabel; hoursLabel = Label(window);
    global hoursEntry; hoursEntry = Entry(window);
    global rateLabel; rateLabel = Label(window);
    global rateEntry; rateEntry = Entry(window);
    global submitButton; submitButton = Button(window);
    global clearButton; clearButton = Button(window);
    global scrolledText; scrolledText = ScrolledText(window);
```

After the execution of function *createWidgets*, all widgets are represented by objects in memory but not yet displayed.

All widgets are created by constructor invocations, such as *Label(window)*, *Entry(window)*, *Button(window)*, and *Scrolled-*

Text(window). An embedded widget is created with a reference to its master widget, which in this particular program is always the main window. As a result, every embedded widget knows its master at widget instantiation time. The main window itself is a widget without a master.

All widgets are assigned into global variables. These variables can be accessed from any function in the program.

Example

The intermediate program produced by this second step can be executed. When executed, the program produces the GUI depicted below. Note that this GUI looks exactly like the GUI displayed by the previous intermediate program. Still, this is a different program: it creates widgets and assigns them into variables without yet displaying them. Widgets will be displayed as a result of the next step.

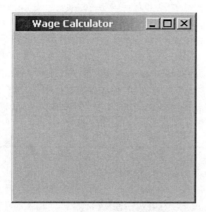

Third Step: Widget Positioning

The goal of this step is to place all widgets at specific positions in the main window.

The main window of a GUI can be viewed as a rectangular grid of rows and columns. The desired position of each widget in the main window can be identified by a row number and a column number.

Example
This is the desired appearance of the main window for the Wage Calculator GUI:

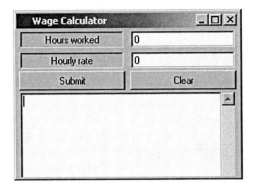

The main window in the Wage Calculator program is a grid of four rows and two columns. The positions of all widgets in this window are specified as follows:
- The *hours label* is in *(row = 0, column = 0)* and the *hours entry* is in *(row = 0, column = 1)*.
- The *rate label* is in *(row = 1, column = 0)* and the *rate entry* is in *(row = 1, column = 1)*.
- The *submit button* is in *(row = 2, column = 0)* and the *clear button* is in *(row = 2, column = 1)*.
- The *scrolled text* starts in *(row = 3, column = 0)*. It is a larger widget that spans two columns.

Remember, every embedded widget is created with a specific master. In the *Wage Calculator* program, for example, the main window is the master of all labels, entries, buttons, and the scrollable text. Every widget has a method named *grid* that can be used to position the widget at a specific row and column within the widget's master.

Example
The following invocation positions the *submit button* widget in row *2* and column *0*:

submitButton.grid(row = 2, column = 0);

The following invocation positions the *scrolled text* widget in row *3*. The widgets will start at column *0*, as specified by the argument *column = 0*. This widget spans across two columns, continuing from column *0* to column *1*, as specified by the argument *columnspan = 2*.

```
scrolledText.grid(row = 3, column = 0, columnspan = 2);
```

In *Tkinter*, keyword arguments, such as *row*, *column*, and *columnspan* are called *options*. All options have default values that allow the programmer to skip setting them. The default value for *columnspan* is *1*. By default, a missing *row* or *column* number is resolved to the first available row or column in the grid.

Several more options are to be used in the *Wages Calculator* program. The *rowspan* option positions a widget that spans across several rows. The *padx* and *pady* options define additional padding to be placed, horizontally and vertically, around the widget. The default value for *rowspan* is *1*, while the default for *padx* and *pady* is *0*.

The *grid* method keeps track of how many grid cells are needed. Cells that are not filled are not displayed.

In the *Wage Calculator* program, a function named *positionWidgets* places all widgets at specific positions in the main window. It does so by invoking the *grid* method of each widget.

```
def positionWidgets():
    global hoursLabel;
    hoursLabel.grid(row = 0, column = 0, padx = 3, pady = 3);
    global hoursEntry;
    hoursEntry.grid(row = 0, column = 1, padx = 3, pady = 3);
    global rateLabel;
    rateLabel.grid(row = 1, column = 0, padx = 3, pady = 3);
    global rateEntry;
    rateEntry.grid(row = 1, column = 1, padx = 3, pady = 3);
    global submitButton;
    submitButton.grid(row = 2, column = 0, padx = 3);
    global clearButton;
    clearButton.grid(row = 2, column = 1, padx = 3);
    global scrolledText;
    scrolledText.grid(row = 3, column = 0, padx = 3, pady = 3,
            columnspan = 2);
```

Example

The intermediate program produced by this third step can be executed. When executed, the program produces the GUI depicted below. Notice all widgets are displayed with some default sizes, without any text on them. At the next step, widgets are configured with proper size, relief, borders, text, and other properties to ensure proper widget look.

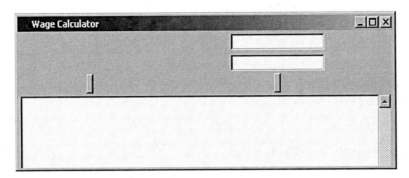

The *grid* method is often referred to as a *grid geometry manager,* or simply *grid manager. Tkinter* supports two more managers, the *pack* manager and the *place* manager. The *grid* manager is chosen for this course because it is versatile and easy to use.

Fourth Step: Widget Configuration

The goal of this step is to configure each widget by specifying various widget properties, such as widget size and relief. For most widgets, we specify what text is to be displayed in the widget. For buttons, we specify actions to be performed when the button clicked.

Each widget has a special method named *configure*. This method can be invoked with various options, depending on the desired configuration.

Example

The following invocation configures the *submit button* to have a width of 20 characters and display the text 'Submit.'

submitButton.configure(text = 'Submit', width = 20);

When you use buttons in a GUI, you must specify what actions are to be performed when the button is clicked. Python functions are a convenient way to define actions performed in response to button clicks and other widget events.

Example

When the user clicks the *Submit* button, your program should take the *hours* and *rate* values from the corresponding entry widgets, calculate the *wages*, and insert them at the end of the *scrolled text* widget. When the user clicks the *Clear* button, you program should delete the entire content of the *scrolled text* widget and reset the *hours* and *rate* entries to 0. In either case, you can specify these actions as Python functions. In this step, we must define two dummy action functions (one for the *Submit* button and for the *Clear* button) that can be invoked but do nothing:

```
def submitAction(): pass;
def clearAction(): pass;
```

These action functions are to be completed at the next step.

To each button, you attach an action function using the *command* option.

Example

The following invocation configures the *submit button* with the *submitAction* function to be executed when the button is clicked:

```
submitButton.configure(text = 'Submit', width = 20, command = submitAction);
```

The *submitAction* function will be automatically invoked upon clicks of the *Submit* button.

A program with a GUI may process events other than button clicks. For example, your program can react and perform actions when the cursor moves or when the user presses a key. Event handling such as this is an advanced topic that will not be discussed further in this course.

An entry widget is used in a program for the sole purpose of getting input from the user to the program. However, you must configure the widget with a *text variable*. You use a special *Tkinter* invocation, *StringVar()*, to create a text variable. You attach a text variable to a widget using the *textvariable* option.

Example

The following statements create a global text variable named *hoursText* with an initial value '0' and attach the text variable to the *hours entry*:

```
global hoursText, hoursEntry;
hoursText = StringVar(); hoursText.set('0');
hoursEntry.configure(textvariable = hoursText, width = 20);
```

A text variable attached to a widget contains the text that is displayed in the widget. If the user types text into the widget, your program can retrieve that text from the widget's text variable. If your program changes the text variable, the text that is displayed in the widget changes as well. Note that the value of a text variable is always a string, even when the string contains numerals. You must convert such string objects into numbers before you perform numeric operations with them. Also, you must convert numeric results back into strings before you put them into text variables to have them displayed in widgets.

Note you can supply configuration options as early as when you create the widget, not only with the *configure* method. Widget configuration options may be supplied in widget constructor invocations.

Example

```
submitButton = submitButton(
        window, text = 'Submit', width = 20, command = submitAction);
```

In the *Wage Calculator* program, a function named *configureWidgets* specifies desired properties for all widgets. It does so by invoking the *configure* method of each widget.

```
# Configure the widgets:
def configureWidgets():
    global hoursText, hoursLabel, hoursEntry;
    hoursText = StringVar(); hoursText.set('0');
```

```
        hoursEntry.configure(
            textvariable = hoursText, width = 20);
        hoursLabel.configure(
            text = 'Hours worked', width = 20,
            borderwidth = 2, relief = SUNKEN);
        global rateText, rateLabel, rateEntry;
        rateText = StringVar(); rateText.set('0');
        rateEntry.configure(
            textvariable = rateText, width = 20);
        rateLabel.configure(
            text = 'Hourly rate', width = 20,
            borderwidth = 2, relief = SUNKEN);
        global submitButton, clearButton;
        submitButton.configure(
            text = 'Submit', width = 20, command = submitAction);
        clearButton.configure(
            text = 'Clear', width = 20, command = clearAction);
        global scrolledText;
        scrolledText.configure(
            width = 40, borderwidth = 2, relief = SUNKEN);
```

Recall that the *padx* and *pady* options define additional padding to be placed, horizontally and vertically, around the widget. The padding is outside of the widget and does not use the space allocated for the widget. The *borderwidth* option defines optional borders with labels, scrolled texts, and other widgets. In contrast to padding, border width is within the widget itself and uses part of the space allocated for the widget.

Example

The intermediate program produced by this fourth step can be executed. When executed, the program produces the GUI depicted below. Notice that you can click on buttons but there will be no consequences to your clicking. At this step the buttons have only dummy functions attached to them. At the next step, the button's action functions are completely defined to ensure proper operation of the entire program.

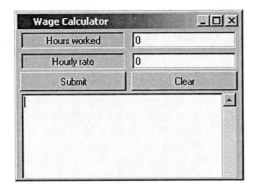

Fifth Step: Action Programming

The goal of this last step is to implement all needed action functions.

For the *Wage Calculator* program, we need to define the action functions to be invoked upon clicks on the *Submit* and *Clear* buttons. These functions are named *submitAction* and *clearAction*. The *submitAction* function receives the *hours* and *rate* values from the corresponding entry widgets, calculates the *wages*, and inserts them at the end of the *scrolled text* widget. The *clearAction* function deletes the entire content of the *scrolled text* widget and resets the *hours* and *rate* entries to 0.

It has already been discussed that a program can communicate with an entry widget through a text variable attached to the widget. Technically, your program uses *set* and *get* methods to update the text variable or to obtain its value.

A scrolled text widget stores and displays lines of text. The index of each character is a decimal number set, such as '1.0' or '7.2'. This index refers to the line number followed by the character position within the line. Line numbers start from 1, while character positions within lines start from 0. A special index named END is used to denote the last character in the formatted text widget.

Your program sends text to be displayed by a scrolled text widget directly by means of a special *insert* method. The program can delete text from the widget by means of the *delete* method.

Example

The following statement appends text to the end of the entire available text:

```
scrolledText.insert(END, 'Hello.');
```

If no text is available, the new text is inserted at the very first position, '1.0'.

The following statement deletes the text between the first character, '1.0', and the END of the text:

```
scrolledText.delete('1.0', END);
```

In the *Wage Calculator* program, a helper function named *fpToString* is used to convert floating point values to string before they are appended to the scrolled text widget. This function rounds the value to a specified number of decimal positions, avoiding the unnecessary output of insignificant digits. The *fpToString* function returns a slice of the entire string representation. When you study the function, remember that the slice *s[0:n+1]* consist of *s[0], s[1],...s[n-1], s[n]*.

Complete definitions of functions *submitAction*, *clearAction*, and *fpToString* are below. The implementation of these functions completes the *Wage Calculator* program.

```
# Clear the scrolled text:
def clearAction():
    global hoursText, rateText, scrolledText;
    hoursText.set('0');
    rateText.set('0');
    scrolledText.delete('1.0', END);

# Input hours and rate, calculate and display wages:
def submitAction():
    global hoursText, scrolledText;
    hours = float(hoursText.get());
    rate = float(rateText.get());
    wages = hours * rate;
    outputString = '\n\tHours worked :\t' + fpToString(hours, 2) + \
        '\n\tHourly rate  :\t$' + fpToString(rate, 2) + \
        '\n\tGross wages  :\t$' + fpToString(wages, 2) + '\n';
    scrolledText.insert(END, outputString);
```

```
# Convert a floating point value to a string with specified
# decimal positions:
def fpToString(value, decimalPositions):
    string = str(round(value, decimalPositions));
    periodPosition = string.find('.');
    if (periodPosition >= 0):
        string = string[0: periodPosition + decimalPositions + 1];
    return string;
    # Example: fpToString(value = 3.14159, decimalPositions = 2)
    # returns '3.14'.
```

Example
The following snapshot depicts a sample execution of the *Wage Calculator* program.

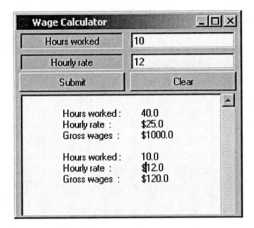

Widgets and Their Properties
The previous section introduces several useful GUI widgets. This section summarizes, in tabular form, the properties of these widgets. The following tables are included:
- A table with names and widget descriptions
- A table with widget-related methods
- A table with common widget options
- A table with widget-specific widget options

Widget Names and Descriptions

A selection of widgets is presented in the following table.

Widget name	Defining module	Widget description
Tk	Tkinter	Top-level widget used as main GUI window.
Label	Tkinter	Displays information.
Button	Tkinter	Displays information. Has a Python function attached. When the button is pressed, the function is automatically invoked.
Entry	Tkinter	Enters or displays a single line of text.
ScrolledText	ScrolledText	Provides multi-line text display. Has a vertical scrollbar.

A widget is created with constructor invocation formed by the widget name. A widget constructor expects the widget master as an argument. The *Tk* widget is an exception: as a top-level widget, it does not have a master, but serves as a master itself.

Example

The constructor invocations create a main window and button:

```
window = Tk(); button = Button(window);
```

A widget constructor invocation may include widget configuration options.

Widget Methods

A selection of widget methods is presented in the following table.

Method invocation	Description
window.title(*string*)	Set main window's title.
window.mainloop()	Display main window and listen for various events, such as button clicks.
widget.configure(*options*,...)	Set *widget* options.
widget.configure()	Without arguments, this method returns a dictionary with all current options for the *widget*.

widget.grid(*options,...*)	Position *widget* in its master.
textVariable.set(*string*)	Assign a value into a *text variable*. A *text variable* that is attached to a widget holds the actual text displayed in the widget.
textVariable.get()	Obtain the current value of a *text variable*. A *text variable* attached to a widget holds the actual text displayed in the widget.
scrolledText.insert(*index, text*)	Insert text at specified position.
scrolledText.delete(*start, stop*)	Delete all text within specified range.

Recall that the position of each character in a scrolled text widget is specified as a decimal separated pair of numbers, such as '1.0' or '7.2'. Such indexes consist of a line number followed by character position within the line. Line numbers start at 1, while character positions within lines start at 0. A special index named END is used to label the last character in the formatted text widget.

Widget Configuration Options

A selection of widget configuration options is presented in the following table.

Option	Widget	Description
width	All	Widget width.
height	Button, Label, Scrolled Text	Widget height.
relief	All	Border decoration. Possible values are FLAT, SUNKEN, RAISED, GROOVE, and RIDGE. Defaults are widget-dependent.
borderwidth	All	Widget border width. Default is platform dependent, but is usually one or two points.
text	Button, Label	Text to display in the widget.

command	Button	A function to be called when the button is pressed.
textvariable	Button, Entry, Label	Associates a text variable (usually of Tkinter's type StringVar) with the widget. The text variable contains the text displayed in the widget.

Note that in the above table, the word *all* stands for buttons, labels, entries, and scrolled texts. The level widget used as main window is excluded from this table.

Grid Options

A selection of widget configuration options is presented in the following table.

Option	Description
column	Insert the widget at this column. Column numbers start with 0. If omitted, defaults to 0.
columnspan	Indicates the widget column span. Default is 1.
row	Insert the widget at this row. Row numbers start with 0. If omitted, defaults to 0.
rowspan	Indicates the widget row span. Default is 1.
padx, pady	Padding to place vertically and horizontally around the widget. Default is 0.

Note that all of the above options can be used in invocations of the *grid* geometry manager.

Widget Resources

This course uses the *Tkinter* module, together with several smaller modules derived from *Tkinter*, to introduce basic GUI programming. You are now prepared to develop adequate GUIs for most Python programs we have already studied. You can continue studying GUIs in a special GUI courses.

If you want to further learn *Tkinter* details, there are adequate online and printed resources. Start looking in the references for this course.

Exercise

Search the Web for information on *Tkinter* fonts.

Import Patterns

At the uppermost level, every module defines various *attributes*, such as functions and global variables. The import-statement makes a module's attributes available to the program.

The import-statement has several forms. Two common forms of the import-statement were informally introduced earlier in the course. These two forms are revisited and summarized in this section.

The first form of the import-statement starts with the *import* keyword, followed by one or more comma-separated module names. The importing program refers to the attributes of the imported module using qualified names. A qualified name consists of a dotted pair of a module name and an attribute name.

Example

```
import math, random;
x = random.randint(1, 100); s = math.pi * math.sqrt(x);
import Tkinter;
window = Tkinter.Tk(); button = Tkinter.Button(window);
```

The second form of the import-statement starts with the *from* keyword, followed by a module name, followed by the *import* keyword and a star. The importing program refers to all attributes of the imported module by means of their names. No qualified names are needed.

Example

```
from random import *;
x = randint(1, 100);
from math import *;
s = pi * sqrt(x);
from Tkinter import *;
window = Tk(); button = Button(window);
```

Although the second form seems convenient, it should not be your immediate choice. Consider two independent modules, each of them defining a function with the same name. To resolve the name conflict, you will need to use the first form of the import-statement (or another, less common import forms not discussed here). Also, the first form of the import-statement forces the use of qualified names, which in many cases makes a program easier to analyze and comprehend.

The *sys* built-in module encapsulates some variables that are used by the interpreter, such as, for example, the *sys.path* variable. The import-statement uses the *sys.path* variable to locate any imported modules.

The *sys.path* variable is a Python list that you can import, observe, and even modify in your programs. You can enhance the *sys.path* variable with your own pathnames, which will help the Python interpreter find and import your own modules.

> Example
>> Assume that in a Windows system, a custom *turtle* module is located in folder A:\Master\08. You can make the *turtle* module available to the import-statement by inserting its parent folder, A:\Master\08, in the beginning of *sys.path*:
>>
>> import sys;
>> sys.path.insert(0, 'A:\\Master\\08');
>> import turtle;
>> ...
>> pen = turtle.Pen();
>> pen.forward(100);

The Global-Statement

The global-statement consists of the keyword *global*, followed by one or more comma-separated names. The global-statement declares the listed names are interpreted as global.

In a function body, it is impossible to assign a value into an existing global variable unless the function specifically declares the variable global.

It is possible to use (but not assign) a global variable in a function body without listing the variable in a global-statement. However, listing all global variables in global-statements makes your program more readable and less error prone.

The Pass-Statement

The pass-statement consists of the *pass* keyword only. When executed, the pass-statement does nothing at all. This statement can be used as a placeholder for statements that will be added later in the program design process.

Example

The following statement defines a dummy function that will be defined at a later step of the program design:

```
def f(): pass;
```

The following loop statement incorporates a dummy loop body that will be defined at a later step of the program design:

```
for i in range(10): pass;
```

The above statement does execute its body ten times, but each execution of the body does nothing.

Sample GUI Programs

Several complete GUI-oriented sample programs are provided with this topic. All sample programs employ some new GUI concepts. The programs are written as self-contained introductions of these GUI concepts.

Study, analyze, and possibly enhance the sample programs. Your independent work with these programs will help you master your knowledge and ability to program.
Brief descriptions of sample programs follow.

Celsius to Fahrenheit Converter

A program named *C2F Converter* converts Celsius temperatures into Fahrenheit. The name *C2F Converter* is an abbreviation for Celsius to Fahrenheit Converter. This program interacts with the user using a simple GUI. Snapshots of a sample interaction with the program are shown below.

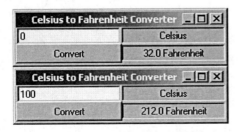

The program's GUI is a 2 x 2 grid of widgets. The first row incorporates an entry for the Celsius temperatures to convert and a label instructing the user what to type in the entry. This label never changes.

The second row incorporates a button to trigger the conversion and a label to display the result of the conversion.

The label displaying the result of the temperature conversion must have its text changed for any new temperature conversion. This is easy to do using the configure method of the label.

Example

The following statements change the text displayed in a label:

```
label = Label(master);
...
label.configure(text = 'This text is displayed initially in the label...');
...
label.configure(text = '... but then replaced by this text.');
```

Recall that the *Wage Calculator* program discussed in a previous section demonstrated how to use scrolled text widget for output. The *C2F Converter* program shows how to use a label widget as an alternative to scrolled text output. A label widget is usually smaller than a scrolled text widget. Output sent to a label widget replaces any previous output.

The main function of program *C2F Converter* is named *init*. An invocation of the *init* function is included at the very end of the program. Thus, you can launch the *C2F Converter* program as you prefer: independently or from within IDLE.

File Copier

The *File Copier* program creates a copy of an arbitrary text file, i.e., a file that consists of lines of characters. The extension of the file does not matter as long as the file is a sequence of lines. Python programs and CSV files are examples of text files.

The most remarkable feature of the *File Copier* is its employment of convenient, ready-to-use GUI software components, known as *file dialogs*, to open and save files. In particular, the program uses an *open file dialog* to retrieve the name of the source file to open. Also, the program uses a *save-as file dialog* to acquire a name for the saved file copy. A reduced size snapshot of an open file dialog is shown below.

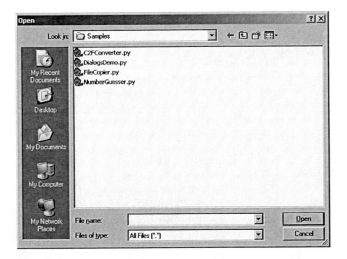

A save-as file dialog is similar to an open file dialog, the main difference being the use of a *Save* button instead of an *Open* button.

Both file dialogs allow you to conveniently browse the file system. When needed, file names can be typed directly in an entry widget incorporated in both file dialogs.

File dialogs are provided as ready-to use GUI components by the *tkFileDialog* module. For each type of dialog, there is a convenient function to initialize and carry out the dialog. Each such function returns a complete string pathname your program can use to open and work with a file's contents. Both functions return empty strings when the user cancels the dialog.

In the *File Copier* program, the file copying is implemented by a function named *fileCopy*. The definition of the *fileCopy* function follows:

```
# Open a file then save a copy:
def fileCopy():
    sourceName = tkFileDialog. askopenfilename();
    # Test if the user clicked on the Cancel button on Open:
    if (sourceName == ''): return;
    inFile = open(sourceName, 'r');
    localData = inFile.read();
    targetName = tkFileDialog. asksaveasfilename();
```

```
# Test if the user clicked on the Cancel button on Save:
if (targetName == ''): return;
outFile = open(targetName, 'w');
print >>  outFile, localData;
inFile.close(); outFile.close();
```

The main function of program *File Copier* is named *init*. An invocation of the *init* function is included at the very end of the program. Thus, you can launch the *File Copier* program as you prefer: independently or from within IDLE.

Exercise

Run the *File Copier* program then open the program file *FileCopier.py*. Save a copy as *CopyOfFile Copier.py*.

Number Guesser

The *Number Guesser* program is designed to:
- Ask the user to think of an arbitrary *secret number*.
- Ask the user to multiply the secret number by 5, add 6, multiply by 4, add 9, and multiply by 5.
- Ask the user to enter the *result* of the above operations.
- Guess the secret number.
- Convey to the user the guessed secret number.

An interesting feature of the *Number Guesser* is its use of convenient, ready-to-use GUI software components that inform the user what operations to perform, input the numeric result from the user's operations, and output the guessed number. The program uses several *message dialogs* to tell the user what operations to perform, an *input dialog* to enter the result of those operations, and another *message dialog* to convey to the user the guessed secret number. Snapshots of a message dialog and an input dialog are shown below.

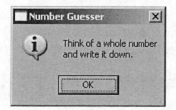 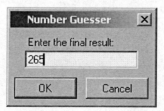

Message and input dialogs suspend program execution and wait for user action. For a message dialog, the user is simply expected to read the message and confirm. For an input dialog, the user is expected to enter a value and confirm.

Message dialogs are provided as ready-to use GUI components by the *tkMessageBox* module. There are several types of message dialogs, such as information dialog, warning dialog, and alert dialog . For each type of dialog, there is a convenience function that will initialize and carry out the dialog. The *Number Guesser* program uses only information dialogs, but other types of dialogs may be used when needed.

Input dialogs are provided as ready-to use GUI components by the *tkSimpleDialog* module. There are three types of input dialogs: integer input dialog, string input dialog, and floating point input dialog. Again, for each type of dialog, there is a convenience function that will initialize and carry out the dialog. The *Number Guesser* program uses only integer input dialog, but other dialogs are introduced by a subsequent sample program.

In the *Number Guesser* program, the actual number guessing is implemented by a function named *guessNumber*. The definition of the *guessNumber* function follows:

```python
# Ask the user to think of a number then guess it:
def guessNumber():
    tkMessageBox.showinfo(
        title, 'Think of a whole number\nand write it down.');
    tkMessageBox.showinfo(title, 'Multiply it by 5.');
    tkMessageBox.showinfo(title, 'Add 6 to the result.');
    tkMessageBox.showinfo(title,
        'Multiply the previous result by 4.');
    tkMessageBox.showinfo(title, 'Add 9.');
    tkMessageBox.showinfo(title, 'Again, multiply by 5.');
    result = tkSimpleDialog.askinteger(
        title = title, prompt = 'Enter the final result:');
    if (result != None):
        original = (result - 165) / 100;
        feedback = 'Hmmm... I guess you original number was ' \
            + str(original) + '.';
    else:
        feedback = 'I guess you are in a hurry...';
    tkMessageBox.showinfo(title, feedback);
```

The main function of program *Number Guesser* is named *init*. An invocation of the *init* function is included at the very end of the program. Thus, you can launch the *Number Guesser* program as you prefer: independently or from within IDLE.

Exercise

Run the *Number Guesser* program and experiment with your preferred secret number.

Dialogs Demo

The *Dialogs Demo* program is designed to demonstrate the following ready-to-use GUI components: message dialogs, input dialogs, color dialog, and file dialogs.

Previous sample programs have introduced some of the message and input dialogs, as well as the two available file dialogs. A most useful feature of the *Dialogs Demo* program is its usage of all seven message dialogs, all three input dialogs and a color chooser dialog that has not been demonstrated in other programs. A reduced size snapshot of a color chooser dialog is shown below.

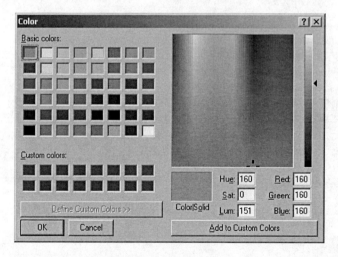

All dialogs are provided as ready-to use GUI components by several modules as follows:
- Message dialogs are in the *tkMessageBox* module.
- File dialogs are in the *tkFileDialog* module.
- Input dialogs are in the *tkMessageBox* module.
- The color chooser dialog is in the *tkColorChooser* module.

For each type of dialog, the corresponding module offers a convenience function to initialize and carry out the dialog. The number guesser program uses only information dialogs, but other dialogs are introduced in a subsequent sample program.

Input dialogs are provided as ready-to use GUI components by the *tkSimpleDialog* module. The *Dialogs Demo* program demonstrates all available dialogs by invocations to their convenience functions. Note that each function returns a value to reflect the user's response.

Example
- Message dialog functions return the string 'ok' after the user clicks the OK button.
- Data input functions return the value entered by the user.
- All functions return some special value, such as empty string or *None*, when the user cancels or closes the dialog.

The main function of program *Dialogs Demo* is named *init*. An invocation of the *init* function is included at the very end of the *Dialogs Demo* program. Thus, you can launch this program as you prefer: independently or from within IDLE.

Exercise
Run the *Dialogs Demo* program and experiment with various inputs.

Synonyms

Some terms that have been introduced in this topic have synonyms. A list of such terms and their corresponding synonyms follows.

Term	Synonym
Text-only interface	Command line interface
Geometry manager	Layout manager

Lab A [Graphics and Interfaces]

Objective; Background; Lab Overview; What to Do Next; Downloading Sample Programs; Uncompressing Sample Programs; Warning; Interactive Experiments; Saving Your Interactive Session

Objectives
- The objective of this lab is to study and get hands-on experience with the *turtle* module.

Background
- The following excerpt from the E-Text introduces the *turtle* module.
  - An easy way to get started with graphics programming in Python is to use a simple module named *turtle*. This module allows you to use a *pen* object that can draw on a *window* object. Pen movements along the screen can be likened to the movements of a little turtle, hence the module name *turtle*. This type of computer graphics is often referred to as *turtle graphics*.
- The E-text contains a comprehensive description of principal turtle graphics concepts and methods. Familiarity with those concepts and methods is required for this lab.
- The *Turtle Demo* sample program illustrates the principal turtle graphics concepts. Careful study of the sample program is a required part of this lab.

Note
The easiest way to start using the custom *turtle* module in interactive mode is to open the *turtle.py* file and then run it. Then you can type various turtle statements in the corresponding shell window. You do not need to keep *turtle.py* open.

Note

Before you draw:
- Close all unnecessary windows.
- Minimize completely or at least reduce partially the size of all remaining widows.

The drawing window must be uncovered at all times.

Lab Overview

To perform this lab:
- Study turtle graphics concepts and methods from the E-Text. Study the *Turtle Demo* sample program.
- In interactive mode, execute all activities listed in the Interactive Experiments section of this lab.
- Save your IDLE interactive session in a text file.

What to Do Next

You are now offered the following choices:
- Follow the detailed lab instructions below.
- Try the lab independently, using the instructions when you require help.
- Perform the lab independently, without any aid from the instructions.

All three approaches are beneficial to students. Choose the approach most beneficial to you.

Downloading Sample Programs

Various Lab Assignments for this course of study are based on ready-to-use sample programs. Such programs are downloadable from the online study pack. Save these files into your *master* folder.

Download sample programs for the current Topic 8 by performing these steps:
- Locate *Topic 8* in the online study pack.
- Open the *Lab Assignment* resource.
- Right-click on the *Sample Programs* link.
- Use *Save As* to store the downloaded compressed (zipped) folder, *08.zip,* within your *master* folder.

Uncompressing Sample Programs

- Uncompress the contents of the downloaded compressed (zipped) folder. Depending on your platform, you may use built-in compression support, or compressing utilities.
    - In Windows XP, use built-in un-compression support as follows:
        - Open your *master* folder using the *File Browser*.
        - Right-click on the downloaded compressed (zipped) folder.
        - Use *Extract All* to extract the contents of the compressed (zipped) folder within the *master* folder.
            - This will create an uncompressed folder, *08*, within the *master* folder. This folder contains your sample programs.
    - Alternatively, you can:
        - *Open* the compressed (zipped) folder.
        - *Cut* folder *08* from within the compressed (zipped) folder, and
        - *Paste* the cut folder *08* outside the compressed (zipped) folder – directly within the *master* folder.
- Delete the compressed (zipped) folder, *08.zip*; keep the uncompressed folder, *08*.
- Open the uncompressed folder *08* and browse its contents.
- Note that Python program files have extension '**.py**'.

Warning

- When you need to close the drawing window, restart the Python shell using *Shell → Restart Shell*. This will safely close the drawing window.
    - The same effect is achieved by closing the shell window.
- Avoid closing the drawing window directly.

Interactive Experiments

- Study turtle graphics concepts and methods from the E-Text.
- In interactive mode, execute all statements below. If you follow all the steps carefully, you should be able to draw this image:

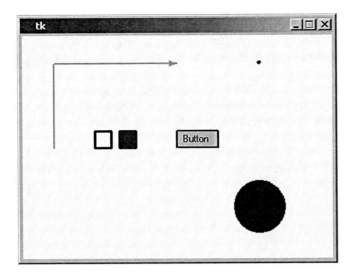

- Execute the following statements in sequence.

    ```
    >>> # Open the turtle.py file from Turtle Demo;
    >>> # Run the turtle.py file (you may then close this file);
    >>> # Type the following statements in the shell window;

    >>> # Create pen and drawing window:
    >>> pen = Pen();
    >>> # Resize and move widows if necessary to see
    >>> # the drawing window:

    >>> # Move left without drawing:
    >>> pen.reset();
    >>> pen.up();
    >>> pen.backward(100);
    >>> pen.down();

    >>> # Draw an empty square:
    >>> pen.width(3);
    >>> for j in range(4): pen.forward(20); pen.left(90);

    >>> # Move right without drawing:
    >>> pen.up();
    >>> pen.forward(30);
    >>> pen.down();

    >>> # Draw a filled square:
    >>> pen.color(0, 0, 1); #blue
    ```

```
>>> pen.fill(True);
>>> for j in range(4): pen.forward(20); pen.left(90);
>>> pen.fill(False);

>>> # Move right and down without drawing:
>>> pen.up();
>>> pen.goto(100, -100);
>>> pen.down();

>>> # Draw a filled circle:
>>> pen.color(0, 0, 1); # blue
>>> pen.fill(True);
>>> pen.circle(30);
>>> pen.fill(False);

>>> # Move up without drawing:
>>> pen.up();
>>> pen.goto(100, 100);
>>> pen.down();

>>> # Draw a tiny circle:
>>> pen.color(0, 0, 1); # blue
>>> pen.fill(True);
>>> pen.circle(1);
>>> pen.fill(False);

>>> # Move right without drawing:
>>> pen.up();
>>> pen.goto(0, 0);
>>> pen.down();

>>> # Fill a button-like rectangle:
>>> pen.width(2);
>>> pen.fill(True);
>>> # Set drawing color to black:
>>> pen.color(0, 0, 0); # black
>>> pen.goto(50, 0);
>>> pen.goto(50, 20);
>>> pen.goto(0, 20);
>>> pen.goto(0, 0);
>>> # Set fill color to light gray:
>>> pen.color(0.8, 0.8, 0.8); #light gray
>>> pen.fill(False);
>>> # Write some text:
```

```
>>> pen.up();
>>> pen.goto(8, 4);
>>> pen.down();
>>> pen.color(0, 0, 0); # black
>>> pen.write('Button');

>>> # Set tracing off, draw, set it on:
>>> pen.up();
>>> pen.goto(-150, 0);
>>> pen.down();
>>> pen.tracer(False);
>>> pen.color(0, 1, 0); # green
>>> pen.goto(-150, 100);
>>> pen.goto(0, 100);
>>> pen.tracer(True);
```

- Use *Shell → Restart Shell* to restart the Python shell.
- Open and study the Turtle Demo sample program.
- Run the Turtle Demo sample program.
- Save your interactive session as explained in the next section.

Saving Your Interactive Session

- Save the interactive session with your all of your experiments in your current labs folder, *08Labs*.
- From the Shell Window, use *File → Save As*.
- Name the saved copy *Session_8A.txt*.
    - **Important Note:** You must explicitly supply the file extension '**.txt**' when saving from IDLE.
- If you perform experiments in two or more interactive sessions, save your work in several files. If you choose to do so, use names *Session_8A_1.txt, Session_8A_2.txt*, and so on, for all saved files.
    - In the beginning of each session, run the *turtle.py* file first.
- Your saved file(s) must be included in your Lab Assignment submission.

Lab B [Graphics and Interfaces]

Objective; Background; Lab Overview; What to Do Next; Studying the Sample Program; Creating a Program File; Developing the New Program

Objective
The objectives of this lab include:
- Developing a *New Patterns* program as a modified version of the *Pattern Designer* sample program.
- Employing the *New Patterns* program to produce new unique patterns.
- Posting a message in this topic's *Forum* that:
  - Describes your experiments with and modifications of the *Pattern Designer* sample program.
  - Contains one sample pattern produced by your *New Patterns* program.

Background
- A sample program named *Pattern Designer* draws various original computer graphics patterns. The E-Text offers a detailed description of this program. Knowledge of this program is required for this lab.
- In the *Pattern Designer* sample program, a pattern is built as a composition of tiny circles produced by the *draw* function. You can produce new original patterns by making specific changes to the *draw* function.

Note
Before you draw:
- Close all unnecessary windows.
- Minimize completely or at least reduce partially the size of all remaining widows.

The drawing window must be uncovered at all times.

Lab Overview
To perform this lab:
- Study the *Pattern Designer* sample program.

- Transform a copy of the *Pattern Designer* sample program into a *New Patterns* program.
- Modify the *draw* function in the *New Patterns* program to produce new, original patterns. Experiment with various modifications.
- Describe in this topic's *Forum* your experiments and modifications; attach one sample pattern designed by your *New Patterns* program.

What to Do Next

You are now offered the following choices:
- Follow the detailed lab instructions below.
- Try the lab independently, using the instructions when you require help.
- Perform the lab independently, without any aid from the instructions.

All three approaches are beneficial to students. Choose the approach most beneficial to you.

Studying the Sample Program

- Open and browse the *Pattern Designer* sample program using IDLE.
- Invoke *pattern* with various arguments, such as 5, 3, and 6.
  - Before each invocation, use *Shell → Restart Shell* to restart the Python Shell.
- Analyze the *Pattern Designer* sample program implementation.

Creating a Program File

Create this program in your current labs folder, *08Labs*.
- Copy the entire *Patterns* folder into your current labs folder; rename the copy to *NewPatterns*.
  - All work will be done in *NewPatterns* folder.
- In the *NewPatterns* folder, rename the *PatternDesigner.py* file to *NewPatterns.py*.
  - This is the program file for your *New Patterns* program.
- In the *NewPatterns* folder, delete all other files, keeping only the *NewPatterns.py* file.

Developing the New Program

- New patterns can be produced by making certain changes in the *draw* function. Here are some possible changes to explore:

- Use alternative expressions to defined the *ez* variable in terms of *a* and *b*.
- Use alternative *ez*-tests in place of *(ez % 2)*, such as *(ez % 3)*.
- Use different drawing methods in place of *circle*, such as the *forward* and *backward*.
- Use multiple selection *ez*-tests to choose a particular color for each point.

○ Perform the following steps with your *New Patterns* program:
- Use *Shell → Restart Shell* to restart the Python Shell.
- Introduce an experimental change in the *draw* function.
- Run the program, observing the created pattern.
- If necessary, resize and move widows to see the drawing window.
- Observe the pattern. If it strikes your fancy, save it as suggested below.
- Repeat the above steps until you produce a new pattern you are particularly found of; always restart the Python Shell between patterns.

○ Update comments throughout the program.
○ Supply additional lines of comments to improve readability.

○ Save your new pattern as a file named MyPattern - within your current labs folder. How exactly you create and save this file will depend on your particular system: Windows, Macintosh, or Linux.
○ In Windows, for example, perform the following steps.
- Click on the title bar of the drawing widow to make it the active window.
- Use *Alt→ Print Screen* to copy the window onto the Clipboard.
  - The above step will have no visible effect to you.
- Start an application that can handle graphics, such as the Paint program.
  - Use *Edit → Paste* to paste the window copied from the Clipboard onto an empty document.
- Save the document as a JPEG file.
  - Use *File → Save As* and choose *Save as type: JPEG*. Save under the name MyPattern in your current labs folder.

- If you have no access to Paint, you can use a word processor, such as Microsoft Office Word or Open Office Writer.
  - Paste and then save as a *Single File Web Page* (.mht) or as a *Word Document* (.doc) under the name MyPattern. Again, save in your current labs folder.
- Post a message in this topic's *Forum*.
  - Attach the MyPattern.htm file containing one sample pattern designed by your *New Patterns* program.
  - Describe how you produced that pattern. For example, specify any alternative expressions or tests used in the *draw* function.
    - Do not post your program; post only the pattern and a brief description of what you have done to produce it.

Lab C [Graphics and Interfaces]

Objective; Background; Lab Overview; What to Do Next; Studying the Sample Program; Creating a Program File; Developing the New Program

Objective

The objective of this lab is to develop an *Order Calculator* program with a GUI. The program should:
- Input a complete *quantity* of items per order, with floating point numbers for *item price* and percentage *tax rate*.
- Calculate the *total price* of the order, the *sales tax,* and the *order total*.
- Display *quantity, item price, sales tax,* and *order total*.

Your *Order Calculator* GUI should look like this:

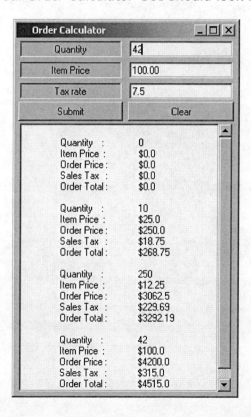

Background
- A sample program named *Wage Calculator* uses a GUI is similar to the GUI needed to design this lab. The E-Text offers a description of the sample program. You must be familiar with the *Wage Calculator* program to complete this lab.
- The following formulae specify the order calculation part of your program:

  *order price = quantity * item price;*
  *sales tax   = order price * (tax rate / 100.0);*
  order total = order price + sales tax;

Lab Overview
To perform this lab:
- Study the *Wage Calculator* sample program.
- Transform a copy of the *Wage Calculator* sample program into an *Order Calculator* program.
- Extensively test the *Order Calculator* program.

What to Do Next
You are now offered the following choices:
- Follow the detailed lab instructions below.
- Try the lab independently, using the instructions when you require help.
- Perform the lab independently, without any aid from the instructions.

All three approaches are beneficial to students. Choose the approach most beneficial to you.

Studying the Sample Program
- Study the *Wage Calculator* sample program from the E-text.
- Open and browse the *Wage Calculator* sample program using IDLE.
- Run the program with various input data; observe the output.
- Analyze the program implementation.

Creating a Program File
Save this program in your current labs folder, *08Labs*.
- Copy the entire *Wages* folder into your current labs folder; rename the copy *Orders*.
  - You will continue your work in the *Orders* folder.

- In the *Orders* folder, rename the *WageCalculator.py* file to *OrderCalculator.py*.
  - This is the program file for your *Order Calculator* program.
- Keep only the *OrderCalculator.py* file in the *Orders* folder; delete all other files;

Developing the New Program

Important Note

It is likely that programming errors will occur as you develop your *Order Calculator* program. Remember, if you try to run a GUI program but the GUI does not behave as expected, **look in the Python Shell window for tips**. The Python Shell window will probably contain an error message that will help you isolate and correct the error.

Perform the following steps with the new *Order Calculator* program.

First Step: Program Initialization

- Modify the *init* function to display title 'Order Calculator' instead of 'Wage Calculator'.
- Run the *Order Calculator* program. Your *Order Calculator* GUI should look like the *Wage Calculator* GUI except for the updated title bar.
- Exit the program by clicking on the *Close* button on the window's right upper corner.

Second Step: Widget Creation

- In function *createWidget*, replace all *hours* widgets with *quantity* widgets.
  - You will need to work with global *quantityLabel* and *quantityEntry* widgets, instead of *hoursLabel* and *hoursEntry* widgets.
    - Simply replace 'hours' with 'quantity' in all variable names in all the functions of the program. This replaces *hours* widgets with *quantity* widgets.
- In function *createWidget*, create *price* widgets.
  - Create global *priceLabel* and *priceEntry* widgets.
  - Create *price* widgets immediately after the creation of the *quantity* widgets, and before the creation of the *rate* widgets.
  - Remember, the new *price* widgets must be global.
- Keep all other widgets as they are.
- Run the *Order Calculator* program. Your *Order Calculator* GUI should look exactly like the one at the end of the previous step. Remember, as explained in the E-Text, at this stage all widgets

are represented by objects in memory. They are not yet displayed.
- Exit the program by clicking on the *Close* button in the window's right upper corner.

Third Step: Widget Positioning

- Work exclusively with the *positionWidgets* function.
- Replace 'hours' with 'quantity' in all variable names if you have not yet done so. This replaces *hours* widgets with *quantity* widgets.
- Be sure the *quantity* label and entry widgets are positioned in grid row 0.
- Position the *price* label and entry widgets in grid row 1, columns 0 and 1 respectively.
- Reposition the *rate* widgets from grid row 1 to grid row 2.
- Reposition the button widgets from grid row 2 to grid row 3.
- Reposition the *scrolled text* widget from grid row 3 to grid row 4.
- Run the *Order Calculator* program. Your *Order Calculator* GUI should like the one below. At the next step, widgets will be configured with size, relief, borders, text, and other properties that create the prescribed widget look. In particular, all widgets will be assigned the correct texts for display.

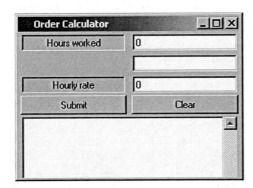

- Exit the program by clicking on the *Close* button in the window's right upper corner.

Fourth Step: Widget Configuration

- Work exclusively with the *configureWidgets* function.
- Replace 'hours' with 'quantity' in all variable names, if you have not yet done so. This replaces *hours* widgets with *quantity* widgets.
- In the configuration of the *quantity* label, use *text = 'Quantity'* instead of *text = 'Hours worked'*.
- Configure the global *price* widgets.
  - The configuration of the *price* widgets is very similar to the configuration of the *quantity* and *rate* widgets.
  - The configuration of *price* widgets should follow the configuration of *quantity* widgets and precede the configuration of *rate* widgets.
  - Now:
    - Define a global string variable named *priceText* and set it to '0';
    - Configure the *priceLabel* and *priceEntry* widgets. Use the *priceText* variable in the configuration of the *priceEntry* widget.
- In the configuration of the *rate* label, use *text = 'Tax rate'* instead of *text = 'Hourly rate'*.
- Run the *Order Calculator* program. Your *Order Calculator* GUI should now look like the one shown below. At this stage, the program displays a proper order-related GUI but still performs the old wage calculations. At the next step, wage calculation will be replaced with order calculations.

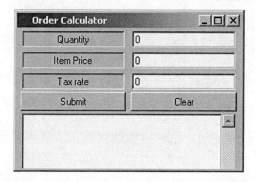

- Exit the program by clicking on the *Close* button in the window's upper right corner.

Fifth Step: Action Programming
- Modify the *submitAction* function to perform order calculations instead of wage calculations. If your program does not behave as expected, look in the Python Shell window for error messages.
  - Get *quantity*, *item price*, and *tax rate* from the corresponding string variables.
  - Use the following formulae for order calculation:
    order price = *quantity* * *item price*;
    sales tax   = *order price* * (*tax rate* / 100.0);
    order total = *order price* + *sales tax*;

  - In the *scrolled text* widget, insert *quantity*, *item price*, *order price*, *sales tax*, and *order total*.
- Modify the *clearAction* function to reset to '0' the string variables for *quantity*, *item price*, and *tax rate*. The *scrolled text* needs to be deleted, as before.
- Run the *Order Calculator* program. Your *Order Calculator* GUI should like the one shown in the very beginning of this lab.

Fifth Step: Action Programming
- Test your *Order Calculator* program.
- Update all comments, adding new comments to improve readability.

Lab D [Graphics and Interfaces]

Objective; Background; Lab Overview

Objectives
- The objective of this lab is to study and gain hands-on experience with the sample programs for the current topic.

Background
A number of sample programs are available to help you learn lists and dictionaries. The following sample programs are available to be studied:

- *Pattern Designer*
- *Mandelbrot Patterns*
- *Turtle Demo*
- *Simple Wages*
- *Wage Calculator*
- *C2F Converter*
- *File Copier*
- *Number Guesser*
- *Dialogs Demo*

The E-text offers descriptions of all sample programs. Two of the programs, the *Pattern Designer* and the *Wage Calculator*, are described in detail. The descriptions of all other programs are overviews. Your task is to analyze all programs and experiment with them.

Lab Overview
To perform this lab:
- For each sample program from the above list:
  - Read the description in the E-Text.
  - Open and browse the sample program using IDLE.
  - Run the program with various input data; observe the output.
  - Analyze the program implementation.

- Pay special attention to the *Dialogs Demo* sample program.
  - In repetitive executions of the program, use different dialog replies, such as OK, Cancel, and Close;
  - Observe value returned by the dialog function for different dialog replies.
- Return nothing for this lab.

Lab E [Graphics and Interfaces, Optional]

Objective; Background; Lab Overview

Objectives
The objectives of this lab are:
- To develop a *New Mandelbrot* program as a modified version of the *Mandelbrot Patterns* sample program.
- To employ the *New Mandelbrot* program in producing new unique patterns.
- To post a message in this topic's *Forum*:
  - Describing your experiments and modifications of the *Mandelbrot Patterns* sample program.
  - Containing one sample pattern produced by your *New Mandelbrot* program.

Background
- A sample program named *Mandelbrot Patterns* draws various original computer graphics patterns. The program offers a possible visualization of the famed Mandelbrot sets.
- Descriptions of the famed Mandelbrot sets are found in many web and print recourses. You must be familiar with Mandelbrot sets visualization to complete this lab.
- In the *Mandelbrot Patterns* sample program, a pattern is built as a composition of tiny circles produced by the *draw* function. New patterns can be produced by changing the *draw* function.

Lab Overview
To perform this lab:
- Research web and print resources to self-study Mandelbrot sets visualization.
- Study the *Mandelbrot Patterns* sample program.
- You may start experimenting with this sample invocation:

mandelbrot(u0= -0.5, v0 = 0, side = 1).

- Create a copy of the *Mandelbrot Patterns* sample program in your current labs folder. Transform the copy into a *New Mandelbrot* program.
- Experiment with the *draw* function in the *New Mandelbrot* program; modify it to produce new original Mandelbrot patterns.
- Describe in this topic's *Forum* your experiments and modifications; attach one sample pattern designed by your *New Mandelbrot* program.

Lab F [Graphics and Interfaces, Optional]

Objective; Background; Lab Overview

Objective
The objective of this lab is to develop a GUI-based *Number Tricks* program that will:
- Ask the user to think of an arbitrary *secret number*.
- Ask the user to subtract 1 from the secret number, double the difference, and add the secret number itself to the result.
- Ask the user to enter the *result* of the above operations.
- Guess the secret number.
- Convey to the user the guessed secret number.

Background
- Guessing method: Add 2 to the result reported by the user and divide by 3. The quotient is the original secret number.
- Sample number trick:
  - The secret number is 18.
  - The player transforms the number as follows: 18 − 1 = 17; 17 * 2 = 34; 34 + 18 = 52.
  - Your program guesses the secret number as follows: 52 + 2 = 54; 54 / 3 = 18.

Lab Overview
To perform this lab:
- Study GUI implementations in the sample programs for this topic; choose a GUI to use as a sample.
  - Although the Number Guesser sample program seems a close fit for the Number Tricks, it is not the only good choice. The Wage Calculator program, for example, can lead you to a nice, clean GUI.
- In your current labs folder, implement and test the Number Tricks program.
- Try to prove the correctness of the guessing method.

Lab G [Graphics and Interfaces, Optional]

Objective; Background; Lab Overview

Objective
The objective of this lab is to develop a *Class Ranker* program that will:
- Accept a *percentage* and display a list of all students whose GPA is in that *percentage* bracket.
- Use a GUI for all communications with the user.

Background
- This program can use a GUI similar to the GUI of the *Wage Calculator* sample program.
  - A GUI for the *Class Ranker* program requires only one entry widget, used for the entered percentage.
- The *Class Ranker* program should use a file open dialog to read records from a file, similarly to the *File Copier sample program*.
  - Each student record should consist of comma-separated *last name*, *first name*, and *GPA*.

Lab Overview
To perform this lab:
- Study the *Wage Calculator* and *File Copier* sample programs.
- Develop this program in a separate folder in your current labs folder.
- Use an Entry widget to input any specific percentage.
- Use a Submit button to trigger computation.
- At the first Submit action, use a file open dialog to read a file containing student records.
- Use a Scrolled Text widget for output.
- Use a Clear button to clear the Entry and Scrolled Text widgets.
  - The first Submit action after a Clear action should open another file.
- Extensively test your program.
- Supply adequate comments for readability.

Lab H [Graphics and Interfaces, Optional]

Objective; Background; Lab Overview

Objective
The objective of this lab is to develop a program that will:
- Play the game *Three Button Monte*.
- Use a GUI for all communications with the user.

Background
- The *Three Button Monte* game is a simplified version of a game known as Three Card Monte.
  - The game of Three Card Monte is described in Web resources.
- A program for the *Three Button Monte* provides three buttons. For each individual game, the program randomly selects winning buttons then asks the user to click any button. The program keeps the score by counting how many times the user has won and how many times the user lost.

Lab Overview
To perform this lab:
- Research the game of Three Card Monte on the Web. This is not required, but will be helpful.
  - This research can give you enhancement ideas for your *Three Button Monte* program.
- Develop *Three Button Monte* program in a separate folder, within your current labs folder.
- Extensively test your program.
- Supply adequate comments for readability.

Classes

Objects Revisited; Introduction to Classes; Stepwise Class Design; Classes and Program Execution; Class Definitions; Class Concepts; Inheritance; Sample Programs; Synonyms

Objects Revisited

The concept of an *object* has already been introduced in this course, and various objects have been studied since then. When a program runs, all of its structures – numbers, strings, lists, and functions - are represented in computer memory in binary form, as sequences of 0s and 1s. Different types of program structures use different binary representation schemes. The memory representation of any program structure is called an *object*. This is a very general yet useful and popular concept.

There are various types of objects. A *numeric object* represents a number while a *string object* represents a sequence of characters. An object can also represent executable code, such as a function. A *list object* is the run-time memory representation of a list. A *widget* object represents a button, entry, label, scrolled text, or any other device used to build a GUI. A graphics *pen* object represents an electronic pen designed to draw on an electronic canvas.

Generally speaking, the term object stands for anything that can be assigned a name: a number, a string, a function, a list, a dictionary, a widget, a pen, and more.

Recall that objects usually have functions attached to them. Such functions are referred to as *methods*. Methods are invoked through their objects, by means of dot-notation.

Example
A number of useful functions are attached to every pen object. Examples of such pen functions are *up, down, forward, goto,* and *circle.* These functions are always invoked through a pen object using dot-notation, as illustrated below.

```
>>> import turtle; pen = turtle.Pen();
>>> pen.up(); pen.goto(75, 100); pen.down();
```

```
>>> pen.goto(0, -100);
>>> pen.goto(-75, 100);
>>> pen.up(); pen.goto(0, 0); pen.down();
>>> pen.circle(20);
```

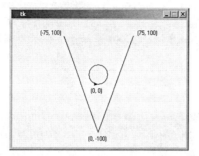

In addition to functions, objects usually have variables attached to them to store necessary data. Variables attached to objects are typically accessed indirectly, by means of methods.

Example

A pen object uses variables representing the *window width,* the *window height*, the pen *color,* the pen *position*, and other data. The width and height of a pen's window can be obtained by invoking two special methods, *window_width* and *window_height*. The pen position is changed by invocations of the *goto* method. For example:

```
>>> import turtle; pen = turtle.Pen();
>>> w = pen.window_width();
>>> h = pen.window_height();
>>> print w, h;
382 269
>>> pen.goto(75, 100);
```

Functions and variables attached to an object are called an object's *attributes*. All object attributes are referred to through their objects, by means of dot-notation.

Introduction to Classes

All objects discussed so far have been predefined and supplied to us through the *Python system*. Various *classes* of objects, such as pens, buttons, labels, entries, scrolled texts and more, can be specified in Python by means of *class definitions*.

Example

Pen and *Button* class definitions look like this in Python:

> class Pen:
>   *... Definitions of various*
>   *pen-specific functions...*
>
> class Button:
>   *... Definitions of various*
>   *button-specific functions...*

Class definitions commonly used are normally packed in modules. For example, various widget classes, such as *Button*, *Label* or *Entry*, are packed in the *Tkinter* module. When you import such a module, you make all class definitions available to your program. Alternatively, you can define a specific class in your program and use it only there.

When there is a class definition available, it can be used to create one or more objects of that class. You can do this by means of constructor invocations. A constructor invocation is like a function invocation, but instead of a function name it has a class name. Each constructor invocation constructs and returns an object of the class.

Example

During the discussion of the topic of Graphics and Interfaces, we imported all classes from the *Tkinter* module. Among others, we imported the *Button* class and created various *Button* objects. The following assignment statements use *Button* constructor invocations to create two *Button* objects and assign the created objects into variables:

> submitButton = Button(window);
> clearButton = Button(window);

A constructor invocation creates a new object and automatically attaches functions and variables to it. What functions and variables to attach is specified in the corresponding class definition.

As you already know, functions attached to objects are commonly referred to as *methods*. Methods are invoked by means of dot-notation.

Example

The *grid* method can be invoked with any *Button* object, as illustrated by the following statements:

    submitButton.grid(row = 2, column = 0);
    scrolledText.grid(row = 3, column = 0, columnspan = 2);

The *configure* method can be invoked with any *Button* object, as illustrated by these statements:

    submitButton.configure(text = 'Submit', width = 20, ...);
    clearButton.configure(text = 'Clear', width = 20, ...);

Remember, more details on these invocations are provided in the topic on Graphics and Interfaces.

Summary of Introductory Terms

A Python *class* defines the attributes, such as functions and variables, of each object of that class. The class definition is used in constructor invocations to create new objects. In this sense, classes are blueprints for objects.

A *class definition* statement, or simply a *class-statement*, consists of a class header followed by a class body. The *class header* starts with the keyword *class* and contains a class name chosen by the programmer, such as *Pen, Button* or *Label*. A typical *class body* is a sequence of function definitions.

A *constructor invocation* consists of a class name followed by a list of arguments, which may be empty. Some constructor invocations include arguments. The invocation of the *Button(window)* constructor uses the window argument to include a master *window* for the newly created *Button* object. Many constructor invocations do not include arguments. An example is the *Pen()* constructor invocation.

What Comes Next

Classes are probably the most complex programming language constructs you will work with. Classes require familiarity with all the other language structures that you have studied so far; this is why they are introduced so late in this course.

At this stage of the course, you are prepared to understand and master classes. The next sections introduce class-related concepts and

techniques by means of sample programs. Your study of these sample programs will lead you to the following worthy results:
- Understanding how classes work.
- Knowing how to define and use simple classes.

It is relatively easy to attach functions and variables to objects of any class. This is outlined in the next section through a sample stepwise class design.

Stepwise Class Design

This section presents a stepwise design process that produces a useful sample class. Recall that studying a program by following its design steps enhances your understanding of the program and prepares you to apply stepwise design to your own programs.

Consider the following programming problem. Develop a program to produce various original computer graphics patterns. A human designer wants to use unusual programmatically generated patterns as inspiration for the design of wallpaper, tablecloth, coffee mugs, and other household products. **The entire program must be implemented as one single class, with all necessary functions embedded within the class.** A snapshot of a possible pattern produced by a possible program is shown below.

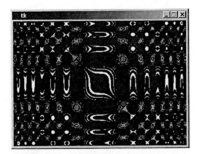

As you can see, the above sample problem is very similar to the pattern design problem from the topic on Graphics and Interfaces. The *Pattern Designer* sample program from the topic on Graphics and Interfaces designs the required original graphics patters. What is new and different about the current problem is the program must consolidate all necessary functions in one single class.

A sample program named *Classy Patterns* solves the above problem.

The *Classy Patterns* sample program consists of a single class incorporating all necessary functions. We refer to a program made of classes as *class-based*. The *Classy Patterns* program is class-based. In contrast, the *Pattern Designer* program from the topic on Graphics and Interfaces was composed of several free functions that were defined directly at the module level. We refer to such a program *function-based*.

The rest of this section describes a stepwise design of the *Classy Patterns* sample program.

The *Classy Patterns* class-based program defines a class named *PatternDesigner*. The *PatternDesigner* class includes the definitions of three functions. At each step of the design process, we add one function to the *PatternDesigner* class. The first and the second design steps produce intermediate versions of the *Classy Patterns* program that can be executed and tested. The third design step produces the final version of the program.

Before we describe the three design steps in detail, it may help to know the final version of the designed class will look like this:

```
class PatternDesigner:
    ... Definitions of functions, such as init, pattern,
    and draw, are embedded within the class...
```

The definition of the *PatternDeisgner* class is included in the *Classy Patterns* sample program.

Exercise

Use IDLE to run the *Classy Patterns* sample program. Running the program will define the *PatternDesigner* class. In interactive mode, create a *PatternDesigner* object:

```
>>> pd = PatternDesigner();
```

Invoke the *pattern* method of the newly created *PatternDesigner* object:

```
>>> pd.pattern(5);
```

The above invocation produces the drawing from the beginning of this section.

Our stepwise design of the *Classy Patterns* program mirrors the *Pattern Designer* program studied in the Graphics and Interfaces topic. It is beneficial to compare the new class-based code for the *Classy Patterns* program to the corresponding function-based code from the *Pattern Designer* program at each step of the *Classy Patterns* program development.

First Step: Initialization

The goals of this step are to create a pen object with an associated drawing window, set the current drawing color to blue, and extract the default width and height of the drawing window. Within the *Pattern Designer* class, this is implemented by a function named __init__. Note that the function name consists of the word *init,* with two consecutive underscores appended before *init* and two consecutive underscores appended after *init*. The __init__ name is mandatory for the initialization function of any Python class.

A new *PatternDesigner* object can be created with a constructor invocation:

>>> pd = PatternDesigner();

The constructor invocation, *PatternDesigner()*, automatically invokes the __init__ function embedded in the *PatternDesigner* class to initialize the newly created object.

The definition of function __init__ is embedded in the first version of the *Pattern Designer* class. The *Pattern Designer* class definition is explained in detail in a Python-to-English translation that follows the class definition itself. You should review the class definition below then acquaint yourself with the class features by studying the Python-to-English translation. As you review the class definition, compare the new class-based code to the old function-based code from the topic on Graphics and Interfaces.

The definition of the first version of the *PatternDesigner* class, with a function __init__, is shown below.

```
import turtle;
# A pattern designer class:
class PatternDesigner:
    # Initialize the pen, and determine the window width and height:
    def __init__(self):
```

```
        self.pen = turtle.Pen();
        self.pen.color(0, 0, 1); # blue
        self.width = self.pen.window_width();
        self.height = self.pen.window_height();
    # End of the PatternDesigner class;
```

The *__init__* function has one special parameter named *self*. This is a required first parameter in all functions that are defined within a Python class. When the function is executed, the *self* parameter represents the object to which the function is attached. Through its *self* parameter, the function can refer to all attributes (variables and functions) of its object.

The following Python-to-English translation provides insight into the definition and invocation of the *__init__* function.

Python Statement	Common English Meaning
import turtle;	▫ Import the *turtle* module.
class PatternDesigner:	▫ Start the definition of class *PatternDesigner*.
def __init__(self):	▫ Within the *PatternDesigner* class, start the definition of function *__init__*. • The *__init__* function has a required first parameter with the mandatory name *self*. • The *self* parameter represents the *PatternDesigner* object that the function is attached to.
self.pen = turtle.Pen();	▫ Create a *Pen* object and assign it into the *pen* variable. ▫ Attach the *pen* variable to *self*. • *Self* now contains a *pen* attribute.
self.pen.color(0, 0, 1); # blue	▫ Change the *pen* color to be (0, 0, 1), i.e. blue. • Use dot-notation to refer to the *pen* attribute.

self.width =
   self.pen.window_width();
self.height =
   self.pen.window_height();
	▫ Determine the *width* and the *height* of the drawing screen and attach them to *self*.
	• *Self* now contains attributes *width* and *height*.

Example

The intermediate program produced by this first step can be executed. When executed, the program defines the *PatternDesigner* class. Once a PatternDesigner is defined, a *PatternDesigner* object can easily be created in interactive mode:

```
>>> pd = PatternDesigner();
```

The purpose of the *__init__* function is to initialize newly created *PatternDesigner* objects. The constructor invocation *PatternDesigner()* automatically executes the *__init__* function to initialize the newly created object. All actions described in terms of *self* are performed with the new object.

Second Step: Pattern Generation

The goal of this step is to implement a *pattern* function that generates, point after point, the entire pattern. The new pattern function is added to the *PatternDesigner* class after the *__init__* function.

The *pattern* function uses two nested for-loops to generate a rectangular matrix of points. For each point, the pattern function invokes the *draw* function that decides whether and what to draw at the point.

The *pattern* function, shown below, is embedded in the second version of the *Pattern Designer* class. At this step, only a dummy *draw* function is developed; a complete version of the *draw* function is designed at the next step.

```
# A pattern designer class:
class PatternDesigner:
    def __init__(self):
        ... rest of __init__ skipped...

    # Given a number, design a pattern:
    def pattern(self, number):
        self.pen.clear();
        # Switch off tracing for speed:
        self.pen.tracer(False);
```

```
            for x in range(-self.width/2, + self.width/2):
                for y in range (-self.height/2, + self.height/2):
                    self.draw(number, x, y);
                # Temporarily switch on tracing to observe drawing:
                if (x % 100 == 0):
                    self.pen.tracer(True); self.pen.tracer(False);
            self.pen.tracer(True);

        # Draw a pattern element at point (a, b):
        def draw(self, number, x, y):
            pass;
    # End of the PatternDesigner class;
```

The *pattern* function and the *draw* function are defined within the *PatternDesigner* class. These functions are automatically attached to all objects of the *PatternDesigner* class.

The *pattern* function has a required first parameter named *self*. When the function is executed, the *self* parameter represents the object the function is attached to. Through the *self* parameter, the *pattern* function refers to all attributes (variables and functions) of the object. The *pattern* function expects *self* to contain the following attributes:
- Variables *self.pen, self.width, self.height*, and
- Function *self.draw*

In the *pattern* function, all attributes of *self* are referred to by means of dot-notation.

The *pattern* function defines local variables named *x* and *y* and a parameter named *number*. Local variables and parameters are not attached to any object; they are referred to by means of their simple names.

Third Step: Point Drawing

The goal of this step is to complete the *draw* function. For each point *(x, y)*, the *draw* function must decide whether and what to draw on that point.

The definition of the *draw* function, shown below, is embedded in the definition of the *Pattern Designer* class.

```
# A pattern designer class:
class PatternDesigner:
    def __init__(self):
        ... rest of __init__ skipped...

    def pattern(self, number):
        ... rest of pattern skipped...

    # Draw a pattern element at point (x, y):
    def draw(self, number, x, y):
        a = y * (number / 100.0);
        b = x * (number / 100.0);
        ez = int(a*a*a + b*b*b);
        # Try ez = int(a*a + b*b) and other expressions.
        if (ez % 2 == 0):
            self.pen.up(); self.pen.goto(x, y); self.pen.down();
            self.pen.circle(1);
# End of the PatternDesigner class;
```

The *draw* function has a required first parameter named *self*. When the function is executed, the *self* parameter represents the object to which the function is attached. Through the *self* parameter, the *draw* function refers to all attributes (variables and functions) of the object.

The *draw* function expects *self* to contain variable attribute *self.pen*. The *draw* function refers to this attribute by means of dot-notation.

The *draw* function defines local variables named *a, b* and *ez*, and parameters named *number, x* and *y*. Local variables and parameters are not attached to any object; they are referred to by their simple names.

The completed *Classy Patterns* program has the form shown below.

```
class PatternDesigner:
    def __init__(self): ...
    def pattern(self, number): ...
    def draw(self, number, x, y): ...
```

The *pattern* function can now be invoked to draw a pattern number *n* as shown below:

    pd = PatternDesigner();
    pd.pattern(n);

All actions described in terms of *self* will be performed with the *PatternDesigner* object held in the *pd* variable. This is valid for all three functions from the *PatternDesigner* class: __init__, *pattern,* and *draw*.

Exercise

Run the *Classy Patterns* program. In interactive mode, execute the following method invocations:

    >>> pd.pattern(5);
    >>> pd.pattern(0.9);

Classes and Program Execution

A program can start with a class definition and end with a statement to create an object of the defined class. Recall that object construction automatically executes the __init__ function defined in the corresponding class. This automatic execution of the __init__ function may be used to launch the entire program.

Example

A sample program named *Hello Printer* begins with the definition of class *Hello* and ends with a statement to create a *Hello* object. The complete *Hello Printer* program is shown below.

```
from Tkinter import * ;
    # A class that prints 'Hello' in response to button clicks:
    class Hello:
        def __init__(self):
            self.root = Tk();
            self.hello = Button(self.root);
            self.hello.grid(row=0, column=0);
            self.hello.configure(text='Hello', command=self.sayHello);
            self.root.mainloop();
        def sayHello(self):
            print 'Hello everyone!'
```

```
# Create a Hello object. This automatically executes __init__:

Hello();
```

When executed, the above program defines a class named *Hello* then creates a *Hello* object.

The construction of a new *Hello* object automatically invokes the *__init__* function. The *__init__* function then displays a button labeled 'Hello', waits for the button to be clicked, and prints 'Hello everyone!' in response to every button click. The user who runs the *Hello Printer* program does not need to explicitly invoke any function to achieve this result. Finally, note that saving the *Hello* object into a variable is not necessary in this case.

Exercise

Use a *file browser* to retrieve the icon of the *Hello Printer* sample program. Click (or double click) on the program icon to execute the program. Click several times on the 'Hello' button to observe the program output in the *shell window*.

Class Definitions

Class definitions are statements sometimes referred to as *class-statements*. They are compound structures that incorporate headers and bodies.

A class header gives a name to the class. The class name can be used in constructor invocations in order to create objects of the class. Although a class body can incorporate arbitrary statements, a typical class body is just a sequence of function definitions.

A function defined within a class can be invoked through an object of that class.

The *self* parameter is a required first parameter in each function. When the function is executed, the *self* parameter represents the object to which the function is attached. Through the *self* parameter, the function can refer to all attributes (variables and functions) of the object. The name *self* is not compulsory; any other name may be used. Note: the majority of programmers prefer the name *self;* the *self* parameter is only used in functions defined in the Python class.

Most classes define a function named __init__. This function is automatically executed anytime when a new object is constructed. The main purpose of this function is to initialize newly created objects. Using any name other than __init__ will fail to trigger automatic initialization.

Example
Consider a class named *ProducerConsumer* that does not define the __init__ function. The class is part of a short sample program that is shown below in its entirety.

```
# A class without __init__ function:
class ProducerConsumer:
    # A function to produce g:
    def producer(self):
        self.g = 100;
    # A function to use g:
    def consumer(self):
        print 10 * self.g;

pc = ProducerConsumer();
pc.producer();
pc.consumer();
```

A *ProducerConsumer* object is originally constructed without any variables attached to it. The execution of *pc.producer()*, however, attaches a variable named *g* to the *ProducerConsumer* object held in variable *pc*. The execution of *pc.consumer()* prints this variable.

Class Concepts
A number of class-related concepts are introduced in the previous sections. For historic reasons, some class-related terms have synonyms. For example, functions that are defined within classes and are attached to all objects of that class are often called methods. Thus, the terms *function* and *method* are used interchangeably.

In order to help you cope with the new terminology, the following table offers common English meanings and examples of principal class-oriented concepts.

Concept	Example	Common English Meaning
Class	ProducerConsumer (see definition in next rows)	A blueprint for objects.
Constructor invocation	pc = ProducerConsumer();	Uses the class as a blueprint to build a new object.

Class definition	class ProducerConsumer:
	    def producer(self): self.g = 100;
	    def consumer(self): print 10 * self.g;
		A statement that formally defines a particular class. Consists of a class header and a class body.

Class header	class ProducerConsumer:	The first part of a class definition. Starts with the *class* keyword and gives a name to the newly defined class.
Class body	def producer(self): self.g = 100; def consumer(self): print 10 * self.g;	The second part of a class definition. Usually consists of function definitions.
Method	Producer Consumer	Function that is defined within a class and is attached to all objects of that class
Method definition	def producer(self): self.g = 100;	Function definition within class body.
Initialization method	def __init__(self, value): self.g = value;	Special function that is automatically executed when new objects are created. Must be named __init__.
self	Self	Required first parameter in method definitions. Represents the particular object to which the function is attached.
Dot-notation	pc.produce(); pc.consume();	Reference to a name defined within a module or a class.

Inheritance

Inheritance is a language mechanism that allows the definition of new classes as extensions of existing ones. We will illustrate the essence of inheritance by means of several sample classes, such as *Human*, *Professor,* and *Student*. The *Human* class defines some basic human attributes. The *Professor* and *Student* classes inherit those attributes and add some professor-specific or student-specific attributes correspondingly.

One common feature of humans is possession of personal names used to introduce themselves. The class of all humans capable of introducing themselves to others is defined below.

```
# A class that describes any human with a name:
class Human:
    def __init__(self, name): self.name = name;
    def getName(self): return self.name;
    def introduce(self): print 'Hello, I am ' + self.getName() + '.';
```

A *Human* object is created with one data attribute, *name*, and three function attributes, *__init__*, *getName*, and *introduce*. The *__init__* function is automatically executed in constructor invocations. The *getName* method can be used to obtain anyone's name. The *introduce* function makes a *Human* object print a friendly introduction.

Example

```
>>> humans = [Human('Jake'), Human('Baldy'),
        Human('Bubba'), Human('Johnny',)];
>>> for human in humans: human.introduce();

Hello, I am Jake.
Hello, I am Baldy.
Hello, I am Bubba.
Hello, I am Johnny.
```

A student is a human with a grade-point average, or GPA. A *Student* object should have all attributes of a *Human* object, extended with GPA-related attributes. Of course, you can copy the *Human* class, rename it to *Student*, and add a few new statements to represent the GPA. Alternatively, you can define the *Student* class to **inherit** the definition of the *Human* class and extend it with new attributes. This approach is implemented using the following pattern:

```
class Student(Human):
    ... All functions from the Human class are available in the Student class...
    ... New student-specific functions are defined in the Student class...
```

This approach is materialized in the following complete definition of a *Student* class.

```
class Student(Human):
    def __init__(self, name, GPA):
        Human.__init__(self, name);
        self.GPA = GPA;
    def setGPA(self, GPA): self.GPA = GPA;
    def getGPA(self): return self.GPA;
```

The newly defined *Student* class inherits the definition of the *Human* class. Inheritance makes the three *Human* functions, *__init__*, *getName*, and *introduce*, readily available in the *Student* class.

The *Student* class implements its own *__init__* function. This function defines a *GPA* attribute and also invokes the old *__init__* function inherited from the *Human* class. The purpose of this invocation is to have the *name* attribute defined for each *Student* object.

Although the *Student* class does not define an *introduce* function, it has inherited it from the *Human* class. This function is used to make any *Student* object introduce itself.

Example

```
>>> s1 = Student(name='Jake', GPA=3.75);
>>> s1.introduce();    # invocation of inherited function
Hello, I am Jake.
>>> s2 = Student(name='Johnny', GPA=2.50);
>>> s2.introduce();    # invocation of inherited function
Hello, I am Johnny
```

The *Student* class implements two additional functions, *getGPA* and *setGPA*, that provide access to the *GPA* attribute of a *Student* object.

Example

```
>>> s1 = Student(name='Jake', GPA=3.75);
>>> s2 = Student(name='Johnny', GPA=2.50);
>>> s2.getGPA();
2.5
```

```
>>> s2.setGPA(3.50);
>>> s2.getGPA();
3.5
```
Functions like *setGPA* and *getGPA* provide access to one specific attribute, such as *GPA*, are called *setter* and *getter* functions.

If class *C1* is defined by means of inheritance from a class *C0*, *C0* is referred to as the *base class* of *C1*, while *C1* is termed a *subclass* of *C0*. The *'is a subclass of'* relation is transitive: if *C2* is a subclass of *C1* and *C1* is a subclass of *C0*, then *C2* is a subclass of *C0*. The relation *'is a base class of'* is transitive too.

A professor is a human with a degree. A *Professor* object should have all the attributes of a *Human* object, extended with degree-related attributes. A *Professor* class can be defined by means of inheritance from the *Human* class. This is implemented in the following definition of a *Professor* class.

```
class Professor(Human):
    def __init__(self, name, degree):
        Human.__init__(self, name);
        self.degree = degree;
    def setDegree(self, degree): self.degree = degree;
    def getDegree(self): return self.degree;
```

As you can see from the above definition, the transition from a *Student* to a *Professor* is very straightforward, consisting of the replacement of the GPA attribute with a degree attribute.

Similarly to the *Student* class, the *Professor* class does not define an *introduce* function but has it inherited from the *Human* class. Of course, this function can be used to make any *Professor* object introduce itself.

A *boasting professor* may start introducing himself as a regular human, by announcing his name, and then continue by announcing his degree. A *BoastingProfessor* class can be defined by means of inheritance from the *Professor* class, as shown below.

```
class BoastingProfessor(Professor):
    def introduce(self):
        Human.introduce(self);
        print 'I have a ' + self.getDegree() + ' degree.';
```

Note that the *BoastingProfessor* class does not define a custom __init__ function because the __init__ function inherited from the Professor class is adequate for the *BoastingProfessor* class as well. In this case, the __init__ function inherited from the *Professor* class is automatically executed to initialize any new *BoastingProfessor* object.

Although the *BoastingProfessor* class inherits an *introduce* function from the *Professor* class, it defines its own *introduce function*. The newly defined *introduce* function invokes the inherited *introduce* function to print the traditional human part of the introduction and then print degree information (hence the boasting part of the introduction).

Example

```
>>> bp = BoastingProfessor(name='Baldy', degree='PhD');
>>> bp.introduce();
Hello, I am Baldy.
I have a PhD degree.
```

A boasting professor might have been a boasting student in his younger years. One can imagine that a boasting student may start introducing himself as a regular human, by announcing his name, and then continue by announcing his presumably high GPA. A *BoastingStudent* class can be defined by means of inheritance from the *Student* class, as shown below.

```
class BoastingStudent(Student):
    def introduce(self):
        Human.introduce(self);
        print 'My GPA is ' + str(self.getGPA()) + '.';
```

All classes discussed in this section: *Human, Student, Professor, BoastingProfessor,* and *BoastingStudent,* contain a function named *introduce*. This function is originally defined in the *Human* class and then inherited by all of its subclasses. Two of the subclasses, *BoastingPro-*

fessor, and *BoastingStudent*, redefine their versions of the inherited *introduce* function. What is important is the object of all classes have an *introduce* method. This method can be invoked for any object of these classes, regardless of the particular class of that object. Such invocations can produce different results for different objects.

Example

The following statements build a heterogeneous list of objects and invoke the *introduce* method for each object from that list:

```
>>> humans = [BoastingStudent('Jake', 3.75), BoastingProfessor('Baldy', 'PhD'),
    Human('Bubba'), Student('Johnny', 2.50)];
>>> for human in humans: human.introduce();

Hello, I am Jake.
My GPA is 3.75.
Hello, I am Baldy.
I have a PhD degree.
Hello, I am Bubba.
Hello, I am Johnny.
```

Sometimes it is necessary to test if an object belongs to a certain class. A built-in function invocation *isinstance(X, C)* can be used to test if *X* is an object of class *C* or any of its subclasses.

Example

```
>>> X = BoastingProfessor(name='Baldy', degree='PhD');
...
>>> isinstance(X, BoastingProfessor);
True
>>> isinstance(X, Professor);
True
>>> isinstance(X, Human);
True
>>> isinstance(X, Student);
False
```

Remember, the *BoastingProfessor* class inherits the *Professor* class which inherits the *Human* class. Therefore a *BoastingProfessor* object has all attributes of a *Professor* object which has all attributes of a *Human* object. This is why it is reasonable to accept, as function *isinstance* does, that a *BoastingProfessor* object is also a *Professor* object and a *Human* object.

The *isinstance* function comes in very handy in the case of a heterogeneous list of objects that may contain not only students, but all kinds of humans. An attempt to increase the GPA of a non-student will cause a run-time error, for a non-student does not have GPA-related attributes. The *isinstance* function can be used to check the class of each object and increase the GPA of *Student* objects only. Consider, for example, the problem of increasing the GPA of a student object.

Example
The following statements build a heterogeneous list of objects and then invoke the *introduce* method for each object from that list:

```
>>> humans = [BoastingStudent('Jake', 3.75), Human('Bubba'),
    BoastingProfessor('Baldy', 'PhD'), Student('Johnny',
2.50)];
>>> for human in humans:
        if (isinstance(human, Student)):
            oldGPA = human.getGPA();
            newGPA = min(oldGPA + 1, 4.00);
            human.setGPA(newGPA);
```

The above for-loop will increase the GPA of any *Student* or *BoastingStudent* object up to one point. In particular, the GPA of 'Jake' will be increased to 4.00, 'Johnny''s will be increased to 3.50.

Sample Programs
Several complete class-based sample programs are provided with this topic. You are advised to study, analyze, and possibly enhance the sample programs. Independent work with these programs will help you master your understanding of class-related concepts and your capability to design class-based programs.

Descriptions of sample programs follow.

Concentric Circles
Consider the following problem. Develop a turtle graphics program to support the following circle drawing tasks:
- The program must be capable of drawing *one colored circle*.
- The program must be capable of drawing *one set of concentric circles*.

- The program must be capable of playing *a circle show*.
  - A circle show is a sequence of randomly colored sets of concentric circles. In the show, each set of concentric circles is displayed for a few seconds then replaced by the next set in the show.

A snapshot of one set of concentric circles generated by the desired program is shown below.

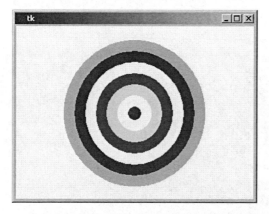

The sample program named *Concentric Circles* solves the above problem. The program defines classes named *Circle, ConcentricCircles,* and *Demo* that serve the following purposes:
- The *Circle* class is a blueprint for individual circle objects.
- The *ConcentricCircles* class is a blueprint for sets of concentric circles.
- The *Demo* class provides a setup for sample program executions.

In order to use the *Demo* class, you need to create a *Demo* object by means of the constructor invocation:

demo = Demo();

Once you have a *Demo* object, you can use it to invoke a *Demo* method. The three available *Demo* methods are outlined in the following table.

Method	Description
demo.circle()	Draw a single circle.
demo.concentricCircles()	Draw a set of randomly colored concentric circles.
demo.circleShow()	Play a show of randomly colored concentric circles.

Exercise

Run the *Concentric Circles* program. Create a *Demo* object then invoke *demo* methods, as shown below.

>>> demo = Demo();
>>> demo.circle ();
>>> demo.concentricCircles(); #... and again ...
>>> demo.concentricCircles();
>>> demo.circleShow();

Observe the circle show as long as desired then exit the program by clicking on the *Close* button on the drawing window's right upper corner.

Concentric Squares

Consider the following problem. Develop a turtle graphics program to support several polygon drawing tasks.
- First, the program must be capable of drawing *one colored polygon*.
- Second, the program must be capable of drawing *one set of concentric squares*.
- Third, the program must be capable of playing *a square show*.
  - A square show is similar to a circle show but consists of concentric squares rather than circles.

A polygon is defined by a sequence of points in the graphics window. The program is supposed to create any kind of polygons the user wises to work with.

A snapshot of one set of one polygon generated by the desired program is shown below.

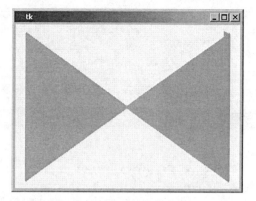

A snapshot of one set of concentric squares generated by the desired program is shown below.

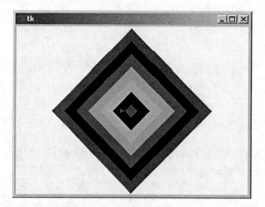

A sample program named *Concentric Squares* solves the above problem. The program defines classes named *Polygon*, *ConcentricSquares*, and *Demo* that serve the following purposes:
- The *Polygon* class is a blueprint for individual polygon objects.
- The *ConcentricSquares* class is a blueprint for sets of concentric squares.
- The *Demo* class provides a setup for sample program executions.

The *Polygon* class allows you to create an empty polygon, then *add* various points to the polygon, then *draw* the polygon defined by those points. A *Square* class is defined as a special case of *Polygon*. Of course, you can use the *Polygon* class to implement other special classes, such as *Rectangle* or *Diamond*.

In order to use the *Demo* class, create a *Demo* object by means of the constructor invocation:

demo = Demo();

Once you have a *Demo* object, you can use it to invoke a *Demo* method. The three available *Demo* methods are outlined in the following table.

Method	Description
demo.polygon()	Draw a single polygon.
demo.concentricSquares()	Draw a set of randomly colored concentric squares.
demo.squareShow()	Play a show of randomly colored concentric squares.

Exercise

Run the *Concentric Squares* program. Create a *Demo* object then invoke *demo* methods, as shown below.

```
>>> demo = Demo();
>>> demo.polygon ();
>>> demo.concentricSquares(); #... and again ...
>>> demo.concentricSquares();
>>> demo.squareShow();
```

Observe the square show as long as desired then exit the program by clicking on the *Close* button on the drawing window's upper right corner.

Note

The *Concentric Circles* and *Concentric Squares* programs use a custom version of the turtle module. The custom version of the turtle module is located in the folder with sample programs for this topic.

Classy Wages

Consider the following sample problem. Develop a wage calculation program with a GUI. The program must use the GUI to input hours worked and hourly rate, calculate the wages, and output the calculated wages. **The entire program must be implemented as one single class, with all necessary functions embedded within the class.** A snapshot of a possible interaction with the required program is shown below.

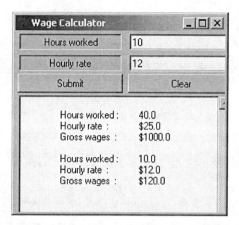

As you can see, the above sample problem is very similar to the wage calculation problem from an earlier topic. Indeed, the topic on Graphics and Interfaces offers a sample program named the *Wage Calculator* that does exactly what is specified above. What is different about the current problem is the program is expected be contained in one single class that incorporates all needed functions.

A sample class-based program named *Classy Wages* solves the above problem.

The *Classy Wages* sample program defines a class that incorporates all functions needed for wage calculations. In contrast, the *Wage Calculator* program from the topic on Graphics and Interfaces consists of a number of free functions that are defined directly at the module level.

The design of the *Classy Wages* program mirrors the design of the *Wage Calculator* program as studied in the topic of Graphics and Interfaces. It is beneficial to compare the class-based code from the *Classy Wages* program to the corresponding function-based code from the *Wage Calculator* program.

Exercise

Launch the *Classy Wages* sample program by either clicking on its icon, or running it from IDLE. Input various numbers and submit them for wage calculation. Exit the program by clicking on the *Close* button on the *shell window's* upper right corner.

Synonyms

Some terms that have been introduced in this topic have synonyms. A list of such terms and their corresponding synonyms follows.

Term	Synonym
Variable attribute	Data attribute
Variable attribute	Instance variable
Object	Class instance
Class-based program	Object-oriented program
Class-based programming	Object-oriented programming
Dot-notation	Attribute reference
Base class	Super class
Base class	Parent class
Inheritance	Subclassing

Lab A [Classes]

Objective; Background; Lab Overview; What to Do Next; Downloading Sample Programs; Uncompressing Sample Programs; Studying the Sample Program; Creating a Program File; Developing the New Program

Objective
- The objective of this lab is to convert the function-based *Mandelbrot Patterns* sample program into a class-based *Classy Mandelbrot* program.

Background
- A sample program named *Mandelbrot Patterns* draws various original computer graphics patterns. The program offers a possible visualization of the famed Mandelbrot sets.
  - Mandelbrot sets visualization is described in many web and print recourses. Research of such publications is not required for this lab.
- In the *Mandelbrot Patterns* sample program, a pattern is built as a composition of tiny circles produced by the *draw* function. You can produce new original patterns by changing the *draw* function.
- The *Mandelbrot Patterns* sample program consists of three free functions that are defined directly at the module level, not within a class. We refer to a program composed of free functions as *function-based*. *Mandelbrot Patterns* is therefore function-based. In contrast, we refer to a program composed of one or more classes as *class-based*. The *Classy Mandelbrot* program developed for this lab must be class-based.
- The *Classy Mandelbrot* program may be organized similarly to the *Classy Patterns* sample program.

Note
Before you draw:
- Close all unnecessary windows.
- Minimize completely or at least reduce partially the size of all remaining widows.

Make sure the drawing window is uncovered at all times.

Lab Overview

To perform this lab:
- Study the *Mandelbrot Patterns* sample program and the *Classy Patterns* sample program.
- Transform a copy of the *Mandelbrot Patterns* sample program into a *Classy Mandelbrot* program.
- Experiment with the *Classy Mandelbrot* program to produce at least one Mandelbrot pattern.

What to Do Next

You are now offered the following choices:
- Follow the detailed lab instructions below.
- Try the lab independently, using the instructions when you require help.
- Perform the lab independently, without any aid from the instructions.

All three approaches are beneficial to students. Choose the approach most beneficial to you.

Downloading Sample Programs

Various Lab Assignments for this course of study are based on ready-to-use sample programs. Such programs are downloadable from the online study pack. Save these files into your *master* folder.

Download sample programs for the current Topic 9 by performing these steps:
- Locate *Topic 9* in the online study pack.
- Open the *Lab Assignment* resource.
- Right-click on the *Sample Programs* link.
- Use *Save As* to store the downloaded compressed (zipped) folder, *09.zip,* within your *master* folder.

Uncompressing Sample Programs

- Uncompress the contents of the downloaded compressed (zipped) folder. Depending on your platform, you may use built-in compression support, or compressing utilities.
  - In Windows XP, use built-in un-compression support as follows:
    - Open your *master* folder using the *File Browser*.
    - Right-click on the downloaded compressed (zipped) folder.

- Use *Extract All* to extract the contents of the compressed (zipped) folder within the *master* folder.
  - This will create an uncompressed folder, *09*, within the *master* folder. This folder contains your sample programs.
- Alternatively, you can:
  - *Open* the compressed (zipped) folder.
  - *Cut* folder *09* from within the compressed (zipped) folder, and
  - *Paste* the cut folder *09* outside the compressed (zipped) folder – directly within the *master* folder.
- Delete the compressed (zipped) folder, *09.zip*; keep the uncompressed folder, *09*.
- Open the uncompressed folder *09* and browse its contents.
- Note that Python program files have extension '**.py**'.

Studying the Sample Program
- Study the *Classy Patterns* sample program in the E-Text.
- Open and browse *Classy Patterns* sample program using IDLE.
  - Analyze the implementation of the *Classy Patterns* sample program.
- Open and browse *Mandelbrot Patterns* sample program using IDLE.
- Run the *Mandelbrot Patterns* program and invoke the Mandelbrot function to produce one or more Mandelbrot patterns.
  - You may start experimenting with this sample invocation:

  mandelbrot(u0= -0.5, v0 = 0, side = 1).

- Analyze the implementation of the *Mandelbrot Patterns* sample program.

Creating a Program File
Create this program in your current labs folder, *09Labs*.
- Use IDLE to create a copy of the *Mandelbrot Patterns* program file. Save the copy in your current labs folder.
- Give the name *ClassyMandelbrot.py* to the saved copy.
  - **Important Note:** You must explicitly supply the file extension '**.py**' when saving from IDLE.

Developing the New Program

Perform the following steps with the newly created *Classy Mandelbrot* program.
- Define a *MandelbrotPatterns* class.
- Right-shift all three functions to form the class body.
- Modify the *init* function.
  - Rename *init* to __init__ and add a *self* parameter.
  - Define the *pen, width,* and *height* variables as attributes of *self*.
    - Always refer to these variables by means of dot-notation.
  - Remove the return-statement.
    - The return-statement is unnecessary in the new class-based program because *pen, width,* and *length* are now attributes of the *self*-object. The attributes of the *self*-object are accessible from all functions defined in the class.
- Modify the *mandelbrot* function.
  - Add *self* as the first parameter; keep the other parameters.
  - Eliminate the invocation of the *init* function.
    - The invocation of the *init* function is superfluous in the new class-based program because *pen, width,* and *length* are now attributes of the *self*-object. The attributes of the *self*-object are accessible from all functions defined in the class. In particular, *pen, width,* and *length* are now accessible in the *mandelbrot* function by means of dot-notation.
  - Replace:
    - All references to the *pen* variable with references to *self.pen*.
    - All references to the *w* variable with references to *self.width*, and
    - All references to the *h* variable with references to *self.height*.
  - Modify the invocation of the *draw* function.
    - Remove the *pen* argument from the invocation. The *pen* argument is unnecessary because the *pen* is now an attribute of the *self*-object. The attributes of the *self*-object are accessible from all functions that are defined in the class. In particular, the *pen* is now accessible in the *draw* function by means of dot-notation.

- Replace the references to the *draw* function with a reference to *self.draw*.
  - Remember, the *draw* function is now defined within the class. The function is automatically attached to each object of this class. Thus, *draw* is now a function attribute of the *self*-object and must be referred to by means of dot-notation.
- Modify the *draw* function.
  - Add *self* as the first parameter, remove the pen parameter, and keep the other parameters.
    - The *pen* parameter is unnecessary because the *pen* is now an attribute of the *self*-object. The attributes of the *self*-object are accessible from all functions defined in the class. In particular, the *pen* is now accessible in the *draw* function by means of dot-notation.
  - Replace all references to the *pen* variable with references to *self.pen*.
- Test the program and experiment with some patterns.
  - You may start experimenting with these sample statements:

    ```
    >>> mb = MandelbrotPatterns();
    >>> mb.mandelbrot(u0= -0.5, v0 = 0, side = 1);
    ```

- Update all existing comments and provide new comments as needed.

Lab B [Classes]

Objective; Background; Lab Overview; What to Do Next; Studying the Sample Program; Creating a Program File; Developing the New Program

Objectives

The objective of this lab is to develop a *Lined Circles* program as a modified version of the *Concentric Circles* sample program. The *Lined Circles* program must support two circle drawing tasks.
- First, the program must be capable of drawing one set of circles, all with the same radiuses, along a horizontal line.
- Second, the program must be capable of playing a circle show. A circle show is a sequence of randomly colored sets of lined circles. In the show, each set of lined circles is displayed for a few seconds then replaced by the next set in the show.

Background

- The E-text contains a comprehensive description of the *Concentric Circles* sample program. Familiarity with the program and the related class concepts is crucial for this lab.
- This is a snapshot of a drawing produced by a *Lined Circles* program.

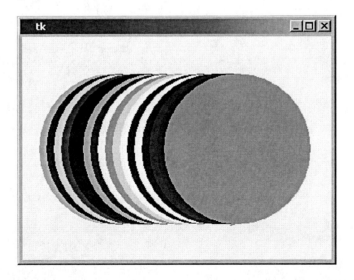

- Note that all circles have the same radius and are arranged horizontally along the same line.
  - Concentric circles have the same center and different radiuses.
- The leftmost lined circle is centered at point *(x, y)*.
- Given some constant distance, consecutive circles are centered at *(x, y), (x+distance, y), (x+2*distance, y)*, and so on.

Note
Before you draw:
- Close all unnecessary windows.
- Minimize completely or at least reduce partially the size of all remaining widows.

The drawing window must be uncovered at all times.

Lab Overview
To perform this lab:
- Study the *Concentric Circles* sample program.
- Transform a copy of the *Concentric Circles* sample program into a *Lined Circles* program.
- Thoroughly test the *Lined Circles* program.

What to Do Next
You are now offered the following choices:
- Follow the detailed lab instructions below.
- Try the lab independently, using the instructions when you require help.
- Perform the lab independently, without any aid from the instructions.

All three approaches are beneficial to students. Choose the approach most beneficial to you.

Studying the Sample Program
- Use IDLE to open and browse the *Concentric Circles* sample program.
- Run the *Concentric Circles* program and create two circles, c1 and c2, using the following statements:

```
>>> c1 = Circle(x=0, y=0, r=100);
>>> c2 = Circle(x= -100, y= -100, r=30);
```

- Set the colors of the two circles from the previous step, *c1* and *c2*, to red and green respectively using the following statements:

  ```
  >>> c1.setColor(red=1, green=0, blue=0);
  >>> c2.randomColor();
  ```

- Create a turtle graphics pen and draw the two circles from the previous exercise, *c1* and *c2*, using the following statements:

  ```
  >>> import turtle; pen = turtle.Pen();
  >>> c1.draw(pen); c2.draw(pen);
  ```

- Run again the *Concentric Circles* sample program and execute the following statement in interactive mode:

  ```
  >>> demo = Demo();
  >>> demo.circle();
  >>> demo.concentricCircles();
  >>> demo.circleShow();
  ```

- Analyze the implementation of the *Concentric Circles* sample program.

Creating a Program File

Create this program in your current labs folder, *09Labs*.
- Use IDLE to create a copy of the *Concentric Circles* program file. Save the copy in your current labs folder.
- Name the saved copy *LinedCircles.py*.
  - **Important Note:** You must explicitly supply the file extension '**.py**' when saving from IDLE.

Developing the New Program

Perform the following steps with the newly created *Lined Circles* program.
- Convert the *ConcentricCircles* class into a *LinedCircles* class.
  - Update the __init__ function.
    - Replace parameters *minRadius, maxRadius* with *radius, distance*.
    - Modify the init loop to calculate the next x-coordinate by adding *distance* to the current x-coordinate.

- Use the *pen.clear()* invocation in the *show* function to clear the graphics window before the display of any set of lined circles. If the graphics window is not cleared, the performance of the pen deteriorates gradually as more and more sets of lined circles are drawn.
○ Modify the *Demo* class.
    - Convert the *concentricCircles* function into a *linedCircles* function that displays a single set of lined circles.
    - Modify the *circleShow* function to play a show of lined circles rather than a show of concentric circles.
    - The background section of this lab offers a snapshot of a lined circles drawing. The following values have been used to produce that drawing:
        - The *radius* of each circle is *self.span / 3*.
        - The center of the leftmost circle is *(x0, 0)*, where x0 = -radius + 10.
        - The *number* of circles is 18.
        - The *distance* between any two adjacent circle centers is *2 * radius / number*.
○ Update all existing comments.

Lab C [Classes]

Objective; Background; Lab Overview; What to Do Next; Studying Sample Programs; Creating a Program File; Developing the New Program

Objectives

- The objective of this lab is to develop a *Dream Figures* program similar to the *Concentric Squares* and *Concentric Circles* sample programs that produces a new, unique figure.
  - Your program may produce an interesting static figure, or a show of changing figures.
- Post a message in this topic's *Forum*:
  - Describing your *Dream Figures* program.
  - Containing one sample drawing produced by your *Dream Figures* program.

Background

- The E-text contains descriptions of the *Concentric Squares* and *Concentric Circles* sample programs. Your familiarity with the program and related class concepts is crucial for this lab.
- This is a list of possible drawings produced by a possible *Dream Figures* program.
  - Embedded diamonds, squares, triangles, or other polygons
  - Lined circles with decreasing radiuses
  - Blinking lights
  - Moving triangles
  - Alternating concentric squares and circles
  - A moving snake that never crosses itself
  - Anything else that you find interesting and reasonable

Note
Before you draw:
- Close all unnecessary windows.
- Minimize completely or at least reduce partially the size of all remaining widows.

The drawing window must be uncovered at all times.

Lab Overview

To perform this lab:
- Study the *Concentric Squares* and *Concentric Circles* sample programs.
- Transform a copy of the *Concentric Circles* sample program into a *Lined Circles* program.
- Thoroughly test the *Dream Figures* program.

What to Do Next

You are now offered the following choices:
- Follow the detailed lab instructions below.
- Try the lab independently, using the instructions when you require help.
- Perform the lab independently, without any aid from the instructions.

All three approaches are beneficial to students. Choose the approach most beneficial to you.

Studying Sample Programs

- Open and browse the *Concentric Circles* sample program using IDLE.
- Run the *Concentric Circles* program.
- Analyze the implementation of the *Concentric Circles* sample program.
- Open and browse the *Concentric Squares* sample program using IDLE.
- Run the *Concentric Squares* program.
- Analyze the implementation of the *Concentric Squares* sample program.

Creating a Program File

Create this program in your current labs folder, *09Labs*.
- Use IDLE to create and save a new blank *Dream Figures* program file. Save the file in your current labs folder.
- Name the saved copy *Dream Figures.py*.
  - **Important Note:** You must explicitly supply the file extension '**.py**' when saving from IDLE.

Developing the New Program

- Use ideas and possibly program code from *Concentric Squares* and *Concentric Circles* sample programs to implement your unique *Dream Figures* program. Remember to add adequate comments.
- Test your program and experiment to produce various figures.
- Save a snapshot of your favorite drawing in a file.
  - The snapshot must be produced by your personal and unique *Dream Figures* program.
- Post a message in this topic's *Forum*.
  - Attach your snapshot file.
  - Briefly describe your unique *Dream Figures* program.

Review

Purpose; Assignment Statements; Print-Statements; Names; Numbers; If-Statements; Boolean Expressions; While-Statements; Break-Statements; Function Definitions; Function Invocations; Parameters, Local Variables, and Global Variables; Return-Statements; Sequences; Objects and Methods; Lists; The Range Function; For-Statements; Dictionaries; Tuples; Strings; Files; Web Resources; Turtle Graphics; Graphical User Interfaces; Classes; Modules and Import; References; Finale

Purpose

This last topic summarizes the most important language structures introduced throughout the course.

The review follows the structure of the course, topic after topic. The review begins with concepts covered in the introduction, such as assignment statements, print-statements, and numbers. The review ends with classes, as covered in the very last topic.

The review is based on numerous examples. For complete coverage of concepts read the corresponding E-Texts.

Assignment Statements

An assignment statement evaluates an expression and assigns the result of the evaluation into a variable. A variable name is defined by the first assignment into the variable.

> Example
>
> ```
> >>> score = 85; # A score variable defined;
> >>> score = score + 10;
> ```

A variable name cannot be used before it is assigned a value. Using a variable that has not been assigned a value is a run-time error.

Example

>>> GPA = GPA + 0.5;
NameError: name 'GPA' is not defined

Print-Statements

A print-statement evaluates one or more comma-separated expressions and outputs the results on the screen. The print-statement replaces commas with spaces and moves to a new line at the end.

Example

>>> print score, score - 10;
95 85

Names

Names are used to identify variables, functions, classes, and other program elements. Names may contain letters, digits, and the underscore character, but cannot start with a digit. Splitting a name by means of a space or in any other way is a syntax error. Names must differ from the Python reserved keywords and, like all Python words, are case-sensitive.

Example

>>> in = 123;   # in is a keyword
SyntaxError: invalid syntax
>>> tax rate = 6.75;
SyntaxError: invalid syntax
>>> celsius = 32; # lowercase 'c'
>>> Celsius = Celsius + 10; # capital 'C'
NameError: name 'Celsius' is not defined

Numbers

Python supports several types of numbers. Among those, integer, floating point, and long integer numbers are most important.

Example

- Integer numbers: 42,, 100, 1
- Floating point numbers: 3.14, 1000.0, 3**E**2, 314**E** -2, 2**e**120
- Long integer numbers: 10000000000**L**, 9999999999**L**

Python supports standard arithmetic operations, such as addition (+), subtraction (-), multiplication (*), division (/), power (**), and remainder (%). When both x and y are integer numbers, their quotient is the integer 'floor' of the mathematical quotient x / y.

Example

```
>>> 2**10;
1024
>>> 9 / 5;
1
>>> 9 % 5;
4
>>> 9.0 / 5;
1.8
```

Python offers useful built-in arithmetic functions, such as *abs, int, float,* and *round.*

Example

```
>>> abs(-42);
42
>>> int(0.99999999);
0
>>> round(0.99999999);
1.0
>>> float(10);
10.0
```

The *input* built-in function can be used to get numbers from the user.

Example

```
>>> score = input('Enter score: ');
Enter score: 100
>>> print score;
100
```

If-Statements

An if-statement tests one or more conditions and, depending on the result of the test, selects one of several possible courses of action.

The general form of an if-statement is:

```
if (condition):      # if-clause header
    statements # if-clause body
elif (condition):    # elif-clause header
    statements # elif-clause body
...
else:           # else-clause header
    statements # else-clause body
```

An if-statement starts with a required if-clause, optionally followed by one or more elif-clauses, optionally followed by one else-clause. The if-statement executes the statements that are associated with the very first true condition. If all conditions are false, the body of the else-clause, if present, is executed.

A one-way if-statement has no elif- or else-clauses. A one-way if-statement does not execute any statements when its condition evaluates to false.

Example

```
>>> score = 75;
>>> ...
>>> if (score < 60): print 'Sorry, you fail.';
>>> ...
```

A two-way if-statement consists of exactly two clauses. A two-way if-statement is an if-clause followed by either an else-clause, or an elif-clause.

Example

```
>>> score = 75;
>>> ...
>>> if (score < 60): print 'Sorry, you fail.';
else: print 'Great, you pass.';
Great, you pass.
```

A multiple-way if-statement consists of three or more clauses.

Example

```
>>> score = 75;
>>> if (score < 60): grade = 'F';
elif (score < 70): grade = 'D';
elif (score < 80): grade = 'C';
elif (score < 90): grade = 'B';
else: grade = 'A';
>>> print grade;
C
```

A sequence of two (or more) if-clauses represents a sequence of two (or more) if-statements that are executed independently of each other.

Example

```
>>> score = 75;
>>> if (score < 60): grade = 'F';
>>> if (score < 70): grade = 'D';
>>> if (score < 80): grade = 'C';
>>> if (score < 90): grade = 'B';
>>> print grade;
B
```

Boolean Expressions

In Python and other programming languages, conditions are called *Boolean expressions*.

To test a condition, in strict Python terms, means to find the value of a Boolean expression. Boolean expression can have two possible logic values: True and False.

Python offers a standard set of comparisons that can be used in Boolean expressions. Comparisons include equal (==), not equal (!=), less than (<), less than or equal (<=), greater than (>), greater than or equal (>=).

Example

```
>>> score = 75;
>>> print score < 75, score == 75, score > 75;
False True False
```

Python offers several built-in logic operations. The most important of these are *and*, *not*, *or*.

Example

```
>>> score = 75;
>>> 70 <= score and score < 80
True
>>> 70 <= score < 80
True
```

The expression *(A and B)* is evaluated left-to-right. If *A* evaluates to false, *(A and B)* is assumed to be false and *B* is not evaluated. Similarly, the expression *(A or B)* is evaluated left-to-right. If *A* evaluates to true, *(A or B)* is assumed to be true and *B* is not evaluated.

Example

```
>>> x = 10; y = 0;
>>> x < 0 and x / y < 1;
False
>>> x / y < 1 and x < 0;
ZeroDivisionError: integer division by zero
```

While-Statements

A while-statement test one condition and, if the test succeeds, executes an action. This test-execute process is repeated until the condition tested fails.

The most common form of a while-statement is:

```
while (condition): # while-loop header
    statements # while-loop body
```

The while-statement repeatedly tests the condition and, while it is true, executes the body. When the condition is false (which may be the first time it is tested) the while-statement terminates.

Example
```
>>> a = 1; b = 5; prod = 1;
>>> while (a <= b):
      prod = prod * a;
      a = a + 1;
>>> print prod;
120
```
The body of any while-statement should modify variables from the statement condition. Otherwise, the condition may remain true forever and the while-statement will execute as an infinite loop.

Example
Consider the while-statement from the previous example. The loop body contains the statement $a = a + 1$. During each execution of the loop body, this statement increments a by 1. Eventually it will reach $a > b$ turning the condition $a <= b$ to false. Therefore, the while-statement from the previous example is guaranteed to terminate. If the statement $a = a + 1$ is missing from the loop body, a and b never change and the condition $a <= b$ remains true forever, causing an infinite loop.

Break-Statements
A break-statement can be used to terminate the execution of its innermost enclosing loop. A while-loop with a break-statement can be used to provide correct input data.

Example
```
>>> while (True):
        hours = input('Enter hours worked (0..168): ');
        if (0 <= hours <= 168): break;
Enter hours worked (0..168): -11
Enter hours worked (0..168): 200
Enter hours worked (0..168): 40
>>> print hours;
40
```

Function Definitions
A function definition is a statement that defines a new function. The form of a function definition is:

```
def function-name(parameters):   # function header
    statements      # function body
```

The number of function parameters can be 0 or more. Two or more parameters are separated by commas.

Example

```
>>> def product(a, b):
    prod = 1;
    while (a <= b):
        prod = prod * a;
        a = a + 1;
    return prod;
```

The pass-statement can be used as a substitute for a missing body. Its execution has no effect. A pass-statement is handy in stepwise program design to create function and class stubs.

Example

```
>>> def configureWidgets(): pass;
```

Function Invocations

A function definition does not execute the function body; it merely makes the function available for invocations. A function body can be executed as many times as needed through function invocations.

A function invocation consists of the function name followed by a list of arguments in parentheses. The general form of a function invocation is:

function-name(arguments)

The arguments are assigned into their corresponding parameters, then the function body is executed. The invoking part of the program is suspended during the execution of the function body.

Example

```
>>> product(a=1, b=5);   # keyword arguments
120
>>> product(b=5, a=1);   # order does not matter
120
```

```
>>> product(1, 5);      # positional arguments
120
>>> product(5, 1);      # order matters
1
```

Parameters, Local Variables, and Global Variables

Variables that are defined in a function are local for that function. Local variables cannot be accessed from outside of their defining function. Also, local variables do not exist before, after, or between function invocations. All parameters are local and cannot be accessed outside of their defining function. There are two exceptions to these rules that are discussed later in this section.

Example
Parameters *a* and *b* are local for the product function and not accessible outside of its body. The variable named *prod* is defined in the function body; it is also local.

```
>>> def product(a, b):
      prod = 1;
      while (a <= b):
         prod = prod * a;
         # variable prod is local for the product function
         a = a + 1;
      return prod;
>>> product(a = 1, b = 5)
120
>>> print prod;
NameError: name 'prod' is not defined
>>> print a;
NameError: name 'a' is not defined
```

As an exception, parameter names can be used outside of their defining function to form keyword function arguments in function invocations.

Example
Parameter names a and b can be used outside of the product function body to form keyword arguments in function invocations.

```
>>> product(a=1, b=5);
120
```

Variables that are defined in a function can be declared as global, by means of the global-statement, and therefore made accessible outside of the function body.

Example

```
>>> def product(a, b):
    global prod;
    prod = 1;
    while (a <= b):
        prod = prod * a;
        a = a + 1;
    return prod;
>>> product(1, 5);
120
>>> print prod;
120
```

Return-Statements

A return-statement ends the execution of a function invocation, sends results to the invoking function, and resumes its execution.

A common pattern of use of the return-statement is:

def *function-name*(...):
   ...
   return *results*;
   ...

The returned result is typically defined by an expression. Note that returned results may be defined by a list of two or more comma-separated expressions.

A return-statement can be used without an expression. In this case, a special built-in value named *None* is returned. It is also possible to use functions that do not contain a return-statement at all. In such functions, a default return-statement that returns the *None* value is inserted at the end of the function body.

Example

```
>>> def f(): print 'Printing Hello';
>>> result = f();
Printing Hello
>>> print result;
None
```

Sequences

Strings are sequences of characters. Lists and tuples are sequences of items of arbitrary types. Syntactically, list and tuples only differ by the use of angle brackets (for lists) and parentheses (for tuples). There is just one difference between tuples and lists but it is significant: lists can be modified, tuples, once created, never change. In other terms, lists are mutable sequences and tuples are immutable ones. Similarly to tuples, strings are also immutable sequences.

Examples

```
>>> sentence = 'a sentence with a 'quote' inside';
>>> weekday = ['Mon', 'Tue', 'Wed', 'Thu', 'Fri'];
>>> weekend = ['SAT', 'SUN'];
>>> date = ('Dec', 8, 2004);
```

A summary of common operations and functions shared by all sequences is presented in the following table.

Operation or Function	Description
len(sequence)	The number of items in sequence.
sequence[i]	Sequence item at position i.
item in sequence	Test if item is a member of sequence.
item not in sequence	Test if item is not a member of sequence.
P + Q	Concatenate copies of the items of P and Q.
n * S	Repeat n times copies of the items of S.
min(sequence)	The smallest item of sequence.
max (sequence)	The larges item of sequence.
sequence[i:j]	A sequence slice: [sequence[i], sequence[i+1], ... sequence[j-1]].

Example

```
>>> weekend[0] = 'Sat'; weekend[1] = 'Sun';
>>> week = weekday + weekend; print week;
['Mon', 'Tue', 'Wed', 'Thu', 'Fri', 'Sat', 'Sun']
>>> print 3 * weekend;
['sat', 'sun', 'sat', 'sun', 'sat', 'sun']
>>> 'Dec' in date;
True
>>> sentence[len(sentence) - 6 : len(sentence)];
'inside'
```

Lists are mutable. In contrast to lists, tuples and strings are immutable.

Example

```
>>> # lists are mutable:
>>> weekend[0] = 'sat'; weekend[1] = 'sun';
>>> print sentence[0], date[2];
a 2004
>>> # strings are immutable:
>>> sentence[0] = 'A';
TypeError: object doesn't support item assignment.
>>> # tuples are immutable:
>>> date[2] = 2005;
TypeError: object doesn't support item assignment
```

You cannot change immutable sequences but you can create their modified copies.

Example

```
>>> Sentence = 'A' + sentence[1 : len(sentence)];
>>> print Sentence;
A string with a 'quote' inside
```

Note that P + Q concatenate **copies** of the sequences P and Q. This operation can be used to make a copy of any sequence.

Example

```
>>> weekendCopy = weekend + [];
>>> weekendCopy.reverse();
```

```
>>> print weekendCopy, weekend;
['sun', 'sat'] ['sat', 'sun']
```

Objects and Methods

When a program runs, all of its structures – numbers, strings, lists, and functions - are represented in the computer memory in binary form, as sequences of 0s and 1s. Different types of program structures use different binary representation schemes. In widespread terminology, memory representation of any program structure is called an *object*. This general concept is very useful and popular concept.

There are various types of objects. For example, a *numeric object* represents a number; a *string object* represents a sequence of characters. An object can also represent executable code, such as a function. A *list object* is the run-time memory representation of a list. A *widget* object represents a button, entry, label, scrolled text, or any other widget used to build a GUI. A graphics *pen* object represents an electronic pen that can draw on an electronic canvas.

Generally speaking, the term *object* stands for anything that can be assigned a name: a number, a string, a function, a list, a dictionary, a widget, a pen, and more.

Objects usually have functions attached to them. Such functions are referred to as *methods*. Methods are invoked through their objects, by means of dot-notation.

Example

A set of useful functions is attached to every list object. Examples of such list functions are *sort, reverse, remove,* and *append*. These functions are always invoked through list objects, using a dot-notation, as illustrated below.

```
>>> scores = [90, 100, 85, 45, 70, 20];
>>> scores.sort();
>>> print scores;
[20, 45, 70, 85, 90, 100]
>>> scores.reverse();
>>> print scores;
[100, 90, 85, 70, 45, 20]
```

In addition to functions, objects usually have variables attached to them to store necessary data. Variables attached to an object are typically accessed indirectly, by means of methods.

Functions and variables attached to an object are termed object attributes. All object attributes are referred to through their objects by means of dot-notation.

Lists

A Python *list* is a finite sequence of items. Placing comma-separated expressions in square brackets forms a list. Items that belong to the same list may be of different types.

Example

```
>>> lst = ['Xena', 3.14, True, [100, 95], (10, 20)];
```

List objects can be modified by a number of list methods. A summary of list methods is presented in the following table.

Method	Description
list.append(*item*)	Append *item* to *list*.
list.count(*item*)	Return the number of times *item* occurs in *list*.
list.index(*item*)	Return the position of the first occurrence of *item* in *list*.
list.index(*item*, *i*)	Return the position of the first occurrence, after *i*, of *item* in *list*.
list.insert(*i*, *item*)	Insert *item* into *list* before position *i*.
list.pop()	Delete and return the last *item* of *list*.
list.remove(*item*)	Delete the first occurrence of *item* in *list*.
list.reverse()	Reverse the items of *list*.
list.sort()	Sort the items of *list*.

Exercise

In interactive mode, create some lists and apply the above list methods to them. Print the lists to observe how methods modify them.

The Range Function

Some useful lists of integers can be created with the *range* built-in function. The invocation *range(n)* generates the list *[0, 1, 2, 3, ... n-1]*. The invocation *range(m, n)* generates the list *[m, m+1, m+2, ... n-1]*.

Example

```
>>> print range(10);
[0, 1, 2, 3, 4, 5, 6, 7, 8, 9]
>>> print range(10, 15);
[10, 11, 12, 13, 14]
>>> print range(10, 20);
[10, 11, 12, 13, 14, 15, 16, 17, 18, 19]
```

For-Statements

The for-statement is indispensable when you need to iterate over the elements of a sequence, such as a list, string, or tuple. We focus on the following common execution of a for-statement:

```
for target-variable in sequence:   # for-loop header
    statements         # for-loop body
```

The body of the for-statement is executed once for each item in the sequence.

Each item from the for-statement sequence is assigned to the target variable before the body is executed. Items are assigned to the target variable in the order of ascending indices. When the items are exhausted, the for-loop terminates. When the sequence happens to be empty, the body is not executed at all.

Example

```
>>> for day in week:
    print day;
Mon Tue Wed Thu Fri Sat Sun
>>> for i in range(7):
    print i;
0 1 2 3 4 5 6
>>> for i in range(7):
    print week[i];
Mon Tue Wed Thu Fri Sat Sun
```

The actual output will contain one day per line. In the above examples, the output days are concatenated in a single line for brevity.

Remember that a break-statement terminates the execution of its immediately enclosing for-loop. This rule applies to both while-loops and for-loops.

Dictionaries

A Python dictionary is a finite set of key-item pairs. Placing comma-separated key/item pairs in curly braces forms a dictionary. Dictionary *items* can be of any type, including lists and dictionaries. Typically, dictionary *keys* are strings. Lists and dictionaries cannot be used as keys.

Example

```
>>> score = {'Johnny' : 85, 'Xena' : 95 };
>>> print score;
{'Johnny': 85, 'Xena': 95}
```

A summary of the most common dictionary operations, functions, and methods, is presented in the following table.

Operation, Function, or Method	Description
{ }	Empty dictionary.
{ k_0 : v_0, k_1 : v_1, ... k_{n-1} : v_{n-1} }	Dictionary of *n* key-item pairs, k_i : v_i.
len(*dictionary*)	The number of key-item pairs in *dictionary*.
dictionary[*key*]	Look-up *dictionary* item for this *key*.
del *dictionary*[*key*]	Delete the *key-item* pair for this particular *key*.
key in *dictionary* *key* not in *dictionary*	Test if *dictionary* contains a *key-item* pair for this particular *key*.
dictionary.keys()	List of all keys in this *dictionary*.
dictionary.values()	List of all items in this *dictionary*.
dictionary.copy()	A copy of this *dictionary*.

Example

```
>>> score = {'Xena' : 95, 'Johnny' : 85};
>>> listOfAllStudents = score.keys();
>>> listOfAllStudents.sort();
>>> print listOfAllStudents;
['Johnny', 'Xena']
```

```
>>> for student in listOfAllStudents:
        print student, score[student];
Johnny 85
Xena 95
```

Tuples

Python *tuples* are similar to lists, for they are finite sequence of items. A tuple item can be of any type. There is just one difference between tuples and lists but it is significant: lists can be modified but tuples, once created, never change. Because tuples never change, they permit more efficient memory representation and faster operations.

Placing comma-separated expressions in parenthesis forms a tuple. Parentheses may be omitted from any tuple of two items or more.

Example

```
>>> t1 = (10, 20, 30);
>>> t2 = 10, 20, 30;
>>> print t1, t2;
(10, 20, 30) (10, 20, 30)
>>> print t1 == t2;
True
```

The *tuple* and *list* built-in functions copy lists into tuples and tuples into lists, correspondingly.

Example

```
>>> tpl = (10, 20, 30);
>>> lst = list(tpl); print tpl, lst;
(10, 20, 30) [10, 20, 30]
>>> TPL = tuple(lst); print lst, TPL;
[10, 20, 30] (10, 20, 30)
```

Strings

Character sequences starting with a backslash character are termed *escape sequences*. Escape sequences are used to specify control characters, such as the new line character, '\n', and the tab character, '\t'. The backslash character itself can become a member of a string literal if preceded by another backslash character, '\\'.

Example

```
>>> path = 'C:\\Python24';
>>> print path;
C:\Python24
```

Single or double quotes prefixed by a backslash character forms an escape sequences. In this way, a single or double quote can become a part of a string literal when needed.

Use the *raw_input* built-in function to input strings from the user.

Example

```
>>> name = raw_input('Enter your name: ');
Enter your name: Xena Zucchini
>>> print name;
Xena Zucchini
```

Python offers four principal groups of string methods:
- Methods to test string contents: *isalpha, isdigit, isalnum*.
- Methods to search substrings in strings: *count, find*.
- Methods to produce changed copies of strings: *lower, upper, replace, lstrip, rstrip*.
- Methods to transform strings into lists and lists into strings: *split, join*.

Refer to the topic on Strings, Files, and the Web for detailed descriptions of the above string methods.

To process string data, first convert them to lists, then process those lists, then convert the results back to strings. Conversions between strings and lists are supported by the *split* and *join* methods.

Example

```
>>> line = 'Zucchini, Xena, 95\n';
>>> line
'Zucchini, Xena, 95\n'
>>> aString = line.rstrip('\n');
>>> aString
'Zucchini, Xena, 95'
>>> aList = aString.split(',');
```

```
>>> aList
['Zucchini', ' Xena', ' 95']
>>> aString = ','.join(aList);
>>> aString
'Zucchini, Xena, 95'
```

Files

In Python, a file object is connected to an external file. The connection between the file object and the external file is established when the file object is created.

A summary of principal file functions and methods is presented in the following table.

Functions and Methods	Description
open(*fileName*, 'r')	Create a file object in reading mode and connect it to the external file *fileName*.
open(*fileName*, 'w')	Create a file object in writing mode and connect it to the external file *fileName*.
file.read()	Return entire *file* as a single string.
file.readline()	Return next line from *file*.
file.readlines()	Return entire *file* as a list of line strings.
file.write(*string*)	Write *string* into *file*.
print >> *file*, *string*	Same as *file*.write(*string* + '\n')
file.close()	Terminate the connection to the external file. If the *file* is in writing mode, save it before that.

Example

```
>>> outFile = open('example.txt', 'w');
>>> outFile.write('Line 1\n');
>>> print >> outFile, 'Line 2'; # '\n' added by print;
>>> outFile.write('Line 3\n');
>>> outFile.close();
>>> inFile = open('example.txt', 'r');
>>> text = inFile.read();
>>> text;
'Line 1\nLine 2\nLine 3\n'
```

Web Resources

In Python, reading files or other resources provided by remote hosts is as easy as reading files located on your computer. A URL Library module, *urllib,* offers a function named *urlopen* that is used to create a file object connected to a web resource. The *urlopen* function expects a URL string as a parameter.

Example

```
>>> import urllib;
>>> inFile = urllib.urlopen('http://www.yahoo.com');
>>> webData = inFile.read();
>>> outFile = open('webData.html', 'w');
>>> print >>  outFile, webData;
>>> inFile.close(); outFile.close();
```

Turtle Graphics

Computer graphics is a general term embracing the generation, manipulation and display of images with the aid of a computer. Turtle graphics is characterized by the use of a *pen* object that is designed to draw on a *window* object. The pen can be programmed to move forward or backward, to make left and right turns. As the pen moves, it draws a line on the window. This way, the task of drawing a shape on the window is reduced to the task of programming pen movements. Pen movements along the screen can be likened to the movements of a little turtle, hence the name *turtle graphics*.

The *turtle* module provides easy-to-use turtle graphics primitives. A *pen* object is created by means of a *Pen()* constructor invocation. The *pen* object comes with a number of methods that facilitate graphics programming, such as *goto, forward, left, right, circle, fill, color, up, down,* and *tracer.* Many of these methods have very intuitive meaning. Their descriptions can be found in the E-Text.

Example

```
>>> pen = Pen();
>>> # Move application windows to see the drawing window;
>>> pen.reset();
>>> pen.color(0, 0, 1); # blue
>>> pen.fill(True);
```

```
>>> pen.circle(80);
>>> pen.fill(False);
>>> pen.goto(0,0);
>>> pen.clear();
```

Graphical User Interfaces

"User interface" is a general term embracing the communication channel between a program and the human user. There are two widespread types of user interfaces: text-only interfaces, and graphical user interfaces (GUIs).

Programs that employ *text-only interfaces* typically output text on the screen and input text from the keyboard. In Python, text-only interfaces are implemented by means of simple statements and functions, such as the print-statement and the input function. Programs that employ *graphical user interfaces (GUIs)* take advantage of the computer's graphics capabilities to facilitate the interaction with the user. Such programs display various widgets on the screen, such as buttons, menus, scroll bars and text areas, all positioned within windows. Typical GUIs involve graphics displays, keyboards, and pointing devices, such as mice.

The popular *Tkinter* module allows you to compose GUIs out of some basic widgets. In *Tkinter*, widgets are defined as Python classes, such as *Tk* (main window), *Label, Button* and *Entry*. These classes define a number of methods that can be used with various options.

Designing a GUI is a complex task that is simplified by breaking it into a sequence of well defined steps. The first step is to configure and display a main GUI window. The second step is to create various widget objects. The third step is to position the widgets in the main window. The fourth step is to configure each widget by specifying various widget properties, such as size, relief, borders. The fifth step is to define particular action functions to be invoked upon events such as button clicks.

Example

The following interactive program creates a GUI with a 'Hello' button. The program prints 'Hello everyone!' upon button clicks.

```
>>> from Tkinter import *;
>>> window = Tk();
>>> hello = Button(window);
>>> hello.grid(row=0, column=0);
```

```
>>> def sayHello(): print 'Hello everyone!';
>>> hello.configure(text='Hello', command=sayHello);
>>> window.mainloop();
Hello everyone!
```

Classes

Various classes of objects, such as pens, buttons, labels and entries, can be specified in Python by means of class definitions. Class definitions are statements, sometimes referred to as *class-statements*. They are compound structures that incorporate headers and bodies.

A class header gives a name to the class. The name of a class can be used in constructor invocations in order to create objects of the class. Although a class body can incorporate arbitrary statements, a typical class body is just a sequence of function definitions.

Example

```
>>> # A class that describes any human with a name:
class Human:
    def __init__(self, name): self.name = name;
    def getName(self): return self.name;
    def introduce(self): print 'Hello, I am ' + self.getName() + '.';
>>> human1 = Human('Xena');
>>> human2 = Human('Johnny');
>>> human3 = Human('Bubba');
>>> humans = [human1, human2, human3];
>>> for human in humans:
    human.introduce();
Hello, I am Xena.
Hello, I am Johnny.
Hello, I am Bubba.
```

A function defined within a class can only be executed throughout an object. Such functions are often called *methods*.

The *self* parameter is a required first parameter in each function that is defined within a Python class. When the function is executed, the *self* parameter represents the object to which the function is attached. Through its *self* parameter, the function can refer to all attributes (variables and functions) of its object.

Most classes define a function named *__init__*. This function is automatically executed anytime a new object is constructed. The main purpose of the __init__ function is to initialize newly created objects. Using any name not __init__ will not trigger automatic initialization. *Inheritance* is a language mechanism that allows the definition of new classes as extensions of existing ones.

Example

In Python, a new class can inherit from another class, or if needed, from two or more classes:

> class Student(Human): ... *Inherits all human attributes*
> ... *Defines specific student attributes*...
> class Professor(Human):... *Inherits all human attributes*
> ... *Defines specific professor attributes*...
> class TeachingAssistant(Student, Professor):... *Inherits all students and professor attributes*
> ... *Defines specific teaching assistant attributes*...

If a class *C1* is defined by means of inheritance from a class *C0*, *C0* is referred to as a *base class* of *C1*, while *C1* is termed a *subclass* of *C0*. A built-in function invocation *isinstance(x, C)* can be used to test if an object *x* is an object of a class *C* or any of its subclasses.

Modules and Import

A sequence of statements saved in a text file is referred to as module. A module defines, at the topmost level, various attributes, such as classes, functions and global variables. The import statement makes a module's attributes available to the program.

The import statement starts with the *import* keyword, followed by one or more comma-separated module names. The importing program can refer to the attributes of the imported module by means of qualified names. A qualified name is a dotted pair module name and attribute name.

Example

> >>> import random;
> >>> print random.randint(0, 100);
> 21

Another form of the import statement starts with the *from* keyword, followed by a module name, followed by the *import* keyword and a star. The importing program refers to all attributes of the imported module by means of their names. No qualified names are needed.

Example

```
>>> from random import *;
>>> print randint(0, 100);
96
```

While common purpose modules such as *random* and *Tkinter* are intended to be imported by other modules, many modules are written to be executed as standalone programs. A standalone program module can import common purpose modules then define its own classes and/or functions. Such a module should end with a function invocation or a constructor invocation to initiate program execution.

Example

```
# Module start
from Tkinter import * ;
# A class that prints 'Hello' in response to button clicks:
class Hello:
    def __init__(self):
        self.root = Tk();
        self.hello = Button(self.root);
        self.hello.grid(row=0, column=0);
        self.hello.configure(text='Hello', command=self.sayHello);
        self.root.mainloop();
    def sayHello(self):
        print 'Hello everyone!'

# Create a Hello object. This automatically executes __init__.
# Init creates the GUI for the program.

Hello();    # Module end
```

References

An assignment statement defines a variable as a *reference* to a specific object. This reference can be changed to a different object by a subsequent assignment into the same variable. At any time, the *value* of the variable is represented by the object referred to by the variable.

Example

```
>>> V = [65, 95, 100];
>>> print V;
[65, 95, 100]
>>> V = [100, 95, 80, 75];
>>> print V;
[100, 95, 80, 75]
```

The above assignment statement defines variable V as a reference to the list *[65, 95, 100]*. The reference change is depicted in the following figure.

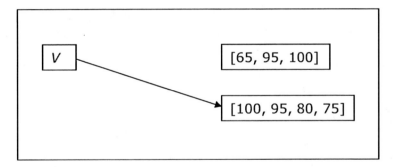

Two or more variables may refer to the same object. When two variables refer to the same object, either of them can be used to modify the object.

Example

```
>>> V = [65, 95, 100];
>>> W = V;
>>> print V, W;
[65, 95, 100] [65, 95, 100]
>>> V[0] = 99;
>>> print V, W;
[99, 95, 100] [99, 95, 100]
```

The first two assignments define variables *V, W* as references to the same list, *[65, 95, 100]*. The assignment *V[0] = 99* updates affects both variables *V* and *W*. The update is depicted in the following figure.

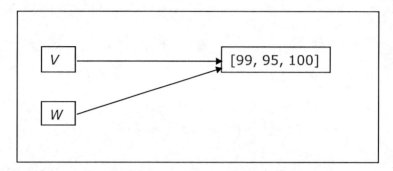

Parameters are similar to variables. A function invocation defines a parameter as a *reference* to a specific argument object. Through the parameter, the function may update the argument object.

Example

The following statements demonstrate how an assignment of a list into a parameter name does not affect the argument.

```
>>> def g(W):
    W[0] = 99;
>>> V = [65, 95, 100];
>>> g(W = V);
>>> print V;
[99, 95, 100]
```

First, the function invocation *g(W = V)* assigns *V* into *W*. This makes both *V* and *W* refer to the argument list, *[65, 95, 100]*, as depicted in the following figure.

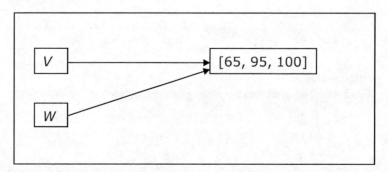

Second, the function invocation $g(W = V)$ executes the body of function g. The function body executes the statement $W[0] = 99$ and thus updates the list referred to by W. The change affects V, which refers to the same list, as depicted in the following figure.

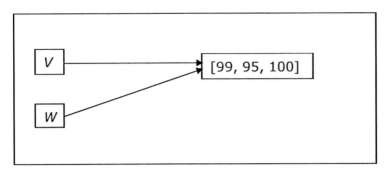

Finale

Learning how to program is like learning how to speak. Both activities are performed at various levels. A little child who only pronounces a few simple sentences is said to speak. An experienced linguist is qualified with the same term: speaking.

Learning how to program like an expert certainly takes longer than one introductory course. Followed this course and doing the work with reasonable quality will have equipped you with the ability to design simple programs, all by yourself.

Of course, many programs covered in the course were not as simple as others. Even if you cannot create more complex programs by yourself, you should be able to understand and modify them. As a matter of fact, this is exactly what a majority of programmers do: understand and modify existing programs. Few people start software design from scratch. Many people reuse existing software and enhance it to solve their unique problems. At this time, you should be prepared to program by retrieving adequate existing software, studying and understanding it, enhancing it, and transforming it into programs to serve your purpose. Enhancing existing programs was the core of most labs for this course.

Last but not least, this course taught something that is more important than practical programming skills. This course helped you gain intuition and understanding of fundamental computing concepts and techniques. Good intuition and understanding is a very solid base to build your future computing studies and practices on. Good intuition and understanding is what makes programming a fulfilling and satisfying activity. Computer programming is fun.

Lab A [Review]

Objective; Background; Lab Overview; Creating a Topic Folder and a Labs Folder; Interactive Experiments; Saving Your Interactive Session

Objectives
- The objective of this lab is to get hands-on experience with the review material.

Background
- The E-text Review summarizes the most important language structures introduced in this course of study. The review is based on numerous examples. This lab contains the review examples. You must have studied the review E-text prior to doing this lab.

Lab Overview
To perform this lab:
- Study the E-Text Review.
- In interactive mode, execute all activities listed in the Interactive Experiments section of this lab.
- Save your IDLE interactive session in a text file.

Creating a Topic Folder and a Labs Folder
- There are no sample programs for this topic.
- Within your *master* folder, create an empty folder and rename it *10*. This is your current topic folder.
- Within your topic folder, *10*, create an empty folder and name it *10Labs*. This is your current labs folder.

Interactive Experiments
- Study the E-Text Review.
- In interactive mode, execute in sequence all statements below.

Assignment Statements

```
>>> score = 85;          # score defined;
>>> score = score + 10;
>>> GPA = GPA + 0.5;
```

Print Statements

```
>>> print score, score - 10;
```

Names

```
>>> in = 123;              # in is a keyword
>>> tax  rate = 6.75;
>>> celsius = 32;          # lowercase 'c'
>>> Celsius = Celsius + 10;   # capital 'C'
```

Numbers

```
>>> 2**10;
>>> 9 / 5;
>>> 9 % 5;
>>> 9.0 / 5;

>>> abs(-42);
>>> int(0.99999999);
>>> round(0.99999999);
>>> float(10);

>>> score = input('Enter score: ');
>>> print score;
```

If Statements

```
>>> if (score < 60): print 'Sorry, you fail.';

>>> if (score < 60): print 'Sorry, you fail.';
else: print 'Great, you pass.';

>>> score = 75;
>>> if (score < 60): grade = 'F';
elif (score < 70): grade = 'D';
elif (score < 80): grade = 'C';
elif (score < 90): grade = 'B';
else: grade = 'A';
>>> print grade;

>>> score = 75;
>>> if (score < 60): grade = 'F';
```

```
>>> if (score < 70): grade = 'D';
>>> if (score < 80): grade = 'C';
>>> if (score < 90): grade = 'B';
>>> print grade;
```

Boolean Expressions

```
>>> print score < 75, score == 75, score > 75;
>>> 70 <= score and score < 80;
>>> 70 <= score < 80;

>>> x = 10; y = 0;
>>> x < 0 and x / y < 1;
>>> x / y < 1 and x < 0;
```

While Statements

```
>>> a = 1; b = 5; prod = 1;
>>> while (a <= b):
prod = prod * a;
a = a + 1;
>>> print prod;
```

Break Statements

```
>>> while (True):
        hours   = input('Enter hours worked (0..168): ');
        if (0 <= hours <= 168): break;
Enter hours worked (0..168): -11
Enter hours worked (0..168): 200
Enter hours worked (0..168): 40
>>> print hours;
```

Function Definitions

```
>>> def product(a, b):
   prod = 1;
   while (a <= b):
      prod = prod * a;
      a = a + 1;
   return prod;

>>> def configureWidgets(): pass;
```

Function Invocations

```
>>> product(a=1, b=5);     # keyword arguments
>>> product(b=5, a=1);     # order does not matter
>>> product(1, 5);         # positional arguments
>>> product(5, 1);         # order matters
```

Parameters, Local Variables, and Global Variables

```
>>> def product(a, b):
      prod = 1;
      while (a <= b):
        prod = prod * a;
        # variable prod is local for the product function
        a = a + 1;
      return prod;
>>> print prod;
>>> print a;

>>> product(a=1, b=5);

>>> def product(a, b):
      global prod;
      prod = 1;
      while (a <= b):
        prod = prod * a;
        a = a + 1;
      return prod;
>>> product(1, 5);
>>> print prod;
```

Return Statements

```
>>> def f(): print 'Hello';
>>> result = f();
>>> print result;
```

Sequences

```
>>> sentence = 'a sentence with a 'quote' inside';
>>> weekday = ['Mon', 'Tue', 'Wed', 'Thu', 'Fri'];
```

```
>>> weekend = ['SAT', 'SUN'];
>>> date = ('Dec', 8, 2004);
>>> weekend[0] = 'Sat'; weekend[1] = 'Sun';
>>> week = weekday + weekend; print week;
>>> print 3 * weekend;
>>> 'Dec' in date;
>>> sentence[len(sentence) - 6 : len(sentence)];

>>> weekend[0] = 'sat'; weekend[1] = 'sun';  # lists are mutable;
>>> print sentence[0], date[2];
>>> sentence[0] = 'A';                       # strings are immutable;
>>> date[2] = 2005;                          # tuples are immutable;

>>> Sentence = 'A' + sentence[1 : len(sentence)];
>>> print Sentence;

>>> weekendCopy = weekend + [];
>>> weekendCopy.reverse();
>>> print weekendCopy, weekend;
```

Objects and Methods

```
>>> scores = [90, 100, 85, 45, 70, 20];
>>> scores.sort(); print scores;
>>> scores.reverse(); print scores;
```

The Range Function

```
>>> print range(10);
>>> print range(10, 15);
>>> print range(10, 20);
```

For Statements

```
>>> for day in week:
      print day;
>>> for i in range(7):
      print i;
>>> for i in range(7):
      print week[i];
```

Dictionaries

```
>>> score = {'Johnny' : 85, 'Xena' : 95 };
>>> print ;
>>> score = {'Xena' : 95, 'Johnny' : 85};
>>> listOfAllStudents = score.keys();
>>> listOfAllStudents.sort();
>>> print listOfAllStudents;
>>> for student in listOfAllStudents:
print student, score[student];
```

Tuples

```
>>> t1 = (10, 20, 30);
>>> t2 = 10, 20, 30;
>>> print t1, t2;
>>> print t1 == t2;
>>> l1 = list(t1); print t1, l1;
>>> t2 = tuple(l1); print l1, t2;
```

Strings

```
>>> path = 'C:\\Python23';
>>> print path
>>> name = raw_input('Enter your name: ');
>>> print name;

>>> line = 'Zucchini, Xena, 95\n';
>>> line;
>>> aString = line.rstrip('\n');
>>> aString;
>>> aList = aString.split(',');
>>> aList;
>>> aString = ','.join(aList);
>>> aString;
```

Files and the Web

```
>>> outFile = open('example.txt', 'w');
>>> outFile.write('Line 1\n');
>>> print >> outFile, 'Line 2';              # '\n' added by print;
>>> outFile.write('Line 3\n');
>>> outFile.close();
```

```
>>> inFile = open('example.txt', 'r');
>>> text = inFile.read();
>>> text;
```

Using Web Resources

```
>>> import urllib;
>>> inFile = urllib.urlopen('http://www.yahoo.com');
>>> webData = inFile.read();
>>> outFile = open('webData.html', 'w');
>>> print >>  outFile, webData;
>>> inFile.close(); outFile.close();
```

Graphical User Interfaces

```
>>> from Tkinter import *;
>>> window = Tk();
>>> hello = Button(window);
>>> hello.grid(row=0, column=0);
>>> def sayHello(): print 'Hello everyone!';
>>> hello.configure(text='Hello', command=sayHello);
>>> window.mainloop();
```

Classes

```
>>> # A class that describes any human with a name:
class Human:
   def __init__(self, name): self.name = name;
   def getName(self): return self.name;
   def introduce(self): print 'Hello, I am ' + self.getName() + '.';
>>> human1 = Human('Xena');
>>> human2 = Human('Johnny');
>>> human3 = Human('Bubba');
>>> humans = [human1, human2, human3];
>>> for human in humans:
human.introduce();
```

Modules and Import

```
>>> import random;
>>> print random.randint(0, 100);

>>> from random import *;
>>> print randint(0, 100);
```

References

```
>>> V = [65, 95, 100];
>>> W = V;
>>> print V, W;
>>> V[0] = 99;
>>> print V, W;

>>> def g(W):
      W[0] = 99;
>>> V = [65, 95, 100];
>>> g(W = V);
>>> print V;
```

Saving Your Interactive Session

- Save the interactive session with all of your experiments in your current labs folder, *10Labs*.
- From the Shell Window, use *File → Save As*.
- Name the saved copy *Session_10A.txt*.
  - **Important Note:** You must explicitly supply the file extension '**.txt**' when saving from IDLE.
- If you perform experiments in two or more interactive sessions, you can save your work in several files. If you choose to do so, use names *Session_10A_1.txt, Session_10A_2.txt*, and so on, for all saved files.
- Your saved file(s) must be included in you Lab Assignment submission.

Please visit StudyPack.com to gain full access to the complete Python First Pack:

sample programs

quizzes

e-texts

lab assignments

forums, and

other digital resources